PURGED

The Wevlian Chronicles – Book 2

Aaron N. Hall

Cover design by Shelbi Tietjen

Map illustrations by Joseph Spangler

Copyediting by Adam Anderson

Beta readers: Russel Haggard, Devan Freebairn, Riley Crofts, Gary Hall

ISBN 979-8-9910978-8-8

Dedicated to Russ.

Thanks for staying with us.

United States National Suicide Prevention Lifeline

1-800-273-8255

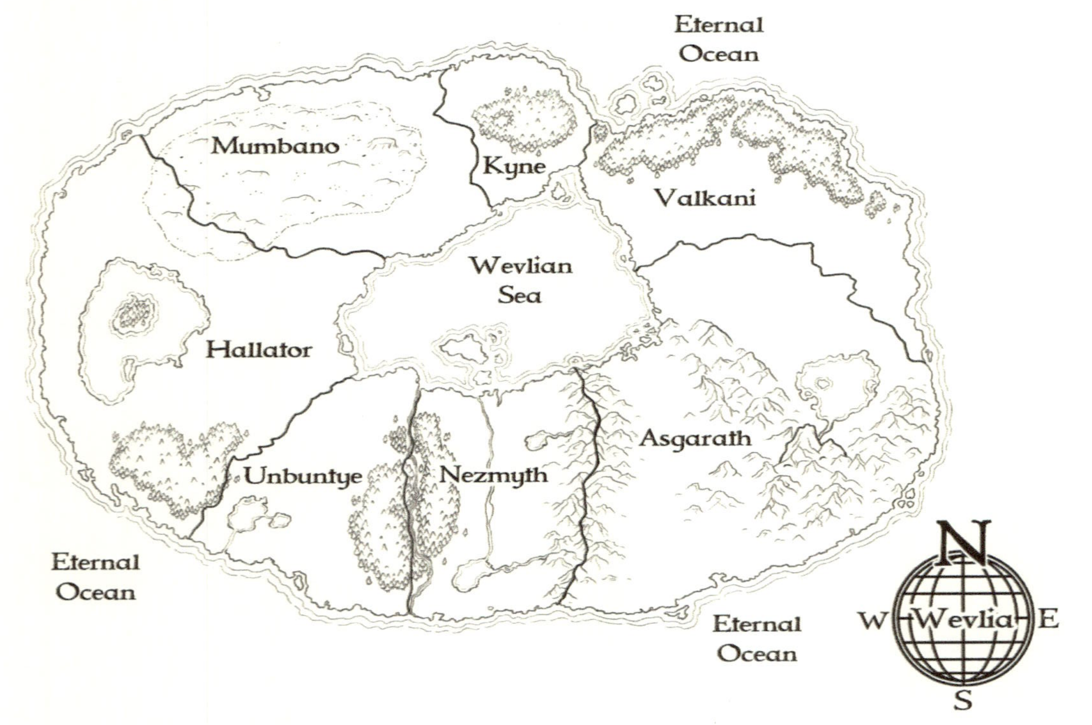

Eternal Ocean
Mumbano
Kyne
Valkani
Wevlian Sea
Hallator
Unbuntye
Nezmyth
Asgarath
Eternal Ocean
Eternal Ocean
N
W Wevlia E
S

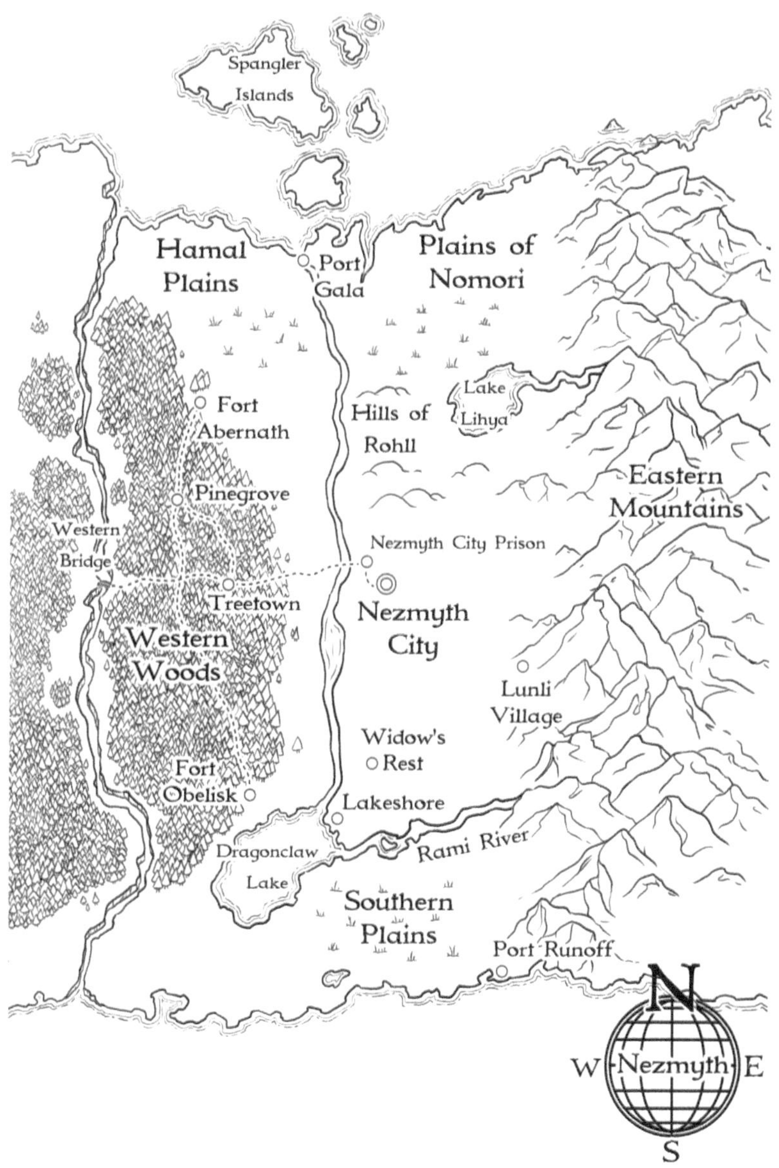

Spangler
Islands
Hamal
Plains
Plains of
Nomori
Port
Gala
Lake
Lihya
Fort
Abernath
Hills of
Rohll
Pinegrove
Eastern
Mountains
Western
Bridge
Nezmyth City Prison
Treetown
Nezmyth
City
Western
Woods
Lunli
Village
Widow's
Rest
Fort
Obelisk
Lakeshore
Dragonclaw
Lake
Rami River
Southern
Plains
Port Runoff
N
W
Nezmyth
E
S

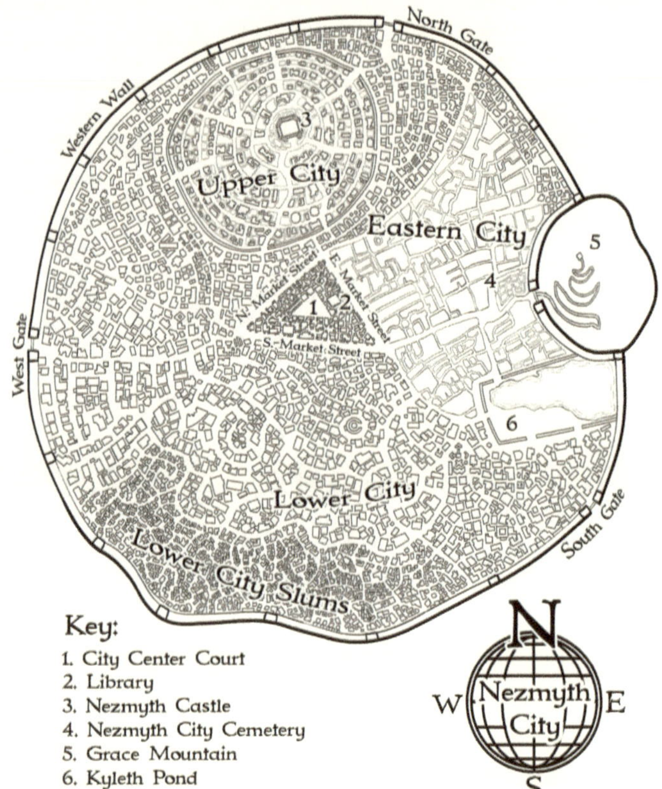
North Gate
Western Wall
Upper City
3
Eastern City
5
N. Market Street
E. Market Street
1 2
4
S. Market Street
West Gate
6
Lower City
South Gate
Lower City Slums
Key:
1. City Center Court
2. Library
3. Nezmyth Castle
4. Nezmyth City Cemetery
5. Grace Mountain
6. Kyleth Pond
N
W
Nezmyth
City
E
S

I

THE VAULT

It was only a few miles west of Nezmyth City—the prison. Dug by captured criminals centuries ago, it breached the ground from the middle of a perfectly round chasm wider than a city plaza and hundreds of feet deep. A round spire protruding from the center contained layers upon layers of barred cells and was nearly as round as the monstrous pit. Four staircases, carved from the edges of the pit, were the only way in or out. If you were to walk it, one side would be a curving stone wall lined with torches. The other side, a seemingly endless drop to the bottom.

Five men were nearly to the bottom of the pit. To them, the sky was just a thin sliver of blue overhead. Two of them carried torches, and as they reached the bottom of the steps, one retrieved a large set of keys from a pouch on his armor. Coughs, curses, and murmurs echoed through the chasm as they approached a thick iron door at the base of the spire. Above the door was a sign, crudely fashioned and centuries old:

VAULT OF THE DAMNED

The first two men passed their torches to the men in the back. One man inserted the key into an enormous lock, turned it, then grunted as he twisted a large wheel until it stopped spinning with an echoing *clack*. The other man at the front placed his hand on the other side of the door and muttered a lengthy phrase in Ancient Nezmythian. The door rippled like water.

With another loud *snap*, the door became rigid and creaked open.

"With all respect, Your Highness," one of the men in the back said. "What do you gain from visiting him? He's a villain."

The man in the middle, Jason, King of Nezmyth, turned slowly to face the questioner, his deep brown eyes probing. A thick beard wrapped around his chin, and his hand rested on the pommel of a silver-hilted sword lashed around his waist. On his hand, he wore a Foreordination ring with a bright orange stone. The man in the back shrunk a little as if realizing he had asked an inappropriate question. The King breathed deeply, then turned away as he exhaled.

"The Dragon compels me," was his answer.

The King stepped forward, and the four guards resumed position, two in back and two in front. Beyond the door, a staircase descended into darkness.

The two torches cast flickering light and tall shadows down the narrow pass as they went. The air was dank and muggy. The only things to be heard were their own footsteps and the chittering of rats. At length, the party reached flat ground where the dancing flames threw feeble light into five cells with rusted bars and locks.

Only one was occupied.

The King strode toward it. He didn't ask for it to be unlocked. He didn't even address the convict immediately. He simply approached it, pulled his cape into a bunch, and sat on the ground, his sword and armor clinking as he did. The four guards looked on, exchanging glances and not speaking.

The prisoner, thin and pale, sat with his back to the King. A mess of gray hair, unwashed for years spilled from his head. The rags that hung from his skin were torn and frayed in various ways. A pile of old hay pushed in a corner was the closest thing he had to a bed. He didn't acknowledge the presence of his visitors.

For a long moment, the only sound was the faint crackle of the torches whispering against the walls. The King glared at the ground between his knees, drawing something abstract with his fingers as his guards watched on. He took a deep breath, then spoke low enough that only he and the prisoner could hear.

"One of them is new," he said. "The guards, I mean. He probably thinks you'll try to attack me in some way. But I know you can't, not even with Dark Magic. This cell is blessed by ancient spells that keeps you from practicing. I know you stopped trying ages ago."

The prisoner said nothing. The King continued.

"That's a good thing, too. I'm sure it clears your mind. With no Dark Magic clouding your soul, you begin to feel joy and peace again." He paused. "At least, as much as you can in a place like this."

No response. The King sighed. His gaze fell to the ground and he wrestled with his thoughts. The Dragon compelled him to come here. But what could he say that hadn't already been said? And if he did, what good would it do? He dropped the hay from his fingers.

"Still not one for conversation?" The King asked.

Same response. The King shook his head.

"Well," he said. "Maybe I'll see you again soon."

He stood from the ground, brushed himself off, and turned about. The two guards retrieved the torches from the metal stands. But as the King began to walk away, something flared up inside him—something that drove him back to the cell. In one stride, he was upon the cell door, gripping the bars. His eyebrows bent and his jaw clenched, as if his mere gaze could make the prisoner face him. He wasn't whispering anymore.

"I order you to look at me, Barnabas!" he said. "I want to see your eyes!"

The response wasn't immediate, but grudgingly, the prisoner placed his feeble arms on the dirt and forced himself around. The ridges of his rib cage were easily visible. Dirt and sweat caked his torso. His messy gray hair hung over his eyes, but through the greasy strands, Jason could make out the icy blue that long ago filled him with so much dread.

Upon seeing his frailty, Jason turned to the guards. "He still refuses to eat?"

"Only small morsels of bread, Your Highness," one said. "Not enough to fill a man."

Jason turned back to the prisoner, looking hard over his sorry countenance. The icy eyes that looked back at him were bleary and old, vacant and lost. Jason's jaw tightened.

"I hated you once," Jason whispered. "Just the thought of you filled me with so much anger and fear. I was seventeen. I had nothing. I was a Lower City boy with barely a thing to my name. You made me *suffer*. And not just me, but everyone that I loved. Now look at you. The Holy Dragon exacted vengeance upon you and your wicked rule through me. And yet," Jason stooped down, putting his eyes level with Barnabas's, "the Dragon compels me to visit you time after time. And for what?"

After a long pause, Jason released the bars, stood up, and began to make his way to the exit. After only a few strides, Barnabas finally spoke.

"Jason," he said.

The King perked like a dog at the sound of a whistle. Barnabas's voice wasn't the deep, cold menace that it once was, but a tired breath, dusty and ancient. He turned about. In the flickering torchlight, the King saw Barnabas turn himself back around to face the wall, his back against everyone else. The next three words were just as tired and dusty as the first.

"Please don't return."

Jason deflated. "That's not your choice."

* * * * *

Jason's legs ached long before he reached ground level. Waiting for him was his crimson carriage and a man sitting on a nearby tree stump. The man's wavy, silver hair billowed from his scalp, and his searing red eyes stayed fixed on the ground as he leaned forward. A rich blue cape fell to his ankles, and a sword was slung around his hip. While he waited, a small rock magically danced in the palm of his hand, occasionally breaking apart and forming back together. Just like Jason, he had a Foreordination ring on his hand. When Jason emerged from the prison, their eyes met and the rock fell to the ground.

"Well?" the Advisor said.

"He spoke for the first time today," Jason said.

The Advisor's eyes widened as he sat up straight. "Oh?"

"He told me not to come back."

All tension left the Advisor's body, and his shoulders sagged. As he shook his head, he said, "I've told you time and time again—"

"That visiting Barnabas is pointless," Jason said as he strode toward the carriage. "I understand how you feel, Nadiel. I still haven't forgiven him either. I haven't forgotten what he's done. But I keep feeling the Dragon's pressings to visit him."

"Jason," Nadiel said seriously as he joined the King's stride. "This is such a small matter—a distraction if anything. Are you sure it is the Sacred Dragon that gives you these feelings? This feels like an improper use of your time."

Jason climbed into the carriage and sat down. "I'm sure of it. At least… at least I think I am. It's hard to tell."

"That, I can certainly understand," Nadiel sat across from him and drummed his fingers on his knee before speaking up again. "Of a truth, you are the only human interaction Barnabas has the hope of receiving currently. Perhaps this is an example of the Dragon's mercy—granting him some sort of company even after the thousands of lives he destroyed."

Jason thought about it for a second. "It could be."

"However, I still believe that this is a pointless venture."

"I know, Nadiel. I know."

After another brief pause, Nadiel asked, "Have you been receiving any other instructions from the Dragon?"

Jason looked down. He imagined Barnabas out of his cage, out of his rags, out of the prison. They were nothing but thoughts—even less than thoughts. Still, they drifted in and out of his mind, and every time they did there was a dull whisper to make the order. He ignored it each time. Because why should he? Barnabas got what he deserved.

So, in response to Nadiel's question, he shook his head.

"Very well, then," Nadiel said. "Whatever you do, I am here as your aid, my King."

"Thank you."

Outside, there was a snap, a "Yaw!" and the carriage lurched to a crawl.

Grassy hills rolled for miles in every direction underneath a sapphire sky and a beaming sun. The view was only interrupted by a wide river cutting through the landscape, the river that stretched all the way from the Northern Seashore to Dragonclaw Lake in the south. To the east, Nezmyth City was just within view, its bustling districts small enough to fit in the palm of Jason's hand.

The venture back to Nezmyth City was slow. As the carriage moved eastward, Nadiel elected to busy himself with the pages of a book. Jason sat across from him quietly, thinking about the visit. At length, the carriage reached the city's outer wall—a tall expanse of stone and mortar. Before them, a thick set of wooden gates just large enough for a carriage sat wide open, guarded by soldiers on either side.

The carriage wheels found cobblestone once they slipped through the gate. Through the streets of Nezmyth City they went. As the townspeople saw the carriage, many waved and huzzahed with bright smiles. King Jason returned these gestures with a polite smile and a genteel wave.

Some wandering the streets with shabbier clothes and dirtier faces scowled at the sight. Jason didn't make eye contact with them. He had done his best to help those in the lowest slums of Lower City. But apparently, it wasn't enough.

After a while, Nadiel closed his book and put his hands on his knees, sitting up straight and closing his eyes. His breathing became deep and measured.

Study and meditation, Jason thought. *Every day. No wonder he's the most powerful magician in Nezmyth.*

The carriage jittered through the streets, passing the bustling Southern Market Street. During Barnabas's rule, this was an area full of street urchins and miserable peasants. But ever since Jason took the throne and the Harvest Tax was abolished, the commoners of Lower City looked cleaner and walked with more energy. Scanty carts and derelict storefronts transformed into healthy, colorful shops with clean displays and fresh wares. Jason couldn't help but smile as he thought of it.

The carriage was on the Southern Market Street for only a short moment. Then it turned onto the posh Northern Market Street, where aristocrats and noblemen did most of their shopping. The people walked about, girded in fine apparel, past storefronts ornamented with lavish materials. During Jason's commoner days, he never found himself venturing here. It was laughable to think a Lower City boy could afford so much as an apple on the Northern Market Street.

After a short venture on that street, the carriage turned north, ascending through Upper City. The mansions that lined the winding uphill streets were extravagant, surrounded by gates and boasting perfectly manicured gardens. Again, Nadiel and Jason barely spoke. Nadiel's eyes stayed closed while Jason opted to stare out the window.

At the top of the Upper City hill, an ancient iron gate surrounded the grounds of Nezmyth Castle. It wasn't what it used to be—Jason had vivid memories of a shadowy cathedral with walls like charcoal. The castle he once knew. But when Barnabas was cast from the throne and a day of torrential rain cleansed the earth, the castle transformed into an ivory white fortress as if the darkness had been washed away. The stained glass windows sparkled with multicolored light, particularly the one on the face of the castle: an ancient knight holding a glorious orange blade to the sky.

As the gate swung open and the guards tipped their heads and wished a good day to the King, the carriage left the Upper City cobblestone and entered the smooth paths of the castle courtyard. What was once a stark courtyard of soil and stone had flourished into a lush, beautiful garden in the past four years. Exotic fruits bursting with vibrant colors grew on trees that had shot up as quickly as they had disappeared decades ago. Scattered throughout the grounds, dozens of commoners —with the groundskeeper's permission—strolled the paths and picked fruit.

In the middle of the grounds, a white marble statue of an Ancient Nezmythian knight pointed its sword to the air. Out of its lips, a steady stream of water spilled into a small reservoir at its feet. Jason knew what it was—a representation of a Knight of the Holy Order, just like him.

As the carriage passed it, he gazed down at the palm of his right hand. There, directly beneath his index finger, an orange triangle was carved into his hand. It seemed to have been carved hastily, with one side of the triangle extending longer than the other two. For eighteen years Jason kept it concealed, unsettled and unsure of its meaning. It wasn't until the day of his Ordination that he understood the power and the sacredness of it. He rubbed it with his thumb and clenched his hand shut.

The carriage lurched to a halt in front of the castle doors. Nadiel's eyes popped open and he took a deep, cleansing breath. Before he and Jason even climbed out, a soldier was banging the castle doors with a giant hammer. After a pause, the enormous doors groaned open. Jason and Nadiel marched through.

The castle interior had remained nearly unchanged for hundreds of years. Soldiers stood sentinel throughout the perimeter of the room. The walls were busy with paintings, windows, and lit torches. Enormous pillars shot up from the floor to the ceiling in a grid, crystal chandeliers dangling intermittently between. On the ceiling, an epic mural depicting the land of Nezmyth and the Sacred Dragon stretched from corner to corner. From the castle entrance, a red carpet extended to a platform on the other end of the hall, with thrones for the King and Queen.

As they marched down the red carpet, Nadiel suddenly stopped. His eyebrows scrunched and his fingers drummed the hilt of his blade. Jason stopped in kind and turned around to face him, perplexed.

"Do you feel that?" Nadiel asked.

Jason's face hardened. "Feel what?"

"Something…" Nadiel's voice trailed. "Like a very subtle squirming in my soul… something I cannot place." His gaze lifted to Jason's eyes. "Sire, if you'll excuse me, I'll be studying in my quarters."

Jason nodded. "Of course."

Nadiel gave a little bow and marched through a door at the far end of the hall. Jason watched him as he went. Now something inside him squirmed as well. If a master magician like Nadiel was sensing something like that, then—

"Your Highness!"

A soldier quickly approached Jason from the other side. She bowed respectfully. "I have messages to deliver, Your Grace."

"Very well," Jason said as he began walking toward his throne. "What do you have for me?"

"The Queen wants to have *the talk* with you again."

A shiver slid down Jason's back. "Immediately?"

The soldier nodded. "I exhausted every excuse I could muster, but I was no match for her wit, sire. She could see right through me. Those silver eyes are like swords."

Jason sighed. "Alright then, I guess there's no use avoiding it. What else is there?"

"Master Ferribolt should be here any moment as well. I told him you should be back before dusk. All he said to tell you is, '*It is his time.*'"

Jason's heart stopped beating and his eyes bore into the soldier, intense and awe-stricken. The soldier immediately tensed up, her jaw tightening and her eyes becoming worried.

"That's all he said?" Jason breathed.

"Yes, Your Highness," the soldier replied with a stiff nod.

It is his time… Jason replayed the four words in his head. Thoughts of his Year of Decision resurfaced—the year in which Barnabas tested him for the throne. That was the last year of tyranny, and the year where Barnabas punished all of Jason's loved ones for his Foreordination. He could remember so vividly that day when he was brought up to the castle in the dead of night. Here, he was told he would be crowned King in one year based upon his virtuous performance… and survival. What a year it was, and what a time it had been since. Jason quickly brought himself back to reality.

"Is that all?" he said.

"Yes, sire."

"Where is my wife?"

"Last I saw her, she was painting in the courtyard."

Jason thanked the soldier for her service and excused himself from the hall. Through a door and down a corridor, he reached the exit to the outer courtyard. All the while, he tried to control his breathing and march firm while he straightened his armor. He pushed the door open and sunlight spilled onto him.

There she was, Queen Saryan, facing the brilliant hills that rolled endlessly northward. Her back was to him, shrouding her face behind a curtain of golden blonde hair. Her figure was covered by a flowing white dress that reached her ankles and elbows; however, she wore no shoes, leaving her bare feet on the courtyard stone. In front of her, an easel propped up a white canvas which had become splotched with greens, yellows, and blues. Even in a painting smock, Jason couldn't help but think about how beautiful she was—he could fully appreciate the moment if he weren't so nervous.

"Haven't you already painted these hills before?" he said as he strolled up to her.

She turned around. Her perfect lips pulled into a smile, accentuating her dimples and the splash of freckles around her nose. She sneered and she said, "Sometimes you need to repeat some things to get the desired effect. Like conversations with your husband, for example."

Jason shriveled and sat on the edge of a garden box not far from her. He picked an angle where he could see her eyes, even though they barely left her canvas. A small tray of paints was propped up on her right side. The front of her dress was stained with a vast assortment of colors.

"It's interesting to me that you chose a white dress to be your painting dress," he said. "The colors are much brighter and more visible when you spill."

"Exactly."

I might as well cut to the chase, he thought. "One of the soldiers said you wanted to talk to me."

"One of the soldiers was right."

"Darling, we've talked about this so many times before."

"And here we are again."

"What is different this time?"

"Hopefully, this is the time you actually listen."

"I've always listened, I just don't agree," Jason said. "Saryan, I don't think now is the right time to have a child. We're both still too young."

"Jason, my mother was twenty when she had me," Saryan replied without looking off her canvas. "We're both twenty-two. It's not uncommon for people our age to start having children."

"What about a King and a Queen?"

At that, Saryan tore her eyes from her painting and jabbed a paintbrush in Jason's direction. "*That* kind of thinking is dangerous. Don't put yourself above those you serve. It breeds corruption. We're all commoners in the Dragon's eyes."

"I think I know a little bit more about being a commoner than you do," Jason said with a raised eyebrow. "Is the son of a Lower City printer more common than the daughter of a Nezmythian Captain?"

"Don't get distracted," Saryan said firmly. "We're talking about having children, Jason."

"Right," Jason said. "What about the kingdom, then? Would I be first a king, or a father?"

"I don't know. But you're not going to be replaced anytime soon. There is no use waiting to start the next part of our married lives. You could be king until we're old and gray for all we know." For once, Saryan set her brush on the tray. She turned about and faced her husband with one hand on her hip. She wasn't angry. Instead, her eyebrows with slightly furrowed and her cheeks were stiff.

"You're scared. You're scared, aren't you? You don't think you're ready to be a father."

Jason sat up straight. His voice raised as a splash of indignation. "I'm not scared! Why would a king be scared of having a baby?"

"I really don't know," Saryan's face softened and she shook her head. "You truly are a wonderful person. I think you would be a marvelous father. You know that the Dragon helps us in times of need. You know that better than most."

To this, Jason had no reply. He knew she was referring to his Year of Decision, the year in which they fell in love and had to endure the constant, watchful eyes of King Barnabas and his spies. Divine intervention was the only way Jason could have survived that year, being a poor boy from Lower City. He subconsciously rubbed the mark on his right hand.

"Saryan," Jason began. "I love you more than anything. But I think—"

At that moment, the door to the courtyard flew open, and another soldier was standing in the doorway.

"Your Highness," the soldier bowed politely. "Master Ferribolt has arrived. I've summoned for Mr. Nadiel and he should arrive in the great hall shortly."

Jason nodded and the soldier departed.

Queen Saryan's shoulders sagged and she picked up her brush again. "Go on. I'm sure it's important."

Jason didn't get up right away. He gazed upon her, his eyes searching. Dejection was riddled across her face, and she seemed to be trying to push down the hopelessness and tender frustration she had been feeling with every brushstroke. At length, Jason stood up, left her a gentle kiss on the cheek, and slipped back into the castle.

2

THE MESSAGE

As Master Ferribolt tilted his head upward to admire the mural painted across the castle ceiling, the torchlight reflected off his bald head and round spectacles. He strolled around, his feet lifting lightly off the carpet as his hands clasped behind his back. The movement accentuated his round belly, even under his flowing orange robes.

Nadiel was at his usual spot by the throne, standing on the side opposite of the Queen's seat. He didn't say anything, but tapped his toes in an impatient rhythm. His face was hard—twisted by a variety of thoughts. He and Master Ferribolt had already exchanged their pleasantries. A door unlatched on the side of the hall, and Jason made his way through. Both he and Master Ferribolt bowed as he entered.

"Master Ferribolt, how are you this evening?" he said as he strode up and embraced him.

"Very well, thank you, Your Highness," Master Ferribolt returned with a genuine smile. "How do you suppose our friend is going to take to the news?"

"I'm not sure," Jason replied as they walked toward the throne. He turned to a nearby soldier and said, "Would you find Master Ferribolt a seat please?" Then he turned back to the Chief Patriarch. "I imagine he'll take to it better than I did to mine."

"Yes, you won't plot to destroy him during the next year, so I would assume so," Master Ferribolt said with a wink.

Jason grinned, but as he passed by Nadiel to sit in his Throne, he couldn't help but notice Nadiel's intensity. His tapping toe and his stoic gaze never stopped. Jason frowned. "Are you okay, Nadiel? I know we only got to work together for a short time."

"My feelings on this matter are irrelevant," Nadiel returned flatly. "The Dragon has set in motion Its mighty purposes, and we as leaders of Nezmyth are charged to follow those promptings in protecting and guiding our people."

Jason sat in his throne and let out a muffled sigh. When he looked to Master Ferribolt, the Chief Patriarch gave him a subtle, helpless shrug.

Nadiel continued, "I suggest we begin discussing what must take place if a new Advisor is to replace me. There is no reason to prolong the purpose for this gathering. Shall we begin?"

The soldier had returned with Master Ferribolt's seat, and after setting it behind him, Master Ferribolt granted him the most genuine thanks. The soldier retreated with a nod and a shimmering grin that could only be directed to the holiest man in Nezmyth.

"So, Master Ferribolt," Jason spoke first. "Was it just today that you felt these nudges from the Sacred Dragon?"

"Indeed," Master Ferribolt replied. "I was kneeling in prayer at the Upper City Cathedral, supplicating the Holy Dragon, asking what Its will may be. I felt as though I meditated for nearly an hour before an answer came as clear as the morning sunrise. It is time for Nezmyth's King to receive his new Advisor."

To this, Jason peered at Nadiel from out of the corner of his eye. Nadiel didn't budge. His gaze remained fixed on the Chief Patriarch.

"I thought it strange at first," Master Ferribolt continued. "I thought, 'He must be around the King's age? That's very young for an Advisor.' But then I remembered that the Dragon had prompted me five years earlier to call the new King to his position. Jason, you were only seventeen at the time. How odd! It seems as though the Holy Dragon is in favor of young leaders at this time."

"It is odd. Nadiel," Jason turned to the Advisor. "What was your Year of Decision like? I know mine was measured a lot based on my virtue, wisdom and strength, but I was Foreordained to become King."

"Becoming a King's Advisor is very different," Nadiel said, his red eyes focused and his hands laced together on his lap. "The Ordination Ceremony at the conclusion of the year is essentially unchanged—the Foreordained's worthiness is measured by the Chief Patriarch's observations, my own, and the Oracle Stone's."

"So, we'll need to retrieve the Oracle Stone before he arrives tonight," Jason confirmed. He turned to a nearby soldier and gave him a nod, signaling the order. The soldier nodded in return and marched away.

"Yes," Nadiel said. "But you, Jason, were simply measured by your efforts to become a better man for the throne. You grew in wisdom, virtue, and strength upon your own accord. That is also true of an Advisor. He must do these things, but this is not all. He must be nothing less than an impeccable scholar. He must be well-versed in history, economics, geography, magical arts, and so forth. That includes Ancient Nezmythian."

"How will he be tutored in the next year?" Master Ferribolt asked. "I took it upon myself during Jason's Year of Decision, but I'll admit it was a little presumptuous to do so."

"You were the only protection I had from a King that constantly sought my life, so I think your actions were justified," Jason said.

Nadiel shifted and said, "Custom dictates that I take it upon myself to teach the boy. It is recommended that my lessons with him should be a daily occurrence."

"If he's supposed to learn all of those things within the year that seems necessary," Jason said. "During my Year of Decision, I met with Master Ferribolt weekly just to learn Ancient Nezmythian and I still wasn't close to fluent by the end of the year."

Nadiel nodded. "As I understand, he is an expert in physical combat, but seldomly uses magic outside of a jeroki. How is his knowledge on the things I had mentioned earlier? History and economics?"

The question was directed to Jason, who replied, "He runs his own shop on the Lower Market Street, so he has a slightly better understanding of economics than most. As for history… only as much as the common man."

"I see," Nadiel said. "Well, is there anything you gentleman think we need to address further?"

Jason and Master Ferribolt agreed in the negative. It was decided that they would fetch him tonight.

"You fetched me in the blue coach at the beginning of my Year of Decision," Jason said to Nadiel. "Is it customary that I fetch him in my red coach?"

"It matters not," Nadiel shook his head. "But I know you would like to."

With that, he grinned at the King genuinely. Jason couldn't help but return the gesture. He placed his hand on Nadiel's shoulder, which was noticeably above his own.

"It has been an honor to work and serve with you," he said. "And I'm grateful that I'll still have you for at least one more year. Nezmyth will forever be grateful for your service."

Nadiel continued to grin, but his eyes lost their gleam with Jason's comment. The King squeezed his shoulder in reassurance, and it was that moment that a soldier marched up to his side.

"Your coach is ready, Your Majesty," he said.

"Good," Jason replied. "Let's pay a little visit to Tarren, son of Gulaf the stonemason. He's got a very big year ahead of him."

With that, Jason and the soldier started toward the main doors. Jason blindly followed the red carpet as he walked, thinking about the honor it would be to serve as King and Advisor with his best friend. Memories of sparring, playing music, and laughing as young boys danced in his mind. It seemed as though the memories they had already forged together were just a dull fraction of what their future held.

However, something stopped him. In an instant, a chill fell over him like a blanket. His fingers and face went cold, making him shudder and gasp. The feeling didn't go away.

"Do you feel that?" Nadiel called from halfway down the hall.

"Yes," Jason said.

"I do as well," Master Ferribolt said.

"It's just as I felt earlier," Nadiel said. "But much stronger."

Jason turned about and faced the two of them. Concern was riddled across their faces. Nadiel's red eyes, burning and serious, were fixed on the doors. His hand was on the hilt of his sword, his shoulders back.

"Something is coming," he said. "I can sense it. I'm not certain, but it can't be far."

He and Jason both ripped their blades from their sheaths in unison. Master Ferribolt merely stood, waiting, his eyes locked on the door. The dark feeling hadn't dissipated in the slightest, but only grew in intensity as the moments stretched on.

With each passing second, the air grew colder.

"Your Highness!"

A soldier scurried into the hall, panting and clutching some parchment. He slid to a halt in front of Jason.

"Sir," he began. "Three messengers have somehow infiltrated the castle grounds and are waiting by the doors! They've requested an audience with you immediately. All of them are heavily armed, but—they aren't doing anything."

Nadiel marched up to Jason, his eyes fierce.

"They made it past the outer gates?" Jason clutched his sword tighter.

"Yes, sir," the soldier continued. "They just appeared out of nothing! The soldiers were ready to fight them, but the messengers didn't draw their weapons. They said their only purpose is to deliver a message."

"Then why the weapons at all?" Nadiel asked flatly.

At this, the soldier had no answer. Jason, Nadiel, and Master Ferribolt all exchanged hard looks. Messengers never stopped by in the evening. And the cold rush that had befallen all their hearts was unmistakable. However, everyone's weapons were drawn, there were only three messengers, and the castle hall was lined with some of the most able-bodied soldiers in the kingdom.

Jason turned back to a soldier and said, "Fine. Let them enter."

The soldier nodded and scurried away again. After a long moment, three great knocks were given, and a small group of soldiers heaved the ancient doors open. They groaned mightily as they swung open inch by inch, pouring the crisp evening air into the castle.

A shiver shot down Jason's back. The sun was fading over the horizon, so little daylight spilled into the hall. It was hard to discern the figures of their intruders, but as they sauntered down the red carpet, their silhouettes cleared. The sight of them made his palms sweat.

The messengers were human-like in the sense that they had arms, legs, and similar features, but the rest of their appearance was undeniably unnatural. Gray, oily skin covered their grotesquely muscular bodies, and their eyes and ears stuck into their skulls as if they were half-melted. The crudely crafted clothes of leather and beasts' fur hanging from their bodies covered little more than their privates. And each messenger carried a small armory on their person—swords, axes, and spears across their backs and daggers in their boots.

As they came closer, they leered at the three Nezmythian leaders. The one in front sneered at the King as he stopped only a few paces away from him. It was then that Jason noticed their teeth—an eroding yellowish gray, coated with saliva. Jason held his ground, blade still drawn, while the chilling cold enveloped him. The three creatures bowed.

"Greetings, Jason, King of Nezmyth," the first had a voice like stone.

"Who are you?" Jason replied firmly. "And how did you make it to the castle doors without detection?"

"We come bearing a message," the first said, "from his majesty, King Nartikis of Unbuntye."

"We have no dealings with the kingdom of Unbuntye," Nadiel shot.

"Now, it seems you will," the beast sneered once more.

The beast held a folded-up piece of parchment and extended it to Jason. With his eyes still fixed on the beast, Jason snatched up the parchment and unfolded it. The message was very short, written with thick black ink.

TO THE FOREORDAINED KING OF NEZMYTH, JASON. WE ARE IN NEED OF YOUR AID. OUR KINGDOM SUFFERS WHILE NEZMYTH ENJOYS PLENTY. I WOULD BE HONORED TO HOST YOU WHILE WE NEGOTIATE A MEANS FOR TRADE. PLEASE ARRIVE AS SOON AS POSSIBLE. MY

PEOPLE ARE IN GREAT NEED. —NARTIKIS, BORN
KING OF UNBUNTYE

Beneath the signature, the seal of Unbuntye was stamped in black wax. Jason stole another look at King Nartikis's servants. The message seemed earnest enough, but the nature of its delivery was questionable to say the least. His eyes narrowed.

"A plea for help," Jason said. "Then why send three armed guards?"

"We are but messengers," the first beast said. "Serving the Born King of Unbuntye."

"Born King..." Jason echoed the letter's signature. "That's right, Unbuntye has followed a succession of bloodline for some time now, haven't they? You're much like the other kingdoms of Wevlia that have abandoned the ancient ways of Foreordination."

The beast didn't reply but continued to smirk with horrible teeth. Jason folded the note back up.

"I take it you need an answer immediately?" he said.

The beast nodded.

"Then you'll allow me to deliberate with my Advisor and Chief Patriarch."

"Of course."

His brow furrowed, Jason marched back to the throne platform, Master Ferribolt and Nadiel following closely behind. Once they were out of earshot, Jason spoke in a low tone. "I don't like this."

"The dark cloud around my heart is unmistakable," Nadiel said. "And the nature of these... messengers... is most unsettling. They are the result of something unnatural— possibly Dark Magic. I believe it would be unwise to visit Unbuntye. I suspect ulterior motives."

Jason turned to Master Ferribolt. "And you, Master?"

"This is not my matter to discuss," Master Ferribolt said. "But since you asked, I must echo what Nadiel has stated. The darkness in our hearts and the chill in our bones is a warning if I've ever felt one."

"Good, then it's decided."

Jason and the others marched back, and Jason held the letter back out to the first messenger. Jason said, "Unfortunately, Nezmyth is not in a position to assist Unbuntye at this time. I'm sorry."

The beast took the note, and its mischievous demeanor dropped. Instead, it ogled over Jason, perplexed. "But Nezmyth is rich with livestock and crops. We have heard of the Southern Plains and its—"

"His Highness has given you his response," Nadiel said with finality. "We now kindly ask you to depart."

The beasts scanned the great hall. Every soldier in the room was squared up, feet apart, swords and spears and magic hands twitching, ready to attack. The messengers pensively closed their smoldering eyes, then bowed and lifted their heads one more time.

"Very well," the beast said. "We shall go."

Nadiel and Jason covertly exchanged glances. The beasts turned about and began to saunter toward the giant doors. After just a few steps, the leading beast stopped. It turned its head toward the Nezmythian rulers and spoke softly.

"The children of Unbuntye starve," the beast purred. "Our crops scorch in the sun and our livestock rot in the fields. Is this the life you curse us to? We had heard much of the goodness and mercy of King Jason. It appears we were misinformed."

With that, the beasts continued their march. Jason's body was consumed with the chill, but he felt his heart sink. Is this the legacy he was choosing to leave? To so quickly dismiss the ruler of another kingdom's honest plea? His face was hard as the gears in his mind turned. He pictured it—the starving Unbuntye children in a kingdom depleted of resources. Could it be true? If it were, those lost lives would be on him.

On that thought, Jason thrust his sword back into its sheath. Nadiel looked on in cautious curiosity, but his curiosity quickly changed to dismay when Jason stepped forward.

"Wait!" Jason called to the messengers.

The soldiers were beginning to pull open the massive doors at the end of the hall. As they continued to pull, the beasts turned around. Jason ignored their unnatural eyes and horrible teeth. When he reached them, he put the palm of his hand on the pommel of his sword.

He asked, "How far is it to the capital of Unbuntye?"

"Four days by carriage," the beast replied.

Jason looked back at his friends. Master Ferribolt's face was dark, and Nadiel's was still bristling and tense. The Advisor slowly shook his head. Jason turned back to the messenger.

"I'll leave tomorrow morning," Jason said. "I'll order bags of seeds and grains and bring it with my caravan. I don't want Unbuntye to suffer. You can tell King Nartikis that."

The beast grinned, and the glint returned to its eye. "Very well, Your Highness. The kingdom of Unbuntye thanks you."

Without another word, the three beasts strode out of the hall. Once they were through, soldiers pushed the massive doors shut. Before they could shut completely, Jason saw them disappear in a puff of purple smoke. When they disappeared, warmth gradually returned to his body. The soldiers in the great hall relaxed their shoulders and sheathed their weapons. Jason frowned.

"What were those things?" he said. "Have you ever seen them before?"

"No," Nadiel said sternly. His eyes bore into Jason. "You directly disregarded my council once again."

"What if they were telling the truth?" Jason said. "What if Unbuntye is suffering? We can't turn our backs on them."

"*Or* it could be a terrible lie. Your Highness, those creatures are teeming with Dark Magic. We all felt the warmth leave our souls when they approached. The fruits of Dark Magic are power, greed, lust, and *deception*. I fear that you're venturing into the mouth of an enemy."

"You fear a lot of things, Nadiel," Jason replied sharply. "Are they the result of Dark Magic? Very possible. If that's the case, we won't have any dealings with Unbuntye. But until then, I need to see for myself."

Master Ferribolt readjusted his robes. "Jason, the Sacred Dragon has not assigned me as your Advisor, but I must say that this whole enterprise leaves me uneasy."

"Duly noted, Master Ferribolt, thank you," Jason said. "Regardless, I gave them my word. Nartikis will be expecting me. I'll hear him out. We won't know the full condition of Unbuntye until I've seen it with my own eyes. I'll alert you both immediately of my plans after I've arrived."

"Would you like some company on the journey, Your Majesty?" Nadiel said, trying to push down his irritation.

Jason looked upon him. Those red eyes were serious, like a strict, protective parent. Jason shook his head. "I don't think so. I need you to stay here to overlook the affairs of the kingdom while I'm gone. After all, I'll be gone for several days."

"The Queen will likely want to go with you," Nadiel replied.

"I won't let her," Jason said with finality. "I think we all know this trip will be unlike any other we've experienced. I want her to stay here." The King paused once more before he said, "But we'll worry more about this tomorrow. Right now, I need to fetch the kingdom's next Advisor."

3

THE ADVISOR

Four years ago, The Cranny Musical Instrument Repair and Shop was nestled in an alleyway just off the Southern Market Street. Though the shop was uncomfortably small, Tarren still made it his home after hours. He had a cramped room in the back of the shop just big enough for a bed and not much else.

However, when King Barnabas was dethroned and the Harvest Tax was removed, business improved steadily for many people across the kingdom, including Tarren. More people had money to afford musical instruments, so he quickly found himself with more customers and more money to save. Over time, he was able to move out of the tiny shop in the alleyway and purchase a bigger, modestly sized storefront not far away on the Southern Market Street.

Nighttime had settled on Nezmyth City, and there was barely a spirit roaming the street. The crimson carriage rolled up to The Cranny and the white stallions jerked their heads as the reigns were pulled. When Jason climbed out, he scanned the new premises that Tarren had become accustomed to. Various drums and stringed instruments stood on display in the window, and a handsome sign with the shop's name hung just over the door. He probably would have made that sign himself if he hadn't become King years ago.

He didn't walk up to the door. Instead, Jason walked around the back of the building where a narrow, slanting staircase led to an upper floor. Each step creaked horribly as he climbed. At the top, a shabby door with a rusty latch stood between him and the inside. He knocked.

There was a short pause, then the sounds of slow, muffled footsteps on wooden floorboards. After a moment, the rusty latch clicked, and the door swung open. Tarren appeared with squinting, sleepy, purple eyes and a long nightshirt. His blonde hair had recently been cut, so it didn't reach his eyes like it used to. However, he was still several inches taller than Jason and had muscle to spare.

He had to blink a few times, and Jason merely stood in his door, grinning. Finally, Tarren's eyes adjusted. "Business hours are from sunup to dusk. If you'd like a custom order, please submit it at least a month in advance."

Jason smirked and a staccato laugh escaped his lips. "I don't know how you're still able to joke when you're this tired."

Tarren half-smiled and said, "It's a gift. Come on in."

"Actually, the carriage is waiting for you."

Suddenly, the sleepiness fled from Tarren's eyes. Color left his face and he swallowed hard.

"So," he breathed. "It's time then?"

Jason nodded. "It is."

Tarren took a deep, heaving breath and cleared his throat before retreating into his flat. He resurfaced not long after with pants, boots, a comfortable linen shirt and two daggers slung around his waist. He locked his door shut before they descended the staircase.

"So now what?" Tarren said. "Am I suddenly Advisor? That's it?"

"No," Jason replied. "You have to go through something called a Year of Decision. I had to do it before I became King.

It's a year in which you're tested and taught how to rule before you make your final decision on your Foreordination. My Advisor, Nadiel, is at the castle right now and he'll explain everything when we arrive."

"So it will be at least a year?"

"One year from today."

They both climbed into the carriage. Tarren sat across from Jason, twiddling his thumbs in his lap, staring at the space between his feet with glossy, vacant eyes. The carriage wheels ground softly on the cobblestone beneath them and the clopping of horse hooves were soft, almost hypnotic.

"How are you feeling?" Jason asked.

"Oh, just fine. Just great. Yep." Tarren said. Then he sighed. "I don't know what to do. I've known this was going to happen for years, but I didn't know *when* it would happen. I'm still so young."

Jason laughed a little. "I understand that feeling."

"What was your Year of Decision like?"

"It was all-consuming. Terrifying. I spent all my time and energy trying to better myself for the Throne. Meeting with Master Ferribolt every week was a great help. I never could have made it without him."

"Your Year of Decision had to be unlike any other, though," Tarren said. "With that murderous madman Barnabas and everything. It's amazing he didn't kill you."

"Dragon knows he tried," Jason replied. "But Nadiel and the Dragon protected me from afar. You have a lot to learn in the coming year, but I know the Dragon will help you too."

"But I'm not allowed to talk about it, right?" Tarren said.

"No," Jason. "But it's mostly for your benefit. Imagine every aristocrat trying to befriend you because of your new position. You'd have a legion of new 'friends' that would want to associate with you just because of your title. You don't need that burden upon you."

Tarren hummed and nodded.

They sat in silence for some time. The once-tawdry shops of the Southern Market Street turned to the fancy and intricate storefronts of the Northern Market Street. All the while, Tarren kept rubbing his hands between his knees and staring at the floor. Suddenly, he asked, "You're the only Nezmythian ruler that's married, aren't you? Master Ferribolt and Nadiel don't have wives."

Taken aback, Jason replied, "That's true."

"Why?"

"Master Ferribolt was married, but she passed five or six years ago," Jason said. "Nadiel has never been married, though. I would tell you the story, but I don't think that's my place. I'm sure he'll tell you eventually."

"I thought it was strongly recommended that a Foreordained ruler be married."

"It is," Jason replied. "But not necessary. It's all in the Dragon's plan."

They sat in silence for a bit longer. The carriage turned toward Upper City, climbing up the hill that led toward the castle. Handsome, symmetrical houses of brick and stone stood in the moonlight. Lit street torches threw a dancing orange glow onto the ascending cobblestone. As the carriage tottered closer to the castle, Jason couldn't help but think of the recent events in the great hall.

"We had a strange happening at the castle just before I came to get you," Jason said.

"The royal chef undercooked your beef?" Tarren said. "No maids to rub your feet?"

Jason would have loved to laugh but couldn't. "We had a few visitors—three messengers from Unbuntye on behalf of their King, Nartikis. He wants my presence immediately because he says Unbuntye is struggling to survive."

"That doesn't seem too strange."

"But the messengers were beastly things. They look like humans, but with gray skin and misplaced eyes and ears. When they entered, all of us felt cold, like the warmth of our bodies just left us. I could even see my breath."

At this, Tarren shivered and his hands subconsciously went to his daggers. "You didn't hear them cast a spell of any sort?"

"No. We think they may be the result of *Tepnoh Edomah*."

"*Tepnoh Edomah?*" Tarren repeated.

"Ancient Nezmythian for Dark Magic."

Tarren's gaze dropped. "I didn't know something like that even existed."

"Good," Jason said. "We try to keep it that way. It's powerful, but seductive and evil. If everyone knew about it, the kingdom would probably fall into chaos." He looked out the window. "I plan on leaving tomorrow. I'm not sure what this trip will hold, but I'm going with a legion of guards. Tarren, I've never seen those creatures before. I felt it—the darkness that was within them. I hope I'm wrong about all of this."

Tarren swallowed and he let out a shaky sigh.

Jason half smiled and said, "I suppose this is what you get to look forward to for the next year."

* * * * *

Tarren sat in a chair not far from the throne platform, his knees together and his hands on his thighs. The past several minutes had gone quickly for him. He entered the great hall trying desperately to breathe evenly and keep a temperate composure. Master Ferribolt magically procured a chair and Tarren sat in it. Nadiel rehearsed all the details for his Year of Decision. Then he brought the Oracle Stone.

When Nadiel placed the Oracle Stone in Tarren's hands, Tarren took it like it was made of priceless porcelain. Jason knew that he couldn't break that stone if he tried, but it was still amusing to see him handle it so carefully. The smoke inside the glassy orb stirred at Tarren's touch, and, after a moment, the smoke swirled vigorously and began to change color.

As it was first a neutral gray, but in Tarren's hands it became a soft, glimmering yellow. It reminded Jason of the color it was during his Ordination Ceremony years ago.

"The Oracle Stone measures the purity of your heart," Nadiel told Tarren as he paced several feet away. "It will be black if you have completely surrendered yourself to darkness, or white if your heart is completely unspotted and pure. It looks as though you have a very healthy spirit."

"Thank you, sir," Tarren said. "I supplicate the Dragon at the Cathedral weekly."

"That is good. What did you make of your Foreordination when you received your Blessing of Fate?"

Tarren scratched his neck. "I didn't know what to think. I didn't understand why the Dragon would want *me* to be an Advisor, but I wished in my heart that my time wouldn't come until after Barnabas was gone." The last few words were hard and heated.

"Understandably so," Nadiel said. "But if the Dragon had called you to fulfill your Foreordination at that time, would you have done it?"

Tarren though about it for a second, then nodded the faintest nod. "Yes."

That word came out with particular venom. Jason knew that Tarren was thinking of his mother, who, if it weren't for Barnabas, wouldn't be living in a faraway village for the incurably insane. She was taken many years ago and thrown in prison, accused of speaking ill of the King. When she was released, she had such frequent flashbacks of her prison beatings that she couldn't live among average people. They sent her to Lunli Village to live with others like her. Tarren's hatred for King Barnabas had been alive and well ever since.

"For the next year," Nadiel said. "You will meet with me every day so I can tutor you in preparation for your position. You'll become well-versed in the arts, literature, mathematics, economics, history, magical arts, and Ancient Nezmythian. It is imperative that you acquire a formidable knowledge of these things in order to properly advise your friend. After all, a King is nothing without his Advisor."

Jason smirked. Maybe Nadiel was patting himself on the back for saying that, but it wasn't far from the truth.

"Every *day?*" Tarren repeated. "But I'm already loaded with so much work! How do I juggle the time it takes to travel to the castle daily and participate in these lessons? What about my shop?"

"The Dragon will provide," Nadiel said. "Your Foreordination takes precedence above all else." Nadiel marched back to the throne platform. "I have nothing further that I need to discuss with Tarren. So, unless either of you have matters you would like to address, I would be happy to escort him home in my coach."

Jason arose from his throne and strolled off the dais, heading for his best friend. He took Tarren in the Nezmythian Grasp of Brotherhood, looked him firmly in the eyes and said, "You'll be an excellent Advisor. The next year will be difficult, but if I can wear this cape, you can too."

Tarren smiled sheepishly.

Everyone at the throne platform exchanged their pleasantries, then Tarren and Nadiel made their way down the red carpet. The doors at the head of the hall opened and closed in their usual manner, and Jason knew that Tarren and Nadiel were on their way back to the Southern Market Street.

Interestingly, Master Ferribolt lingered, even though it was much later than he preferred to stay awake. He stood by the throne platform, his hands clasped behind his back, admiring the mural on the ceiling once again. Then he turned to Jason and smiled like a wise and patient father.

Jason knew that look all too well. He had been on the receiving end of that gaze dozens of times before—particularly during his Year of Decision.

"This must bring back memories for you."

Jason slumped down and propped his head in his hand. His eyes felt heavy and his bones ached. "It sure does," he responded. "Many visits to your mansion in which you taught me the ancient language and the dangers of Dark Magic. I told Tarren that I wouldn't be in this throne without you."

"You learned much, and you grew significantly," Master Ferribolt said. "You were humble. You had faith. You were willing to rise to your responsibility and take the throne, despite your fear. Your story is truly remarkable."

Jason squinted just a little. "You know, usually you precede some sort of criticism with compliments."

Master Ferribolt's belly bounced as he chortled. "I know. You find yourself short of surprises once you reach my age." He paused. "Jason, I worry for you occasionally."

"How so?"

"You came in and began to rebuild a crumbling kingdom. You've seen much success. You're beloved by your people and you judge righteously. It's clear that the people of Nezmyth are much happier now than they were years ago."

"But?"

"But I'm afraid a seedling of pride has been growing inside you. And I fear that it is because of your success."

Jason tilted his head. "Explain."

"Your disregard to your Advisor's council today was an example, among other things," Master Ferribolt said. "It's impossible to be perfectly humble as King—with legions of soldiers at your every beck and call, it can be difficult to hear dissenting views when you're surrounded by so many that tell you 'yes.' You seem to do more and listen less than you did when you took the throne years ago."

"I've learned a lot since then."

"True, but considering yourself wise leaves little room for wisdom at all."

A spark of anger lit up Jason's chest. As quickly as it appeared, it faded. His hands tightened and then loosened.

"I understand, Master Ferribolt," Jason said. "Could we continue this conversation another time?"

"Of course. I apologize," Master Ferribolt bowed respectfully. "I do hope you know my words come from a place of love. I'm so grateful to have you as my King. I just worry. That's all."

Jason smiled benevolently. "And I'm grateful for you. Truly." He got up from his throne, stepped off the dais, and gave Master Ferribolt a hug. They exchanged their farewells before they exited the great hall.

Dragging his feet, Jason ascended through several hallways and staircases that led to the castle's master bedroom. As he went, soldiers nodded to him and wished him a good night. He hardly noticed them. His mind was occupied on Master Ferribolt's recent words. Had he become too prideful and overconfident? Perhaps, but compared to Barnabas? No. Jason was a perfect angel in comparison. Right now, maybe that's all that mattered.

He opened the door to his quarters as quietly as he could and latched it shut. Across the room, in their large four-poster bed, Queen Saryan slept. Her golden blonde hair spilled over her pillow and onto the sheets. Jason untied his cape and hung it on a hook by the door, then proceeded to slip off his armor and put on his night clothes soundlessly. The stone floor was cold against his bare feet, and he walked on tiptoes toward the bed.

He slipped under the covers, being careful not to disturb the Queen. She stirred, not reaching the threshold of waking, and exhaled a deep, peaceful breath.

Jason fell asleep quickly. In his dreams, he saw warriors with oily gray skin.

4

THE FOREST

When Jason exited the castle the next day, he found several servants already packing things into a supply carriage. His red carriage waited for him not far away, his driver leaning back in his seat smoking a pipe and looking as pleasant as ever. He tipped his hat to the King as he passed. Among the carriages, nearly one hundred soldiers stood armed and ready for march.

Spring was slowly creeping into summer, and the sun had a fresh golden tint as it rose over the Eastern Mountains. The chill of the morning was bracing, and Jason's arms sprouted into goose bumps as he marched across the castle grounds. Plants and trees swayed in the breeze as he walked by, almost as if they were bowing to him.

Nadiel was outside overseeing the packing affairs, arms folded, watching the servants like an unimpressed supervisor. His blue cape wafted around his ankles and shuddered in the early morning breeze. Jason walked up beside him, adjusting his own cape. When he stopped, he placed his hand on the hilt of his sword.

Nadiel spotted him out the corner of his eye. "Good morning, Your Highness."

"I don't feel good about this," Jason said.

"Nor do I. Yet here we are."

"I'm just looking forward to getting it over with," Jason said. "I feel better having all these guards come along. How was Tarren on the trip home last night?"

"As well as can be expected," Nadiel replied. "Very nervous. Very unsure of himself. Just like another young man who was tested not long ago."

"He'll be alright—better than me, I would say. He's a hard worker, one of the hardest I know, and I know he'll put in a valiant effort."

"His heart is pure, too," they heard from behind.

They turned and discovered that Master Ferribolt had suddenly appeared on the edge of a garden box not a dozen paces away. His legs were crossed, and his hands sat laced on top of one knee. Overall, he looked very pleased.

"I listened to the Dragon's whispers as we talked last night," Master Ferribolt continued. "Tarren is of course very unsure of himself, but he's ready and willing to do whatever he can for the kingdom. I think in time he will make a fine Advisor."

"How long have you been sitting there?" Jason narrowed his eyes.

Master Ferribolt didn't reply, but just smiled a crafty smile. Jason shook his head and turned to Nadiel. "What are you planning on teaching him tonight?"

"History and Ancient Nezmythian," Nadiel replied. "He's most interested in magical arts, which will come along with the ancient language."

"Of course," Jason replied. "I'm looking forward to hear how the lessons fare." He glanced at the sun to check the time. "I should probably leave soon if I'm to reach the Western Woods by nightfall. Have either of you seen my wife?"

"*I'm right here!*"

And there she was indeed, stomping her way over to them. Her face was red and hot, and her hair was tied up as if she had recently finished sparring. Her hand wrapped tightly around her favorite staff—the one that Jason had made her years ago—as she thrust it into the ground. Her other hand was on her hip, and her scowl could have set Jason ablaze.

"What's all this about?" she half-yelled, motioning to the caravan.

"Excuse us," Nadiel said to the King while shooting a glance at Queen Saryan. "Erm—Master Ferribolt, do you mind?"

"Certainly not!" Master Ferribolt slid off his perch.

They both scurried away without looking back at whatever storm was brewing. Jason gazed into those burning silver eyes and tried to remain collected.

"Saryan, my love," he said calmly. "I meant to tell you, but when I came in last night you were asleep and when I awoke you were already out—"

"*Eight days, at least!*" she said, leaning in. "That's what they told me, Jason! Eight days! The entire castle knew before I did! Where are you going?"

"Unbuntye."

"Why?"

"Unbuntye is struggling—or at least the King claims it is. I don't know." Jason sighed. "I'm going to Unbuntye to measure their affairs. If they need help, we have carriages packed with supplies and we'll send more later. If there are ulterior motives, we'll have a large battalion of soldiers at the ready."

"I'm going with you," she said.

"No, you're not," Jason returned with just as much finality.

"Jason—!"

"Saryan, I *don't* have a good feeling about this trip!" Jason said. "I need you here. In Nezmyth. What if—Dragon forbid—something were to happen to me? You're my Inheritor, so you'd be left to rule the kingdom. Please stay."

"If you have a bad feeling about this trip, why are you going at all? That could be a warning. Just stay home."

"I gave them my word. My mind wouldn't rest if I didn't at least see for myself."

Saryan huffed and threw her staff over her shoulder. "*Your* mind. Of course. Well then…" She dropped her staff, letting it clatter to the ground. Gracefully, she stretched out her hands and gave a theatrical bow, her matted hair hanging down her face. Her voice was unmistakably sarcastic. "Forgive me, Your Excellency! I only wanted but a morsel of your time!"

"Stop," Jason glowered.

Saryan scooped up her staff, flipped around, and said "Happy travels!" without so much as looking at him as she stormed away.

"Saryan!" Jason whined.

It was no use. The conversation was over. The hundred soldiers that lingered by the carriages watched the Queen saunter away spitefully before the castle doors opened and closed behind her. Then all eyes were on Jason. He clenched his jaw and breathed deep, trying not to think about how red his face probably was.

Now that the storm was over, Nadiel crept over to Jason. He cleared his throat and said, "Your Highness, the carriages are fully stocked now."

Jason breathed deep, looked up at the sky, then at Nadiel.

"Well then," he said. "No use wasting time. I'll see you in eight or nine days."

* * * * *

When the carriage reached the western gate, a small battalion of soldiers hurriedly opened the doors. The carriage bustled through, but not without engaging the distasteful glares of shoddy-looking townspeople. In his carriage, Jason caught the gaze of one scowling mother clutching to her young daughter, whispering something in her ear. Then the daughter scowled too. Jason pursed his lips and looked away.

Outside the city, it was rolling green hills for miles. It would be hours before the Western Woods would come into view—an expanse of coniferous trees that covered the western quarter of the kingdom. Deep in the Western Woods on the road toward the kingdom's border lay a village: Treetown. That's where they would stop for the night. A messenger was sent earlier alerting village chief of their arrival.

As the carriage climbed the first large hill, Jason looked out to the right. In the distance, he could see the chasm that was the Nezmyth City Prison. He couldn't help but think of Barnabas in the Vault of the Damned, buried deep below all the other convicts. What was he doing right now? Sitting on his knees, facing a wall, wallowing in the encompassing silence? What was he thinking?

The carriage door clicked open and ripped Jason out of his train of thought. A man wholly comprised of chiseled muscle and perfect posture slipped into the carriage and sat across from him. He was clad in a special bronze armor that signified the rank of Chief Captain in the Nezmythian Army. He took off his helmet, revealing peppery gray hair. His familiar silver eyes fixed on Jason as a knowing father would.

"I heard my daughter was a little upset this morning," he said in a thick, baritone voice.

"Good morning, Garrit," Jason replied. "She was. Understandably so. I didn't have the chance to talk to her at all about this trip since our little visitors came so late yesterday. I'm glad you were able to put this battalion together so quickly."

"Of course, Your Majesty," he said. "After all, it's not often that I get this kind of time with my son-in-law."

Jason half-smiled. "I'm sure Saryan is jealous of you right now. Sometimes I wonder if I spend more of my time in a carriage or by her side."

"She knew what she was getting into when she married you," Garrit replied. "Don't doubt that she still adores you,

Jason. Her passion just tends to bubble near the surface at times. Always has."

Jason thanked him for his reassuring words before Garrit saluted and exited the carriage.

The rest of the day's journey was uneventful. Grassy hills extended everywhere. The sun crept across the sky. After some hours, the Western Woods finally appeared. Jason could catch a glimpse of it every time the carriage rose over the crest of a hill. He spent some of the time studying Ancient Nezmythian texts that Master Ferribolt had let him borrow. As the afternoon wore on, he grew tired of the ancient books and hopped out of the carriage to stretch his legs.

The dirt crunched under his boots as he walked. Before and behind his carriage, nearly one hundred soldiers marched. All that noticed him nodded respectfully when they made eye contact, which Jason returned. It felt good to walk after sitting in a carriage for so long. He looked over his shoulders. The Nezmyth City Prison was far in the distance.

He craned his neck. "Garrit!"

In the carriage just ahead, Garrit hopped out and met Jason, walking shoulder to shoulder with him. As Garrit's eyes probed him, Jason could almost feel Saryan's probing him in kind.

"Garrit, do you think I'm a good King?"

Visibly taken aback, Garrit scoffed and said, "Of course I believe you're a good King. What's caused your confidence to falter?"

"A list of things," Jason sighed. "My relationship with Saryan… Master Ferribolt had some words for me last night about pride. This trip. Maybe I'm not doing enough for the kingdom."

"You're doing more than enough," Garrit said. "The kingdom is prospering now more than it has in decades. Remember, Your Highness, I had to serve under *Barnabas* for years. He killed people or threw them in prison at the drop of a hat, and I had to carry out those orders. It was terrible. Now that you're King, I can sleep well once again. You're a blessing to Nezmyth and I trust your judgment completely."

Jason grinned. As Garrit said it, the knot inside him loosened. Nezmyth *had* been prospering greatly in the years since Jason took the Throne. Poverty had decreased dramatically. The people seemed much happier. The prisons weren't full anymore. His decisions and decrees had brought peace and plenty. Maybe Master Ferribolt was just overreacting.

Jason thanked Garrit and they both clambered back into their individual carriages. But thoughts of Barnabas still trickled through Jason's mind.

Dusk fell over Nezmyth before the carriage creeped into the Western Woods. Tall conifers towered over the road and became more dense as they ventured deeper into the forest. The warm sunlight gave way to the coolness of shade, and sweet pine needles tickled Jason's nose. A sign was posted beside the road.

TREETOWN – 4 MILES
WESTERN BRIDGE/UNBUNTYE – 23 MILES

Perfect, Jason thought. *We'll be there just before nightfall.*

As they ventured, the sounds of animals became more frequent and varied. In the distance, Jason spotted deer on multiple occasions, and he noticed a fox poke its head out of a hole and look at him before embarking in search of a meal. Old, yellow pine needles were strewn everywhere, and the soft brown soil was quiet under the carriage wheels.

"Your Highness!" he heard a soldier call. "To your right!"

He sounded more excited than alarmed. Jason thrust his head out the window just in time to see it—a bear-sized, hairy, lumbering brown mass hurrying away at the sight of the caravan. At first glance, it appeared to be headless, but before it disappeared, Jason realized its face was part of its torso. It had only three fingers on its massive hands and thick, bare feet. It was tough to tell where exactly it disappeared to, but nonetheless, it was gone with surprising speed.

"Lampi!" one of the soldiers called. "The Guardian of the Western Woods! What is it doing so close to Treetown and the forest's edge?"

"It obviously wanted to see the King!" Garrit called with a cheerful air.

Jason grinned. He was sure the ancient creature was out there, watching him. As the caravan crawled by, he winked. The only reply was the distant rustle of a pine branch.

Through the trees, the stars began to populate the sky as the sun retired. Chirping crickets began to creak in chorus all around them as the cool night air drifted through the trees. After a while, the caravan could hear sounds of hollering men, clanking metal, and crying babies. Lights flickered between the trees as the dark blanket of night enveloped them.

The road opened into a large clearing nearly a mile in diameter. A quaint, handsome sign indicated the obvious: they had reached Treetown. Wooden cabins of various sizes packed in tight for the entire area of the clearing. Near the entrance, two guards clad in bear fur and toting axes of considerable size stood by the road. As they both saw the royal caravan, one pulled out a horn and blew. The sound echoed through the trees.

Instantly, voices sprouted through town. "The King is in town!" "King Jason is here!" "Come out, the King is coming!"

Like bees swarming in a hive, the people of Treetown gathered to the main road to greet the caravan. Jason returned the waves and cheers with his own tired wave and smile. The caravan pulled into the center of town where the main road opened up to a wide circular plaza. In the middle of the plaza, a stone well stood with its bucket drawn to the top—clearly the town's main water supply. The caravan pulled into a circle and lurched to a stop.

The applause didn't stop when Jason hopped out. He continued to wave and grin as he thought, *I'll never get used to this.*

It was then that he noticed two women approaching him. The first was massive and garbed in the skins of what had to be a half dozen different woodland creatures. Like the men guarding the city, she herself had a large ax slung across her back. Her beady black eyes accompanied a smile and laugh that could shake the earth, and her hands were as close to a giant's as Jason had ever seen.

The second woman was Jason's height. She had shaved her dark hair on the sides and pulled the rest into a tight ponytail. Everything about her seemed strong and dense, from her wide shoulders to her thighs. Despite her strength, the glasses on her nose and the parchment in her hand made her appearance radiate intelligence as well as strength.

The first woman lifted her giant arms and with a booming voice said, "Long live Jason, Fore'dained King o' Nezmyth!"

The people of Treetown cheered.

With that, the woman continued to lumber jovially over to Jason with a robust laugh. She threw her arms out and scooped Jason up in a bear hug. The town looked on with delight as the woman nearly broke Jason in half. When she released him, he inhaled sharply and coughed.

"Chief Patu!" Jason said, still coughing. "Thank you for making arrangements for us on such short notice. I apologize for any intrusion."

"No apologies nes'sary, your 'ighness!" Chief Patu replied. "Adria is ever-p'pared for such things!" Her face beamed as she motioned to the woman beside her.

Adria nodded and shook Jason's hand firmly. "I hope your venture through the woods was peaceful."

"Very, thank you," Jason replied.

"Come!" Chief Patu said. "The trip from Nezmyth City's a full day's journey! I'm sure yer exhausted. Let us feed ya some supper. Come!"

Chief Patu and Adria led Jason to the village chief's cabin. Meanwhile, the battalion of soldiers took their stations throughout town and the people returned to their homes. Garrit and two soldiers followed behind Jason a few paces but said nothing. The cabin was an intricate work of timber with the flag of Treetown hanging on the roof's crest. The King's cabin was next door, a very similar edifice, but hardly ever used.

Jason and Chief Patu made idle conversation about the goings-on in Nezmyth City as they entered the cabin and made their way to the dining quarters. A splendid meal of venison and cooked vegetables already waited for them. Chief Patu and Jason sat at the table and began to dine while Garrit and the soldiers stood silently at the entrances to the room. Adria served a similar position to Chief Patu, standing over her shoulder.

"'Ow are the Lower Ci'y folk?" Chief Patu asked as she stuck a fork full of vegetables in her mouth.

"Still not in favor of me," Jason said lowly as he dabbed the corner of his mouth with a napkin. "I don't know what to do. I got rid of the Harvest Tax and distributed Barnabas's riches, but many of them are still poor. I'm at a loss. I think they believe that I'm still hoarding lots of Barnabas's money for myself. And you know that's not true."

Chief Patu nodded. "Send 'em here. We'll teach 'em to be people o' the woods."

"I'm not sure they'd appreciate that," Jason said with a gleam in his eye.

Chief Patu motioned to Garrit and the others with her fork. "'Ave they 'ad anything to eat yet?"

"No," Jason replied. "And they won't take anything if you offer. They'll eat when I return to my quarters this evening. My Chief Captain is a very by-the-books individual. Pretty stuffy and insufferable if you ask me."

Jason smirked. Garrit's expression barely changed, but a spark flashed through his eyes.

"Adria's the same 'ere," Chief Patu pointed at her over her shoulder. "N'matter 'ow much I 'nvite 'er to dine when there's guests, she refuses. Swears by th'old customs."

Adria bowed just a little. "I'll help myself when you both have concluded your meals, Your Majesty."

"Ope. I'm done," Chief Patu said. "Might as well join us, then."

Adria punched Chief Patu's shoulder, which barely budged. Chief Patu grinned broadly.   "So what brought ya t' Treetown so sudden, your 'ighness?"

Jason took a gulp of cider and said, "We had a group of strange visitors last night at the castle. Three men… at least I think they were men. They had a dark feeling to them that made the warmth leave our bodies—my Advisor and the Chief Patriarch felt it, too. They were messengers from Nartikis, King of Unbuntye. He said their kingdom is suffering and is in need of supplies. I'm traveling to see for myself."

As Jason told the story, Chief Patu's appetite became less and less ravenous. Her fork moved slower to her mouth and her eyes fixed on Jason, unblinking. When Jason noticed this, he said, "You've seen these creatures too, haven't you?"

Chief Patu wiped her lips. "Reckon I 'ave. Only once. We was on our way back from huntin' in the woods not many weeks 'go and we saw one o' them. Made our insides cold. Big, strong thing with gray skin an' unnatural features, yeah? Somethin' jus' didn' sit right when I saw it. As soon as it realized I saw it, *poof.* Gone."

"In purple smoke?"

Chief Patu nodded. Across the room, Adria and Garrit traded glances.

Jason put down his fork. "So strange. What are they doing in the Western Woods?"

"I dunno, but your 'ighness," Chief Patu said. "These woods 'ave been strange lately…like they feel somethin' we don't. The 'oly Dragon gave th' creatures a special sense—they c'n feel evil 'fore we can, and everythin' west o' here has been 'avin the jitters lately. Somethin' could be brewin' over there in Unbuntye, your 'ighness… somethin' very strange."

45

5
THE CAPITAL

Chief Patu and Adria made sure Jason and the guards had a hearty breakfast of sausage, eggs, and potatoes before they left town. They also contributed a considerable amount of dried meat and tree seeds to the supply carriages. The people of Treetown cheered and waved all the way to town's edge.

But the forest didn't greet them warmly as they continued their westward journey. Chief Patu was right—the farther west they traveled, the jumpier and more anxious the animals became. The few rabbits and foxes Jason spotted looked around suspiciously and darted away as if something were prickling their senses. Even the way the trees rustled was unsettling.

Jason stuck his head out the carriage window and beckoned Garrit inside. Once Garrit joined him, he asked, "What did you think about what Chief Patu said last night?"

"I think she's right," Garrit said with serious eyes. "These woods seem to be fighting a dark force settling on them. I feel it as well. It's unnerving."

"We should reach the edge of the kingdom by nightfall, right?"

"Yes," Garrit replied. "The Western Bridge is the only way between Nezmyth and Unbuntye, and this is the only road that connects to it."

Jason paused. "I hope that's not a problem for us later."

Throughout the day, Jason continued to study the Ancient Nezmythian text, sleep, and stare out to the forest. Morning turned to afternoon, and afternoon turned to dusk. Jason's legs ached from so much sitting, and he pushed out his arms in a mighty stretch. A sign alerted them that they would be approaching the Western Bridge in two miles. Jason exhaled a shaky breath when he saw it.

In no time they had reached the Western Bridge—a feat of engineering pioneered by the people of Nezmyth and Unbuntye long ago. It was constructed entirely of stone, several hundred feet long and wide enough to squeeze four carriages side-by-side. Beneath it, a chasm stretched down thousands of feet, where a raging river curved through the canyon like a snake. Jason could hear the current's hiss from the bridge.

Before the carriage left the soil, Garrit left his carriage and joined Jason. As the wheels rolled onto the stone, Jason couldn't help but realize that this was the first time he had left Nezmyth's borders. And from the trip so far, he hoped it would be his last.

The uneasy feeling that resided in the westernmost part of the Western Woods didn't subside as they crossed into the realm of King Nartikis. The other side of the bridge was also accompanied by a forest... or at least it used to be.

Bare tree stumps stretched on for miles, scattered among an expanse of parched, cracked soil. The carriage creaked along a narrow road that clearly hadn't been used in years. Every soldier tensed as they looked about the wasteland.

Jason looked back at his own kingdom. Across the expanse, the Western Woods were rich with growth. But dead ahead, stark destruction.

"They've chopped down every single one," Jason said. "How does a kingdom get that desperate for lumber?"

Garrit's reply was detached. "I'm not sure."

The soldiers marched cautiously as the caravan traveled through the murdered forest. There weren't any creatures to be seen—no foxes, rabbits, wolves, or even insects. The only trace of life came from the wind, and even then, it had an unwelcome bite to it. Jason shivered in response. His thumb traced the hilt of his sword.

Nightfall was upon them long before they reached any village. And truthfully, their first find was hardly a village at all. It was more of a large collection of makeshift tents, rounded together in a small cluster beside the main road.

The inhabitants perked up as they watched the caravan pull along. Their filthy, sunken faces and milky, tired eyes—the faces of vagabonds and drifters—were curious, but not inviting.

Jason frowned when he saw them. *Definitely no room to lodge tonight. But maybe we can help.*

He ordered the carriage to stop. As it did, one hundred soldiers ceased their march, and Jason hopped out. The villagers ogled at the caravan, awestruck. Jason scanned their faces as he walked toward them. He locked eyes with one—a woman, presumably in her mid-thirties, wearing a dirty gray bonnet around her head. She stared at Jason with wonder and fear as he approached.

"Hello," Jason said softly, bowing to her slightly. "My name is Jason, King of Nezmyth. I'm on my way to the kingdom's capital for a meeting with King Nartikis. Tell me… what happened here? How long has it been like this?" Jason motioned to the destruction that surrounded them.

Her skin went even more pale. "Uh—the forest is gone, sir! Started not two years ago! King Nartikis, the Mighty and Great, commanded the forest to be chopped and burned, sir!"

Jason's face scrunched. "The whole forest? For what purpose?"

The woman swallowed hard. Her eyes darted to the side. Jason furrowed his eyebrows, looking back at Garrit, who had his hand on his sword.

"For what purpose?" Jason asked again.

"Turn back!" An elderly voice piped up from the crowd.

Everyone stiffened and all eyes focused on an old woman nestled in creaky chair a dozen yards away. The wrinkles on her face compressed into a scowl as she gazed upon Jason. Jason returned the gaze with just as much perplexity as heat. Someone edged up to the old lady and held her hand to sooth her, but the old lady's gaze held firm.

"Nartikis is a snake!" The old woman raved. "He is vermin! Filth! He killed the forest! He—"

"Gran," the woman next to her stroked her hand more lovingly. "Gran, it's okay…"

Jason kept his eyes locked on the sight and his hand on his sword. As he continued scanning the crowd, he said, "Nartikis has requested that Nezmyth provide aid to Unbuntye. We have provisions in the caravan. I'm happy to impart some to you, though I must save some for whatever purposes Nartikis has."

The village exhaled a collective sigh of relief and gratitude, then everyone lined up to gather what could be shared. Soldiers handed out portions of grain, wheat, cheese, and dried meat. The villagers immediately went to work making bread and tearing into whatever food was already prepared.

When they had what was given to them, they seemed to forget that the King of Nezmyth was in their midst. And on that note, Jason made his way back to the carriage. As he went, Garrit walked with him.

"Garrit, do you think that was an omen?" Jason said.

"The old woman?"

"Yes."

"The way she was handled, I might have to question her sanity," Garrit replied.

"Maybe we *should* turn back," Jason thought out loud. "Everything about this trip has been dark, like a constant shadow. I feel the cold getting stronger the closer we get to the kingdom's castle. This could be a mistake."

Garrit stood up straight. "Your order is my duty, my king. Whatever you wish."

Jason stopped and surveyed the villagers one more time. From how eager they were to take their provisions, it's clear that they were struggling. It was probably like that all over the kingdom as well. Jason's caravan was armed with one hundred soldiers. He was protected. And Unbuntye obviously needed help.

"We've already come this far," Jason resolved. "We move forward. But I'll be grateful when we leave this Dragon-forsaken place."

$$* * * * *$$

The next two days involved long hours of nothing. They left the remnants of what was once a forest in a day's journey, and after that, it was all wasteland. The caravan and the red carriage were nothing but a splotch moving across bleak grassless, treeless plains.

Occasionally, they would pass through other communities of derelict people with dirty faces, wearing dingy rags and walking with hunches in their backs. Without fail, they would gaze at the red carriage and the caravan as if it were something incredibly curious, even magical. Jason and the others stopped as briefly as they could to distribute supplies, and the people of Unbuntye always accepted the offer hungrily.

Jason was eating an apple and reading through more of the Ancient Nezmythian text when Garrit let himself into his carriage.

"We see the capital of Unbuntye on the distance," he said as he closed the door.

"How long until we'll be there?"

"One hour. Maybe two."

"Very well."

"Your Highness," Garrit began slowly. "The kingdom of Nezmyth is a beautiful place—I would say the most beautiful kingdom in Wevlia. All of it lives and radiates because of a noble King that rules with love and integrity."

"Please don't patronize me, Garrit."

"But *this*," Garrit's tone instantly changed. "This kingdom is forsaken. I have been to Unbuntye on only a few occasions many years ago and it was never like this. This is a wasteland. I think this says something of King Nartikis's character."

"I suspect the same," Jason said.

"I'll be watchful," Garrit said. "I would admonish you do the same." He motioned to the sword by Jason's hip.

Garrit returned to his own carriage, and Jason couldn't focus on reading after that. He stuck his head out the window only for a moment, but in the distance he could see walls around what had to be a city. He tried to picture King Nartikis—the man that allowed his kingdom to fall into such decay, even more so than Barnabas ever did.

What kind of King is this? He wondered. *He destroyed an entire forest, and every subject looks like some of the poorest of Lower City. What happened here?*

At long last, they reached the gates of the capital. A stone wall stretched for miles around the perimeter of the city, which seemed to be significantly smaller than Nezmyth City. The walls were charcoal black, with tall ugly spikes protruding from the top that reached dozens of feet high.

The caravan didn't have to stop on its way through the gate. A battalion of massive gray men—the same kinds of messengers that visited the castle—hoisted the massive wooden doors open. The doors themselves, however, were falling apart. Full of pock marks and holes, they barely clung onto giant rusty hinges and squealed horribly as they swung open.

The gray creatures by the gates leered at the caravan as it passed through the gates. Their sickly yellow teeth gleamed in the dim sunlight and Jason couldn't help but grimace in return. He suddenly felt chilly again, like he did at the castle when those beasts first arrived. He brushed at the goosebumps that sprouted on his arms.

The inside of the Unbuntye capital was the same as the villages they had passed. Signs of civilization remained, like the ruins of old houses and storefronts. The citizens had clearly done their best to create makeshift shelters from these remains, but most relied on bits of canvas and wood to create huts and tents. All of them stared as Jason's caravan rolled through.

What Jason found most unsettling was the mixture of massive gray beasts to humans. The ratio was almost one to one. The humans were unarmed, filthy and derelict, while the beasts traveled in pairs, scantily clad in animal fur and heavily armed. The townspeople didn't make eye contact with any of them and often scurried away from them like abused dogs escaping their tormentors.

It's like Barnabas's reign, Jason thought. *But worse.*

One by one, gray beasts began walking with the caravan on their way to the castle. Jason looked around, his hand resting on the hilt of his sword, his face hard. The beasts continued to assemble like flies gathering around a carcass. He met the gaze of one, which sneered at him before flipping its head back and looking forward. Jason clenched his jaw held the hilt tighter.

The castle wasn't far inside the city walls. The caravan curved into a semi-circle and lurched to a halt. After a moment, the driver stepped down to open the carriage door for Jason and quietly asked, "Your Highness, what would you have me do while you are in there?"

"I'm not sure, my friend," he replied lowly. "But try to be safe."

Jason took a deep breath before he pushed himself to his feet and exited the carriage. His heart dropped when he stepped outside and saw the castle.

He had never seen a building so black and foreboding. Its collection of spires towered to the sky like pointed spears, daring the sun to shine. No door led inside, just a tall expanse of iron bars across the threshold. No windows of any sort were to be seen, and the stone itself was so dark that it seemed diseased.

As Garrit climbed out of his own carriage, he and Jason traded looks. It was clear that they were having similar thoughts.

At once, all the beasts that surrounded the caravan marched into two perfect lines, creating a trail leading straight to the castle. Jason, Garrit, and a small group of elite Nezmythian soldiers made their way toward the iron bars, glancing at the beasts that stood at either side of them.

When they were about halfway there, the beasts began stomping in place, perfectly in unison. The Nezmythians slowed their walk, and Jason's heart rate quickened as he looked around, ready for anything to jump out. His palms sweated, and he subconsciously rubbed the mark on his right hand.

When they were upon the iron bars, every beast finished marching in place with one final stomp, then they all drew their weapons and thrust them to the sky with a mighty "*Rah*". The bars to the castle magically retreated into the ground, and three persons exited from the shadow.

Two of the three figures were gray beasts, but bigger, stronger, and more grotesque than any of the others. The third was a boy, no older than fifteen, with a scrawny, thin body. His face was pale, with a hooked nose and blue eyes that were devoid of any expression. He wore no armor and carried no weapon, but was clad completely in black, including a cape the spilled from his shoulders to his ankles.

The realization struck Jason hard. He knew who this boy was. Garrit's eyes hardened and he flexed his hands. Every beast that had lined up outside the castle suddenly fell to one knee as the boy crossed the castle entrance.

With his chilly eyes focused on Jason, the boy said, "Greetings, Jason, King of Nezmyth. I am Nartikis, King of Unbuntye."

6

THE NEGOTIATION

How long has this kid been King? Jason thought. *He looks even younger than me when I took the throne!*

Despite his thoughts, Jason bowed and said, "Greetings, Your Highness. I hope the day finds you well."

He said these words and forced a polite smile. King Nartikis didn't return it. Jason frowned and couldn't help but glance at the gray beasts on either side of him. They stood completely erect, moving almost entirely in sync to one another. He tried not to narrow his eyes. Standing to the side of Jason, Garrit still never took his hand of the hilt of his blade.

"It is my honor, King Jason," King Nartikis said. "Come and dine. I am sure you are weary from your journey."

With that, the King and his guards slowly turned and slunk back into the dark of the castle. Jason gulped and Garrit put his hand on his shoulder as they followed, their battalion of guards close behind. A frosty shiver dropped down Jason's back as he crossed the threshold. When he and his guards were fully submerged in the shadow, the iron bars sprang up with a *clang* faster than they had come down.

As the sound reverberated off the walls, Jason couldn't help but shudder—not just from nerves. The temperature in the castle was noticeably colder than outside.

The hallway they found themselves in was hardly lit. Garrit charged a jeroki in his right hand and held it there, allowing it to emit a little white light throughout the hall. Jason scrunched his nose. A smell hung in the air that was unbecoming of a royal edifice. He struggled to place it, but it rested somewhere between dead rats and rotting flesh.

This feels more like a dungeon than a castle, he thought.

Eventually, the hallway turned and opened into a large dining hall lit with a dozen torches. A long table with just two chairs stretched nearly the entire length of the room. A lit fireplace crackled on the opposite wall but barely threw any heat. Surprisingly, the walls were devoid of paintings and sculptures. Instead, King Nartikis opted for weapons as decorations: swords, shields, spears, axes, maces. Around the perimeter of the room, gray beasts bearing ugly smirks full of rotting teeth stood and watched the Nezmythians enter.

One beast approached them, holding out its hands and grunting, "You won't need your weapons while you dine."

Garrit tensed, his eyes scanning the room. But this was the only move he made. Jason glanced at him out of the corner of his eye, proud and satisfied.

Always on guard, He thought. *As he should be.*

"If it's well enough for you," Jason told the beast. "It's custom in our kingdom for everyone to carry a weapon when they reach a certain age. You might as well separate us from our legs. If you don't mind, we'll keep them while we dine."

The beast's eyes panned to its master, who had already sat at one end of the table. King Nartikis nodded faintly. The beast bowed and retreated to its perch by the entrance.

Jason sat down, slid his chair in, and immediately King Nartikis began to dine without a word. The clink and tinkle of dishes and silverware were quiet against the crackling of the fireplace. Cautiously, Jason picked up a fork.

It was quite a magnificent feast to be prepared for just two people. Cooked pheasants, steaks, peas, squash, corn—Jason clenched his teeth behind his lips as he stared at it all. Didn't Nartikis summon him here because his kingdom was struggling? Then why such a lavish spread? He jabbed his fork into some meat, trying not to appear rude. Meanwhile, Garrit and his soldiers stood behind him, fully at attention.

Across the table, King Nartikis ate mechanically, his icy eyes perpetually faint and lifeless, but focused on his plate. Jason nodded and wiped his mouth. "Again, I thank you for inviting me to your home, Your Highness. Before we dive into our plan for aiding Unbuntye, I must admit I have several questions. Would now be an acceptable time to address them?"

"As ever," King Nartikis said.

"You're remarkably young for a King," Jason said. "What is your age?"

"I have been King of Unbuntye since the age of nine," King Nartikis replied. "Six years. That was when my mother died."

Jason bowed his head. "I'm sorry for your loss. That must have been very difficult."

King Nartikis didn't reply.

Jason wiped his mouth as the silence hovered. Then, clearing his throat, he motioned to one of the guards standing over the King's shoulder. "And your servants… they're like nothing I've ever seen. What…" he stammered as he corrected himself. "Who…?"

"The Ash," King Nartikis said. "That is what they are called. They are bred to serve me and only me. That is their sole purpose. They have no other choice or desire."

Jason traced the bottom of his fork uncomfortably, his eyes hardening as he gazed around the room, surrounded by a small army of them. "That's very interesting. How are they… bred?"

"From ashes, of course," King Nartikis replied. "And very ancient magic. Hence, their name."

Tepnoh Edomah, no doubt, Jason thought. *Just looking at King Nartikis, he seems completely drained of emotion. I wonder how long he's been practicing.*

"Is that what happened to the eastern forest?" Jason asked. "You took the wood from the forest to create them?"

King Nartikis's gaze on Jason sharpened, and Jason couldn't help but shiver again. Finally, he said, "Yes. The forest was dying regardless. It might as well have been put to use."

"I see," Jason nodded. He looked at his mostly filled plate of delicious food, but his appetite had all but disappeared. He set down his knife and his fork and laced his hands on the table, leaning forward slightly.

"So," he began. "Shall we begin our plan to aid Unbuntye? We had interactions with several villages on the way here that are in dire need of—"

"Before we discuss those particular matters," King Nartikis interjected. "I have a few questions of my own."

Surprised, Jason leaned back in his chair. "Alright then."

"Tell me what has become of Barnabas, the former King."

Jason had another flash of Barnabas, sitting alone in his cell. It was only days earlier that he had seen those bleary, vacant eyes and stringy white hair. He shifted in his chair before he answered.

"Barnabas is in the deepest, darkest cell in the Nezmyth City Prison," he replied. "He is paying a life sentence for the thousands of lives he destroyed during his rule. His relentless taxes threw the entire kingdom into poverty, and he slaughtered thousands on suspicion of treason and treachery. The kingdom is still recovering from his negligence."

With this, King Nartikis's pale face locked on Jason, blank and unmoving. And suddenly... those eyes looked familiar. And the hooked nose. Could it be? No. Impossible. The wonder must have been apparent in Jason's face, because Nartikis cut right to it.

"Barnabas was once the King of Nezmyth," he said. "And I am his only son—his heir, you might say."

Jason's mouth went dry. He stayed silent, watching King Nartikis, whose bored gaze had become razor sharp ever since the mentioning of his father. After a tense moment, Jason felt as though it was his turn to speak. "You are his son?"

"Yes," King Nartikis said. "His blood is my blood. The blood of a King." He leaned back in his seat and wiped his mouth with a napkin. "I hardly knew him. I saw him infrequently, and he never stayed in the kingdom long. He was a strong man, a mighty warrior from what my mother told me."

"One of the mightiest Nezmyth has known in recent years," Jason said. "He was the Chief Captain over the Nezmythian Army."

"But obviously you were mighty enough to defeat him," King Nartikis said. "You must be quite a warrior yourself. Have you studied the arts of war much, Your Highness?"

"I've studied the history of our kingdom, which includes many wars from the past, but I don't consider myself a warrior by any means," Jason said, thinking of the mark on his right hand.

For the first time, King Nartikis's mouth twitched into a half smile. "Nezmyth is a beautiful kingdom. Do you not fear those who would wish to take it from you?"

"I suppose I would if I knew any," Jason said. "But Nezmyth is a peaceful kingdom. We have no enemies."

"Why does everyone carry a weapon in a peaceful kingdom?"

"It's a matter of custom, along with battle training from an early age. Everyone is required to do it for a short number of years. It's what we've been doing for centuries."

"Why do you continue?"

"The Dragon hasn't prompted us to change anything."

"Interesting," King Nartikis said curiously. He took a sip from his goblet. "I have visited many parts of Nezmyth, you know."

Jason's eyebrows furrowed. "Really? I never heard anything of your excursions. I don't believe we'd had the pleasure of hosting any Wevlian royalty in many years."

"I do not seek to draw attention to myself," King Nartikis replied after taking another sip from his goblet. "Why do you suppose that is? Your lack of visitors, I mean."

"Our culture is so deeply rooted in the Old Ways," Jason said. "We still believe the Holy Dragon rules over us. And I believe that repels a lot of people living in other kingdoms. They see it as old fashioned."

Another half-smile from King Nartikis. There was nothing comforting about it.

"I fancy all parts of Nezmyth. It teems with life. I am particularly fond of the Western Woods."

Jason forced a smile. King Nartikis's familiar eyes flashed, and his chair creaked as he leaned forward. The tone of cordiality he had been producing was fading, and the cold, bleary emptiness of his countenance was returning.

"On the matter of the aid Unbuntye requires of Nezmyth," he began. "This is my proposal: Unbuntye is starving. We have run out of resources. Crops scarcely grow, lakes and rivers are drying up... but Nezmyth is rich and abundant in all things. It is rich with life from the trees, the animals, the people..."

Jason found himself nervously stroking his fork again. The Ash standing around the perimeter in the room stirred excitedly, as if they knew exactly what Nartikis was building up to. Sinister smiles were slashed across their faces.

"I hope you will forgive me for misleading you, Your Highness," King Nartikis said. "But in truth, I do not desire aid from Nezmyth. I desire Nezmyth itself. Unbuntye follows a royal succession based on bloodline. Barnabas was my father and is no longer King, so it should come as no shock to you that I consider myself the rightful King of Nezmyth. The kingdom belongs to me."

Jason's blood turned to ice and his mouth went dry again. The Ash were becoming antsier. Their fingers twitched by their sides, and some of them rose and fell on the balls of their feet. Jason's hand found the hilt of his sword.

"The army of Ash I have raised in recent years is insurmountable," King Nartikis continued. "Resistance is suicide. I plan to send them into Nezmyth to take control immediately. I do not wish to spill quality blood, so you have two choices. You can stand back as I march through your kingdom and take it, or you can die. Choose now. Regardless, Nezmyth is mine."

At this, the Ash were on the brink of eruption. For some reason, the mention of violence shot an excited buzz through the lot of them. King Nartikis continued to glare at Jason with stoic indifference, awaiting his response.

Across the table, Jason couldn't believe what he was hearing. Nartikis's cordial veneer had dropped completely. He was the direct offspring of Barnabas—something he didn't know existed—and he had concocted an entire army of dark warriors for the sole purpose of taking over his kingdom. Every other problem he worried about seemed small and insignificant now. A massacre awaited Nezmyth.

"I..." Jason stammered, quickly trying to process everything King Nartikis had said. "You... uh—Nartikis, please. We can help your kingdom rebuild. We can provide you resources and training. There's no need for w—"

"You misunderstand me," King Nartikis said, his voice rising. "Nezmyth is *mine*, Jason. The only death that will occur is to all those who will oppose me. Now, will you stand aside? Or die?"

This was it. The Ash grunted as they held in excited whoops and hollers. Behind him, Garrit's hand was already wrapped around the hilt of his sword, ready to strike. The soldiers accompanying them stood with their feet apart in like fashion. Jason took a deep breath. With the mark on his hand resting on the pommel of his sword, he looked King Nartikis squarely in the eye.

"Nartikis, I must warn you, if you attempt any sort of invasion of Nezmyth, the Dragon will defend it. And ultimately that is a force you cannot conquer. You may have success for a time, but it will not last. You must reconsider."

King Nartikis's shoulders drooped. He reached for his goblet, brought it to his lips, drained it, then dropped cup with a loud *clang* on the plate below. Jason watched without blinking as the King stood from his chair and turned to exit the dining hall. The King may have finished his meal, but the Ash were looking as hungry as ever.

King Nartikis reached the door to exit the room but didn't pull the latch. Instead, he turned about to face everyone, then uttered three words.

"Kill them all."

7

THE ESCAPE

Every Ash rushed upon Jason and his guards in an explosion of barbaric shouts. Jason and Garrit ripped their swords from their sheaths and brandished them, hearts pounding.

Garrit fired several well-aimed jerokis at advancing Ash, hitting each one squarely in the head. Necks snapped and Ash toppled to the floor, their swords and spears clanging on the ground.

Jason followed suit, hurling jerokis, most not hitting with near the accuracy of Garrit. He shouted *"Mohlah Eelohda matah!"* and his blade burst into flames. It didn't deter the Ash in the slightest. They advanced like a swarm of angry bees, murder flashing in their terrible red eyes.

I've never truly killed anyone before, Jason thought. *Is today that day?*

As he thought these things, another thought instantly replied, calmly and firmly as the wind, *These are born of fire and darkness. Feel no remorse.*

Jason bared his teeth and gripped his flaming sword tighter.

With shouts and whoops, Jason tore through the Ash. As his fiery blade ripped through their flesh, no blood spilled from their bodies. Instead, black ashes flew into the air in dusty clouds. Limbs fell and the beasts kept coming, determined to kill.

Whack!

A beast kicked Jason to the floor. The King, staring down the end of a jagged black sword, landed hard on his back, the beast's foot on top of him. The beast pulled back, ready to strike, but Jason launched a beam into its chest that sent it howling in pain, burning and melting its torso. It finally fell backward, convulsing.

But more Ash were coming, and Jason was still on his back. Thinking quickly, he did a series of quick gestures and shouted in Ancient Nezmythian. Just in time, a flame shield shot out from his body, pushing the Ash back and setting their bodies ablaze. Jason stammered to his feet. The smell of burnt, rotting flesh filled the air. Several feet away, Garrit was fending off the army of Ash better than Jason was. Half of the Nezmythian guards had already fallen, their blood pooling on the black stone floor.

Jason jerked his head to King Nartikis, still standing by the door, eyeing the spectacle with his hands behind his back. His jaw tightened, and he thought, *Should I attack? He's corrupted by Dark Magic… I can't change his mind now. If he lives, he'll be determined to take over Nezmyth. Thousands will die. It's either him, or thousands of my people.*

Jason charged and launched another burning beam, this one directed at King Nartikis. The beam sailed across the room, but Nartikis held out his hand and deflected it, exploding a nearby wall into bits of stone and dust.

Seeing that Jason was determined to attack, King Nartikis flicked his hands from out of his cape and snapped his fingers. Instantly, Jason's flame shield extinguished.

His heart sank. King Nartikis held out two fists, and in a flash of purple smoke, two black swords shot out from his grip.

He shot across the room toward Jason, his feet flying just inches above the ground. With the fraction of time Jason had, he remembered something important. The mark on his hand. What it represented. The power that awaited him if he simply called for it.

Silently, he did.

As soon as King Nartikis was upon him, their blades met with a mighty *clang*, but Jason's blade was the Blade of Nezmyth. Its heavenly orange steel glowed fiercely in the darkness and his hand was wrapped around a hilt of the finest silver. Around the cross guard, an inanimate dragon snarled.

Jason's body burst into flame. Black, swirling marks sprouted on his arms and hands, his eyes turned a shimmering orange along with his hair and beard. When he exhaled, thick smoke billowed from his mouth.

Nartikis looked him up and down and said, "Interesting."

He lashed out in a series of quick attacks, which Jason parried. Garrit looked over from atop the dining table several yards away and saw the two Kings battling as he fended off the army of Ash. Several cuts had sprouted on his face and arms, and he was breathing heavily. Ashes were strewn around the floor around him, accompanied by the bodies from whence they came. Almost all the Nezmythian guards had fallen.

Jason shot a jeroki into Nartikis' stomach point-blank, slamming him into a wall across the room. Nartikis recovered fast, still blank-faced. His swords disappeared and he lifted his hands to the air, conjuring a giant snake that fell to the floor with a mighty *thud*. It quickly slithered toward Jason. When it was in range, it arched up on its back and struck with lightning speed.

Jason dodged out of the way, missing it by inches, and decapitated it with a swipe of his blade. The beast's grotesque head fell to the floor, followed by the rest of its body, and it disappeared in a giant puff of purple smoke.

Somehow, Nartikis had shot forward and was upon him, grabbing Jason by the throat before he could react.

As soon as Jason looked into those icy blue eyes, he was sucked in. They became bigger until he was completely engulfed in the pupils. He was surrounded by darkness, no longer a Knight of the Holy Order, bitter cold enveloping his body. He was in his filthy craftsman clothes, seventeen again with no sword slung over his back.

He turned around, and there was a body on the ground, blood oozing from its neck. It was Saryan. But there was another—Tarren. And others... Nadiel, Master Ferribolt. His heart dropped into his stomach and his teeth chattered, but, looking about, he tried to fight off the darkness that was settling on him.

This isn't real, Jason thought. *It's like the Dreamslayer spell Barnabas used on me years ago... maybe I can Overcurse him... It isn't real...*

Jason sat down in the darkness, his legs crossed, his hands on his knees. Suddenly, a dozen giant snakes materialized around him, all slithering toward him, hungry. Jason eyed them, waiting for them to strike.

"Stop the games and face me without your dark magic, coward," he said.

The snakes reared back and struck, each latching onto a different part of his body. The pain was exquisite. His head was in one of the snakes' mouths, its fangs latched into his neck. Jason howled with raging pain, blood spilling into his mouth.

Yield, he heard Nartikis whisper in his hear.

Jason almost succumbed, but inwardly begged the Dragon for an escape. Suddenly, he felt something in his hand—the hilt of his sword. He gripped it tight and thrust the blade into the head that engulfed him. The snake hissed and released, letting his head hit the floor. The blade in Jason's hand was gone, but the ember inside him was starting to burn brighter. Clenching his teeth, he thrust his hands at the snakes that ripped his body. Fire erupted from his palms, sending them reeling and covered in flame.

As the beasts recoiled, Jason stood to his feet and shouted to the air, "*Release me!*"

"Very well," came Nartikis's reply.

Jason was suddenly back to his own body, his Knightly power fading but still present, and Nartikis's face just inches from his. He released Jason's throat and dashed back several feet.

Again, oily black blades sprouted from Nartikis's fists, and with a devilish smirk, not panting and no sweat on his brow, he asked, "One more go, Your Highness?"

Breaths came in mighty gulps for Jason. *I have to finish him right now.* He sucked in a mighty breath of air and roared with all that he was. Just as he had hoped, flame erupted from his mouth, forming into the shape of a dragon soaring toward Nartikis, its lips snarling menacingly and its claws outstretched.

Nartikis dug his heels in the ground, inhaled a feverish breath, then roared with equal ferocity. In a haze of purple smoke, curling horns shot out of his head, and his eyes glowed an eerie purple. The dragon collided with him, pushing him across the floor as they clenched fists, grappling and roaring at each other.

Jason tried to stay standing, directing the dragon with his hands as Nartikis pushed back from yards away. Great drops of sweat fell from Jason's face. Fevered, perverted words—not his own—slithered into his ears mysteriously. He was certain they had to be coming from Nartikis, but it was like they were surrounding him, invisible to his eyes. Jason could feel his Knightly power fading little by little.

Finally, Nartikis toppled the dragon. One of his dark blades materialized in his hand, and he stabbed the dragon through the head. The dragon vanished in a puff of white smoke, and

Nartikis flexed his shoulders and neck, taking another chilling breath in and out. The horns on his head disappeared, and he leered at Jason delightedly. It made Jason's blood cold.

Jason held the Blade of Nezmyth tightly, panting hard. *He's toying with me!*

"Of course I am," King Nartikis's reply came. "Your magic is so limited, even with the pathetic help of your Dragon. I am still deciding whether to end you now or keep sparring with you for sport. It has been much too long since I have had such a spirited opponent."

Jason swallowed. It was no use. Even as a Knight of the Holy Order, King Nartikis's power surpassed his. If he stayed here and tried to battle, he and Garrit would both die, then King Nartikis would be free to run over Nezmyth. There was only one option. Jason tried to act on it before King Nartikis could read his thoughts.

Jason threw out his hand and furiously thought of the most intense paralyzing curse he could muster. King Nartikis's expression became rigid, his body spread eagle and he was thrust flat onto the floor, pinned for a moment. Jason, still glowing as a Knight of the Holy Order, threw his head back and yelled to Garrit, "We can't stay here! He's too powerful!"

That's when Jason noticed it—the blood caked against Garrit's side. A fatal wound for sure. His face and neck shimmered with sweat, peppered with ashes, as he blinked hard and swung against the onslaught. He was losing strength fast. But he had enough strength to throw a jeroki large enough to blow a hole in the wall.

Boom!

Rubble burst into the dining hall and sunlight spilled in. Jason looked toward Saryan's father with horror, knowing the inevitable but refusing to believe it.

"*Fly, Your Highness!*" he yelled. "Don't stop until you've reached the border! Destroy the Western Bridge! Tell Saryan I love her!"

This was it for him. Jason's eyes stung. Maybe he could save him. But Nartikis's body was already starting to stir. There was no time for thinking. He gritted his teeth behind quivering lips.

Garrit yelled more viciously, *"Go!"*

Jason nodded and he leapt. As his body careened toward the hole, he thought of Garrit and held out his arm. Garrit reached up to take Jason's hand.

No use. Jason's fingertips only brushed with Garrit's as he flew over, bursting into the sunlight. Wind snapped through his hair and around his cape. He climbed higher and higher into the sky until he was nearly with the clouds.

The kingdom of Unbuntye moved slowly beneath him, vast and empty. His orange hair flicked in the wind as he soared eastward as quickly as he could for Treetown and the Western Bridge. He clenched his teeth and tried to swallow the lump from his throat as he thought of Garrit back at the castle. He could feel his Knightly power diminishing as fear and anguish grew inside him—he hoped that he could last until he reached the border.

But he wasn't alone.

Something large collided with Jason as he soared through the air, sending him tumbling. His eyes watered and his back throbbed, but he was able to get his bearings just enough to right himself and continue flying. As he tumbled, he saw what had hit him. Nartikis had caught up to him, darting through the air. He had just hurled an enormous jeroki at Jason from behind.

Jason's heart dropped and he hurled a jeroki back at Nartikis. Nartikis dodged it and threw another one back at him, which narrowly missed Jason . He felt the heat of it graze his body as it zipped passed him.

Jason charged a jeroki and each hand and launched two blue beams at Nartikis. The beams blasted toward the dark King, but Nartikis jolted forward and dodged both by inches. He was gaining on Jason rapidly. In a flash of purple smoke, a blade appeared in his hand. Jason couldn't fly fast enough to evade. Nartikis raised the blade, poised for a killing stroke.

But just then, there was a flash of light and a deafening crash. It made his ears ring and the hair stand up on his arms. And with the flash, King Nartikis was blasted out of the sky.

The evil King hurtled toward the ground like a wounded bird, limp and unconscious, his black cape bunched and flapping about him. Before he hit the ground, he somehow came to and shot back toward the castle, retreating from the mysterious attack.

Unsure of what had happened, Jason flew on. He looked around as he soared, trying to see where the flash of light had come from, but saw no one in the sky.

What he didn't see was a mass of swirling clouds that had dissipated just as quickly as they formed.

8

THE GUARDIAN

Jason clung to what strength he had as he flew across Unbuntye. From the clouds, he saw it all—the dried-up rivers and lakes, the parched, cracked fields, the miles of tree stumps that were once forests. Villages were few. Most of them were just wreckage.

The sun behind him was beginning to set when the Western Bridge finally came into view. Luckily, he hadn't seen any advancing masses of Ash as he soared over the kingdom. He descended gradually, barely clinging onto his Knightly powers. His breathing strained, and his entire body ached for rest. Nezmythian soil was coming closer.

Jason managed to sail to a sufficiently slow speed before his power gave out. He toppled to the earth, bumping and bruising his body as he tumbled across the soil and pine needles. He didn't stop until he crashed into a bush just off the side of the road, the Western Bridge directly behind him.

There were still several miles until Treetown, but all energy left Jason's body. His eyes rolled back into his head and he lost consciousness. The sword in his hand was his own again, and his features returned to their normal state.

* * * * *

He couldn't tell if he was awake or dreaming, but the treetops moved over Jason's head. Pale moonlight smothered his face. He wasn't in the back of a carriage or cart, though—his face was against something much too soft, and he felt as though he were being cradled like a child. Whatever was carrying him was moving with tremendous speed, but Jason's eyes were too bleary and his body too weak to decipher what it was.

At length, the force stopped and laid him on the ground. Whatever carried him let out a loud but beautiful whistle then darted off as quickly as it had carried him. It made no sound as it went, excluding the rustling of branches and the occasional snapping of a fallen twig.

From the opposite direction, a barrage of footsteps rapidly approached the King. His consciousness was fading again. Right before he lost it, he heard Chief Patu shout, "Your 'ighness!"

* * * * *

Jason's vision cleared, but his limbs were still stiff and aching. Completely sapped of energy, indistinct sounds slipped from his lips. He was lying down, covered in animal fur, and staring at the ceiling of a log cabin—his cabin in Treetown. A few people whispered around him.

As soon as he realized where he was, he gasped and sat up so quickly his eyes filled with sparkles. He propped his body up while his head swam. At his bedside, Chief Patu and Adria watched over him.

"Careful, your 'ighness!" Chief Patu said. "It ain't 'ard to tell that yeh exhausted yer magical energy. 'Ere, eat this. Fix yeh right up."

Chief Patu handed him a bowl of thin green soup that burned Jason's nostrils. He blinked hard, took the bowl by both hands, and tipped it into his mouth. The liquid was bitter and hot, but as it trickled down his throat, he felt his energy replenish. It had to have been made from some herbs that only grew in the forest. He took larger gulps.

"Your Highness," Adria said quietly. "What were you doing unconscious outside the village? Where's the rest of your caravan?"

Jason wiped his mouth, the soup now half drained. "Back in Unbuntye, probably dead."

His eyes started to sting as he thought of Garrit, fighting to protect him, the brush of his fingertips as he flew over him. *Tell Saryan I love her.* He tried to push the thought away before the lump in his throat became too big. His eyes became intense as they locked on Chief Patu and Adria.

"Chief Patu, get your most powerful magicians, warriors, whatever necessary and destroy the Western Bridge *immediately*. King Nartikis has conjured an army of creatures known as the Ash—those gray warriors you've seen before—and plans to take over Nezmyth by force. He'll kill anyone who resists him."

Chief Patu's shoulders became square and rigid. Then she clenched her teeth like an angry bear. Without hesitation, she stood her chair and bellowed, "You 'eard the King! Assemble our mightiest! We need the Western Bridge at the bottom o' the ravine *now!*"

A couple of messengers scurried out of the cabin. Everything jovial about Chief Patu evaporated, replaced by the brutal ferocity of a woman determined to defend her people.

"Do yeh know 'ow long it'll be 'till the beasts are upon us?" she said.

"I don't," Jason said, pushing himself to the edge of the bed. "I couldn't see any of them as I fled back here. I can only assume they're assembling as we speak."

Adria stepped forward. "I'll alert our men and women for battle. With some luck and the Dragon's help, we can destroy the Bridge before the Ash arrive, but we must be ready just in case."

"May th' Dragon bless yeh, Adria," Chief Patu growled. "Please be careful."

Adria nodded and left the room.

Jason's heart thumped hard as he thought of what was to come. The slaughter that took place at Unbuntye Castle. Coming here. Coming to Nezmyth. A peaceful kingdom. He and Chief Patu let the silence hang for a tense moment. Then, softly, Chief Patu asked the glaring question.

"So war's upon Nezmyth, then?"

Jason didn't want to say it, but the answer was clear. "Yes. I'm afraid so."

More silence. Not even the crickets chirped outside. Revived, Jason quickly strapped on his armor and slung his sword around his waist.

"Your 'ighness," Chief Patu said seriously. "We can 'andle things out 'ere in the forest. We c'n destroy the Bridge before the Ash arrive. Ride back to th' castle and let the rest o' the kingdom know what we're facin'. I'll send ya with my fastest carriage and a couple o' brash men to guard yeh. We'll keep ya 'nformed with messenger hawks at th' ready."

Jason frowned and said, "I can't just leave you the night before battle."

"Your 'ighness, I insist," Chief Patu said. "The kingdom needs yeh. Ride."

Jason battled within himself at Chief Patu's words. *What if the people of Treetown don't last the day? What if they don't destroy the Western Bridge before the Ash start spilling into the kingdom?*

"Go, your 'ighness!" Chief Patu again pleaded.

This was the second time Jason had been commanded to flee. The second time he knew it was the best choice. The first time, he lost someone that he dearly loved. Who would he lose this time? But what else could be done? He had to alert the rest of the kingdom. He gritted his teeth and said, "Fine. I'll alert you as soon as we arrive to the castle."

Chief Patu clapped him on the shoulder with an enormous hand. "We'll fight 'em with th' fire 'n strength of the Dragon Itself. Grum and Klan 'll protect yeh. May the Dragon bless yeh, your 'ighness! Ride for Nezmyth City!"

With that, they were out the door. The carriage was ready in a flash—a roofless, dart-like vessel toted by two steeds clad in carefully crafted plate armor. Jason's bodyguards were twin brothers—two large, muscular men covered in hair and rich with body odor. Each armed himself with axes and arrows. Plentiful scars marked their arms and faces.

Men and women spilled from their cabins clad in whatever armor they had, toting weapons as they ran for the west side of town. Jason shuddered as he imagined a legion of Ash falling upon them.

The moons were full and brilliant above the treetops, and the stars were bright and clear. Jason bunched up his cape as he clambered into the carriage, keeping one hand on his sword and the other tightly gripping his seat. Inwardly, he prayed for the safety of his countrymen.

"Are yeh ready, Yer Majesty?" Klan shouted.

"We don't stop until Nezmyth City," Jason replied.

"Hold tight, Yer 'ighness!" Grum said.

Snap!

The horses whinnied as they broke into a sprint, tearing through the village and breaking into the forest. The echoing shouts of battle preparations became more and more faint as they flew. Now all they could hear were the jittering creaks of the carriage and the barrage of horses' hooves. Jason craned his neck about and watched the flickering candlelight of Treetown vanish through the trees. The cool breeze drifting through the conifers brought little comfort. No animals were out to make a sound. Either they were all sleeping, or they could feel darkness that was quickly approaching.

Maybe I came back soon enough, he thought. *Maybe we can get the Western Bridge destroyed before any of the Ash arrive.*

"Yer 'ighness!" Klan said as he turned about in his seat. "At this speed we c'n reach th' castle 'n just a few hours! These 'orses are bred for 'ndurance!"

"The sooner, the better!" Jason called back. "We can't risk any—!"

Whoosh

Something whisked by Jason's face—something long and rigid. Jason's head flipped about to see an arrow lodged in a tree, the feathers in its end still quivering. He felt another one fly just behind his head.

And suddenly, the forest was cold.

"*They're here!*" Jason yelled as he ripped his sword from its sheath.

Instantly, Klan shouted an ancient phrase and thrust out his hands. A shell of shimmering transparent blue enveloped the carriage. As arrows collided with it, they bounced off as if it were metal.

"It'll withstand th' arrows fer a time, Yer 'ighness!"

"How long?" Jason yelled in reply.

"'opefully long 'nuff for us to outrun 'em! It c'n only take th' blows for s'long!"

Grum snapped the reigns and shouted again. The horses whinnied. Arrows continued to rebound off the blue shell, and Jason's grip remained tight on his sword. Around the carriage, bursts of purple smoke lit up the air as Ash materialized. Some of them were dangerously close.

Boom!

An Ash threw itself against the side of the shell, causing the carriage to lunge. Grum swore loudly and quickly regained control. Jason fell on his back and found himself staring into the face of the Ash that was still clinging onto the side of the shell. Drool dripped onto the shell from its rotting teeth.

"You won't escape!" it growled.

It pulled out a dagger and thrust it into the shell. The blade crushed through the cocoon, cracking it like a spiderweb. Jason fumbled for his blade and jammed it through the shell, sending it through the stomach of the Ash. The Ash's body drooped and toppled to the dusty ground, its sickly smirk fading as it went. The cracks spread through the shell until it all fell to pieces, disappearing into the air.

"It's broken!" Grum called. "Get ready, Yer Majesty!"

Jason was already back on his feet, his fist tight on his sword. He saw Ash up ahead, pelting toward the road, ready to intercept the carriage. There were nearly a dozen of them.

"*For Nezmyth!*" Klan shouted as he pulled out his battle axe, ready to strike.

"*For Nezmyth!*" Jason echoed with just as much fire.

It wasn't necessary.

At that moment, an enormous brown mass the size of a bear came hurtling through the trees. Its massive hands and feet made no sound as it blasted through the foliage.

Lampi! Jason thought.

It was over quickly. Lampi picked up one of the soldiers with a single hand and hurled it into another. The other soldiers raised their weapons in retaliation but were met with crushed skulls and broken backs at the mercy of Lampi's beastly hands.

More Ash swarmed Lampi as the carriage sped through the trees. Amazingly, no more Ash appeared. Lampi took all of them.

"Was that Lampi?" Klan called. "I've never seen it 'fore! Took all the soldiers at once! Dragon be praised!"

Before Jason could reply, he heard a voice in his head. A deathly young voice. It made his palms clammy and the hair on his neck stand. The last voice he wanted to hear.

"You can run for now," King Nartikis's voice slithered between his ears. *"But the Ash know no rest. You will die, along with all those who stand beside you. Nezmyth is mine."*

9

THE PRISONER

Jason's thrashing heart didn't subside even after they crossed the edge of the forest. The horses panted mighty billowing breaths as they continued to race toward Nezmyth City. The sun was just rising over the Eastern Mountains, throwing its familiar orange glow over the kingdom as it slowly climbed the sky. The grass swayed on the hills, shuddering at what was to come.

After hours that felt like days, the carriage found itself at the gate of Nezmyth City. They had raised a siren call signaling an emergency to the guards, so the carriage was able to pass through the gates without stopping. In the distance, Jason could see the Nezmyth City Prison. Anger bubbled up in his heart.

The carriage's pace barely slowed as it rushed through the city streets. Townspeople dodged out of the way, startled and concerned. Normally, Jason would have hated disturbing his people in such a way. But there was no time for that. They had to reach the castle.

Through the Upper City streets they went, until they passed through the castle gates and some very confused soldiers. The horses whinnied and slid to a stop just before the castle doors. Jason hopped out of the carriage and fought his tired legs as he ran to the doors. The guards at the gate stared at him, stiff and confused.

"Your Highness—" One started to say.

"*Open the doors!*" Jason commanded.

The soldier swallowed and scooped up his hammer. Three knocks and the doors creaked open.

Jason bolted through the doors as soon as there was a crack wide enough for his body. The soldiers guarding the perimeter of the great hall turned and gazed at him with the same worry and concern as the gate soldiers. Morning sunlight spilled through the stained glass windows, but they brought no warmth.

Nadiel was standing near the throne, conversing with Saryan, who was doing more yelling than talking. She was wearing her sparring attire, and her face was red and sweaty— just as Jason left her days before. Both of their eyes widened as the King ran down to the throne platform.

"Jason, what happened?" Saryan said.

Jason threw his arms around her, holding on to the version of her that didn't know that her father was dead. He closed his eyes, trying to soak in that moment. This startled her. She hugged him back after some confused hesitation.

"You're back early," Nadiel said without an ounce of brightness. "Jason, what happened over there?"

Many things—too many things. Barnabas had a son who is now the King of the bordering kingdom. That King is launching an attack to take over our homeland. Garrit is dead. Treetown has been overrun. And all of Nezmyth is ignorant of the danger that awaits it.

After a tense pause, Saryan unwrapped herself from Jason's embrace and asked the horrible question. "Jason, what's wrong? Where is my father?"

When Jason peered into those silver eyes, he saw Garrit's. Flashes of his last battle resurfaced in his mind. Garrit's face, coated with sweat and blood and dust, his teeth baring at him, commanding him to flee. One hundred of Nezmyth's best soldiers had fought and died that hour. And Jason couldn't save any of them.

With great effort, Jason forced out the words. "He told me to escape. There were so many that attacked all at once. I'm so sorry, Saryan. We tried, but—he…"

All color drained from Saryan's face. She hovered backward, her eyes glassy, radiating with pain, still processing the words. Nadiel clenched his teeth and his eyes fell to the floor before he covered his heart and closed his eyes, conveying a silent prayer. Saryan's body shook.

"I'm sorry," Jason said, his eyes stinging and his chin tightening. "Saryan, I'm so sorry. We were ambushed—"

It was no use. Before Jason could finish his sentence, she sprinted out the nearest door. A thick silence ensued. No one in the great hall made a sound. Jason kept replaying Garrit's last moments in his head, trying to think of anything else that could have been done to save his father-in-law. If he would have flown just a few inches lower, maybe he would have been able to grab his hand. But what good is that now? He was gone, and there was no question.

"Jason," Nadiel finally said. "Tell me everything. Tell me what happened."

Jason rehearsed the entirety of the trip through stinging eyes and a tight throat. He covered everything from the ragged people of Unbuntye to the nature of King Nartikis's parenthood. When that detail was explained, Nadiel's face shone with less surprise and horror than Jason was expecting.

"Of course," he said.

"What do you mean 'of course'?"

"Almost a decade into his Kinghood, Barnabas took frequent trips into Unbuntye," Nadiel explained. "He never explained the nature of the journeys, and I never bothered to ask. After so many years of his unsavory reign, I had lost the desire to pester him on his motives. Having an affair with a Queen in a neighboring kingdom? I had my suspicions."

Jason wiped his eyes one more time. "I want to hear it from his own mouth."

"When?"

"Immediately."

"You wish to see him at a time like *this?*"

"What better time?" Jason shot back just as fiercely. "We need answers. Perhaps he knows something about the Ash as well."

Nadiel was firmly silent for a moment before saying, "Very well. I'll accompany you to the prison."

"No, stay here," Jason said. "I need someone I trust at the castle in case any important messages arrive. But I'll be back soon enough."

* * * * *

In the Vault of the Damned, a crusty and tired Barnabas lay down on a meager pile of hay and watched a mouse scurry across the floor. The mouse ignored him, instead choosing to sniff for the human's latest droppings of breadcrumbs. Its stringy tail dragged across the dirt as it scampered about.

Barnabas lifted his index finger, pointing it at the mouse. Slowly, a tiny ball of magic formed on the tip. He could feel the heat radiating from it, and its tiny gray light gave off just as much light as a candle.

When it reached the size of a pea, he shot it at the mouse. He missed by nearly a foot. Startled, the mouse fled to a nearby hole, abandoning its bounty of breadcrumbs. Barnabas sighed.

Suddenly, he heard the door ripple and open from above. He sat up and turned himself against the wall. Only one person would have the audacity to visit him, and he had already visited him only days ago. Had it been days? The hours were difficult to track down here.

The steps came down the staircase faster than usual. Rushed. What could be the hurry? He wasn't going anywhere.

The cells began to illuminate with the flickering orange light of torch fire. Barnabas had to blink to let his eyes adjust. It was then that he heard footsteps crunch on the dirt behind him.

"Get up," he heard Jason say.

Barnabas didn't move.

"*I said get up!*" Jason bellowed.

Finally, Barnabas attempted to push himself up, leaning on the wall to keep his balance. His knees quaked beneath him and he coughed.

"War is upon us, Barnabas," Jason said loudly. "Thanks to your son."

With this, Barnabas perked up. He almost turned completely around. "Nartikis…?"

"Yes, Nartikis!" Jason hollered. "He considers himself the rightful heir! He's created an entire army of Ash soldiers to take over the kingdom. And they're here. I need you to tell me everything there is to know about him."

Barnabas still wouldn't look Jason in the eye but instead shook his head.

"I hardly know him," he said.

"You know more about him than we do," Jason said. "Tell me about Unbuntye. About his mother. Anything. I need all the information you can give me."

After a shaky breath, Barnabas forced himself to turn around. He held a pair of rusty prison bars to keep his balance but still wouldn't look Jason in the eye. After another shaky breath, he asked, "What is Unbuntye like now?"

"Ruins," Jason answered. "The entire kingdom is a wasteland. The castle is dark and loathsome. Everyone is starving."

"It wasn't always like that," Barnabas's voice was dusty as he leaned his head against the bars. "Unbuntye was much like Nezmyth last I was there. That was many years ago. Green hills, forests, rivers, lakes… quite beautiful. But not as beautiful as Nezmyth."

"Tell me about Nartikis and the Queen."

"I was never in love with Queen Belzeje," Barnabas looked away. "When I became King, she came to visit and congratulate me on my new position. She was intoxicating. And she loved my raw drive for power. Our physical chemistry was undeniable. On occasion, she would visit Nezmyth, or I would visit Unbuntye for several days at a time. No one would disturb us. It was several years into my Kingship that she bore a son."

"Nartikis," Jason said.

"He was always quiet," Barnabas continued. "Frail. I hardly spoke to him. Our escapades became much less infrequent after she bore him, then stopped completely before he was old enough to remember much. I don't know what she taught him of me."

"What about the Ash?"

Finally, Barnabas looked at him. "The what?"

"The Ash!" Jason said. "He's made an army of them from fire and magic! They're hideous creatures that only live to serve him. Garrit and I got attacked by a legion of them." Jason paused. "He's dead."

Silence. Then, Barnabas looked down. "I don't know anything about that."

"So, he could be using techniques that even you didn't utilize?"

"Perhaps."

More silence. It wasn't a lot of information that Barnabas had to give, but it was all they were going to get. With that, Jason stormed out of the Vault. The door closed shut with a resounding *boom*.

Barnabas sat back down and waited for his eyes to readjust to the dark.

* * * * *

Teardrops fell from Saryan's chin and gathered at her feet. She sat in the courtyard among the sunflowers, illuminated by two moons that hung against the black sky. The guards patrolling the grounds respectfully kept their distance.

A door against the castle swung open and Jason came out dragging his feet. His head swiveled as he surveyed the courtyard. Saryan wasn't in bed when he retired to their quarters that night, and she wasn't anywhere in the castle. She had to be out here.

But she wasn't sparring. The battle court was empty except for a couple of patrolling soldiers. As Jason continued to scan, he spotted an askew patch of sunflowers in a nearby patch. She had to be there. He started for it.

But as Jason made his way to the sunflower patch, a guard approached him with a worried look. He swallowed before he addressed Jason.

"Forgive me, Your Highness, but I'm afraid I must stop you."

What? Jason's chest puffed out and his eyebrows scrunched. The soldier held his ground.

"Excuse me?" Jason snarled. "Under whose order?"

"The Queen's, sir," the soldier swallowed again. "She… doesn't wish to speak to you."

Jason's body sagged. The words drove through his heart and made the lump appear in his throat again. He gazed into the soldier's eyes earnestly.

"Please," he said. "Let me speak to my wife."

The soldier shook his head. "I have my orders, sir."

The lump in his throat was getting bigger. Jason looked away from the soldier so he wouldn't see his eyes well up. He pursed his lips and nodded. As he began walking back to the courtyard door, he stopped and looked over his shoulder. He wanted to say something. Anything. But no. She didn't want to speak to him, so strongly about it that she ordered their guards to stop him. And that was that.

Jason went to bed alone.

IO

THE REFUGEES

Jason didn't sleep that night. Too many thoughts ran through his head. His dead father-in-law. The war aggressively thrust upon his kingdom. The onslaught at Treetown. Barnabas rotting in his cell. Saryan's pained silence.

After hours of tossing and turning, Jason finally pushed himself out of the empty bed. He jabbed his arms through his robe sleeves and marched out of the master bedroom. The guards that stood sentinel throughout the halls stayed at attention as the King hastily swept by them, not speaking a word. The stone floors were cold on Jason's bare feet.

Dusty moonlight spilled through the castle's ancient windows, casting fragmented light onto paintings and statues that lined the walls. Sunrise was still a few hours away. The kingdom slept, many still peaceful and unaware of the horror that awaited them. The thought of it made Jason's stomach turn.

Silently, he continued to sweep through the halls with heat and purpose. Down a circular staircase and through several doors he went. The guards became more and more frequent in this section of the castle. None of them spoke to him, but they nodded as he marched by.

Finally, the King reached a wide double door with a massive golden emblem of the Dragon gleaming on its surface. He gazed into the Dragon's eyes for just a moment, taking note of the power, might, and majesty they emulated. Then he put his hands on the doors and pushed them open.

The room on the other side wasn't too large or too small—ten paces long and ten paces wide. Its gray stone walls and floor were no different than the rest of the castle. No furniture was in the room except for a granite pedestal protruding from the center of the floor. On that pedestal, a glassy orb filled with swirling gray smoke rested, emanating a strange energy.

The Reader of Souls. The Conduit to the Sacred Dragon. The Oracle Stone.

But Jason wasn't the only one in the room.

Nadiel was already on his knees, his eyes closed and his hands on his lap, facing the Oracle Stone. He popped one eye open and turned his head as he heard the door open behind him. Even without getting a better look, he knew who it was.

"It seems as though you're sleeping as well as the rest of us," Nadiel said.

Jason sighed. "Saryan is still distraught. I don't know what to say to her." Jason paused for a moment, then continued. "I need to talk with the Dragon."

At this comment, Nadiel arose to his feet. He brushed the dust from his knees and turned to face his King. As he moved his feet toward the door, he placed his hand on Jason's shoulder.

"I hope you have more luck than I," he said quietly. "Nothing. I feel as though I've supplicated myself for hours without so much as a whisper. The Dragon has been silent to me tonight."

"We must be patient," Jason said. "I don't think the Sacred Dragon will allow Nezmyth to fall to ruin."

Nadiel and said, "I do hope you're correct."

With that, he strode out of the room.

Jason took a deep breath and knelt where Nadiel was just moments ago. He put his hands on his knees, closed his eyes, and took in another deep breath. In. Out. When he opened his eyes, his gaze was fixed squarely on the Oracle Stone. The gray clouds continued to swirl and billow inside its glassy, spherical housing. Jason spoke to it but thought of the Dragon.

"Sacred Dragon," he began, "war has befallen Nezmyth—a terrible force of the likes I've never seen before. The opposition is evil in its purest form, even stronger than what Barnabas once was. And Nezmyth is the last kingdom that still holds to the Ancient Ways. Your ways. Please, protect us. What must we do?"

Nothing happened. Then, his insides began to glow. His head swam, not uncomfortably—but like the gentle moments that exist right before you drift off to sleep. The stone walls around him melted away as a white light grew brighter and brighter around him, shrouding everything in the room except for the Oracle Stone. Within moments, Jason appeared to be kneeling in endless white with nothing around except for the floating Oracle Stone.

He stood up, getting his bearings for his surroundings. All was quiet. He walked in a small circle, then a personage appeared on the opposite side of the Oracle Stone.

Jason recognized him immediately. He had only seen this man once before, but the experience was unforgettable. The man was strong but not muscular, tall but not towering. Black curly hair spilled from his head and his brown eyes were soft and patient.

"King Thomas!"

King Thomas smirked. "This is your first time having a revelation like this, isn't it?"

"It is," Jason said as he continued to look around. "I just wish it weren't under such circumstances."

"So war is upon Nezmyth, is it?"

Jason nodded.

"I must admit, I never had to deal with war while I was King," King Thomas said, his hands clasped behind his back. "But I held close relationships with people that did. And they taught me much."

Jason thought of Barnabas in his cell. Then he tore his mind away from it.

"Your thoughts have been on Barnabas lately," King Thomas said as he walked up to the Oracle Stone, never taking his eyes off Jason.

Jason frowned in response. "Of course they have. His son is waging war on us."

"But even before then. You've been visiting him for months, have you not? Descending into the depths of the Nezmyth City Prison to visit him as a broken vagabond? One who refuses to even look you in the eye?"

"This is true," Jason muttered.

"Why do you suppose that is?"

"I don't know," Jason tapped his foot. "I just feel as though the Dragon has been prompting me to. I don't want to. *Barnabas* certainly doesn't want me to."

"Think hard about it," King Thomas said. "The Sacred Dragon will always nudge you to make choices by divine design. So there must be a reason for it," He let the question hang, then said, "Do you think there's a possibility the Sacred Dragon has been trying to prepare you for something? Prepare Barnabas for something? Possibly this war?"

Jason drummed his fingers on his elbow. "Are you implying that I should set Barnabas free to help with the war?"

"Are you implying that is something you'd be unwilling to do, even if the Sacred Dragon required it?"

Jason didn't speak. His eyes absently fixed on the Oracle Stone as he mulled over King Thomas's words. The Sacred Dragon would never prompt him to free a wretch such as

Barnabas. The man killed thousands of innocent people and nearly destroyed the entire kingdom. A man like that would never deserve freedom.

And yet, something stirred inside Jason. He didn't like it.

"Something to consider, Your Highness," King Thomas said. "The Dragon may command you to do things you don't understand. Listen to your feelings. They'll tell you what is right."

Jason's head started to feel light again. The white room was dissolving. The Oracle Stone stayed in place, but everything else around him darkened. The stone walls and floor returned. Within a matter of seconds, he was back at Nezmyth Castle.

Short and poignant. Not what Jason wanted or expected. In a huff, he marched back up to his quarters and tried unsuccessfully to fall asleep.

* * * * *

"Treetown is overrun, as far as I know," Jason said.

He, Nadiel, Master Ferribolt, Tarren, and Saryan all gathered around a table placed squarely in the middle of the great hall. On the table, a map of Nezmyth stretched from corner to corner. The map detailed major roads and rivers that connected all the kingdom and included all landmarks and villages. Nezmyth was separated into four major regions: the Western Woods, Northern Seashore, Eastern Mountains, and the Southern Plains. Nezmyth City was in the center of it all.

Small flags were pinned into different dots on the map representing Nezmyth's villages. A red flag was placed on top of Treetown. Every other major village had a blue flag on top.

"Are we certain Treetown is overrun?" Nadiel said.

Jason nodded. "There's no doubt in my mind. The Ash were chasing us miles out of town. We wouldn't have escaped if Lampi didn't attack them."

"Lampi?" Tarren asked in awe.

Saryan jabbed a finger at Port Gala, the city on the Northern Seashore. "If Nartikis is smart, this is where he'll send the Ash army next. The Great Nezmyth River starts at Port Gala feeds most of Nezmyth its water, and that river is used for transportation, too. Once they take Port Gala, taking the rest of Nezmyth would be easy for them."

"Is Port Gala protected?" Tarren asked with a twinge of worry.

"Port Gala is walled off in a way very similar to Nezmyth City," Nadiel replied. "The stone walls surrounding it are over thirty feet high—not remarkably tall, but they'll still give some protection from the onslaught. Besides, the army must work its way through the rest of the Western Woods and Fort Abernath before it can reach Port Gala."

"This is, of course, assuming that this is even King Nartikis's plan," Jason said darkly.

Nadiel paused. "Yes."

Suddenly, three booms echoed from the castle door. The doors pulled open and a soldier popped into the doorway, panting. Everyone turned to look.

"Your Highness!" the soldier began. "Survivors from Treetown are approaching the city!"

No one hesitated. They abandoned the table and map. Nadiel and Master Ferribolt marched for the entrance as they commanded Nadiel's carriage to be prepared. Saryan ordered for food to be cooked and for dining tables to be laid out in the great hall. Tarren stood back, a little bewildered and lost as his friends hurried about.

Jason turned to the messenger that arrived at the entrance. "I'll go out to meet them as they enter the city. Bring them back here and make sure they're well fed and clothed. These people have just lost everything."

"Of course, sir!"

Nadiel's and Jason's carriages were ready within minutes. Tarren rode with Nadiel while Master Ferribolt and Saryan joined Jason in his carriage. The carriages galloped through the Nezmyth City streets while the drivers blew on brass horns to warn people of their coming. City-goers split to the edges of the street as the caravan blew past.

Jason cleared his throat as he stole a glance at Saryan. "Darling, how are you feeling this morning?"

She didn't reply. Jason sighed through his nose.

Suddenly, the carriages skidded to a halt just after the Southern Market Street. They must have reached the survivors. Saryan threw the door open and jumped out of the carriage before Jason could. He followed closely behind. What he saw made his heart drop.

There were only a few dozen of them, and they looked terrible. Faces with sunken, red eyes. Feet that shuffled across the cobblestone, aimless and lost. Every single one of them had at least one bloody bandage somewhere. On top of it all, they were covered head to toe with soot, ashes, and sweat.

Jason tried to keep his voice from quivering as he spoke.

"Where is Chief Patu?" he called to the crowd.

"'Ere, yer 'ighness," a weathered voice replied.

There she was, in a handcart being towed by three people. The handcart creaked horribly as the giant chief forced herself into a sitting position. Her jolly nature was completely gone, and one of her arms was in a sling and half of her head was bandaged up. The animal skins that she wore as armor were torn and cut in several spots—stained with blood.

Chief Patu grimaced and inhaled sharply through her teeth. She tried to scoot herself forward to climb out of the handcart.

"No!" Jason dashed forward to stop her. "Stop right there. Keep resting. You can tell us everything at the castle." He looked around, then said, "Where's Adria?"

Chief Patu clenched her mighty jaw, pursed her lips together, and shook her head. Two villagers crowded her and rubbed her arms as she tried not to weep. Jason's throat tightened. He took another look around. Everyone from the castle was standing outside of the carriages, fear and sadness ridden across their faces.

Is this just a taste of what's to come? Jason thought.

He tried to push the thought out of his head. "Get all the children in the carriages. We can walk with the rest of you. You! Guards, over there! Come push this handcart. As for you, send for more carriages and some healers. Let's bring these people to the castle as quickly as possible."

Not much as was said as they trudged through the city. The carriages came and went with hasty succession, taking loads of Treetown refugees with them. As they made their way through the streets, the locals looked on with the same sadness and fear that the others felt. Several rushed into their homes to rummage around their belongings, then returned carrying loads of food, blankets, and clothing. The refugees accepted all these gratefully, and often with tears and hugs.

At length, the refugees arrived at the castle. Jason and his friends arrived last. By this time, the great hall had been furnished with three long rows of tables with dozens of chairs to match. The cooks did the best they could to cover the tables with food. The people of Treetown began dining as soon as they reached the castle, one group at a time.

Chief Patu sat at the head of one table. She didn't dig into her meat, potatoes, and greens like Jason remembered at the village. She was quiet. Distant. Jason and the others sat near her, watching, waiting for whatever she had to say. She didn't look up much. Instead, she kept her head down, staring at her food.

All the while, Saryan held Chief Patu's hand tightly, her eyes misty.

"Chief," Jason began slowly. "Please. Tell me what happened."

Chief Patu sniffed. She silently wiped her nose with her big, meaty fingers. When she finally looked into Jason's eyes, her own were full of hurt. Full of recent memories.

"They appeared outta nowhere," Chief Patu began. "In those purple clouds o' smoke. Right on top of us. Had to 'ave been a 'undred of 'em. We weren't fast 'nough." She paused. "Yer 'ighness, Treetown used to 'ave 'bout three 'undred people. What you see now is what's left of us."

Jason looked around. The tables that lined the great hall didn't seat more than forty people, including children. His eyes stung again. Images of destruction flashed across his mind—dark beasts ravaging the people of Treetown with weapons, falling upon them like a dark wave of death.

"My people…" Chief Patu muttered pitifully. "So many of 'em… and Adria…"

With that, she buried her face in a giant hand. She sniffed and her body shook as warm, salty tears dripped into her dirty palm. Jason exchanged looks with Nadiel, Master Ferribolt, and Tarren. Nadiel bowed his head in respect for the dead while Master Ferribolt uttered a quiet prayer. Tarren looked on with a pale face and a hanging jaw. The rest of the Treetown refugees looked upon their strong leader. Their own eyes became misty and two children started crying.

Slam!

Chief Patu smashed her fist onto the table, leaving a splintering dent. Her beady eyes, wet and swollen, were now full of fire as they locked onto Jason. Her teeth ground together in her skull.

"So 'elp me, yer 'ighness," Chief Patu seethed. "I'll kill Nartikis m'self if I 'ave to. We 'ave to stop 'em. We 'ave t' avenge our people."

Jason met her gaze with just as much intensity. "Chief, I want to bring Nartikis to justice and stop the Ash as much as you do. All of us do. But we don't know where to start. We have theories of what Nartikis's plan might be, but not much else."

"Kalyk is on it, isn't she?" One refugee called from another table.

Another refugee chimed in. "Yeah! Kalyk will let us know!"

Jason exchanged puzzled glances with the rest of his friends. Chief Patu almost smirked but wiped her nose and eyes instead.

"Kalyk is a special warrior 'n our village," Chief Patu said. "She's one o' the best bloomin' archers I ever seen. Cunning. Sharp. Most 'mportantly, she moves like a fox 'n the dark." She paused. "Just after yeh left, yer 'ighness, I called fer Kalyk and gave 'er a special task. Hide. Make 'erself invisible. Listen t'what the enemy 'as in store and send us word."

"She's amazing!" One refugee stood from his chair. "She can jump from tree to tree without breaking the softest branch! And I once saw her shoot an apple off a cart at a hundred yards!"

"Kalyk is incredible!" A Treetown youth piped up.

Chief Patu nodded. "She's got a pet 'awk named Justice. The bird's always with 'er. It's trained to deliver messages over long distances. While Kalyk is 'iding in the trees, she'll send us messages with th' bird lettin' us know anything she 'ears from the enemy. That'll teach us their plans."

Jason exchanged glances with his friends again, this time with a spark of hope.

"It appears as though we'll know the enemy's plans after all," Nadiel said with a hint of confidence.

"Thank the Dragon," Master Ferribolt said half to himself.

"The Western Bridge was destroyed?" Jason asked Chief Patu.

Chief Patu shook her head. "Dunno. Our town's best m'gicians managed t' be on their way 'fore the Ash arrived. I hope to th' Dragon that they got the Bridge destroyed. They have no way of communicatin' with us, though. If they did, they came back t' Treetown to find it in ruin. They might even be dead."

"Wait," Tarren said. "But, if the Ash suddenly appeared, what difference does it make if the Western Bridge got destroyed or not?"

"Transporting a living thing takes a great deal of magic," Nadiel said with his arms folded. "It likely took a great toll on Nartikis to transport enough Ash to Treetown. I'm sure a creature like the Ash can't practice magic on its own—it's born from magic itself. If our friends managed to destroy the Western Bridge, that might have been our first victory in this war. It means the Ash can only appear in Nezmyth as long as Nartikis has the energy for it."

"If Kalyk can stay 'idden, she'll be a great asset," Chief Patu said. "If she c'n stay low 'n' observe th' Ash, we may learn their weak spots and discover th' enemy's plans. I must warn yeh, though…"

A hush fell over the room. Chief Patu leaned over the table again, and the tone of her voice got as serious as ever. Her face had never been more stony or hard.

"I never seen anythin' fight like these," she said. "They strike w'thout thought, reason, 'r hes'tation. They're fast. They're strong. 'Nd if we don't stop 'em or keep more forces from comin', I don't know what else we can do fer Nezmyth."

II

THE MAGICIANS

A sudden chill fell upon the Western Woods. There were dozens of them—tall, muscular, and hungry. Ash appeared in puffs of purple smoke, armed with all sorts of weapons, eyes burning for blood. Arrows pelted through the trees. Growls and hisses sounded as their bare feet stamped across the forest floor. They shouted at each other, their target clear and moving fast.

Three horses sprinted down the Western Woods road. In the dark, the horses' breaths billowed like smoke against the cold the Ash brought. The horses were ridden by two men and one woman all garbed in gray cloaks—the symbol of a magician in their home of Treetown.

As the arrows pelted through the air, one found its mark in a rider's leg.

"*Augh!*" the man cried out, clutching his leg. With a sharp, painful yank, he pulled the arrow from his thigh. He inspected it quickly. The arrow was jagged and black, unlike anything he had seen before. He tossed it aside before he slapped his hand onto his wound and uttered an ancient phrase. His leg started to tingle.

"Alix! Are you alright?" The female rider called from his side.

"I'll be fine, Natalia!" Alix responded. "I could heal faster if we weren't moving! Cast a barrier—"

"On it!" Natalia responded.

She shouted a spell, and a transparent blue shell encased the three riders. It followed them as they flew along. Arrows rebounded off the barrier, causing scrapes and scratches that continued to crack and grow.

"It won't hold forever," the rider in the front said, his voice deep and authoritative. "Look alive! These monsters keep appearing! To the Western Bridge!"

They barreled along, their eyes darting around the trees as Ash continued to appear in billows of purple smoke. All around them, the beastly roars and hisses of Ash surrounded them like a cruel nightmare. They seemed to be aware of the magicians' mission—aware that if they succeeded, the Ash's victory could be stopped, or at least slowed.

As arrows and rocks continued to assault the shell, one section finally gave way. One arrow stuck into the shell, causing it to ripple and crack until the fractals covered the entire surface. Finally, the blue shell trickled and collapsed around them, the pieces disappearing into the air.

They were exposed. Arrows continued to zip around them.

Natalia's magic arm was tingling, and her head swam. "Alix! Can you cast one?"

"Maybe!" Alix replied. "I think I've healed enough."

"I'll do it!" the man in front called.

As he raised his hand to cast the spell, an arrow lodged into the head of his horse.

The horse buckled and toppled to the ground at breakneck speed, the rider along with it. Alix and Natalia watched in horror as they blew past the wreckage.

"*Murtag!*" They both cried.

It was too late. Murtag's broken body was already dozens of yards behind them. As they looked back, they saw a battalion of Ash descend upon him, then fall into darkness. Natalia and Alix exchanged looks. No room for tears.

Alix thrust his arm into the air and cast another barrier spell. They were again protected by a transparent blue shell. And again, that shell became a victim of an arrow bombardment. Both Alix and Natalia wiped tears from their eyes as they galloped along, refusing to look back.

"What do you think has become of Treetown?" Natalia said over the barrage.

"Don't think of that, Natalia," Alix replied darkly.

"It was only yesterday that Nezmyth was at peace! What now?"

"I don't know! But if we don't reach the Western Bridge, Murtag won't be the only one to die. Ride!"

"Alix! We're here!"

There it was. The Western Bridge—the monstrous expanse that stretched over the chasm separating Nezmyth and Unbuntye. The bridge they were sent to destroy. In the pale moonlight, the stone appeared ghostlike. Alix and Natalia knew what to do.

Both of them yanked the reins as hard as they could. Their horses stumbled to a stop after a painful whinny, and they both hopped off, casting off their cloaks and surveying the scene. The bridge was hundreds of feet long. Destroying it would be no minor feat.

And behind them, an army of Ash was approaching.

"Natalia," Alix said softly.

Natalia turned to face him. His blue eyes were tender and full of pain. He blinked and said, "I think this is it for us."

Natalia's bottom lip shook. The stampede of Ash was coming closer. She didn't say anything. She just nodded, holding back tears.

Alix cracked his knuckles and said, "I'm with you to the very end, my love."

Natalia didn't hold back. She held Alix's face and planted a kiss firmly on his lips. He pulled her close, her fiery red hair tickling his face one last time.

Finally, Natalia released him and said, "Defend me. I'll destroy the bridge. I love you."

With that, they flipped back-to-back—Alix facing the incoming onslaught, Natalia facing the bridge.

Alix planted his feet apart, keenly aware of his bleeding leg. He stuck out his arms and swirled them in a calculated pattern, muttering under his breath. From the ground, two embers sparked and burned and grew. After a few seconds, each ember had grown into an individual firehound—burning, snarling, and hungry to sink its teeth into whatever was coming. They barked angrily, sparks falling to the ground by their paws.

With another swish of his arms, Alix cast a barrier to protect him and Natalia. A flat wall of transparent blue.

Natalia lifted her arms with her palms down, feeling the reverberations in the ground. Her heart and soul connected with the living things around her. In her spirit, she could feel each stone of the Western Bridge—each very large and thousands of years old. Her eyebrows bent.

"It's so big," she said despairingly. "I don't think I can do it."

"Yes, you can!" Alix shouted. "I know you can! The Dragon will give you strength!" He paused. "They're here."

And they were. Dozens upon dozens of Ash, their weapons raised to the air as they howled girthy cries of bloodlust, descended upon the two magicians. Both firehounds took off, darting across the ground and barking with fury. They were quick, dashing through feet, dodging sword swipes and spear jabs. They bit through the jugulars of several and distracted many others, but it wasn't enough.

Alix lifted both palms vertical and blasted the front ranks with rays of scorching blue beams. They took it hard and toppled to the ground, but more Ash trampled the bodies of the fallen and rushed.

Meanwhile, Natalia bared her teeth and grunted as her arms trembled in the air. She could feel the mortar shaking between the stones in the bridge. Sweat beaded on her forehead.

Alix fired more beams into the crowd, causing more Ash to falter and fall. Sweat poured from his forehead and his injured leg shook. Both firehounds had fallen, stabbed and beaten by the Ash. Their bodies evaporated into the air.

The Western Bridge was shaking. The sound was like a distant thunderstorm. Natalia's arms shook violently as the sweat dripped from her chin.

"*Alright then!*" Alix shouted.

He cried another ancient phrase and punched his fists together. Like water rippling in a pond, his skin turned to metal, starting at his knuckles and growing out to his arms, torso, and legs. After a few seconds, every inch of him was shimmering like steel. He clapped his hands with a mighty *clang*. As he pulled them apart, a fiery orange broadsword grew out from his right hand. Alix let the Ash fall upon him.

The steel of swords and spears rebounded off his metallic skin as he swung his fiery sword. Surrounded, Alix stabbed and sliced at dozens of Ash, killing few and wounding many. Several feet away, the blue transparent barrier guarded Natalia. Ash pressed up against it, pounding on it with fists and weapons, making it quiver and crack.

The Western Bridge rumbled horribly as chunks of rock and stone separated and fell for thousands of feet, plunging into the raging river below. Natalia's knees knocked and drops of sweat fell from her face. Her arms remained outstretched, quaking. Pained grunts slipped from her lips.

Fire burned in the eyes of the Ash. The transparent blue wall cracked and shook until great sections began to fall apart.

Dozens of feet away, the press of Ash tightened around Alix. As he swung his fiery sword, his whole body ached and tingled. The magic was wearing him down. His vision blurred and the metal covering his body became brittle.

The Ash took notice of this. Two soldiers grabbed each of his arms, restraining him. A soft spot had opened near Alix's belly.

Shing!

A dark, jagged sword found its mark through. Alix gasped horribly and his body tensed before losing all strength and slumping to the ground.

"*Nooo!*" Natalia cried.

She heard the noise. She heard the gasp. She knew what had just happened. She knew it was inevitable, but that didn't make the shock any less real.

Natalia's entire body quaked under the weight of the bridge. With Alix's death, the shield he cast would quickly fade. She had to act fast. She had to hold nothing back.

"*For Nezmyth!*" she bellowed.

For a second, her entire body burned with the brightness of the sun. A ripple of white light shot through the Western Bridge, illuminating the cracks between each rock. A series of deafening cracks and snaps rang through the ravine, then the middle of the Western Bridge collapsed.

A torrent of rocks and mortar cascaded to the canyon below. It started in the middle then spread to the edges, a barrage of boulders that had stood for numberless generations. No more. The Western Bridge was gone.

Natalia looked on it with satisfaction, completely exhausted. She couldn't stand. She fell to her knees, teetering on the brink of consciousness, her entire body tingling horribly. The mission was complete. This was a victory for Nezmyth. She was about to collapse, but an Ash blade ripped through her before she could even close her eyes.

As she crumpled to the ground, Ash gathered around her overlooking the ravine. One spat on her body before peering over the edge of the cliff.

"Master will not be pleased," one soldier said, its voice harsh and worn.

"No," the other beast replied. "But this is a small thing. That pathetic town in the woods will fall within hours. And there we will begin." The beast paused to give its comrades a nefarious grin. "The seed has been planted. And it is us."

* * * * *

The jail cell. The long, frail, pale body. The mess of tattered gray hair. The dark, dancing torchlight illuminating it all.

Barnabas turned about slowly to face him. As soon as Jason felt those icy blue eyes upon him, he heard a voice.

"Listen to your feelings."

Jason gasped.

He jolted up in bed, breathing hard, a thin layer of sweat covering his whole body. The image of Barnabas alone in his cell was still branded on his mind. Those chilling eyes lingered on him, waiting for what was supposed to happen next.

Jason looked next to him. Saryan was gone again. Moonlight spilled into their bedroom as it hung over a dark Nezmyth sky dotted with stars. He threw the covers off his legs. He couldn't take the burning in his mind any longer. He shoved his arms through his robe and burst out the door into the hallway, marching quickly.

Everything happened in a flash. His coach was assembled, Nadiel and Tarren were fetched, and everyone met at Master Ferribolt's mansion in Upper City. The three of them were escorted into the study, where books lined the walls from top to bottom and a fire crackled in the fireplace a dozen feet away. A mahogany desk was pressed into the corner and a bear rug snarled at the men's feet. There would still be a couple of hours before dawn, so the tall windows had curtains drawn over them.

All of them sat in a circle, seated in plush armchairs not far from the fireplace. Nadiel blinked the sleep out of his eyes while Tarren rubbed his own. Master Ferribolt was sleepy as well, but barely swayed in his chair. Jason sat tight and alert, however, sleep having fled his eyes nearly an hour ago.

"I'm sorry for bringing you all here at such a late hour," Jason said seriously. "Master Ferribolt, thank you for letting us use your home. It was the quickest, since Tarren still lives on Southern Market Street."

"Of course," Master Ferribolt said as he yawned and covered his mouth.

"What's this about?" Tarren asked bluntly as he stretched in his chair. "I only got an hour of sleep before soldiers showed up at my door."

"Up late reading your assignments?" Nadiel asked.

Tarren let out a hefty sigh. "Yes, sir. All twelve volumes."

"Excellent."

Jason said, "It's about Barnabas."

The tone in the room shifted immediately. Both Nadiel's and Tarren's eyes hardened. Master Ferribolt leaned forward in his seat, intrigued.

"Oh?" Master Ferribolt said. "What about him?"

Jason dug his hands into his hair and scratched his head, then pushed himself out of his chair and paced the floor. The crackle of the fireplace would normally be soothing, but not tonight. Every pair of eyes was on him.

"I had a vision recently through the Oracle Stone," Jason said. "I spoke to the spirit of King Thomas. He told me I might have been prompted to visit Barnabas for some divine purpose—as if he has a role in this war. For the last few months, the feelings have been quiet, but for the past couple of days... they've been undeniably strong."

"Feelings about Barnabas?" Tarren quizzed, his eyebrows creased. "What does that mean?"

Nadiel's jaw tightened and his head dipped. Tarren looked on with his mouth agape. Master Ferribolt waited with his hands in his lap.

Jason rubbed his face before gazing upon his friends. He took a deep breath. "I think… I think I'm supposed to set him free."

Silence. No one exchanged looks—they just ogled at Jason with a mix of confusion, concern, and disgust. Everyone except Master Ferribolt. He frowned in a way that wasn't dissatisfied, but thoughtful and contemplative. He stroked his chin and stared at the floor.

Tarren said breathlessly, "You can't be serious."

"Do you honestly think I'd joke about something like this?" Jason said severely. "I have as much reason to hate him as anyone else in this room. But these feelings are so strong that I can barely sleep anymore. There is something—something that we need from him. I don't know what it is. But there must be something."

Nadiel didn't look at Jason. He asked, "Have you thought about the repercussions this would have across the kingdom?" He paused. "The effects of his tyranny are still fresh in the minds of the people. Nezmyth has entered a war, and the people need to have as much confidence in you as possible. You are their leader—their King." Another pause. "Jason, once word got out that you set Barnabas free, the people would lose their confidence in you. And this is a time where you must have their full support. Nothing about this seems wise."

Jason brushed his arms. "I know. It seems insane. But what can I do? I've been getting these feelings, and I can't deny them."

Another long silence. Jason paced with his arms folded, staring at his feet with every step. It felt like a knot had tied itself in his chest, tense and unyielding. Meanwhile, Tarren's purple eyes could have burned a hole in the bear rug at his feet. Nadiel rubbed his face in his hands, and Master Ferribolt stayed contemplative and unmoving.

"My advice would be that prolonging the Dragon's council will surely be unwise," Master Ferribolt said.

"Spoken like a true Patriarch," Nadiel said half bitterly.

Master Ferribolt ignored him. "Jason, if that is the direction that you have received, the course of action is clear. You must release Barnabas. No matter how absurd or inconceivable it may seem or how much the rest of us disapprove. But you are the Dragon's ordained King of Nezmyth, so you must make the final decision."

Jason didn't reply, he continued to pace. The tension in the deepest parts of Lower City was still strong against him. The poorest of the poor had remained destitute even after he became King and removed the Harvest Tax. With the release of Barnabas, he knew the distrust and the resentment against him would spread. And Nadiel was right—Nezmyth is entering into war. Is this the ideal time to make a drastic decision like freeing Barnabas? What do the people need right now?

Jason stroked his chin some more. Then he looked up.

"I think I have a solution," he said. "I'll free Barnabas… but not right away."

No one responded. They waited for Jason to continue.

"We'll fight this war with all that we have—snuff out the forces of the Ash and bring Nartikis to his knees. Imprison him just like we did Barnabas. Then, Barnabas will be a free man. The war that is on our doorstep seems to me to be a much higher priority than the life of one treacherous man. This way we put the people of Nezmyth first and still follow the Dragon's command of freeing the former King. What say you?"

"Agreed," Nadiel said quickly.

"I trust you, Jason," Tarren said.

Everyone looked to Master Ferribolt. His arms were folded and his eyes half-closed behind his round spectacles. He took a deep breath and gazed deeply into Jason's eyes. The tone of his voice was resigned.

"You are the King, Jason," Master Ferribolt said. "Choose what you feel is right. I'll be in full support of your decision."

"Good," Jason said with finality. "Then we're in agreement." He stopped, then said, "Everyone get some rest. Move forward. Fight with all we are. Goodnight."

With that, everyone exchanged their goodbyes before they departed and returned home. During the carriage ride back to the castle, the knot in Jason's chest didn't subside. He couldn't help but remember the words of King Thomas just one night ago.

"Listen to your feelings."

Even as he lay in bed, he tried to push those words out of mind. He still didn't sleep much that night.

12

THE TIP

It was hard to believe the Treetown refugees arrived in Nezmyth City only yesterday. The plan was to have the people sleep on the floor of the great hall since there wasn't enough room for them anywhere else. Saryan offered the royal bedroom to Chief Patu, who respectfully declined. She preferred to sleep among her people. Jason was not consulted on the matter.

However, the whole affair wasn't necessary. Jason sent a decree to the people of Nezmyth City as soon as the refugees arrived. Gradually, people of the city turned up at the castle gates to offer their homes to the refugees until Treetown could be retaken. Some of these even came bearing blankets, baskets of food, and extra clothing. By the end of the day, not a single refugee was left at the castle. Every last one had a place to rest their head. The sight made Jason's heart swell.

But the mood in Nezmyth City had shifted drastically in the last day. War was upon them, and the whisperings in the marketplace could not be denied. Who would be called to fight against the Ash? Why would Nartikis choose to go to war against Nezmyth now? Can the Ash be stopped? How many villages will they lay in waste before that happens?

When Jason awoke to a sunrise grazing his face, he turned over in bed. The space next to him was empty yet again. He frowned.

He got dressed and made his way down to the back courtyard. He skipped his traditional armor and instead went with an old shirt and pants—the kind of clothes he used to wear when he was a commoner. His bare feet clapped against the stone floors as he made his way downstairs and through hallways, passing several pairs of soldiers.

The morning sun was bright and harsh as he pushed a set of double doors leading to the courtyard. The flowers and shrubs rustled in the springtime breeze, laid out in rows and patches organized by carved stone. In the middle of the courtyard, a large expanse was outlined as a sparring space. Currently, it was inhabited by none other than the Queen, swinging and jabbing her staff as she battled with two soldiers. Guards stood around the perimeter, watching intently.

Jason wordlessly made his way to the spectacle. As he approached, Saryan quickly dispatched two of the soldiers, knocking each of them to the ground.

The guards around the perimeter clapped. One guard silently gave two Bars to another while the recipient smirked. Another guard marched out to the Queen to hand her a canteen full of water, which she drank from liberally.

By this time, Jason had reached her. He said, "Watching you spar reminds me of when I first knew you. Your battle class down by the Market Streets."

Saryan stopped drinking and wiped her mouth. She gave the canteen back to the soldier and glared at Jason coldly, then put her hand on her hip and leaned on her staff.

"Five years, Jason," she said. "I must have really lowered my standards to end up with you." The corner of her lip twitched upward, almost teasing a smile.

"I'm glad you did," Jason said. "I don't know what I would be without you." He paused. "Saryan… I keep going over the battle in my head. I wish there was something more I could have—"

"Don't," Saryan interjected. "Don't. Jason, I know he's gone. And I *know* you would have done something if you could. Somehow I knew that he would go out like this. It just…" she took a deep breath. "It doesn't make things easier."

Without another word, Jason wrapped his arms around her. He didn't care that her face and hair were matted with sweat or that her body radiated heat. He just held her. In kind, she wrapped her arms around his neck, holding him close, not speaking. They embraced for a long moment before letting go. Saryan quickly wiped her eyes with the back of her hand, not wanting the soldiers to see. Then she cleared her throat.

"Well, what are you waiting for?" she said. "Grab a sword!"

Jason smirked. He walked back to the perimeter of the courtyard to grab a wooden sword, but a soldier bustled out and handed one to him. He made his way back to the center of the courtyard where Saryan was waiting for him.

They faced each other. They bowed. Jason lunged.

Saryan backpedaled and parried each blow with ease before she took a turn lunging at Jason. Likewise, he deflected each strike. They crossed their weapons and stared each other down from inches away.

"Do you know who I really blame for all of this?" Saryan said almost amiably.

Push. Swipe. Duck. Counter. Block.

"Me?" Jason replied through the cross in their weapons. "For becoming King and turning your life upside down?"

Another push. Lunge. Block.

"No," Saryan said darkly. "Barnabas."

She pushed against Jason and he backpedaled out of her reach. They both lowered their weapons together.

"Really?" Jason said, half-present.

"Isn't it obvious?" Saryan said. "He threatened you and held my father hostage during your Year of Decision. He went to a kingdom and had a bastard son that killed my father and is waging war on my home. Except my mother's death, all of my suffering comes back to him."

Jason stared at the ground. "I suppose it does."

When Jason didn't say more than this, Saryan dipped her head down, trying to catch his eye. "What's wrong?"

He almost told her. He hesitated, held his tongue, then opened his mouth. But that was when a soldier came running.

"Your Highness! My Lady!" The soldier shouted as it came to a stop at the edge of the sparring court. "Chief Patu just received a message from Kalyk! Her hawk arrived just moments ago!"

Jason and Saryan immediately followed the soldier back into the castle. Chief Patu and Nadiel were waiting for them in the great hall. There, a black-and-red hawk with a sharp, hooked beak and round eyes perched on Nadiel's shoulder, its head swiveling around as it observed its surroundings. Nadiel leaned to one side, almost like he was trying to get away from it. In Chief Patu's hands was a small roll of parchment, unraveled as her eyes darted across it.

"What does it say?" Jason asked.

Chief Patu finished the letter. She glanced at Jason, then held it out to him. Jason took it in both hands. Saryan read the letter over his shoulder.

My chief,

Please forgive late letter. Traveled to the Western Bridge. Traveling amid treetops is slow.

Western Bridge destroyed. Can't find Murtag, Alix, or Natalia. Likely taken by Ash. They make more from us.

Ash going north through Pinegrove. Will travel there to warn village. Please send help. I will fight with you.

May the Dragon protect us.

-K

They make more from us.

Jason read that sentence over and over again. Did that mean what he thought it meant? No. It couldn't. Could it? A shiver slid down his spine.

He creased his eyebrows and handed the letter back to Chief Patu. "So, we were right then. They plan on advancing northward."

"And they plan to move immediately," Nadiel said, still leaning away from the hawk on his shoulder. "Jason, we must rally as many willing hands as we can and march out at once. The journey from Treetown to Pinegrove takes less than a day on foot. If we leave now, we could add to the forces of Pinegrove before the Ash arrive, but we must leave *immediately*."

Jason only stopped to consider it for a moment. "Agreed. We prepare to leave at once." He turned to Saryan. "We'll be back in a few days. I'll send you—"

"Don't be ridiculous," Saryan said sternly. "I'm coming with you."

Jason knew he was treading in dangerous territory, but this was too serious. "No, you're not. I need you to stay here. You haven't seen what these things are—"

"You may be the King, but I am the *Queen!*" Saryan stamped her foot. "I will not be ordered around like one of your guards! I'm coming to Pinegrove and you cannot stop me!"

Everyone in the room stiffened and stole glances at each other. Jason didn't know how to respond. His cheeks blazed with embarrassment—no one wants to have an altercation like this in front of their friends. He swallowed, trying to think of the words to say. But Chief Patu beat him to it.

"Yer 'ighness," Chief Patu spoke softly.

Saryan reared on her, her eyes white hot.

"Please, listen to th' King," Chief Patu said. "I lost Adria yesterday. I know 'ow 'e would feel if 'e lost you."

Saryan's scowl didn't subside, and her face burned so much that it made her eyes water. She folded her arms, stared at the floor, and marched out of the great hall. The doors opened and slammed loudly, filling the hall with furious finality.

Jason took a breath. He'd rather continue the silent treatment if it meant Saryan was safe. *She can sulk and cry in their bedroom all she wants. She needs to stay here. She's the Inheritor. She needed to be protected.*

"Let's bring some of our best soldiers," he said. "Send a decree immediately."

* * * * *

The decree was sent out. Hundreds of men and women answered to call without hesitation. In Center Court, civilians from Upper City and Lower City tearfully gathered to wish their families goodbye, equipped with what armor and weapons they had.

Through the buzz, Jason looked on, admiring the courage of his people but dreading what was ahead. The royal coach waited behind him, along with a caravan of carts and horses that snaked around the perimeter of the court. As people loaded their meager supplies, Jason rubbed his sagging, sunken eyes.

Nadiel put his hand on Jason's shoulder. He hadn't been standing there until only a moment ago, appearing magically without a sound. Jason stopped rubbing his eyes.

"Are you sure it's a good idea for you to come with Tarren?" Jason asked darkly. "It seems risky to put an upcoming Advisor onto a battlefield."

"In my heart, it seems the right choice," Nadiel said.

"How are his studies?"

Nadiel sighed. "I'm worried for him. In his heart, he means well. But he has no thirst for knowledge, and he struggles with the literature of the ancients. We are much farther behind than where I would like to be."

"And his Ancient Nezmythian?"

"Likewise."

"Be patient with him," Jason said. "He'll come around. He's one of the hardest workers I know."

"Hopefully it is enough," Nadiel said.

A small child timidly crept up to the two of them. The girl had dark, short hair and pinned a small, stuffed horse in the crook of her elbow—she couldn't have been older than eight or nine years. She never took her eyes off Jason as she edged her way toward him.

Jason, surprised, got down on one knee to look the girl in the eyes. She spoke first.

"Your Highness?" Her voice was small and delicate as porcelain.

"Yes?"

"Will you keep my dad safe?"

Jason's heart shriveled. He clenched his teeth and swallowed, then reached out and took the girl's hand, rubbing her tiny fingers tenderly. She watched him expectantly, still waiting for an answer.

"Where is he?" Jason said, looking over her head.

She turned around and pointed. Not far away, a man firmly embraced another woman carrying a baby over her back. Surrounding them, three other children clutched onto his legs, sniffling and burying their faces in his clothes. The little girl right before Jason must have been the oldest. Jason looked her in the eyes.

"What's your name?"

"Emilee, daughter of Thomas the blacksmith."

"Emilee," Jason said resolutely. "I will do everything that I can to protect your father. You have my word."

At this, Emilee's bottom lip shook. She gave a little curtsy, two tear drops fell to the stone beneath her worn-out shoes, and she said, "Thank you, King Jason. May the Dragon bless you."

She darted away. Jason stood up. He watched young Emilee throw her arms around her father one more time. Behind Jason, Nadiel was frowning.

"Do you really believe you can protect that man's life when there are hundreds of men on a battlefield?" he said.

Jason frowned in kind. "I gave her my word, so I'll do my best."

"You're as reckless as you are kind."

"There are worse things," Jason retorted. After a brief pause, Jason made the decision. "We should be off. Is Tarren in the carriage?"

"Yes."

"Then let's not wait any longer."

There was no speech. No banners of glory or rousing songs of victory. Jason and Nadiel slipped into the red carriage that led the way for the rest of the caravan. A long snake of horses and carts made its way through the Nezmyth City streets, heading for the western wall, comprised of hundreds of Nezmythian men and women armed with what they had.

Husbands, wives, and children threw flowers in the streets as their loved ones rode by, their faces dripping with worry and sadness. Many of the children buried their sobbing faces into their mothers. Jason didn't look at any of them. He kept his head down, his eyes focused between his boots.

Which ones aren't coming home?

13
THE MARCH

Most of the journey westward was carried in silence. Nothing was heard but the soft clopping of horses' hooves, the grinding of handcart wheels, and the tinny clink of armor. As the carriage climbed over a hill headed for the Western Woods, Jason looked out to his right to see the Nezmyth City Prison in the distance. He quickly looked away.

Nadiel and Tarren sat across from him in the carriage. Most of the time, Nadiel kept his eyes closed but his posture immaculate, deep in meditation. He would need all the meditation he could get to channel his magical power prior to battle. As for Tarren, a small stack of books lay at his feet. Currently, his face was halfway through one volume, staring at the page as if intimidating it would yield more information.

He almost looks like he's in pain, Jason thought with a frown.

Tarren snapped the book shut and leaned back, rubbing his eyes with his palms. Nadiel didn't open his eyes or budge at the sound of Tarren's frustration. His hands stayed clasped on his knees and he spoke:

"*Gaytah emglay,* Tarren?"

Tarren cleared his throat. "*Elu maytesho—*"

"It's *mayteshu*," Nadiel interrupted. "*Mayteshu* means 'I'm well'" while *maytesho* means 'I'm nauseous.'"

"Well, not far off then."

"You will learn," Nadiel said, still not opening his eyes. "Many struggle with Ancient Nezmythian. The rules of grammar and vocabulary may come across as a bit arbitrary and convoluted, but your mastery will come in due time."

"I just don't see why this dead language is necessary," Tarren murmured.

"It's actually very important," Jason interjected. He leaned forward in his seat. "I didn't know this during my Year of Decision, but most of the Ancient Texts are in Ancient Nezmythian. That includes a lot of prophecies and ancient law —things that you'll need to know as my Advisor."

"Master Ferribolt is fluent in Ancient Nezmythian," Nadiel volleyed. "He spends the majority of his time tending to the Cathedrals in the Nezmyth City area and scouring the Ancient Texts for prophecies pertaining to our time. Just weeks ago, he found a prophecy about a creature and flames..." Nadiel trailed off as he tried to remember.

"*The creature that feasts on the flesh of the dead will rise to save Nezmyth from a future of flames*," Jason recalled.

"Indeed," Nadiel nodded.

Tarren leaned back in his seat again, staring helplessly at his stack of books as the carriage continued to jitter along. Jason rubbed his palms together, staring into Tarren's eyes, thinking that maybe this wasn't the best course to motivate him. He leaned back, stroked his beard, then folded his arms.

"Tarren, you still spar regularly, right?" Jason asked.

Tarren shrugged. "As often as business allows. It's hard with the shop. And with *this* now." He pointed to the books.

"Remember years ago, when you taught me how to do the jeroki beams?" Jason held out his palm. "Learning Ancient Nezmythian improved my ability to cast magic noticeably.

Something about Ancient Nezmythian works as a catalyst for magic. It'll make you stronger."

"The King is correct," Nadiel said. His eyes were still closed. "And it's not limited to combat magic, Ancient Nezmythian accelerates magic in communication, conjuring, healing, what have you. Quite literally, there is no limit of what could be accomplished through magic with willpower, spiritual fortitude, and imagination."

Tarren stared at the space between his knees. Then something went off. A light in his mind. A flash that jumped across his eyes. His head popped up and his body stiffened.

"Wait," he said, "there's no limit to what can be done with magic? Any kind of magic?"

Finally, Nadiel opened his eyes and peered at Tarren out of the corners of his. He spoke softly. "Theoretically, yes."

"What about healing madness?"

Tarren's jaw was tense. He turned to face the Advisor, his purple eyes serious. For Jason, it suddenly all clicked. Tarren's mother had been living in Lunli Village ever since she had been driven insane years ago, her madness caused by the beatings that were inflicted on her at Nezmyth City Prison after someone accused her of speaking against King Barnabas. Tarren hadn't seen her since he and his father traveled down to the village to leave her with those like her. Now this was a chance to erase the disease from her mind—to bring her back home.

Nadiel thought about it for a second, then nodded slightly. "Yes, I suppose it is possible."

Tarren remained stiff for a moment, processing Nadiel's response and its implications. There was a resolve in his eyes that Jason had never seen before. It was the determination of a man at the foot of a mountain, completely committed to conquering the peak. His fists clenched, then slackened. Then he snatched the book back up and continued to read.

Jason smirked with satisfaction, then his smile faded as he remembered why they were on the road. They had been sitting in the carriage for a few hours. He pushed himself to his feet.

"I'm going to step out for a moment," he said.

Tarren was already engrossed in his book and didn't answer. Nadiel simply nodded. With that, Jason unlatched the door and slipped out.

The pine needles didn't crunch under his boots—they had just crossed into the Western Woods. Conifers towered overhead, reaching toward the sky, which was red and orange with the setting sun. A chill whisked between the trees that made Jason's arms sprout into goosebumps. The gentle scent of pine sap welcomed Jason's nose, but something about the woods was off.

There was no sound except for the grunts, coughs, and murmurs of the Nezmyth City reinforcements. No birds chirping. No tree branches snapping. No scampering of foxes or rabbits or squirrels. Just eerie, tense silence.

Jason put his hand on the pommel of his sword. He didn't recall the woods being this chilly before. As he took a deep breath, he also noticed that the air didn't seem as clean and fresh as it did days ago.

Days ago? He thought to himself, astonished. *Has it really been a matter of days since I was here last? Everything has happened so quickly...*

"These woods aren't th' same."

Jason turned to see Chief Patu approaching him. She lugged a battle axe across her back that would have taken Jason both hands to wield. She already had black streaks painted across her cheekbones. Not an ounce of joy could be seen behind those beady eyes.

"We should reach Pinegrove in th' dead o' night," she said. "Few more 'ours. After that, the forces might 'ave a few 'ours to rest 'fore the Ash arrive."

Jason didn't reply immediately as the Treetown chief walked shoulder-to-shoulder with him. Then he said, "Do you want to know something that's troubled me since we read Kalyk's letter?"

"Hm?"

"She wrote it all in such a rushed way. But there was one sentence that I found haunting. *'They make more from us.'*" Jason paused. "What do you think that means?"

Chief Patu shuddered visibly. "I 'ave one idear, but I 'ope to th' Dragon I'm wrong."

Jason frowned. *Nartikis said the Ash were made from fire and magic… maybe that's not the only thing.*

Jason shivered more violently. The cold became thicker the deeper they delved into the woods. The road soon split into a fork—one way heading west, one way heading north. The caravan turned right, heading northward.

Every man and woman in the caravan clutched their weapons for the next three hours, squinting their eyes, peering into the dark. They couldn't know for sure if the Ash were staying in Treetown. At any moment, a swarm of them could appear with weapons drawn. They had to be ready.

Jason climbed back into the carriage. When he shut the door behind him, Tarren stirred—he had fallen asleep with a book open in his heads, his head lolling around on his shoulders. Nadiel was exactly as before, sitting up straight, his hands on his knees, and his eyes closed. Frankly, Jason couldn't tell if he was asleep or still meditating.

The third hour passed, and then Jason heard the carriage driver call. "We've reached Pinegrove, Your Highness."

Jason threw open the door. Nighttime had fully enveloped the forest. Stars danced in the infinite distance, easily visible above the clearing that Pinegrove carved out of the woods. It was similar to Treetown, with a small plaza in the middle of the village, a well serving as its centerpiece. Almost a mile in diameter, the rest of the village was cabins and huts. The only exceptions were a mansion-like home near the plaza for the town chief and eight lumber mills.

At a time where everyone in the village should be asleep, nearly every hut and cabin in town was lit with candles in the windows. As the hundreds of men and women from Nezmyth City trickled into town, the people of Pinegrove almost paid them no heed. Everyone was bustling about, scrounging up whatever armor and weapons they had, preparing for what was to come.

Jason marched into the town square and scanned the darkness with Chief Patu by his side. Pinegrove's village chief had to be close by. He remembered meeting him for the first time soon after he became King—Chief Markus. A tall and lanky man who liked to dress in fine clothing. He was never at a loss for money, seeing as his village provided most of the kingdom with its lumber. The trees in the Western Woods grew unusually fast, and in the area around Pinegrove, a 100-foot conifer could grow in as little as three years.

"Your Majesty!"

The sound came from his right. The woman jogging up to him made hardly a sound as each foot stamped the ground. A bow and quiver were slung around her shoulders and wavy brown hair fell from her head, framing her slender jaw. Her eyes were a dark green as if the very forest were inside them. Jason only wondered who this woman was for a second.

"Kalyk!" Chief Patu threw her bear-like arms around her, squeezing her tightly. "Yer tip is helpin' us save th' kingdom! May the Dragon bless yeh!"

When Kalyk was released from Chief Patu's crushing embrace, she coughed and turned to Jason. "Thank you for the extra forces, Your Highness. Every one of them will be needed."

"Where's Chief Markus?" Jason shot.

"Gone," Kalyk's face grew hot. "Fled as soon as he heard of the danger. I've been doing my best to rally the town and prepare them for the Ash."

"Th' coward," Chief Patu growled.

"As you can see," Kalyk said. "Pinegrove has no outer wall like Port Gala or Nezmyth City. The Ash will likely come from the south—hundreds of them. We'll have archers on the rooftops near the town's edge. There, they can weaken the forces before they charge into the city."

Jason just nodded as Kalyk explained the plan. It seemed like a wise course of action. Still, he couldn't get the question out of his mind. "Kalyk, what did you mean by *they make more from us?* In your letter."

Kalyk's face turned white and she swallowed.

"As I was hiding in the trees, listening to them, I watched them. I saw how they grow their forces. I don't know what the Unbuntye King told you, Your Majesty, but I've never seen anything so... so—" she closed her eyes. "They are *us*, Your Majesty.

"The Ash create a fire. A large one. Then they take bodies of the slaughtered... and throw them in the fire. The fire turns purple and burns for a while, and when it settles, there they are. More Ash... naked, gray, and evil." Kalyk paused. "I'll never forget the faces of those thrown into those fires. All of them were people I knew. Many were my friends."

"So yeh mean Adria might be...?"

Kalyk clenched her teeth and nodded.

Jason's blood turned to ice. Beside him, Chief Patu fell to her knees, gazing into Kalyk's evergreen eyes, disbelieving the horror that was described. With a dangling jaw and wide eyes, Jason imagined the Ash dragging the slaughtered bodies of his people through the dirt, only to be horrifically burned and transformed. He bowed his head, letting a tear fall to the soil by his boots. He put his hand on Chief Patu's back as the woman dropped her chin and let the tears fall to soil.

"Your Majesty," Kalyk took a step forward. "We *must* stop the Ash *here*. Every defeat Nezmyth sees will add to their forces. They grow and spread like a plague—like a disease. But I know we can defeat them. You and the Sacred Dragon can lead us to victory."

"I swear by th' Dragon's Fire that Treetown will be *avenged!*" Chief Patu roared as she got to her feet. "Yer highness, you have my axe! We'll show Nartikis what th' fire that burns in th' heart of Nezmyth! This war ends *t'night!*"

Several people who scuttled by cheered at Chief Patu's bravado.

"We'll find whatever food we can for the Nezmyth City troops," Kalyk said, turning to Jason. "I'm sure we can find some bread to give them strength." Her voice suddenly got dark. "Unlike us, the Ash have no need for rest. They move and attack with speed and hunger. We must kill every last one of them, or they will take Pinegrove like they did Treetown. Your Highness," she put her hand on Jason's shoulder again, "this war ends *tonight.*"

Jason couldn't think of anything meaningful to say. So, all he said was, "Thank you. Let's show them the fire of Nezmyth."

With that, Chief Patu and Kalyk ran off to join the rest of the forces on the south side of town. As more forces from Nezmyth City marched quickly to join them, Jason looked up to the sky.

The endless black looked the same as it always had. Like before the time Garrit was dead. Or before Nartikis vowed to take over Nezmyth. But somewhere, in that infinite cosmos, the Sacred Dragon looked down upon Nezmyth, the last standing kingdom that clung to the Ancient Ways.

Dragon, help us, Jason thought.

Then he thought of a wispy old man, alone in a prison, dozens of miles away, and he pushed the thought from his mind.

14

THE ONSLAUGHT

The people of Nezmyth worked tirelessly for the next few hours creating a crude barricade on the south side of town. They felled trees and stacked them into a shabby wall that acted more like a fence, reaching only shoulder's height—hardly any real protection from the Ash. If nothing else, they hoped its presence would give the rooftop archers a better chance to thin the first wave.

Those that weren't fighting were ordered to hide in the homes on the north end of town and arm themselves with whatever they could. Just past those homes on the northern border, carriages and horses waited, ready for an escape. Women and children scrounged up shields, swords, knives— whatever they could use if the Ash broke through their doors and windows. Inside, they huddled in corners and held each other, nervous and shaking.

Jason marched up and down the barricade and counted the forces. He lost count somewhere around five hundred. And how many people lived in Pinegrove? Almost a thousand?

Behind the barricade, Tarren and Nadiel stood beside each other. Nadiel's eyes were closed and focused as he listened and felt his surroundings, still meditating. Both his hands wrapped around the hilt of his sword, point stuck in the ground. Tarren, wearing the armor of a royal guard, ground his teeth together and felt at the daggers slung by his hips. He never took his eyes off the quiet woods stretching southward.

Jason peered to a large tree that towered higher than the others just out of town. He knew that Kalyk was perched in the top of that tree, watching. She told Jason that Justice would caw loudly when the Ash army was approaching.

Everyone shuffled their tired feet as they crowded the barricade. As Jason marched by, they all nodded in respect. Jason kept his hand on his sword.

One person caught Jason's eye, a familiar face from Center Court: Emilee's father. He looked like a shorter version of Tarren. He had the strong arms of a blacksmith, greasy blonde hair, and an angular jaw. He nodded at Jason just like all the others as he walked by. He was perplexed when Jason stopped in front of him.

"You," Jason said. "Your daughter spoke to me before you left. It's Thomas, isn't it?"

Thomas cleared his throat and said, "Yes, Your Majesty."

"That's a noble name."

"Thank you, Your Majesty."

Jason couldn't help but think of the black, curly hair and beaming face of King Thomas. He half-smiled. "He was a wonderful King." He looked to the south, then looked back at Thomas. "I promised your daughter that I would do my best to protect you. And I don't intend to make myself a liar."

Thomas nervously smirked. Jason turned and pointed at Nadiel.

"You see that man over there?"

"The one with the gray hair and the red eyes?"

"Right. That's my Advisor. His name is Nadiel. He's a gifted and powerful magician." He leaned in closer to whisper. "And he's been meditating for the entire day, focusing his power. I recommend that you stay close to him."

At this, Thomas stared at Nadiel, jaw dangling, then nodded stiffly. Jason patted Thomas on the shoulder before he moved along. After Jason walked away, Thomas subtly shuffled away to stand closer to Nadiel.

A tense hour passed. The clinking of armor shuffling from side to side was the only sound, aside from a few scanty whispers and raspy coughs. No crickets. Not even the wind rustled in the trees. Just the blazing silence of the woods fallen into thick, murky darkness. Jason scanned up and down the length of the barrier, taking note of all the men and women who were willing to fight for their kingdom. Pinegrove had few guards—fewer even than Treetown—and they were scattered amid the crowd.

Is this going to be enough? Jason thought.

Caww!

Justice's echoing cry pierced the night. The entire barricade tensed, gripping their weapons tighter and bending their knees. Jason's heart rate picked up—he could feel the blood pumping inside his throat. He extracted his sword slowly from its sheath, letting the steel grind and shimmer in the moonlight. The whole forest stiffened.

And suddenly, the air got colder. People began to shiver. Jason could see his breath as he exhaled. His left hand twitched by his side, ready to throw jerokis.

Then the rumbling started. At first it was subtle, then it grew like a stampede. It was hard to see them through the trees, but the first thing that appeared was their eyes—red and shining in the dark.

Jason brandished his sword.

Sacred Dragon, he thought. *Give me the power of the Knight of the Holy Order! Help me defend our people!*

Nothing.

The stampede rapidly approached. Jason stood directly behind the barrier, blinking. His sword was still his hand—not the shining orange Blade of Nezmyth. The black marks of the Knight didn't snake their way down his arms. His body didn't erupt into fire.

Holy Dragon! Jason thought more desperately. *Grant me the power of a Knight of the Holy Order! Please!*

Still nothing. Jason's body didn't change.

The roar of footsteps was stronger than ever. People's heads swiveled to Jason, anxious to hear his orders. Jason swallowed. His Knightly power wasn't coming. He'd be left to fight the Ash just like the others.

They were coming faster. The ground was shaking harder. The bodies of the Ash were now visible against the dark; oily gray, towering, and muscular, sprinting toward Pinegrove.

Jason scowled and threw his gaze to the nearest roof. "Fire when in range!"

The archers knocked arrows and pulled their bowstrings.

Jason's jaw clenched as he uttered another silent prayer, staring at his sword's steel. *Why won't you do this?*

"For Nezmyth!" one soldier from the front called.

"*For Nezmyth!*" The army roared in reply.

The Ash were upon them. The archers released the first wave. A volley of arrows rained down to the ground, covering the Ash at the front. Ash crumbled to the ground, skewered with multiple shafts. Some, having taken only one or two arrows, kept running.

And those that kept running leaped over the fence like tigers.

The onslaught was tremendous. Immediately, the air was filled with clashes and clangs and the pops of jerokis. And screams. Many Nezmythians fell when the first wave of Ash slammed into the ground. Jason dove in, slashing and shooting as he went. On the rooftops, archers were frantically knocking their next round of arrows.

Not far away, Nadiel unleashed his power.

As soon as the first wave of Ash jumped over the barrier, Nadiel thrust his sword into the ground and lifted his hands above his head. His eyes glowed yellow. His palms sparked. Then, in an instant, electric bolts shot from his palms in every direction. The bolts found the hearts of at least a dozen Ash, killing them immediately while expertly bending around the humans that stood in their way.

More arrows flew and dusty soot filled the air, but the army of Ash poured into the village like a terrible flood. The thunderous rumble of footsteps became all-encompassing. Bodies of Ash and humans were strewn across the ground punctured, covered in ashes, and twisted from broken bones. Jason swung his sword all about him and shot jeroki beams at every Ash that got too close. The body count around him was climbing.

Tarren darted through the crowd, his large frame uncannily fast, slashing and gutting every Ash he could. He dodged sword swipes and ax swings. He broke bones, slit throats, and left a trail of fallen Ash as he tore through the multitude.

But not everyone fought with such fire and expertise. The Ash were fast, powerful, and thirsty for death. They attacked with a singular goal, not to overcome or conquer, but simply to kill, and to kill as much as possible. Many fell by their hands.

Jason saw this. And he knew that with every fallen Nezmythian, the Ash added to their ranks. As his head darted about to observe the carnage. For every Ash killed, another two Nezmythians fell. And the dark soldiers were still pouring into the town from the south. There had to have been hundreds of them.

So many… Jason thought with horrific awe.

He noticed Thomas the blacksmith struggling to fight several yards away. He sparred one-on-one with an Ash much larger than him, and he was clearly outmatched. Jason dug in his feet and darted toward him.

At that moment, Thomas was knocked to the ground. The Ash towered over him, ax raised with both hands, ready to end it all. Jason shot a jeroki that connected perfectly with the ax's head, throwing it off balance. As the Ash struggled to regain control of it, Jason leaped and slashed at the beast's neck.

The wound shot soot into the air in a dusty black cloud. The beast clutched its neck, then toppled. As Thomas lay on his back, looking up in shock and wonder, Jason snatched his hand and pulled him up.

"Go to the north!" he commanded. "Take your sword and defend the villagers!"

Thomas nodded, then scooped up his sword and dashed away.

Screams of women and children rang out from the village. With enough Ash fighting the humans on the south end of town, the homes in the north were defenseless. The rest of the Ash made a gang rush into the north end of town. They passed up the homes on the south side altogether, as if aware that they were empty. The blood of humans drew them in—somehow, they could sense it. They knew where to find them. It called to them.

We should have been guarding them better, Jason thought.

They smashed doors and shattered windows, cackling and grunting as they went. Sounds followed by the muffled screams of women and children. The sound made his spine rattle.

"Defend the houses!" Jason bellowed. *"They're getting through!"*

Chief Patu came charging, roaring like an angry boar. Her bear-like frame moved with passionate fury as she swung her ax with grace and precision. She tossed Ash bodies against walls and into windows as she went, leaving a trail of gray wreckage behind her. Of all the warriors Jason had seen this night, Chief Patu was the only one that instilled any sense of fear in the Ash.

The Nezmythians abandoned the southern wall and darted north, frantically trying to kill as many Ash as possible before they reached their loved ones. Many soldiers were overtaken by the stampede.

Still by the barrier, Nadiel shot fire and lighting in all directions. No Ash could get close to him, but dozens managed to slip by him. He was encased in a cloud of soot and ashes, the black dust caking his arms and face. His entire body tingled. The magic he had expended was immense by anyone's standard, but he had to hold on for a little longer. He eyed the logs comprising the barrier, and his gaze sharpened.

With a swoop of his arms and an ancient phrase, he was surrounded in a sphere of fire, guarding him from the incoming Ash. Protected by his flame shield, he planted his feet and stretched his hands toward the barrier.

The logs that lay horizontal against the south stirred, then shivered, then rumbled. With a series of deafening cracks and bursts of splinters, two massive logs shot arms and legs like great jagged branches. The two logs pushed themselves up to their wooden feet in a great swoop, turning and bounding into town. Each step boomed against the night, and as they went, they swung their mighty arms at the Ash, hurling them dozens of feet into the air, breaking bones and smashing skulls.

Nadiel smirked, his head swimming. But his smile quickly dropped. He wasn't far from the King.

"Jason!"

Jason decapitated an Ash, then flipped around to face Nadiel. There was a long cut beneath one of his eyes and his hair was matted. His chest rose and fell with each breath.

"The ranks are falling! We must retreat!"

Jason knew it. It was impossible to deny. As he cast his eyes about, he saw the fallen bodies of dozens and dozens of Nezmythians. Their arms and legs lay in haphazard, unnatural ways, and blood soaked into the dirt beneath them. Meanwhile, the screams of women and children echoed through the night along with the clashes of battle.

His eyes misted. His teeth bore together behind cracked lips.

"I've cast two tree golems," Nadiel shouted. "But my magic is near its limit. We must evacuate everyone and venture north to Fort Abernath. Help me cast a barrier on the north end of town to give us more time!"

"Let's go!" Jason said.

They wasted no time. They belted through the streets, calling for a retreat. Nezmythians, armed and unarmed, dashed out, heading to the horses and carriages to the north. Every soldier fought to hold back as many Ash as possible. Through the town, the two tree golems trudged up and down the streets, smashing and throwing Ash like rag dolls. The Ash fought back, slashing and chopping at their tree legs.

Husbands, wives, and children held hands as they flew through the soot-laden streets, scattered with broken windows and the splinters of doors and walls. Archers clambered down from rooftops and joined the crowd, running for the northern end. Some rooftops were catching fire. The Ash were already starting to collect bodies, throwing them over their shoulders and laying them in the center of town. Bile crept up Jason's throat as he ran by, knowing what would become of them.

At last, they reached the northern end of town. People frantically untied their horses from trees and hopped on, careening northward through the woods. Little by little, survivors managed to escape.

Jason looked back. The Ash weren't done with them yet. There was more death to be wrought. He fired several jeroki beams, slaying some of the Ash that advanced toward them. A small battalion of brave soldiers insisted on staying on the northern border to afford their friends and family more time. Among them were Nadiel, Jason, Tarren, Chief Patu, and Kalyk. They gripped their weapons tighter.

All of them fired magic and arrows into the crowd of incoming Ash. They slayed several, but not nearly enough.

They were still coming, tireless and strong. And they could run through the forest all night if they needed. Something had to stop them permanently.

When they were less than a dozen feet away, Nadiel and Jason's gaze met. Nadiel's red eyes were nearly exhausted, bleary, stinging. But he had just enough left in him. They both knew what to do. Without a word, they both clapped their hands and stretched them out, palms outward. As they each uttered ancient incantations, ripples of blue light stretched out their hands like translucent glass, quickly spreading through the air.

The Ash crashed into it, toppling to the ground, then stammered back to their feet. They raged at the barrier with their axes and swords, but it was spreading too quickly. They couldn't get through.

Satisfied, Jason and the others backed away. To his side, Nadiel's knees quaked and he collapsed. Tarren caught him and draped his arm over his shoulders. In the near distance, the two tree golems toppled in the middle of town and smoke began to rise. A second fire was building. The jeer and cackles of Ash could be heard.

"That ought to hold them for a while," a soldier to Jason's right said.

Jason's stinging eyes popped. He knew that voice. His head jerked to the right. The soldier's face was shrouded by an iron helm, and their entire body was guarded with thick armor. When the soldier sensed Jason's eyes, she shriveled—almost as if she had unwittingly spoken out of turn. But it was too late. Jason reached out and tore the helmet from off her head.

It was Saryan. Her face was stained with soot and sweat where the helm didn't protect her. Her golden blonde hair was tied in a tight bun and her silver eyes were bloodshot and exhausted. She locked eyes with her husband, exposed and defeated.

The anger ripped through Jason so hot that his body shook. Cocking his arm back, he turned and hurled the helm into the darkness.

"*Why are you here?*" He bellowed. "*I told you to stay home! You could have been killed!*"

"And so could you!" She roared in reply, her lips shaking.

"Guys," Tarren said firmly, holding Nadiel up, who was barely conscious. "We need to go."

He didn't let his eyes off the Ash that stood around the edge of the blue barrier. They snarled and smirked at the Nezmythians' pathetic state. Wordlessly, the crew turned about and retreated to the remaining carriages. The horses whinnied, the wheels spun, and they were off, rushing through the endless black.

In the carriage, Jason and Saryan refused to look at each other. Jason propped his head on his hand and looked out the window as the carriage sped through the trees. He couldn't look back at the remains of Pinegrove. It had fallen. As they retreated to Fort Abernath, he knew that the Ash were building a fire to cremate those who had died. He knew that those bodies would be bent on their destruction in the next battle. And that thought made his stomach churn.

And another thought came to his mind. The thought that had been plaguing him for days. The long, pale, slim body. The wispy and grimy white hair. The hooked nose and icy blue eyes peering out at him. He was the key. Jason didn't know why—but *he* was the key to winning this war. Somehow, he knew it. The words of King Thomas now beat into his mind like a war drum.

"*Listen to your feelings.*"

"Jason…"

Nadiel sat next to him in the jostling carriage, barely clinging onto consciousness. The eyelids over his piercing red eyes fluttered and his head drooped, but he managed to force out one sentence:

"I'm sorry… I didn't… do more."

"No, Nadiel, *I'm* sorry," Jason said.

With that, Nadiel slumped down, out cold. The eyes of Saryan and Tarren were both on Jason. Saryan didn't know what Jason's words meant, but Tarren had an inkling. He frowned and looked at his boots, his jaw clenched, thinking of the fallen King.

They rode through the darkness, leaving the ruins of Pinegrove behind.

15
THE RESOLVE

Calling Fort Abernath a fort was generous. The walls that surrounded the town were barely ten feet tall and not even wide enough for a man to walk along. The town served as a scanty stopping point at the edge of the woods for people heading to Port Gala. Inside the walls, there were maybe a dozen log cabins, two inns, a tavern, a lumber mill, and a dozen merchants with various carts and stands.

The refugees from Pinegrove completely overran the town, and nearly all the merchants' goods were gone within minutes. Both inns were filled beyond capacity, then the townspeople took in whatever survivors they could. The latecomers rested in the streets, their blankets and packs caked with mud as they rested their soot-stained heads.

They had all arrived before dawn. The rising sun didn't even wake them after their long march. The residents of Fort Abernath woke in the morning and went to work caring for the battle-worn, sparing whatever food they could and fetching water to wash the blood and ashes from their bodies.

Those that fought didn't awake until the afternoon sun scraped at their faces. Their eyes fluttered open, praying that what they had seen was just a terrible nightmare. Their demeanor was detached and distant, the horrific scene fresh on their minds. And now, nothing was left. Pinegrove was no more.

Sniffs and whimpers were frequent. They couldn't help it. And now, those that fell back in Pinegrove would return as Ash, hungry and eager for death, oblivious to the memories that once bound them together.

"Leave this place and retreat for Port Gala," Jason commanded. "Take only what you can. If we stay here, the Ash will overrun this place in no time. Once we reach Port Gala, we'll rest, gather what forces we can, and make a stand there. Understood?"

Jason spoke to an army Captain stationed at Fort Abernath. The man nodded his head, said "Yes, Your Highness," then was about to march away when Jason stopped him.

"Also, I'll need your fastest carriage and four of your best soldiers," Jason said. "They'll come with me to the Nezmyth City Prison for a special mission, then rendezvous with the rest of the forces at Port Gala. Quickly."

A puzzled glance flashed through the Captain's eyes, then he nodded and left. They stood outside the entrance to one of the inns. As soon as Jason was done speaking, he pulled the door open and trudged inside.

Sunlight poured in from murky windows, illuminating the dust in the air. The floorboards creaked, and there should have been a roaring fire in the middle of the inn, but there wasn't. What should have been a place filled with food and song was devoid of either.

There was hardly any room to stand. Every square foot was taken by a resting or injured person. Several healers tiptoed around the wounded, applying bandages and whatever healing magic they could. But not everyone could be healed immediately. As a backup, many of the healers crushed special herbs into elixirs to revive their strength, but it wasn't enough.

Jason carefully stepped between the coughing, broken bodies of his people. Many looked up at him with bleary, swollen eyes as he went past and tried to nod out of respect. Among the crowd, he spotted Thomas, sitting up against a wall with a bloodstained bandage that covered one of his eyes.

As Jason walked by, Thomas noticed him. He smiled.

"Your advice saved my life, Your Highness," he said weakly. "I've never seen that kind of magic in my life. It was incredible."

Jason frowned and knelt by him. "How's your eye?"

"Gone," Thomas sighed as he patted bandage. "A slash from a sword. But I got him, though. Right in the stomach." He made the stabbing motion.

"I'm sorry," Jason said, his frown deepening.

"Don't be," Thomas said. "I'll still make it home. It could have been much worse."

Thomas's gaze became vacant as he looked across the room of injured friends, coughing and groaning where they lay. Then he painstakingly pushed himself to his feet, propping himself against the wall.

"I'm going to see what I can do."

With that, Thomas hobbled over to the nearest healer. Jason almost smiled, but instead, hung his head and walked up a nearby staircase.

Most of the rooms on the upper floor had left their doors open, which housed more wounded. Those that were conscious nodded or greeted Jason weakly as he walked by. He made his way down the hall, one step after another, as he passed more and more injured. It was becoming harder to look at them. He hated seeing his people in this state. It shouldn't be necessary.

As he approached a door at the end of the hall, an elderly, experienced healer left a room and closed the door behind her. She bowed slightly as Jason approached her.

"I've made a special mixture to replenish his magic," she said with a dusty voice. "But he still needs to spend the day resting. He overexerted himself. He should be well enough to fight again by the time the Ash reach Port Gala, but he mustn't practice any magic until then."

"Understood," Jason said. "Thank you for your efforts."

The elderly healer bowed again and slipped away, off to tend to the others. Jason opened the door that she came out from.

Inside the room, shades were pulled over the window, letting just a little light seep in. A bed was pushed into the corner of the room, the sheets removed, leaving only a thin pad suspended by a web of tightly pulled rope. Nadiel lay on that pad, hands resting on his chest, feet outstretched, face pointed to the ceiling. As Jason closed the door behind him, Nadiel's face tilted to the door ever so slightly, his eyes opening just a sliver.

"How are the others?" his voice was raspy and exhausted.

Jason pulled a creaky wooden chair next to the bed and squatted down. "Devastated. We lost half of Pinegrove back there. So essentially, the Ash's army has doubled."

Nadiel's nose scrunched and his eyes closed as a burdened sigh left his nostrils. "Jason… why didn't you call upon your Knightly power last night?"

Jason looked down. In the palm of his right hand, an orange triangle was carved just below his index finger. His brand. His mark. He stared at it and rubbed it with his thumb, thinking about the battle.

"I tried," he said. "The Dragon wouldn't give it to me."

Nadiel made an effort to turn his head and look at Jason. His gaze was probing. "Why?"

"Because I've been disobedient," Jason said, still rubbing his mark. "I need to let him go, Nadiel. I don't want to. But something tells me he's the key to winning this war. I'm going to go retrieve him immediately."

Nadiel looked away from Jason again and let out another prolonged sigh. "You remember what I told you. The kingdom will hate you for it."

"I know."

"They will curse you and despise you."

"I *know*. But I don't know what else to do. We can't let Port Gala fall like Treetown and Pinegrove. That will seal Nartikis's victory."

Nadiel paused, then said. "Then it appears your course of action is clear." He reached out a feeble arm with an open palm. "May the Dragon bless you, Jason. Be safe."

Jason took Nadiel's hand and clasped it tightly. "I'll see you in Port Gala. There, we will make our next stand. May the Dragon bless you, Nadiel."

Jason released Nadiel's hand, and Nadiel brought it back on his chest to rest. He took a deep breath and let out another exhausted sigh. Jason exited the room and made his way down the hall as the boards creaked underneath his scuffed and muddied boots. After a minute, he walked down the stairs and through the crowded dining hall, eventually pushing the door open to the afternoon sun.

As the inn door slammed behind him, a personage stood before him that made Jason's blood freeze. Every inch of his body was garbed in black, including the cape that cascaded to his ankles. The pale skin. The vacant expression. Above everything, his eyes were the worst. Those cold eyes tore right through him.

Nartikis. Jason's hand immediately shot for his sword.

"You could try," Nartikis mused. "But what you see before you is a projection of my true self. Your blade would merely phase through me."

Jason clenched his teeth and let his hand fall to his side. "So, you send your filthy monsters to do your dirty work? Refuse to lead from the front?"

"It is more effective," Nartikis responded flatly. "Something you clearly do not understand. From my understanding, my small group of Ash have managed to ravage two Nezmythian towns with no problem." Nartikis looked around, observing the injured Nezmythians that limped around Fort Abernath. "How many more do you think will die because of you?"

"Because of *me?*" Jason advanced on Nartikis to where their noses were only inches apart. "Your nerve! Don't feed me those lies. This is *your* doing and nothing less."

"Wrong," Nartikis replied, unphased. "I gave you the chance to step down peacefully, but you refused. Now look. And this is only the start, Your Highness. How many more thousands will lay waste because of your stubborn pride? Your desire for power?"

Jason couldn't believe what he was hearing. Stubborn pride? Desire for power? Everything in his body wanted to reach out and strangle Nartikis's scrawny, pale neck. He was the cause of all this suffering. All this madness. To pin it on Jason for refusing to step down from his Foreordained responsibility was ludicrous.

"We'll crush your forces in time," Jason seethed. "You have yet to see the Dragon's might."

"The Dragon's might," Nartikis repeated, almost smiling. "Am I supposed to be frightened? This Dragon won't even let you use the same powers you faced me with."

To this, Jason had no response. Absently, his thumb stroked the birthmark on his right hand. Nartikis's eyes flashed. His tone became almost a purr, and Jason could feel his mind getting foggy. The sounds of Fort Abernath died down, and Nartikis's voice reverberated inside his head.

"But it is not too late. Step down now, Jason, and I will call off the Ash. Your people will be safe. And I will rule rightfully as Nezmyth's King. Do it for your people."

Jason's eyes were half closed, and his head continued to swim in some strange, dreamy haze. He felt like sleeping. Most of all, he felt compliant and complacent.

Why not? He thought. *I can stop all this death. Maybe it really is my fault. Maybe I can end all the suffering right now. Maybe I can—*

"Jason!"

It was Saryan. As soon as she called his name, his head jolted out of whatever trance he was put under. Jason clenched his teeth again, his eyes baring into Nartikis's pale, emotionless face one more time.

"Leave me."

Nartikis gave a gentle bow, and his projection faded. Gone. The people in town went about their business, completely unaware of dark King's projection. Maybe Nartikis had made it so only Jason could see it? It made Jason's eyebrows crease.

Finally, Saryan trudged up to him. The soot and blood had been washed from her face, but she was still mostly dressed in her armor. She frowned as she approached him.

"Hey. We need to talk."

"Not right now," Jason said, marching toward the stable where his carriage was prepared.

"Yes, right now! Where are you going?"

"To the prison."

"Why?"

"*Saryan,*" Jason flipped out to face her. He had to stop himself from shouting. "You shouldn't be here! You see what the Ash did? *Half* of Pinegrove is now *dead*. And they'll come back as Ash to fight us at Port Gala!" His voice fell to a whisper. "Do you want to become one of them? Is that why you're here?"

Saryan's bottom lip shook, but her eyes were tougher than steel. She advanced on Jason even more, their faces just inches apart. Her hands shook, and she tried not to bare her teeth as she talked.

"No. I'll tell you why I'm here," she hissed. "My father is dead. My kingdom is under attack. And now the *one man left in my life* is throwing himself into the jaws of death. And during all this, he expects me to stay home like a sweet little cabin maid?" She scoffed. "*That's* why I'm here. You don't get to choose whether I stay home or not. I'm staying here and I'm *fighting*. Nothing is going to change that. I am the Queen, and you *will not* give me orders. Do you understand?"

Jason was silent. He swallowed. Looked at his feet, then sighed. "I just... I don't want to lose you." He shuffled his feet. "Not like we lost Garrit."

Saryan took his chin and lifted his eyes to hers. "Even if you did, this wouldn't be the end for us, remember? We're Melded together for eternity." She gave his cheek a playful slap. "Besides, I'm a much better fighter than you. If either of us is going to die, it's definitely going to be you."

Jason half-smiled. "I love you even when I can't stand you."

"I feel the same. We must be insane."

"You might think I am before too long," Jason said. His smile faded as he squeezed her hand with finality. "I'll see you in Port Gala."

16

THE RETRIEVAL

In the Vault of the Damned, Barnabas couldn't tell if it was night or day. Everything was darkness. It always was. The single flickering torch in the room's center was the only light, and even then, the guards didn't light it every day—only when they felt like it. But Barnabas's eyes adjusted to the dark. He had become completely nocturnal for all he knew.

A rat scurried through one of the cells on the other side of the Vault. Number fifteen. Or maybe he was seeing number four again? The tail was similar. From across the room, he pointed his finger and charged a small jeroki the size of a pea, letting its gray light dance in the darkness. He scooted up to the bars and put his hands between two rungs then flicked the tiny ball of magic at the rat several yards away. He missed. The rat sped off in the opposite direction.

Barnabas sighed through flaked lips, blowing some of the stringy hair out of his eyes. His long fingernails scratched his thin, hairy legs that protruded from his burlap covering.

BOOM. CREEAAKK

Barnabas's head popped up. The opening of the Vault door sounded just as quick and urgent as it did days ago.

Light trickled down the staircase and Barnabas had to squint his eyes to keep them from hurting. The sound of boots clomping on the staircase was rapid, and within seconds, King Jason was standing before Barnabas with four guards behind him. None of them bothered to close the door to the Vault.

Barnabas peered up with bleary eyes as Jason towered over him, his hand on his sword. He wasn't wearing his red cape as usual, and his armor was heavily scratched and dented. Barnabas remembered when Jason had visited him not long ago, asking him about his son and telling him that Nezmyth was on the brink of war. He swallowed.

"Get up," Jason commanded.

Again? Barnabas thought, wondering if he heard correctly.

"I said *get up!*" Jason ordered again.

Startled by the heat in Jason's voice, Barnabas latched his hands onto two bars and forced himself to his feet. His knees quivered as they strained to carry the weight of his body. Finally, he stood completely vertical, holding onto the bars for support, and Jason shot an order to a nearby guard.

"Unlock it."

Barnabas's eyes grew wide.

"Sir," one guard replied timidly, "when you became King, you ordered us to throw away the key."

Jason paused, then looked at the lock. "How old are these locks?"

"Hundreds of years, sir."

"Good."

Without hesitation, Jason lifted his arm and shot a steady blue beam of magic. It erupted from his palm with a loud *pop*, causing Barnabas to stumble backward and fall on his backside to avoid the blast. Pale blue light plastered the walls and heat emanated from Jason's hand. After a few seconds, Jason ceased, leaving nothing but a hole of molten metal where the lock once was. The door creaked open on its own accord.

"Come on," Jason said.

With hesitation that came only from intimidation and amazement, Barnabas pushed himself to his feet again. His back hunched over, and he kept his eyes on the ground as he forced each foot forward. He stopped just outside the cell door, directly in front of Jason, still clinging to the bars for support.

Wordlessly, Jason grabbed his arm. His whole hand wrapped completely around his bicep. He pulled Barnabas out until two soldiers snatched him by the arms, holding him up and marching him along. His bare feet slipped quietly across the stone floor as they escorted him toward the staircase. Up they went, one step at a time, as Jason led the pack.

Finally, they emerged into the light. Barnabas had to completely close his eyes—the sunlight was too strong. He would open them a squint at a time, then close them again, trying to readjust. As his eyes became accustomed, he noticed that the sky was beginning to tinge with red and orange. It was sunset.

BOOM

The door to the Vault slammed shut behind them. And with that, they ascended the long circular climb to the surface. Behind him, two soldiers followed, glaring at him intensely. Barnabas couldn't help but look around confusedly, squinting his eyes and baring his yellowed teeth.

"Where… are you taking me?" He asked.

"To be with the others, fighting for our survival," Jason said flatly.

Barnabas bowed his head. "To die?"

Jason frowned. "That will be for the Dragon to decide."

As they ascended, they passed dozens of cells with other prisoners. The prisoners had seen King Jason descend somewhere down to the depths before. Rumors had spread around that he had been visiting Barnabas, but the guards didn't tell them anything about it. When they saw the wispy old man that Jason brought up from the depths, that erased all doubt. The old man was thin and frail, but they recognized the hooked nose and the blue eyes and the square jaw. It was him, alright. The treacherous former King.

They blasted Barnabas with profanity and curses. Many inmates—vagabonds and villains in their own right—remembered their own suffering at his hands. They came up to the bars, stuck their heads between the rungs, spat on him, and reviled him without mercy.

Then, they turned and cursed Jason. Spat on him. Insulted his parents, his cape, his Queen. They cursed him for visiting the fallen King and not them. They cursed him for taking the King out of his cage and for not just killing him when he had the chance.

Jason and Barnabas ignored the insults and abuse all the way to the top of the prison—ground level.

When they reached the surface, the guards released Barnabas. He collapsed. The fall was painful, but the pain was quickly overtaken by the cool feeling of grass on his skin. *Grass.* As he lay there, panting, gathering his strength, he took the grass in great bunches and pressed them against his face. He turned his nose into the ground so Jason wouldn't see his eyes water.

Jason looked down on him and let out a loud sigh. He turned to one of the soldiers. "Bring him some bread, some cheese, and some water."

Cheese? Barnabas thought, his mouth salivating.

Jason let Barnabas lay there for a long moment while a soldier fetched the food. When the soldier returned, he dropped the food next to Barnabas's face like an animal. Barnabas didn't care. He eagerly scooped up the bread and cheese and ripped into them. The bread wasn't hard and crusty like the bread he was used to. And the cheese... he couldn't remember cheese tasting so wonderful. As he ate, drops rolled down from his eyes down to the tip of his nose.

One soldier leaned over to Jason and whispered, "You don't think he'll try to attack us, sir?"

Jason shook his head and said, "Of course not. Look at him."

Barnabas tore into his food, laying on his side, curled up. Jason frowned. He almost pitied him, but not as much as the people that were on their way to Port Gala. The red carriage wasn't far away. He jerked his head toward it, his eyes on the soldiers.

"Get him inside. We have no time to waste."

The soldiers grabbed Barnabas by the arms again and hoisted him to his feet before he could drink his water. His toes barely touched the grass as they hauled him to the carriage. They nearly threw him inside after Jason had clambered up to his seat. Barnabas still had the remains of his bread and his cheese in his hands, ignoring his scraped knees and elbows. He sat opposite to Jason. Then the soldiers filled up the carriage, sitting side by side with Jason and the former king. The carriage shuddered and they were off.

As the carriage shook and jostled, heading north on the dirt path, a wave of exhaustion hit Jason. He had barely slept in two days, he had fought through the battle of Pinegrove, and now he had fulfilled his errand in retrieving Barnabas from the Vault of the Damned.

Barnabas licked his fingers while Jason squinted at him, arms folded.

"I want you to understand two things, Barnabas. And I want there to be no mistake."

Barnabas paused, saying nothing, and nervously glanced into Jason's eyes.

"One," Jason said. "You are a free man. But that doesn't mean that you are forgiven of your crimes. Until this war is over, you'll be guarded by a team of highly trained soldiers day and night. You won't do anything without their permission or without their watch. And when the war is over, you may very well go back to your cell. That's still being decided."

Barnabas said nothing. Jason continued.

"Second, I want you to know that I don't *want* you here. You and I both know you deserve to rot down in that prison where you belong. But the Dragon has compelled me to set you free, so you can thank It for your freedom. You play some sort of piece in winning this war, but until we figure out exactly what that is, you will play the role of a diligent and humble soldier. That is *all.* Am I understood?"

Without looking Jason in the face, Barnabas nodded, almost imperceptibly.

"Good," Jason said. "We'll reach Port Gala in just less than two days. There, you'll suit up and prepare to fight with everyone else. The army that your son has concocted is the most evil and dastardly thing I've ever seen. It'll take a miracle to overcome them. Until then, I plan to sleep. Don't wake me."

With that, Jason leaned his head back and quickly dozed off. The occasional jerking and grinding of the carriage didn't disturb him. The knot in his chest was gone. The tension inside him had dissipated.

Meanwhile, Barnabas kept his eyes fixed on the spot between his filthy bare feet, trying to ignore the searing glares of the soldiers surrounding him.

* * * * *

"Sire. Sire, wake up."

It took great effort for Jason to pull his eyes open— sleeping in a moving carriage is not comparable to sleeping on the feather mattress back at the castle. His arms were still folded over his chest, and his mouth was dry. Across from him, Barnabas was still staring at the ground with his hands clasped between his knees.

"We're here," the soldier to his left said.

Jason didn't need to look through the window to see it. He had been to Port Gala before—a bustling hive slightly smaller than Nezmyth City, but just as dense. It was the port city on the lip of the Wevlian Sea, the sea that touches all kingdoms of the world. And as such, the city was a web of industry and enterprise. Nearly all foreign goods and valuables were imported through Port Gala; the Eastern Mountains were impossible to traverse, and the Western Bridge was almost never used.

From here, goods were transported down the Great Nezmyth River. The river fed from the sea and cut through half of Port Gala, separating the city into its Eastern and Western Districts. The river then sifted through a gigantic, retractable iron gate that allowed smaller ships to sail through. The river snaked south down the entirety of Nezmyth before opening into Dragonclaw Lake in the Southern Plains.

For centuries, Port Gala had been surrounded by a stone wall three stories high and twenty feet wide. Along that wall were only three gates into the city—one to the west, one to the south, and one to the east. The gates were monstrous, and soldiers always patrolled the upper wall.

It was the keystone of Nezmyth's economical infrastructure, and as such, it was heavily guarded.

We might actually stand a chance here, Jason hoped.

The South gate opened with bone-rattling creaks as the carriage rolled through, meeting a street of refined cobblestone. Immediately, a local Port Gala soldier scurried up to the carriage, sticking his face in the window.

"Your Highness," he said hurriedly. "The forces from Pinegrove just arrived hours ago."

"Good," Jason replied, trying to cast the sleep from his eyes. "What forces can you add?"

"Uh—some five hundred, sir."

"Excellent," Jason nodded. "The Ash will likely be upon us in a day or two. Tell your superiors to provide whatever lodgings and food they can for our forces until they arrive."

"Sir," the soldier replied timidly. "Most of the inns are full. There isn't much room to house the—"

"Then *make room*," Jason growled.

The soldier gulped and nodded dutifully. "Of course, sir. Right away."

As the carriage continued, Jason observed the city through the window. Trees lined the road on both sides of the street. Past the trees, the ground abruptly dropped into the Great Nezmyth River, which stretched for five hundred feet before rising quickly to the edge of the city's Eastern District.

The Western District was noticeably shabbier than the Eastern. There were a lot of gruff and scraggly dock workers walking the streets. The homes and shops were smaller, made of local materials like Western Woods lumber and bricks. Even from the distance, Jason could see many Eastern District buildings constructed from imported materials that screamed luxury.

Makes sense, he thought. *Most of the Eastern District is business leaders and trade experts, aside from Chief Taliman and his friends.*

The people of the Western District ogled at the red carriage is it rolled by. Occasionally, they would shout things like "Hail the King!" or "Dragon bless the King of Nezmyth!" Jason overheard some people muttering to each other about the arrival of the soldiers. Every whisper was delivered with an air of confusion, as if they had no idea why so many people had arrived. And as Jason thought about it, there didn't seem to be more guards on patrol than usual. The thought made his eyebrows furrow.

At length, they reached the Western Plaza, a large expanse of cobblestone with a fountain in the middle. It wasn't far from the docks at all. The plaza was surrounded by shops and inns and peppered with street merchants selling fish, foreign fruits, jewels, and clothing—at least those that were too cheap to sell on the east side of town.

The plaza was completely packed, and not by anyone from Port Gala. Those who packed the plaza were the survivors of Pinegrove—the same ones Jason had left behind at Fort

Abernath. Many of the survivors stared intently at the sight of the red carriage. They had heard rumors of the King's errand, but no one could confirm the reason.

The carriage slowed to a stop. The horses whinnied. Before Jason hopped out, he shot a look at Barnabas and ordered, "Stay here. You two, guard him."

Barnabas said nothing. Jason stepped onto the street, followed by the two guards that sat beside him. He looked around, breathing in the salty sea air and hearing the seagulls caw in the distance. As he marched toward the crowd, many of the people nodded and greeted him reverently.

From among the crowd, Nadiel, Chief Patu, and Kalyk emerged. Nadiel's red eyes were flashing and serious—even more so than usual. Kalyk and Chief Patu's expressions were similar. Jason could see Chief Patu grinding her teeth behind closed lips. Even Justice, perched on Kalyk's shoulder, seemed displeased about something.

Jason was the first to speak. "The soldier at the gates told me there wouldn't be much room for the survivors before battle."

"It seems as though Port Gala is ill prepared at every turn," Kalyk replied as she tightened her jaw and drummed her elbows.

It was then that Nadiel noticed someone approaching nearby, coming from the eastern docks. Whoever it was made the corners of his mouth pull into a frown. Jason pointed his eyebrows in kind and turned around.

When he saw who it was, he muttered, "Why am I not surprised?"

A man with sun-kissed skin and dark eyes quickly approached. Luxurious silk robes covered him from his neck to his ankles, and gold rings glinted on his fingers as he rubbed his hands together. Gold necklaces and chains jingled on him with every step. Behind him, a small entourage of similarly dressed nobles followed closely behind, their faces riddled with nervousness and perplexity.

"Your Highness! My King!" The man reached out his hands to shake Jason's. "If I may have a word with you in private?"

Jason skipped the handshake and invaded the Chief's space, his nostrils flaring and his face just inches away. "You got the decree, Chief Taliman. I know you did."

Taliman held his hands up defensively. "Sire, I'm sure you're under a lot of stress—"

Jason snatched him by the collar. He leaned in to whisper, despite Taliman's wild and frightened eyes. "They have no idea, do they? This whole city is absolutely oblivious to the state of the war we're in, aren't they?"

Suddenly, the fear left Taliman's eyes. His hands shot up, grabbed Jason's, and yanked them free of his collar. The action surprised even Jason.

"What was I supposed to do?" Taliman hissed. "Port Gala is the economic *backbone of Nezmyth*. What would happen if the neighboring kingdoms caught wind of our current state? The imports would stop. Trade in the city would slide to halt. People would be without work. Struggling."

"Some skipped imports are the last of our worries right now," Jason said venomously. "The Ash are likely on their way here as we speak."

"And who's fault is that?" Taliman's eyes narrowed. "From what I hear, the enemy's forces started out very small. Why was it that *you* could not stop them, in your infinite strength and wisdom, Your Highness?"

He had gone too far. Taliman knew it as soon as he said it. His whole body shrunk as he saw the fire flare up behind Jason's eyes. Behind Jason, Nadiel bristled at the sound of the insult. Chief Patu's hands flexed at her side. Jason was quiet, then said, "Taliman, you are no longer Chief of Port Gala. You are relinquished of your duties with shame and dishonor."

Taliman's entourage had been silent up until this point, but now they were speechless. Taliman's cheeks burned red. Jason didn't notice. He turned on his heels and strode toward the refugees gathered at the plaza. All of them watched the exchange, and now they gazed in wonder. The conversation was out of earshot, but the outcome was clear by the reaction of Port Gala's now former Chief.

"I've served this community for nearly a *decade!*" Taliman bellowed as Jason marched away.

"And now it is *over!*" Jason flipped about so quickly his cape snapped. "Death is at your doorstep, Taliman! There will be no money left to spend when the Ash have laid waste to Port Gala and all of Nezmyth! You have failed in your pivotal duty of defending Nezmyth's most influential keep! With that, you are irrevocably discharged *without honor!*"

Taliman's whole body shook. As Jason flipped back toward the crowd, Taliman raised his hands. Around his fingertips, blue sparks begin to form and leap, hissing and buzzing. His eyes were locked on Jason's back.

Jason's guards noticed and dug their feet in, charging spells of their own, but Nadiel was the fastest. He threw out his arm and instantly, with sickening cracks, each of Taliman's forearms snapped into right angles. The sparks stopped and Taliman fell to his knees, howling.

Jason's guards marched forward. "We'll put him away, Your Highness." They took Taliman, healed his broken arms, then carried him away bound in ropes.

Jason put his hand on Nadiel's shoulder. "Save your magic for battle."

"A 'thank you' would be appropriate."

"Are you feeling alright?"

"I'm well enough," Nadiel said. He sighed. "I will be after another day or two of rest." He motioned toward the red carriage. "How is he?"

"A shell of what he once was. He hardly spoke."

"Is he in any condition for battle?"

"Definitely not."

"This doesn't help us."

"Who is this you speak of?" Kalyk asked curiously.

"Hopefully the answer to the war, if my feelings serve me right," Jason replied. He was quiet for a second. Then he said, "Where is Tarren and my wife?"

"Both 'elping the wounded," Chief Patu said.

With that, Jason strode toward the crowd. People nodded as he passed by. They all looked as awful as they did when he last saw them—two days' march hadn't done them any favors. Bandages were getting dirty and red, and their faces were still unwashed. Members of the crowd directed Jason to Tarren and Saryan. He found them just a few paces apart, using healing spells and changing bandages.

Tarren looked over his shoulder and noticed Jason approaching. He sat up straighter. Saryan didn't notice. Jason put his hand on her shoulder.

"Saryan."

She recognized his voice. She quickly finished dressing the wound, stood up, and embraced him. "Where did you go?"

"I had to go get someone. Someone who should help us win this war."

"Who?" Saryan said as she unwrapped herself from his arms.

17

THE BLESSING

Like a frail, hibernating rodent emerging from a cave, Barnabas crept out of the carriage. The two soldiers guarding him stayed an arm's length away. Everyone was there to see when the sunlight hit his face. He blinked his pale blue eyes painfully and kept his face to the ground.

Saryan's entire body shook. A dozen emotions flashed across her eyes, ranging from shock, to confusion, to anger. She spun toward her husband.

"*Why is he here?*" She roared.

Jason swallowed. "The Dragon kept pressing my mind that Barnabas is going to help us win this war. I'm not happy about it either."

"Win the war? Jason, *look at him!*"

She threw both her arms in Barnabas's direction. As usual, Barnabas didn't say anything, but kept his eyes on the ground between his dirty, bare feet. Dozens of yards away, townspeople started to whisper and mutter. That frail old man from the carriage looked familiar… could that really be the disgraced former king? But why? Would King Jason really release him?

"Your Highness," Kalyk said quietly. "If the rumors are true, the former king put you through so much before you took the throne."

"Did you know he was going to do this?" Saryan spat at Nadiel.

Nadiel paused before he said, "I made the King aware of my feelings concerning the matter. It did as much good as it's ever done."

"What's all the commotion?"

Master Ferribolt mysteriously appeared in their midst. Jason jolted when he heard his voice just a few feet away. His orange robes flowed down to his ankles, and his round spectacles glistened in the sunlight, illuminating the smudges he hadn't cleaned off. Although startled, seeing him at the eve of a battle was strangely comforting.

"Master Ferribolt!" Tarren said. "When did you get here?"

"Just now," he said brightly. He nodded his head toward Barnabas. "Is that who I think that is?"

When Barnabas lifted his eyes to the Chief Patriarch, he shrunk even more.

Master Ferribolt strode up to the prisoner. Barnabas stayed still and frail like a starved street dog. The Chief Patriarch reached with a gentle hand and placed it on the prisoner's shoulder, then bent down to look him in the eye. Timidly, Barnabas returned the gaze. Master Ferribolt smiled.

"You've had much to think about, haven't you?" he whispered.

Master Ferribolt placed his other hand on the rope binding Barnabas's wrists together. As if done by invisible hands, the ropes unraveled and fell to the ground. Barnabas rubbed his sore wrists, which were red and swollen. Master Ferribolt turned to the group.

"My friend and I are going to go on a brief walk," he said. "Just the two of us. Your Highness, if you don't mind, I would like you to call off your soldiers for a brief time so Barnabas and I may speak privately."

Every eye was suddenly on Jason. He didn't like the idea of leaving Barnabas unguarded for any period of time, but his trust for the Chief Patriarch outweighed his apprehension. Besides, the likelihood of Barnabas overpowering the Chief Patriarch was low—he couldn't even overpower a child like this. He nodded.

"Thank you," Master Ferribolt said. "Let us walk to the pier, shall we? It's been years since you've seen the sea."

Master Ferribolt slipped his arm around Barnabas's dirty, rag-laden shoulders and walked him northward. As they strolled, Barnabas kept his face down and Master Ferribolt made chitchat that became harder and harder to hear.

Over Jason's shoulder, Nadiel muttered, "I do hope your feelings are correct."

Jason didn't reply. He couldn't help but think of how Saryan had said all her suffering was caused by Barnabas. He turned to her. "Saryan—"

"I'm going to help the wounded," she said as she marched into the crowd.

As she stormed away, Tarren walked away in kind, chewing his tongue and shaking his head. The townspeople couldn't take their eyes away from the scene. The whispering hadn't died down.

One person had the gall to shout, "Was that *King Barnabas?*"

Then the whispering came to a hush as everyone awaited an answer. Jason swallowed and his shoulders stiffened. Many eyes were still following Master Ferribolt and Barnabas as they walked to the shore. But all the other eyes were on Jason, expectant and probing. He swallowed again.

"Yes, it is," he said. "He is going to fight in this war like any one of you. The Dragon has commanded it."

Immediately, the crowd buzzed with more whispers. And more people took enough courage to ask more questions.

"Why would the Dragon command such a thing?" "He's going to fight? He's an old husk now!" "Are you *mad?*"

Among the displeased chatter, Chief Patu mumbled, "I'll 'elp the Queen."

"Thank you," Jason replied.

Nadiel's eyes shifted from Jason to the outlines of Barnabas and Master Ferribolt walking to the sea. He shook his head, then followed Chief Patu and Saryan as they helped the survivors. That left Jason and Kalyk. With mild trepidation, Kalyk took a few soundless steps until she was shoulder to shoulder with him.

Over the noise of the insatiable crowd, Kalyk asked, "Have you forgiven him?"

"Absolutely not," Jason said with resolution.

"Why?"

Jason shot a look at Kalyk. "What do you mean, *why?*"

"Forgive me, Your Highness," Kalyk replied, dipping her chin as she watched Master Ferribolt and Barnabas walk off. "But I don't believe that man is the King Barnabas any of us knew. He's broken. Powerless. How can you resent something so frail and weak?"

"Because *that man* is the very reason this war is happening," Jason pointed at him. "His greed. His lust. Those things gave birth to what's threatening our lives. That's aside from the torment that he put me and my loved ones through before I took the Throne. I don't care if he's not the menace that he used to be. That doesn't change what he's done."

Kalyk was quiet for a second, then said, "I see."

With that, she walked away. She readjusted the bow slung over her back and Justice clicked his beak on her shoulder. Jason let a long sigh escape his lips as he looked out on the disappearing figures of Barnabas and Master Ferribolt.

* * * * *

The hours went by quickly. There was much to do, since Chief Taliman had left virtually everyone in the dark when it came to the war. Jason and Nadiel briefed a band of soldiers and commanded them to ride through both districts, alerting the townspeople of the dangers that awaited. It wasn't long before the entire city was in commotion with frantic preparations.

Meanwhile, the refugees of Pinegrove and Fort Abernath slept. Many townspeople (mostly on the poor side of town) granted them water for washing, food for replenishment, and beds for rest while the locals made fortifications. They calculated that it would likely be one or two more days before the Ash came to attack—likely the time it would take them to burn new bodies and march to the city from the remains of Pinegrove.

During this time, Jason tried to speak to Saryan. It was no use. Her wrath had returned, this time colder. With so much going on in the city, Jason finally gave up and busied himself with helping his subjects.

It was a couple of hours before Master Ferribolt and Barnabas returned from the shore. Jason and Nadiel were outside one of the larger inns at the outskirts of the Western Plaza. Their posture straightened and their attention locked on the Chief Patriarch and the fallen King. Master Ferribolt was bright as ever. Barnabas walked more sure-footedly but kept his gaze to the ground and stayed a few paces behind Master Ferribolt. Four soldiers had found him on the way back from the shore and snapped up to guard him.

When Master Ferribolt reached Jason and Nadiel, he kept his voice low so Barnabas couldn't hear. His eyes twinkled.

"You, Your Highness," he said. "Were indeed inspired. Barnabas and I had a lovely chat."

"What did you tell him? What did he say?"

Master Ferribolt shook his head. "That is between him, I, and the Sacred Dragon. What I will tell you is that he's going to be fine."

"It's not *him* I'm worried about," Jason said lowly.

Master Ferribolt turned to Barnabas. "My friend, is there anything you need at this time?"

Barnabas shuffled his feet, then looked up between the strings in his hair. "Meat."

Jason frowned. "Meat?"

Barnabas nodded. "Lots."

Master Ferribolt smiled and turned toward the guards. "Not only that, but give him a bath and bring him some new clothes." Then he paused and said, "Oh, and bring him a sword as well."

"No, don't bring him a sword," Jason overrode.

"Your Highness, how is he supposed to prepare for battle if he can't train?" Master Ferribolt said.

Jason tapped his finger on his sword, thought for a minute, then said, "I suppose you're right. Don't worry." His eyes became slits. "I'll train him myself."

* * * * *

Three maids washed and groomed Barnabas in the nearest inn while a guard stood in each corner of the room, watching him. From outside, the sound of war preparations—muffled shouts and scuffling feet—drifted in. Silently, the inn workers wished they could have been among them. After all, who wants to scrub and clean a tyrant?

They didn't spend more than half an hour—they didn't give the usual relaxing treatment they gave most of their guests. But by the end, Barnabas nearly looked like his old self, if it weren't for his bony frame and gaunt complexion. His beard was trimmed and neat. The hair on his head had nearly been all shaved off. The years of grime and dirt were scraped away, even under his fingernails and feet.

As the maids labored, Barnabas ravenously tore into eight thick slabs of steak. He used no knife or fork. Just his hands. Blood dripped into the bathwater from the bite marks, and his hands were gnarled and greasy. The inn workers looked on in disgust as he devoured each one. By the time he had finished them all, his stomach barely grew, but somehow, his bony structure somehow seemed less bony.

When they were done, the inn workers tossed Barnabas an oversized tunic and pair of cotton pants, then barked at him to be on his way. Barnabas obliged as his guards led him out of the room.

They escorted Barnabas to a nearby combat gym not a quarter mile away. As they went, the hurried townspeople shot him venomous stares and curses as they ran by. Barnabas said nothing. Instead, he absorbed them like a sponge, fully aware of what he was.

The guards pushed open the gym doors, and the stench of leather and sweat hit them all. The entirety of the floor was mapped out into four separate sparring mats, each teeming with people brushing up on their skills before battle. Around each mat, dozens of people gathered, waiting their turns with wooden practice weapons and leather armor. One of the mats had the more spectators than the others. It was occupied by King Jason and a few of his friends.

As Barnabas and the soldiers walked in, they untied Barnabas's wrists, and someone thrust a wooden sword into his hand. He took it. Practice weapons were heavier than he remembered. The soldiers surrounding him fastened leather practice armor around his torso, shoulders, arms, and legs.

The cracking of wooden weapons died down, along with the chatter. In a matter of moments, everyone's eyes were on Barnabas like vengeful daggers. Barnabas didn't look at anyone, let alone speak. Once he was prepped for sparring, the soldiers led him to the mat where Jason stood, their clinking armor the only noise in the gym.

Jason, Tarren, and Saryan looked on as Barnabas approached. Tarren took a deep breath. Saryan's grip on her staff tightened.

The soldiers left Barnabas's side and spread themselves to the four corners of the combat mat. Everyone in the gym dropped what they were doing and migrated over to the mat, surrounding it completely, eager to see what would unfold. Barnabas's bleary eyes stayed on the ground as he stiffly went over and stood at the side opposite of Jason, holding the sword by his side.

Saryan and Tarren had taken their place among the crowd. Jason looked Barnabas up and down. Somehow, his body had filled out a little since his bath and shave, but he was still nowhere near the beast that he was four years ago. The broad shoulders and thick muscle were gone. The menacing black cape was nowhere to be seen. Instead, there stood a frail, broken man with ill-fitting leather armor and a wooden sword.

"The last time you picked up a weapon was against me," Jason said.

Everyone held their breath. Barnabas didn't speak.

"And what have you learned since that day?" Jason pursued.

Barnabas still didn't open his mouth.

"My strength has multiplied since then," Jason said. "I hope you're ready."

"*Wait!*"

Everyone turned. The owner of the voice was already marching out onto the mat—Saryan. She strode with a resolution and a fire that snapped everyone to attention. She didn't stop until she stood in front of Jason, blocking his view from the fallen King.

"Let me," she said.

With Saryan's foul mood, Jason was in no position to argue or debate. It was only with minor hesitation that he slipped away and took her spot on the edge of the mat.

Everyone watched as Saryan stared down Barnabas, unblinking, focused, and sharp. Barnabas bowed to Saryan respectfully, as was custom before any sparring match. Saryan didn't bow in kind. No one breathed.

When Barnabas bent upward, someone rang a bell to signal the start of the match.

Ding!

Saryan dashed forward and swung her staff three times. Barnabas managed to parry the first two blows but took the third hard. He doubled over and fell to his hands and knees, coughing. The crowd roared and applauded.

Saryan walked circles around him. *"Get up!"*

With shaking knees, Barnabas pushed himself upward, gripping his sword with both hands. He swung it mightily around him. Saryan ducked the blow. She swung her staff and swept Barnabas's feet from under him. He toppled to the floor, facing up, coughing again.

Everyone was laughing now—everyone except for Jason and Tarren.

Barnabas lifted himself to his feet one more time. He hesitated, waiting for Saryan to make the first move, but she didn't budge. He swung the sword over his head. She blocked it with ease. With another swift move, she wrenched the sword out of his grip, grabbed Barnabas by the wrist, and threw him over her shoulder.

Thud!

Barnabas's eyes teared up as the wind was knocked out of him. He lay there, sputtering and breathing hard, as the crowd roared their approval.

Nothing about this moment was triumphant for Saryan. Her face burned scarlet. Her eyes welled with tears. She took her staff in both hands, hoisted her arms back, and threw it at the floor beside her. The staff clattered along the padded floor.

Saryan towered over Barnabas, jabbing an accusing finger at him. "This is *your fault!*"

The roars and cheers died again. Barnabas lay on his back, speechless. Above him, Saryan's golden hair spilled down her face as she roared.

"My father is *dead!*" She screamed. "Treetown and Pinegrove and Fort Abernath are destroyed! We were at peace, but now Nezmyth is at war! All because of *you! You! You did this!* When the Ash arrive and you're one of the first to die, *I'll thank the Dragon!*"

She spat on him, and Barnabas flinched. Her teeth ground together. She wiped her eyes, scooped up her staff, and stormed off before the tears could flow freely. The locals made a path for her as she darted out of the combat gym. The silence still hung even after they heard the doors slam shut.

Like tar receding, the locals slowly shuffled back to the different combat mats, shaking their heads and muttering under their breath. Jason tried to ignore the dozens of people that stole looks at him.

Beside him, Tarren turned to him and whispered, "You still sure you did the right thing?" Then he slipped through the crowd.

Among it all, Barnabas sat up quietly, propping up his body with skinny arms. His gaze turned to Jason out of the corner of his eye. The darkness across his face almost made Jason feel sorry. Kalyk was right—this clearly wasn't the same man that he had imprisoned four years ago. He was broken. How could this weak old man be expected to fight? Regardless, the absurdity of it was irrelevant.

Jason walked out onto the battle mat. "Pick up your sword and stand up, Barnabas. We'll start slowly."

18

THE HISTORY

Jason trained with Barnabas for only an hour. Surprisingly, Barnabas began picking up old swordplay techniques quickly. He regained a portion of the balance, dexterity, and confidence that he once had, almost to the point of being impressive for a weathered old man.

Everyone else in the combat gym carried on with their own training. The overall tone of the room was grave and angry— grave because of the impending danger that was quickly approaching, and angry for the silence of Chief Taliman and the presence of Barnabas. For the hour that Jason and Barnabas sparred, the whispers and the disgusted glances didn't stop.

When they were done, Barnabas and Jason placed their wooden swords on a rack near the battle mat. The soldiers guarding Barnabas went to work on both of them, unstrapping their practice armor.

Jason spoke without looking at Barnabas. "Do you feel ready for battle?"

Barnabas shook his head. "No."

At that moment, Barnabas's stomach growled loudly. Jason turned and looked at him.

"Was that your stomach?" Jason said. "I thought we fed you eight steaks just an hour ago?"

"Yes. But… I may need more." Barnabas hesitated. "Perhaps ten."

Jason furrowed his eyebrows. As the guards took off Barnabas's armor, it became obvious that Barnabas's muscle mass was growing. When he retrieved him from the prison yesterday, he was bone thin. Now his shoulders, arms, and legs were mysteriously thicker—like a man just slightly underweight.

"What did Master Ferribolt say to you?" Jason shot.

"He blessed me with strength to fulfill my purpose," Barnabas replied.

That seemed to be the end of Barnabas's explanation, and the guards had fully removed both of their sets of armor. Now they wore just simple street clothes. The guards fastened Jason's royal armor and his cape, and as they did that, Jason commanded them to feed Barnabas his requested steaks.

* * * * *

Nighttime in Port Gala was usually festive. Parties with travelers drinking some of the finest ales across Wevlia were typical, but not tonight. The clink and shouts of battle preparations could be heard late into the evening. All the armor and weapons from all the blacksmiths in town had been purchased. Many ships set sail, returning to their respective kingdoms with unsold goods. Guards kept constant watch along the city walls—it had been two days since the battle at Pinegrove, meaning the Ash could be rushing the gates at any time.

Port Gala was a welcome opportunity for the refugees of Pinegrove and Fort Abernath to replenish their strength. The inns bore them without trifle or fuss, and many of them rested soundly throughout the day. When night came, they filled their bellies and did what they could to help the citizens of Port Gala—at least the citizens that chose to stay and fight. Many of the wealthier citizens hopped aboard their own personal ships to flee the kingdom until the war was over.

One of the more extravagant inns in the Eastern District volunteered to house the King and his friends, even non-royalty such as Tarren, Chief Patu, and Kalyk. The building was constructed with granite and fine woods and featured the artwork of many prominent painters and sculptors from across Nezmyth. After a long day of directing preparations, Nadiel and Tarren retired to a room on the top floor. They sat at a round table with ancient books sprawled open, nearly covering its entire surface. A single lamp threw harsh orange light on both of their faces.

Tarren's face was just inches from the pages of one book. *"Gayda may alah tomah..."*

"Your annunciation has improved significantly," Nadiel said patiently. He refused to let Tarren see the sleep plaguing his eyes. "Ever since your conversation with the King on the way to Pinegrove, it seems as though you've found the motivation you previously lacked."

"If it means I can heal my mother, I'll do anything," Tarren said as he leaned back in his chair and rubbed his eyes. "She was driven insane in the Nezmyth City Prison years ago. Back when Barnabas ruled. Back when the prison was an evil place full of abuse."

Nadiel bowed his head. "I'm deeply sorry."

"I am too. That makes it harder to see him out in the open like this." Tarren thought for a second. "How did you stay your hand all those years when you were his Advisor? You could have stopped him at any moment."

"I was tempted every day," Nadiel said, slowly closing one book shut. "One flick of my finger could have ended him. Ended his reign. Brought justice upon his head—but no. It wasn't my place. The Sacred Dragon made it very clear to me in my mind and in my heart that I must await the next Foreordained King, then I must do everything I can to protect him. And so I did. I waited all those years."

"How do you feel to see him walk around freely like this?"

Nadiel leaned back and crossed his legs. "I still don't know. It does not change what he's done, but the man that we saw today clearly isn't the same man that King Jason imprisoned years ago. He's stripped down. The power he once knew has left him."

"But what about his... special magic?" Tarren asked. "Don't you think he's holding back, waiting for the right moment to use it?"

Nadiel frowned and stared hard at Tarren. "My young friend, I'm grateful that you're unfamiliar with the workings of Dark Magic. That is to your benefit. I will have you know that Barnabas couldn't use Dark Magic right now even if he desired it."

"Why?"

"Because he hasn't killed in so long."

Nadiel let that statement hang as Tarren's eyes grew wide. Then he leaned in and put his elbows on the table. His red eyes were serious as they shifted from the door, to the window, then back to Tarren. He spoke in a low tone.

"Be careful about the information I'm about to share with you. The royalty of Nezmyth has worked very hard for very long to rid the workings of Dark Magic from existence. If Dark Magic became commonplace, it would prove the destruction of our society as we know it. It will be one of your responsibilities as Advisor to fight against and destroy it. Do you understand?"

Tarren gulped and nodded. Nadiel continued, "Barnabas cannot exercise *Tepnoh Edomah* because the powers of Dark Magic are predicated upon the death that you inflict. And that goes for any source of life—trees, animals, humans. When you kill, it fills a dark reservoir in your heart. From that reservoir, you can draw to use *Tepnoh Edomah*."

"But why not use normal magic, then?" Tarren said, his eyebrows bent. "Normal magic is just as powerful as Dark Magic. You're walking proof of that."

"This is true, Tarren, but I've had a lifetime of study and discipline. Dark Magic is seductively easy to master. Not only that, standard magic renders no euphoric feelings upon use—as a matter of fact, it can be downright exhausting. *Tepnoh Edomah* does offer that euphoria. Even a simple task like throwing a dark jeroki can give you a small rush of pleasure. The larger the spell, the larger the stimulation. You begin to crave it. Your body and your soul need it. And that will lead you to kill more. And to practice more *Tepnoh Edomah*. Thus begins a vicious cycle, and you'll become a shell of what you once were. Very powerful and fearsome, but hollow... and sad."

"Barnabas is a shell of what he once was right now," Tarren said bitterly.

"In a different way. *Tepnoh Edomah* deprives you of what positive emotions you have. Your capacity to love, to be patient and kind, are instead replaced with fear, greed, and lust. That was Barnabas four years ago—sapped of his positive emotions due to the thousands of deaths wrought by his hand. Now, after years of isolation in an ancient chamber that blocks Dark Magic, the dark reservoir inside him has been drained. He has been left weak and powerless. He may have to relearn standard magic, which will be a challenge for him."

Tarren was quiet, then he said, "Are you afraid that he'll start doing it again?"

"I'm sure it will be tempting for him, but that remains to be seen," Nadiel replied. "I'm sure four years in isolation has given him chance to clear his mind. He has literally and figuratively left the dark cave and stepped into the light. It would be hard to imagine him wanting to return."

Tarren was quiet for another long moment, letting everything he heard sink in. He drummed his fingers on the book in front of him. Then he said, "I heard Barnabas used to be a great man."

"He was."

"What do you think pushed him to start using Dark Magic?"

With that, Nadiel's eyes fell. He pulled open the book that he had previously closed. "Perhaps you should ask him yourself sometime. Now recite to me again your Ancient Nezmythian."

19
THE WAIT

Two days went by. The Ash still hadn't arrived.

Since they were expecting a speedy attack, Port Gala had been fortified significantly in those two days. The anti-ship cannons on the north shore were moved along the southern wall. Double the guards patrolled the wall day and night, keeping wary and watchful eyes on the southwest. But nothing stirred over the grassy plains that separated them and the forest.

As such, a blanket of tension covered Port Gala. By now, anyone living outside the kingdom had already escaped on what ships were left. Even some smaller boats were stolen by terrified merchants hailing from other kingdoms, eager to escape the incoming carnage. All that was left were those that loved Nezmyth as much as their own lives.

Jason sat at a large table in his suite, his elbows propping his head up. Under the table, his knees bounced up and down. He tapped his hands on his knuckles just underneath his chin.

"Why haven't they attacked already?" he wondered.

The other people in the room were Chief Patu, Kalyk, and Nadiel. Chief Patu leaned her back against the wall, her arms folded, her black eyes staring intently at the ground in front of her. Nadiel paced up and down the room with his hands behind his back while Kalyk sat sideways in the windowsill, one foot dangling out.

"How intelligent are these creatures?" Nadiel asked pointedly. "Is it likely that they would construct objects to climb the wall? Or barge through the city gates?"

"Kalyk," Chief Patu said. "Yeh've seen 'em more than the rest of us. 'Ow sharp are they?"

Kalyk took a deep breath and exhaled. "I don't know if they're smart enough to make a planned attack on the city. They attack like a swarm of bees—all of them all at once, just like in Pinegrove. I imagine it will be the same here."

"We have the benefit of a massive wall between us," Nadiel said. Then he added, "What is the possibility of a naval attack from the sea?"

Jason shook his head. "This city hasn't seen ships from Unbuntye in decades. I seriously doubt the possibility of a naval attack."

Chief Patu hummed, then said, "Yer 'ighness, where's the Queen?"

Jason shrugged. "Probably sparring. She's been avoiding me since I brought Barnabas here. I think she's still adjusting."

"As we all are," Nadiel said.

The sounds of clomping footsteps rushed closer and closer from outside the room—someone was running toward the King's quarters. They all heard it and exchanged glances just a moment before the door burst open.

It was Tarren. He was panting and his face dripped with unease. He was dressed in leather sparring armor and two wooden daggers were holstered at his hip. Everyone stood up as he threw the door open. He searched the room, and his eyes fell on Jason.

"Everybody, come to the square," Tarren said seriously. "There's a mob."

"What are they doing?" Jason shot.

"They're going to tar and feather Barnabas."

Jason clenched his teeth, and everyone raced out the door. In a matter of minutes, they were at the Eastern Plaza.

Indeed, a large mob had gathered in a circle, all hollering and jeering, facing whatever was happening in the center. Just outside the circle, the four soldiers that were guarding Barnabas had been disarmed and wrestled to the ground. It took four or five citizens each to do it. None of them seemed to notice the King had arrived.

"*What's going on here?*" Jason bellowed.

The crowd promptly fell silent. As they turned and saw the King, dressed in royal armor, armed, with fists trembling at his sides, their faces reverted to those of scolded children. The mob released the armed guards, who jumped to their feet and grabbed their weapons. But they didn't retaliate—they just watched. The people in the circle sagged their shoulders, and they shuffled out of the way, forming a corridor from the edge of the circle to the very center.

At the center, Barnabas sat on his knees, his back hunched and his hands bound. Half of his body was covered in scalding black tar and littered with plucked chicken feathers. His face was to the ground, and his breathing was labored. All of the clothes had been torn from his body except some cotton pants that were ripped at the knees.

Jason could have ground his teeth into powder. He marched through the crowd, his chest rising and falling with each breath. The townspeople looked on, barely breathing. Jason arrived at the center of the circle, standing next to Barnabas. He crouched down, then held Barnabas's chin in his hand. Those icy blue eyes held no ounce of resentment or anger or bitterness. Instead, they seemed resigned to a deserved fate.

Jason stood back up, turning about, observing the crowd. No one looked at him. They looked anywhere else, just not in his eyes.

"*Who led this?*" Jason continued to roar like a lion. "*Answer me!*"

"I did!"

Jason veered around to face the man. There was nothing special about him—a pudgy frame, dark hair, and a beard that needed trimming. His eyes were nervous, but he tried to overpower his unease with stony confidence. His hands twitched apprehensively at his side.

"Where do you get the audacity?" Jason shouted.

"Where do *you?*" The man shot back. He swallowed as he looked around. "We trusted you, King Jason! We trusted you to lead us into war! So why is *he* here? Why does he walk among us?" He pointed to the tar-smeared Barnabas just a few feet away. "Don't you remember his rule? His soldiers killed my son *in front of me!*" The man's eyes stung, and his jaw quivered. "And that's something I'll never forgive. I thought I could trust you to be wise. I thought we all could… but I was wrong. Down with King Jason!"

The man leaned forward and spat in Jason's direction. Several in the crowd gasped. Jason's friends watched from outside the mob, fuming with anger, but waiting to see Jason's reaction.

Jason felt the wad of saliva slap his cheek as flecks of spit showered him. He didn't flinch. He closed his eyes, his teeth still grinding together, and lifted his hand to smear the warm, sticky projectile from his face. As he cleared the disrespect from his cheek and beard, he flicked it to the ground. His eyes met the stranger's, and he glared with a white-hot stare.

No one said a word. Then Jason said, "Remove him."

Immediately, some soldiers swept forward and snatched up the man by the underarms, dragging him away. Jason's gaze circled the crowd again. "Anyone else?"

No one replied. Gradually, the mob dispersed, leaving Barnabas alone on the cobblestone. The shuffle of footsteps evaporated as the mob drew farther apart. Jason stayed close to Barnabas, but his friends stayed several paces away, still watching.

Jason bent down again. The tar covering half of Barnabas's body had nearly cooled. He knelt there with glassy eyes, staring at the ground like a ghost. Jason touched his fingers to the tar and plucked some of the feathers off, dropping them on the ground.

"You didn't even fight back, did you?" Jason asked.

Barnabas didn't move. No words. Not even a shake of the head.

Jason looked back to the soldiers that were guarding him. "Take him and make sure he gets cleaned up. He's still going to fight."

＊ ＊ ＊ ＊ ＊

Neither Jason nor his friends were there when two maids scraped the tar from Barnabas's skin. They weren't there to see the winces or hear the groans. They weren't there when broken feathers were littered across the floor. It was just Barnabas, the two maids, and his guards perched in the corners of the room.

Dusty sunlight spilled into the room. The wooden floors creaked with every step as the maids drew warm, soapy bath water to clean Barnabas of the last remnants of tar. As he settled into the bath, he winced. The warm water should have been delightful, but on raw skin, it stung.

The maids dipped rags in the soapy water and scraped the residue of abuse from Barnabas's body. After several quiet minutes, filled with no sound but the creaking of the floorboards and the sloshing of the bathwater, one of the maids spoke up.

"You've gotten thicker the last few days," she said.

Barnabas looked at her out of the corner of his eye. She still wasn't really looking at him. He hadn't wanted to make chitchat with anyone as of late, and certainly not when he was sitting naked in a porcelain tub. He didn't answer for a long moment.

"Yes," he finally said.

"What have you been doing in Port Gala? I'm sure the King has you doing something."

Again, Barnabas took his time to reply. "I train."

The second maid didn't chime in but slid a disapproving glare at the other. The first maid paid no heed. She hummed in recognition.

"Must be working, I'd say," she continued. "You were naught but bones and skin when you came, and now you're almost filled out proper."

Barnabas had noticed it. He still wasn't as strong as he was when he had the Throne, but his recent growth had been astonishing, if not miraculous. When he wasn't training, he was stuffing his face with meat, bread, cheese, and milk. And when he was training, it was nonstop. Endless running and sparring. Somehow, he had the energy for it.

The bath was done. One of the maids released a valve that drained the bath water into a pipe that ran across the floor and out of the building. They ordered Barnabas to stand up, and he complied. They dried him with the soft towels, and although they were luxurious, the fibers were still prickly and coarse on his raw skin. He stepped out of the bath and the maids dressed him in commoner clothing.

"All done," the kind maid said as she brushed Barnabas's shoulders.

Barnabas tried to clear the dust from his throat. Then he said, "Thank you."

As the two maids walked to the door, the guards advanced, surrounding Barnabas as usual. Before the kind maid walked out the door, she turned around. Her eyes were dark and soft.

They reminded Barnabas of someone he once knew—a beloved kinship that ended with murder and betrayal. He clenched his teeth and frowned at the thought.

"I've forgiven you," the maid said.

Suddenly, a pang in Barnabas's chest grew. *Forgiven me? The next thing he said was the easiest to say. "Why?"

"Because bitterness is poison," the maid replied. "I felt its sting every day. You never did. So, I let go."

She grinned and her dark eyes twinkled. With that, she closed the door behind her. A small lump had formed in Barnabas's throat, but he couldn't let the guards see. He was thankful for the woman. But he also pitied her.

Bitterness is a fuel, Barnabas thought. *If only she knew.*

* * * * *

Stars filled the sky over Port Gala. Guards marched up and down the city walls, their eyes fixed on the south. The cannons were loaded. The torches were lit. But nothing stirred on the horizon.

Back in his quarters, Jason gazed upon the city. Through the glass, he counted the flickering candles dancing in the windowsills as he stroked his beard and let his mind mull over a multitude of thoughts. Most of his thoughts centered around Barnabas.

Did I make a mistake?

Additionally, why hadn't the Ash attacked already? Surely they've had enough time to burn the victims of Pinegrove and charge to the city. That should have happened days ago. What's taking so long? And what of his lost power? His ability to transform into a Knight of the Holy Order?

Jason gazed at his palm and rubbed his birthmark with this thumb. Although the tension in his heart loosened when he freed Barnabas, a new tension had arrived. Would that be enough? Could he even call upon his power again in the next battle? What would happen if he couldn't?

And above it all, the crowd gathered at the Eastern Plaza today, tarring and feathering Barnabas... this was how his kingdom thought of him now. He freed Barnabas—the withered remains of a treacherous and powerful king. And by doing so, he had lost the trust of his people. And his wife.

Just as soon as he thought of her, a pang of hurt entered his heart. The silence. The coldness. The silver eyes filled with hurt and resentment.

As if on cue, the sound of footsteps came outside the door. The doors swung open and Saryan marched in, clad from head to toe in leather sparring armor. Her staff, constructed of Golden Oak, rested on her shoulder. She crossed the room and leaned it by her side of the bed. Then she began unstrapping her armor, revealing her street clothes underneath.

Jason largely ignored all of this. He knew she wouldn't want to speak with him. So he opted not to pursue it. He kept his eyes out the window, mulling, letting his thoughts and feelings swirl as he breathed in and out.

Coldly, Saryan readjusted her armor on a wooden mannequin by a tall bookshelf. She dragged her feet to the window and sat in a chair just a few feet away from Jason. Her gaze fixed on him. Jason noticed this and forced a half-smile. She didn't smile back, but folded her arms.

"The Ash could attack any moment," she murmured. She paused before she continued. "I don't want to stay mad at you."

Silently, Jason nodded. "I don't blame you for feeling this way." He breathed deep, then let the air out through his nose. "I hate this. All of this. I hate that we're here."

"Me too. It doesn't matter how beautiful Port Gala is. It's all wrong."

Jason thought about it for a moment, then said, "I'm sorry for freeing him. I suppressed the feelings for so long. I feared how it would make me appear to others—especially you."

Saryan leaned her head against the wall. "I hate seeing him walk about in the open, even if he's surrounded by guards. If you were really prompted by the Dragon to free him, I support you." She paused. "But if he dies in battle, I won't be sorry."

"He very well might," Jason replied. "If that's the case, my conscience is clear. I did as the Dragon commanded." He walked over to the bed and sat down. His face got darker. "I know there's nothing I can do to keep you away from the battle. But please, *please* be careful. Don't be a hero. I can't lose you."

"Speak for yourself."

He almost smiled. "I love you, Saryan."

"I love you, too."

As he looked around the extravagant bedroom, Jason noticed something small. When he realized what it was, he couldn't help but grin. He stood from the bed and strode over to the nearest nightstand where a small flute the size of his pinky finger lay next to an unlit lantern.

Jason smiled and took it between his fingers. It was much finer even than the one Tarren gifted him during his Year of Decision. It was carved out of ivory with small emerald inlays.

"Saryan, look," Jason said.

Saryan's tone brightened. "A flyra! I remember you had one of those when we first started courting. It hardly left your pocket."

Jason smirked. He put it to his lips and blew. The high whistling notes filled the room as they bent and curved through the air. Jason's fingers covered and uncovered the small holes on the flute's surface, reawakening the sleeping memories of past songs he used to play.

Saryan's eyes sparkled. "I miss hearing that music in the castle walls when you were first made King." She walked over and slipped under the covers, nestling herself comfortably onto the feather mattress. "Will you play me to sleep?"

Jason slipped into bed next to her. "Sure."

And so he did. He didn't have to play long. The soft notes continued to fill the room as the clinks and murmurs of soldiers echoed through the city. Once Jason saw that his wife was soundly asleep, her chest rising and falling with each breath, he set the flyra on the nightstand next to him. He leaned over and kissed her head before he turned over and fell asleep next to her.

20

THE STAND

A sudden chill swept northward.

Jason and Saryan awoke when a Port Gala soldier burst through the door, eyes wild, panting. Both of them popped up in bed with a start.

"Your Highness! My Lady!" the soldier shouted, "The Ash are advancing in the distance! They'll soon be upon us!"

Jason and Saryan leaped out of bed without hesitation, hearts racing. Immediately, a small group of soldiers poured into the suite. They furiously tied knots, buckled buckles, and tightened straps. Within minutes, Saryan and Jason were dressed for battle and marching down the hall.

"How many are there?" Jason asked the nearest soldier.

The soldier's face was white. "So many."

"Hundreds? Thousands?"

"At least a thousand, sir."

Jason frowned. "Sounds about right, considering the people we lost in Pinegrove. How far out are they?"

The soldier said, "I don't know, sir. But I've been instructed to take you directly to the southern wall."

"Lead the way." Jason thought for a second. "Instruct those guarding Barnabas to bring him directly to us."

The soldier looked to another soldier, who nodded and swiftly darted away.

Before the party even left the walls of the inn, Nadiel and Tarren had joined them, armed and ready for battle. The inn workers were running up and down the halls, waking up the tenants. Many of the guests burst forth with whatever armor and weapons they had themselves, ready to come to Nezmyth's aid.

The band burst onto the street and immediately traveled south, headed for the walls. The streets filled with people belting for the south wall, armed with whatever they could scrape up. As the crowd flew through the spider web of streets, Jason, Saryan, Tarren, and Nadiel made no chatter.

Kalyk and Chief Patu should be on their way to the gates, Jason thought. *Each one will lead a battalion of soldiers to guard those entrances. They're both warriors and strategists. We'll be okay.*

Through the decorated streets of the Eastern District they went. The nobles that came out to battle had much finer armor and weapons than the people they saw in the Western District, but from what Jason could see, the aristocrats and nobles weren't as represented. As they climbed the stairs to the massive southern walls, Jason noticed it was filling with people garbed in secondhand, unpolished armaments.

Townspeople separated themselves as they noticed the royal party ascending the steps. Many shouted "Make way for the King!" or "The King approaches!" Jason and the others climbed and climbed until they stood at the brim of the southern wall, overlooking the plains that stretched for miles.

What they saw made their blood freeze.

No more than a mile away, the Ash rushed northward in a frenzied sprint—but it wasn't just humans. Even from the distance, they could see the outlines of bears, wolves, and other forest creatures that had been transformed—gray, oily, and large. There had to be nearly a thousand of them.

Not only that, but the Ash carried things with them. Tree trunks thirty feet long had been chopped down and lashed into makeshift ladders. And there were dozens of them. Each ladder was lugged by a hoard of soldiers, sprinting at full force, the weight barely slowing them down.

"They'll climb the walls with those, no problem," one soldier to Jason's left grumbled.

The sight made Jason gulp horribly. But then he noticed something else. Some of the Ash bears were organized, with their mighty paws and lumbering frames running uniformly, carrying something. The bears were separated into three groups, and each group hauled a log nearly three feet wide and twenty feet long. As they got closer to the gates, they spread apart. Each of the groups were heading for a separate gate.

They're going to ram the gates open, Jason thought.

With the incoming onslaught, the cold grew thicker, sending a spine-tingling chill throughout the crowd. Everyone could see their breath when they exhaled.

Jason looked left and right. Nearly the entire wall was populated with Port Gala residents armed with bows, swords, axes, and spears. Below them, all three gates to the city had been barred and fortified. But now, those fortifications felt small and insignificant. The Ash had a legion of ladders to scale the wall, and they had three enormous battering rams. It would only be a matter of time before the dark soldiers flooded the streets.

Jason frowned as he looked about more. Nearly every citizen's eyes were on him, hoping and expectant, so he tried desperately to hide his fear. He looked to his friends. He knew they were thinking the same thoughts as him. This was where they had to attain victory. This had to be where the war had to end. If not, Nezmyth would be overrun.

But there was someone missing.

"Where is Barnabas?" Jason uttered.

"*Your Highness!*"

The crowd parted enough to allow for a trail leading up to the King. Five people darted up the stairs at full speed. Four of them were soldiers, and the fifth was Barnabas himself. He was the first one up the stairs, skipping every other step as he bounded upward. Behind him, the soldiers struggled to keep up, following behind him at a full sprint.

No one could believe their eyes when they saw him. All Barnabas wore were some worn-out boots and some cotton trousers cinched up at the knees. Sweat coated his entire body, but he didn't breathe heavily. He had fully returned to his former glory: a thick, towering specimen of wide, hard muscle. He had grown so much muscle in such a short time that nearly his entire body was coated in long, horizontal stretch marks. And his eyes—his eyes were as piercing and icy as ever. They focused on Jason. A sword protruded from his right hand.

The soldiers made it up the stairs just in time to hear Barnabas say, "Ready for battle, Your Highness."

Jason's jaw dangled. According to Barnabas, Master Ferribolt's blessing stated the Dragon would lend Barnabas whatever strength he needed to fulfill his purpose. It looked as though the Sacred Dragon, in its infinite wisdom, had delivered in spades. Jason closed his mouth.

"You didn't even wait to get your armor on," Jason said softly.

Barnabas shook his head. The soldiers running after him had a breastplate and shoulder guards in tow. They immediately started putting them onto the fallen King. He acted as if he didn't even notice.

"You're a soldier now," Jason said seriously. "Join your people on the wall and be ready."

Barnabas nodded. No one said a word as the soldiers finished fastening the armor and Barnabas slipped into the crowd, squeezing into the front and overlooking the plains to the south. The townspeople around him stared and squirmed away from him, not wanting to be too close. Jason still felt incredulous. He turned to one of the soldiers that had been guarding Barnabas. "Did he sleep at all?"

The soldier shook his head. "No, sir. Ever since the incident yesterday, all he's done is eat and exercise. He's hardly stopped to breathe. I've never seen anything like it."

"He never gave you any trouble?"

"No, sir," the soldier replied, "To be perfectly frank, he's been the most compliant prisoner I've ever guarded."

Jason's reply felt absent. "I see."

The rumble of the Ash was getting louder. As the stampede ascended northward, coming closer and closer to the metropolis of Port Gala, the sun crept over the Eastern Mountains, throwing soft orange light onto the kingdom. It should have been beautiful. But not today.

People shifted nervously as they stood along the wall, packed shoulder to shoulder, awaiting what was to come. Teeth chattered and knees quaked. Some looked ahead, unmoving, eyes serious, ready for the onslaught.

The stampede was now only half a mile away, and with it, a stronger chill. They didn't stop. They didn't slow down. There were no organized lines or war drums—just a flood of gray, armed monsters ready to climb the wall or break through. Whichever came first.

As Jason exhaled, he could see the smoky breath pluming from his lips. His arms sprouted into goosebumps. Before him, the archers and cannons lined the front of the forces.

"Attack when in range!" Jason shouted the order.

The archers pulled back their bowstrings. The army was getting closer. Jason's heart thumped in his chest. He stole a look at Barnabas over to his left. Barnabas's gaze could have vaporized the Ash, his grip on his sword tight and his other hand balled into a fist. Silently, Jason wondered what he must be thinking at a time like this.

The rumble was now deafening. The army was within range. Everyone held their breath and their teeth chattered from the cold. Palms were sweaty. The ground shook beneath them. At the front of the line, the archers let loose their first volley and the cannons fired.

BLAM BLAM BLAM!

The explosions erupted across the wall. Cannonballs soared through the air until they found their marks, crushing through Ash and or kicking up dirt. Arrows whistled as they found their targets. Some Ash fell, but most didn't. Many took arrows in the shoulders or torso and kept running. They didn't even slow down.

"There are too many, sir!" One soldier agonized.

"Fire more!" Jason commanded.

They knocked more arrows and loaded more cannonballs. More flicks of bowstrings and more exploding cannon fire. The same result. The Ash kept running. They were nearly at the wall. Everyone could hear the growls and roars beneath them.

The Ash were here. Within moments, the Ash stuck the ladder heads in the ground, and the rest of their comrades hoisted the ladders up in mighty swings. Every heart raced with terror and adrenaline as the thick, crude ladders slammed into the wall's edge. The Ash began crawling up them like vicious, bloodthirsty spiders.

Jason didn't know who said it, but someone did.

"For Nezmyth!"

Then the whole wall replied in an echoing chorus, *"For Nezmyth!"*

BOOM!

The first boom of a battering ram on the southern gate echoed through the city. Moments later, booms from the eastern and western gates echoed through the city as well. The Ash were fighting to break in. The archers rained volleys of arrows into the crowd with little effect. Ash continued to scurry up the ladders hungrily. Many of them were cut down, beheaded, or skewered just as their bodies reached the top.

"Yes! Hold the line and keep striking them down!" Jason shouted. Then he thought, *Sacred Dragon, give me the power of a Knight—*

Not yet, came the immediate response in his heart. *Wait.*

Jason's hands tightened. *Wait? Why?*

He looked over at Barnabas. At the edge of the wall, Barnabas gripped his blade tighter. "Burn the ladders! Use your magic!" he barked. Two began launching fire from their palms. Barnabas stood between them, feet planted on the wall, cutting down every Ash that dared ascend. After a long moment, the ladder was inflamed. The Ash refused to climb it. They let it topple to the ground, scattering out of the way.

Jason thought, *He's still a leader after all.*

"Earth golems!" One soldier called out.

Beneath the Ash, several hundred yards away from the wall, the earth trembled and shook. Great mounds arose from the soil, making the Ash fumble and fall around them. Then, bursting from the grass, two massive shapes stood, sentinels made of stone and soil, emerging from the earth's surface. They were each twenty feet tall and faceless, with long, thick arms and legs that ended in massive stumps. Somehow, they made noise like a deep rumble—mighty giants of magic and nature.

Jason looked to his right. Amid the insanity, Nadiel stood not far away, his arms outstretched, his eyes closed, sweat forming on his forehead. Jason smiled. Hundreds of yards away, the earth golems dove into the fray, swinging their arms, sending Ash broken and careening through the air. More people were starting to get Barnabas's hint—they burned the tops of the ladders and pushed them over as the Ash tried to climb.

We could do it. We could win, Jason thought.

Suddenly, a soldier nearby Jason turned around. His eyes filled with terror as his gaze turned northward.

"Look!" The soldier yelled. "Toward the sea!"

Jason flipped around. What he saw made his heart drop.

Five ships sailed toward the harbor of Port Gala. Each ship floated with great, terrible black sails pocked with holes and tears. The bodies were constructed of an oily black wood that appeared diseased. And even from the distance, it was clear to see that each ship was packed tightly with hundreds of Ash. Within minutes, they would reach the city.

No! Jason thought, *We moved our anti-ship cannons to the southern wall, and we're barely staying them off as it is! Once those ships land, there will be nothing stopping the Ash from overrunning the city and killing everything here.* He paused. *Could I destroy them all with my Knightly powers? Is it possible? Who would lead the army then?*

The ships were edging closer to the harbor. The clock was ticking. Annihilation was on Nezmyth's doorstep. Once the Ash took over Port Gala, there would be nothing stopping them from destroying all of Nezmyth. Those ships had to be destroyed.

That's when the voice came in Jason's heart. The feeling. The spark.

Now, it spoke. *Destroy them.*

He knew what he had to do. He uttered the prayer in his heart. He called upon the power of the Sacred Dragon. And then, it was granted.

21

THE INTRUDER

Jason flew down the stairway and into the bowels of the city. He could feel the power coursing through him as he sprinted—the power of the Knight.

The soldier from the wall shouted, "Your Highness! Where are you going?"

Nadiel heard this and turned around, looking for the commotion. His face was drenched in sweat, and his breathing was deep and fast. He watched as Jason sprinted up the street below.

Jason's body burst into flames. His eyes torched into vibrant orange, and his hair ignited into the same color, swaying as he pelted through the street. He looked down. In his right hand was the Blade of Nezmyth, shimmering, bright, and ready to wreak holy vengeance. Jason felt the raw, celestial power crash through his blood and bones. He took two more sprinting steps then leaped into the air.

As Jason's body shot through the sky, Nadiel smirked then looked back toward the fray.

The wind took Jason through the air as the buildings of Port Gala slid by hundreds of feet below. He gripped the Blade of Nezmyth tighter, fixed on the five ships creeping into the harbor. His cape flicked in the gale as he soared. There were hundreds of Ash in those ships, packed shoulder to shoulder and armed for a massacre. As he got closer, their volume was undeniable.

How do I fight every single Ash on these ships? Jason thought. Then it hit him. *Maybe I don't.*

He let go of the Blade of Nezmyth, and it disappeared in a puff of white smoke. His body straightened like a spear aimed directly for the ships.

That's when the arrows started. The Ash saw him coming. They knocked arrows and fired at will, lobbing their shafts in the sky. He spun and dodged as the arrows whizzed by him, missing him by inches. As a Knight, he could sense them coming. He could feel the changes in the air and the matter moving through space. Everything was heightened.

He was so close to the first ship that he could hear the grunts and shouts coming from the deck. The first thing he did was pull his arm back and launch an enormous magic beam at the mast. It connected with the base, sending out an explosion of splinters and wood, skewering the nearby Ash with broken bits.

As the dark mast toppled like a felled tree, Jason aimed right for the hull of the ship. He shielded his face with his forearms.

Crash! Crash!

Jason's body blasted holes in each side of the ship's hull as he pelted through, sending more blasted wood into the sea. For good measure, he spun around and launched a massive jeroki at the hull, widening the size of the scar. The success was nearly immediate. Water began seeping into the ship. It would sink before it even reached the harbor.

The Ash panicked. They scuttled and shifted about the deck like frightened roaches, and many of them jumped overboard. After they hit the water, they struggled to the surface and swam hard for the harbor, but the soldiers were so burdened with heavy weapons that most sunk. For those who abandoned the weapons, it was still slow going.

But that's no reason to hesitate, Jason thought. He flew toward the next ship.

Back at the wall, the Ash were making headway. They weren't being immediately cut down when they reached the tops of the ladders. Clangs and clashes could be heard up and down the wall as the humans fought with all their might. The Ash's towering, oily bodies stood above the heads of the Nezmythians, and each Ash was able to stave off three Nezmythians at once.

By the East Gate, Chief Patu and her battalion stood with their knees bent, weapons at the ready, their eyes glued to the double doors. In front of them, a barrier of anti-ship cannons were trained on the gates, loaded and ready to fire. Every few seconds, the gates shuddered horribly as the weight of a battering ram crashed into it.

SLAM! SLAM!

"Stand yer ground!" Chief Patu roared, clutching her ax. Her beady eyes were stone cold as they locked on the gates. Memories of Treetown flashed through her mind. The screams. The blood. The broken bones. With every crash of the battering ram, the Ash got closer and closer to breaking through. Her eyes scanned the wall overhead. Some of the Ash were muscling their way onto the wall's surface. If they got into the city, it would be all over.

The war had to end here. It had to.

Two miles to the west, Kalyk and her battalion guarded the West Gate with a similar barrier of anti-ship cannons and an additional regiment of archers training their bows on the gates. On the ground, a battalion of soldiers stood with their swords drawn behind the cannons. Kalyk stood at the lip of the nearest building, her own bow drawn, staring unblinkingly at the shuddering gate. Dust shook from the rungs with each blow.

"Steady!" she commanded.

On a rooftop across the street, Tarren stood in typical Nezmythian armor, not drawing too much attention to himself. His daggers were at his side, but he'd do his best not to use them today. Instead, his hands were in front of him, his fingers apart. He concentrated, clenching his jaw and pointing his eyebrows. His thoughts focused one element, then jumped to another. The product was sparks, then flames, and ice flecks leaping between his fingertips.

Near the South Gate, sweat poured down Nadiel's face. The earth golems fought and scrapped outside the wall, killing hundreds of Ash, but the magic was dying. The earth golems were bogged down with the blows of the surrounding Ash. In a matter of moments, they would be nothing but mounds of soil outside the Port Gala walls. Nadiel breathed in great gasps. He threw lightning bolts all around him, striking any Ash that got close. He had some magic left, but he wasn't sure how much longer he could last.

If those ships get destroyed, Nadiel thought has he shot blasts and swung his sword. *We might be victorious. Just perhaps. Please, Sacred Dragon, give Jason strength.*

He looked over his shoulder. In the distance, he saw the distant dot of King Jason careening through the sky, sending blasts of magic at the ships. The water was becoming gray and turbulent as Ash swam hungrily for the harbor.

Nadiel didn't notice that all the Ash ladders had burned away. But Barnabas did. All of them were reduced to long, smoldering heaps laying outside the city walls. He watched without expression as the Ash clambered on top of each other thirty feet below, trying to make ladders of themselves. But they scurried about like insects with minimal success.

Barnabas scowled. The Ash that had managed to climb the top of the wall were sorely outnumbered by Nezmythians and would be stricken down soon. And thankfully, the people had only experienced minor wounds. Not a single Nezmythian had been killed according to what he could see. At least not yet.

As Barnabas looked over the edge of the wall, he noticed the switch. It was instantaneous, like the entirety of the Ash communicated without a single word. The Ash that were bunched against the walls dispersed and spread out. They sprinted away in three directions, forming three large bodies of soldiers. They followed the edge of the wall. Barnabas knew what they were doing, and he knew they needed to act quickly.

"They're heading for the gates!" Barnabas flipped around and roared. *"Get to the gates! Get to the gates!"*

All the soldiers nearby flipped on their heels. The stairways heading to ground level became congested. The stampede dispersed as they reached the ground, and Barnabas stood back to make sure every Ash on the wall was killed.

Through the scuffle, Barnabas locked eyes with Nadiel. He was standing only fifty feet away, casting healing spells at injured soldiers and shooting lightning at whatever Ash remained on the wall. When Barnabas felt those red eyes on him, he remembered the fear that coursed through him back when he was King—knowing that this man was so much more powerful than he, even with his use of Dark Magic. Silently, he was grateful they were on the same side this time.

Nadiel nodded. Barnabas nodded back. Together, they peeled down the stairs among the other soldiers.

"How… how is your magic?" Barnabas asked.

"Sufficient," Nadiel responded.

"Can you cast barriers behind every gate?"

"You can only cast barriers on areas you can see," Nadiel said as they reached ground level. "I can't see all gates at once."

Barnabas frowned. "They'll break through. We'll be overrun."

"Our greatest hope is fighting over the Wevlian Sea," Nadiel said as he cocked his head to the north.

That's when Barnabas looked. His eyes popped as he saw Jason careening through the air. He counted half a dozen ships just outside the harbor of Port Gala. Currently, only two ships weren't sinking.

Over the sea, Jason crashed through another hull of an Ash ship. He tossed another couple of jerokis. The ship began to sink, casting more and more Ash into the sea. His arms and face were coated with cuts and splinters. He pulled an arrow stuck in his thigh and dismissively tossed it before he went hurtling toward another ship.

He breathed hard. Even in his heightened state, he was getting tired. He had to at least destroy the ships. But what would stop all the Ash with swimming into the harbor anyway? Some of them from the first ships were getting uncomfortably close.

He shot for the last ship through another barrage of arrows and exploded the mast as he blasted a hole through the ship. It was sinking. All six ships were destroyed. Now, the Ash slashed at the water, swimming furiously for the harbor.

Jason's head felt light as he pulled three arrows from his shoulders and arms. He felt himself falter in the air; he had to get to shore. He straightened his body and shot for land, the wind flicking at his torn cape. As he flew, he saw scores of his people running for the three gates, moving like a hoard of ants through the streets. He frowned. Did the Ash not climb the walls? Why?

Jason came to a halt at the harbor. The air carried him neatly down to the ground, his boots just inches away from the water's edge. The closest Ash were still hundreds of yards offshore, but they swam with a blind fury that was frightening. For nearly a mile, the waters to the north were white and turbulent with thrashing gray limbs.

Breathing came in great breaths as his heart thumped in his chest. Jason looked down at the birthmark on his right hand— the triangle on his palm just beneath his index finger. He frowned. His Knightly power wasn't dissipating, which means there was still some work to do.

"But what?" he thought out loud.

"*Don't you remember your escape from Unbuntye?*" A voice came in his head. "*Call the elements.*"

That's right. He remembered it. As King Nartikis shot toward him in the air, a burst of something shot him out of the sky. Could he call that at will? Right now?

Not knowing what else to do, Jason raised his hands to the sky. He didn't know how or why, but he could *feel* the particles in the air. Every drop of rain. Every bird. He made a swirling motion with his hands. Above Port Gala, storm clouds began to churn. Soldiers on the ground stopped to watch as the sun hid behind a swirling mass of dark clouds. Jason could feel it all in his arms and chest. Electricity was forming. He didn't breathe—not knowing how much of the power was in him.

That's when he felt it. The charge. As if the clouds had reached their peak power. The spark ignited in his chest. He clenched his teeth. For a fraction of a second, his eyes glowed electric blue. Then the blast came.

CCRRAASSHH

It was mighty and sudden. Deafening. Seven white lightning bolts shot from the clouds, aimed directly for the water just outside the city. Sparks leaped from the seared bodies of Ash as they convulsed along the water's surface. As quickly as the storm clouds formed, they melded away, revealing an azure sky. In their wake, a mile-long emblem of death floated in the water. The water was no longer turbulent with the waves of crashing limbs. It was still and coated with an ugly gray. Thousands of Ash floated face down and lifeless among a layer of dust and soot.

Jason made a pushing motion with his arms. With it, the water circulated. Gurgling swells twirled under the surface, pushing the surface casualties away from the city. It was slow at first, but in time, the current picked up. The bodies of the Ash and the wreckage of the sunken ships were carried out to the open sea. In its wake, the clear blue water sparkled in the Port Gala harbor.

As the bodies and wreckage sailed into the distance, Jason exhaled, and with it, his body returned to normal. He staggered a bit where he stood, cradling his forehead, shutting his eyes to fight the dizziness.

He knew there wasn't time to rest. There was still a battle raging across town. The Ash didn't manage to climb the walls, but he could hear the booms of battering rams slamming into the city gates. He had to move. He picked up his feet and sprinted southward.

BOOM

At the East Gate, Chief Patu turned to Saryan. "Do yeh think it's 'nuff to 'old 'em?" Her face nodded toward the gate.

Another resounding *boom* came from the gates as they shuddered again. Saryan's head, shrouded by an iron helm, swiveled on her shoulders. There had to have been two or three hundred soldiers here inside the gates, weapons drawn, bodies armored, and teeth chattering. She frowned and shook her head.

BOOM

The South Gate cracked under the repeated weight of the rams. The metal bindings holding the beams together were popping.

"Hold your position!" Barnabas barked.

Barnabas had done a lot in the short time just inside the South Gate. A barrier of anti-ship cannons were loaded and aimed. Behind the cannons, Barnabas had rearranged the soldiers strategically—shields and spears in the front, swords behind, archers in the rear. On nearby rooftops, archers were poised with their bows aimed at the gates. They planned on sending volleys in turns, providing a near-constant rain of arrows.

BOOM

The battering ram finally broke through. Just below the rung, broken chunks of wood fell onto the street. The snarling gray faces and red eyes of forest creatures filled the holes as their jaws snapped and salivated.

The soldiers gulped, gripping their weapons with sweating hands as they awaited the onslaught.

BOOM

The hole grew bigger. Ash stuck their hands through, frantically feeling around for the rung that kept the gate sealed shut. They could feel it. Their hands snapped at it hungrily, only pulling out right before the battering ram sailed into the door one final time.

CRASSHHH

The gate buckled. They were through. The battering ram dropped to the ground with a mighty boom, and the Ash flooded into the city. Every last one of them were armed, wild, and sprinting. Their roars and growls rebounded off the buildings.

"*Fire!*" Barnabas roared.

Cannon fire tore through the air. Bursts of flames erupted from their mouths as cannonballs belted through the street. The burning of black powder filled the nostrils of everyone nearby, and at the gates, the cannonballs ripped through the bodies of incoming Ash. Black soot leaped into the air, filling the sky with dust as their maimed bodies fell onto the cobblestone.

Through the clouds and dust, more Ash blindly trampled the bodies of the fallen. As the cannons were frantically loaded at the front line, the archers released a volley of arrows that rained death on the incoming Ash. Through the rain of arrows, more Ash fell among their comrades. Very few broke through.

At the East Gate, the Ash finally broke through and rushed in. The cannons fired haphazardly. No archers on nearby rooftops provided any rain of arrows as the Ash poured into the streets. The Nezmythians shouted battle cries and barbaric roars as the Ash fell upon them. Carnage ensued. All was madness as the sounds of clanging swords and ripping flesh filled every ear.

At the West Gate, it was a similar story. The cannon fire and arrows alleviated more of the danger for the Nezmythians, but the uncoordinated defensive allowed much of the Ash to slip through to fight the defenses on foot. Swords were drawn and shields were splintered as the Ash poured in.

Kalyk never missed as she fired arrows from the rooftops. Even Tarren, with his arms outstretched, found success as he brought pillars of fire and lighting down on the Ash forces. But the force of it all! With every spell he conducted, more perspiration formed on his brow, and his chest heaved as if a bear sat on it. His head swam. After casting several deadly spells for nearly a minute, he fell to one knee, huffing and clutching his head.

How does he do so much? he thought of Nadiel, bewildered.

To the north, Jason sprinted toward the wall. It wasn't far now. He could see the incoming Ash breaking through the South Gate, but they couldn't get far due to the cannon fire and archers. He couldn't see the West and East Gates, but he knew that those were where Tarren and Saryan would be fighting. Silently, he prayed for their safety.

Barnabas's eyes were stone as they locked onto the gates. The Ash were now struggling to climb over the mound of dead that rested just inside the gate. The Nezmythians aimed the cannons upward to get better trajectories on the climbing forces. The archers continued to rain arrows. Each group of soldiers listened for Barnabas's orders as they released their attacks in sequence. When any Ash broke through the line, soldiers with swords and shields were quick to snuff them out. It was methodical. Calculated.

Then, another turn. Another silent shot of communication. As if a switch were turned, all the Ash forces abandoned their pursuit. They turned about, sprinting with just as much zeal and energy away from Port Gala.

They were retreating.

All across Port Gala, the Nezmythians couldn't believe it. The Ash swung their weapons and roared with rage, but as their forces were cut down, they turned on a coin and bolted toward the gates. The clangs and crashes of weapons ceased, replaced only by the stampede of footsteps heading southward —away from the Nezmythians and out of the city.

"*Victory!*" One soldier yelled. "*Victory!*"

The other soldiers began to jeer and celebrate the Ash's stampede. But at the East Gate, Saryan and Chief Patu exchanged worried looks. If the Ash escaped, it wouldn't take much for them to create more. Each and every one of them had to be destroyed, or the war would only continue.

"*Don't let 'em 'scape!*" Chief Patu bellowed at the soldiers. "*Cut 'em down! Fight!*"

It was no use. The soldiers were already celebrating so loudly that even Chief Patu's voice was drowned out. She and Saryan gave each other looks again, defeated and worried.

Jason finally came to a stop as he reached the wreckage just inside the South Gates. The air made him cough; it was thick with the stale scent of black powder. An enormous pile of dead Ash rested just inside the wall, soot scattered among the broken remains. None of the Nezmythians seemed to notice him approach—they were all on the wall, looking out to the south, jeering and celebrating their hard-earned victory.

Jason smiled. He couldn't help it.

They're gone. We won.

"Enjoy it now. It will not last."

He knew that voice. There he was, standing on his left not a yard away. The projection of King Nartikis was fixed on the celebration. His vacant blue eyes reeked with disinterest inside his pasty white complexion.

Jason's jaw clenched. "I told you the Dragon would defend us, and it did. Your forces are defeated."

"Regrouping," Nartikis corrected. "You and these people are fools to revel in a victory marred with the sting of inevitability. You know that the Ash will continue to grow and spread like wildfire." His head nodded to the crowd. "They clearly do not."

He's right, Jason thought bitterly. "We've sent word of your armies to every village in the kingdom. All of them have been making fortifications."

"And when they discover the futility of such measures, I will revel in their anguish," Nartikis said. He turned. "My offer still stands. I do not wish to rule a crippled kingdom. Grant me the throne, and I call off the Ash. You can stop this death now, Jason. Make the wise choice."

"You're barbaric and savage," Jason seethed. "And I'd rather die than see Nezmyth in your hands."

"Then so it shall be."

Suddenly, he vanished. Jason kept staring to his left, even after Nartikis disappeared. He clenched his jaw again, letting Nartikis's words echo through his mind. *The sting of inevitability…*

How do we exterminate a force like this? He thought.

The thought hung in his mind as he watched his people continue to celebrate. He exhaled through his nose, letting them revel in their ignorance for just a moment.

It appears this war is far from over.

22

THE REJECTION

Port Gala spent the rest of the day removing Ash remains from the streets. As the locals cleaned up the mangled, dusty bodies, they clapped each other on the backs, embraced, and counted themselves grateful to be alive. The Ash weapons and armor were collected and stored for future use. The bodies were lifted into giant carts then hauled outside the city for burning.

Although the town rejoiced over the victory and crinkled their noses at the sight of the Ash, Kalyk and Chief Patu tried not to look into the faces of the dead. These bodies were once the people they loved. Their friends. But they were slain, corrupted, and used as puppets for a vile purpose. For that reason, they worked silently.

The Nezmythians labored until eventually the sun set. As the local leaders took account of the casualties from the battle, they discovered something magnificent—there were none. Many soldiers were wounded or otherwise hurt, but not a single Nezmythian lost their life at the battle of Port Gala. What was most curious of all was that the soldiers at the South Gate experienced the fewest injuries by far—the battalion led by Barnabas.

As the sun set over the west, a red-orange glow shimmered over the Wevlian Sea. The candles and lanterns of Port Gala illuminated, and as darkness fell, the city returned to its usual festive self. Celebrating townspeople filled the taverns and pubs, reveling in their miraculous victory. The dimly lit streets became abuzz with the dull noise of clinking glasses, singing, and dancing.

In one particular tavern in the East District, several residents tried to cajole Jason and Saryan into joining the festivities. They politely declined. The locals were disappointed, but weren't about to tease their royalty about it, so they let the King and Queen leave, shouting "Hail King Jason!" and "Dragon bless the King and Queen!"

Jason and Saryan began the short walk to their inn, side by side, wearing street clothes that were plastered with ashes. Their hands, forearms, and faces were also covered with soot from the day's labors.

"Everyone is celebrating," Jason said. "If only they knew. We should have killed every last one of them today."

Saryan's tone was equally dark. "I don't think we can even consider this a victory. You know they'll be back again. It's inevitable."

Jason didn't speak.

"You know the worst part?" Saryan asked. "This."

She stopped and held out her fists, accentuating the dark dust that clung to her sweaty arms. It was all over her, from her neck down to her boots. Nearly every inch of her clothes.

"I can't stop thinking about *who* is on me," Saryan said. "Who from Treetown or Pinegrove? Whose children? Or fathers? Which of our people did I kill today?" He paused as she swallowed. "And they're not even anyone I know. But what about Chief Patu and Kalyk?" She swallowed again. "Before the battle… Chief Patu told me she was worried she would see Adria's face in one of them."

A shiver slid down Jason's back. He couldn't help but imagine himself fighting the onslaught through Chief Patu's eyes. Having to fight the cremated, possessed bodies of those he once directly knew and loved. He imagined awaiting Saryan's face in the army that was hungry to slay him. He shivered again and tried to force down the lump in his throat.

"Let's get this washed off," he said hollowly.

By now, they had reached the inn. They climbed to the top floor and made their way to their quarters. Down the hall, the door to Nadiel's flat was open. It was faint, but they could hear Tarren eagerly talking to Nadiel about his use of magic during the battle. Nadiel congratulated him but kept trying with little success to turn his attention back to Ancient Nezmythian.

"At least his lessons are coming along," Saryan said.

He and Saryan found the washroom just down the hall, and both of them were quickly cleaned up by a small group of maids. They flushed out the dirty bath water and dried off the royal couple, giving them both a set of fine sleeping garments. He and Saryan trudged barefoot down the hall before they reached their quarters.

When they crossed the threshold to their room, Jason asked, "Did Master Ferribolt stay in the city during the battle? Or did—*huh?*"

He nearly jumped out of his skin when he saw Master Ferribolt sitting at the round table just inside the door. The Chief Patriarch's legs were crossed, and his glasses sat on the tip of his nose. His eyes scanned a book propped in his hand, but he looked up as the royalty crossed through the door.

Oddly, he wasn't alone. Barnabas sat next to him at the table, his hands laced together, staring intently at the space between his wrists. He had soldiers guarding either side of him.

Jason put his hand on his heart, which had started thumping uncomfortably. "Do you get some sort of thrill from surprising people?"

Saryan half smiled, but nothing more. The sight of Barnabas in her living space sapped the pleasure from her eyes. Instead, she slipped around the perimeter of the room, making her way for the bed. Meanwhile, Master Ferribolt smirked and placed his book down. "It would be dishonest to say I don't, Your Highness. It's an innocent thrill, though, is it not?"

"Innocent or not, it won't be long before I order you as King to knock that off," Jason smirked in return. Then his smile dropped. "I hope you stayed safe during the battle today."

"You and I both know that my tether to the Sacred Dragon gives me a host of magical techniques," Master Ferribolt said. "But as a spiritual leader, I lean away from those techniques suited for combat. Yes, Jason, I stayed away from the battle today. From what I heard, our friend Barnabas did an exceptional job of defending the South Gate."

"Everyone did an excellent job," Jason said as he glared at Barnabas. "Chief Patu and Saryan, Kalyk and Tarren… but yes, Barnabas's strategic placement of the soldiers led to minimum injuries." He paused. "Why is he here?"

"He has a request."

Jason's eyebrows bent. "Seems presumptuous for a prisoner to request anything from his King, doesn't it?"

"I want to go after them," Barnabas said flatly.

He didn't look up. He hardly moved. His eyes stayed locked on his clasped hands. Cautiously, Jason pulled up a chair opposite of Barnabas and nestled into it.

"You want to pursue the remnants of the Ash that got away?" Jason echoed.

Barnabas nodded.

"By yourself?"

"He would need a battalion of soldiers to accompany him," Master Ferribolt added.

"Regardless," Jason said. "All we know is that they're probably going back to the Western Woods. We don't know where their next target is. It would essentially be a wild goose chase. Do you have any sort of tracking skills? Hunting skills? Do you know how you'd survive in the woods while you pursued their trail?"

Barnabas nodded. "I know enough."

Jason rested his chin on his thumbs, thinking. Then, after a prolonged silence, he said, "Barnabas, if you can find a battalion of soldiers that's willing to follow you into the Western Woods by sunup, you have my permission. This doesn't change the fact that you'll be guarded constantly, but you'll be in command of as large of a squad as you can muster. Is that sufficient?"

Finally, Barnabas looked in his eyes. He said, "Yes, Your Highness."

"Good. Now leave."

Barnabas stood from the table, gave a nod, and slipped out of the room, guarded by his usual soldiers. As the door shut, Jason waited to hear the distant clomps of footsteps before he spoke up again.

"He won't find anyone."

"I wouldn't be so sure of that, Your Highness," Master Ferribolt cocked an eyebrow. "He earned the trust of many residents today, particularly those who fought at the South Gate. You may be surprised."

"I doubt it. But time will tell."

"Indeed. Until then," Master Ferribolt leaned forward. "What do *you* plan to do?"

Jason laced his hands together as he leaned forward, his eyes fixed on the grains in the wood. "I don't know. I have no idea where the Ash intend to go next. All we know is that we saw them retreat into the Woods. They'll probably kill more animals to add to their forces. From there… I don't know. I just don't know."

"If I may, Your Majesty?"

Jason nodded.

"Did you not pray to the Sacred Dragon through the conduit of the Oracle Stone in your most recent time of need?"

"Yes."

"It seems as though Nezmyth may be in its most desperate strait yet. For this, I feel like it would be wise to supplicate the Sacred Dragon in the most direct manner available." Master Ferribolt took a breath. "This is an uncommon and unorthodox solution, but I believe as Nezmyth's spiritual steward that this may be appropriate in times such as this. I would submit that you bring the Oracle Stone to Grace Mountain to supplicate the Dragon for direction."

Jason sat up straight. Of course! Grace Mountain was the place where the Sacred Dragon first laid its holy claws to build the world of Wevlia—the most sacred place in the kingdom. Why hadn't he thought of that before? It just might work.

"Has anyone done that in the past?" Jason asked.

Master Ferribolt nodded. "Yes, but not many times. That sort of thing requires the Chief Patriarch's approval—which you have. And it must only be done in a time of dire need. After all, the Oracle Stone is only supposed to leave the castle walls during an Ordination Ceremony. But in centuries past, the results have been… marvelous."

Jason and Saryan traded looks. Jason folded his arms.

"Master Ferribolt, this army is nearly unstoppable," he said. "I think we could definitely use some marvelous results at a time like this."

* * * * *

Jason and the others packed their things and prepared for the hasty trek down to Nezmyth City before dawn even rose over the Eastern Mountains. Most of the Port Gala residents were fast asleep in their homes after a long night of revelry. Some sweet souls had even passed out in the street after wandering in a victorious, drunken haze. Tarren wanted to take a writing stick to doodle mustaches and glasses on their faces, but Jason persuaded him otherwise.

The soldiers loaded everyone's belongings onto a caravan. Everyone was planning on going straight back to Nezmyth City —at least, almost everyone.

To Jason's astonishment, Barnabas managed to find over twenty strong and able-bodied volunteers. Not only that, but they were familiar with the woods, skilled at wilderness survival, and eager to follow his lead. What wasn't surprising is that nearly all of them fought beside him at the South Gate. They were refreshed, alert, and willing to fight.

And they weren't the only ones that were willing to follow Barnabas's lead. Kalyk and Chief Patu were also among the ranks.

"You too?" Jason's eyes were wide.

Kalyk nodded. "It's not that I doubt Barnabas's leadership, especially after yesterday, but Chief Patu and I know the woods better than anyone here—likely in Nezmyth. He'll need us. I can send messages to you through Justice, just as I did before. We have to know where the Ash are heading. And with every passing hour, they get farther and farther away."

"We'll be fine, Yer Majesty," Chief Patu said as she placed her massive hand on Kalyk's shoulder. "We're people of th' woods. We'll survive."

Jason frowned, but knew they were right. "Fine. But be careful. I still don't trust him," he muttered. "If things get too hairy, make for Nezmyth City immediately."

Kalyk and Chief Patu both said things to the effect of "Yes, Your Highness," then joined the other soldiers.

Jason couldn't help but mull over the peculiarity of it all. Barnabas actually did it. He found followers. It was so easy to imagine him booed and spat on before being cast out of every tavern in town. But no. Two dozen people were willing to follow him—to put their lives in his hands. Jason didn't know what Barnabas looked like before he became evil and took the throne, but this must be close.

"Your Highness?"

Jason turned around. A soldier stood before him with a small wooden chest in her arms.

"What's this?" Jason asked.

The soldier extended the chest forward. Jason reached out and lifted the lid.

Inside, there was an assortment of trinkets and gifts: flowers in an array of dazzling colors, fresh bread, carved wooden ornaments, and a host of other things. The only problem was that they were all broken. Petals were torn from flowers, the trinkets smashed, the bread crumbling… everything in disarray.

"What were these for?" Jason asked, frowning.

The soldier nodded toward Barnabas. "For him. Throughout the night, townspeople came by his room to give these to him. He was out recruiting soldiers, so we collected them and gave them to him when he came back. When he opened the box, he destroyed everything. While people were watching."

Jason's cheeks burned. "Is that all?"

"Yes, sir."

"Thank you. I'll take those."

Jason reached out and took the chest from the soldier. The soldier nodded to her King, then marched away. Jason lifted the lid to look once again upon the destroyed treasures. Anger bubbled inside him. He snapped the lid shut and turned toward the battalion, which was just about to march out of the city.

"*Barnabas!*"

Everyone turned and looked. When he made eye contact with Barnabas, he beckoned him over. Barnabas, guarded by his typical soldiers, marched over without hesitation. When he saw the wooden chest in Jason's arms, he scowled. Once Barnabas was only a few feet away, Jason let him have it.

"The people of Port Gala gave you some lovely treasures," he said, "You should have been grateful."

Barnabas said nothing.

"I'm making sure that we take the remnants of them back to Nezmyth City," Jason continued. "The next time your former subjects bestow gifts upon you, I expect you to accept them more gracefully. *Do you understand?*"

At this, Barnabas's eyes got harder, but he still said nothing. Jason let that order hang in the air before he slowly turned on his heels and made his way to the carriage. He didn't get far.

"Jason."

Jason stopped in his tracks and flipped about, nearly making his cape snap. Around him, Barnabas's guards glared at him, surprised at the audacity to address the King by his given name.

As soon as Barnabas realized he had Jason's attention, he asked, "When is it acceptable to reward a monster?"

Jason advanced on him until their noses were just inches away. It didn't matter that Barnabas was several inches taller than him. The heat radiated from Jason's face.

"One," Jason stuck a finger in the air. "You will refer to me as *Your Highness, Your Majesty,* or *Sir.* My name is for those close to me, which doesn't include you. Secondly, I believe that those monsters should be grateful for whatever kindness they receive, especially from a kingdom they nearly destroyed. I can throw you back in your cage like *that.*" He snapped his fingers. "But I won't. Now go and end this war."

With his square jaw clenched, Barnabas nodded curtly. "Yes, Your Majesty."

Barnabas retreated to the head of his battalion, and in a matter of minutes, they were galloping out of the city toward the Western Woods. They blasted through the gates, past the smoldering piles of burnt Ash bodies that trickled thick gray smoke into the morning sky. Jason breathed in deeply. As he watched Barnabas and his battalion ride out of the city, he prayed that he wasn't making another mistake.

23

THE SUPPLICATION

The trip back to Nezmyth City felt longer than just two days. They stopped to set up brief camps for breakfast and dinner on the first day. Their meals weren't lavish, but they were filling enough. As they packed their things and continued venturing south, Jason stole frequent glances at the Western Woods in the distance. Had Barnabas, Kalyk, and Chief Patu found the Ash army again? If so, where were they going?

Nadiel spent both days either resting or in meditation, hardly speaking a word. He carried himself more like an old man after the battle of Port Gala, moving slowly, his eyes drooping. Meanwhile, Tarren kept himself deep in his books. He seemed to have picked up enough of Ancient Nezmythian to read old spell books with minimal frustration. Even when they stopped to eat, Tarren scarcely stopped reading. When Jason would try to speak to him, his responses were short and lagging.

The second day was more of the same. They ate breakfast and lunch and made it back to Nezmyth City before nightfall. Jason had never felt so thankful to see the city gates, but he wondered how well they would fare if the Ash descended upon them. A legion of stone masons was fortifying it the best that they could, but it looked like the progress was slow going. Would it be enough?

The townspeople applauded and cheered when they saw the King's carriage return. The caravan snaked through the streets of Nezmyth City until they turned onto the Northern Market Street, heading northward for the castle. By this time, darkness was falling, and the night lighters were out to ignite the street lanterns of Upper City.

The caravan pulled into the castle grounds. The greenery swayed in the summer breeze, bidding a well return to the royal residents. The fountain of the Knight spewed water from its lips, filling the nearby air with the soft trickling noise. The company piled out of their respective carriages as soldiers began unloading supplies.

Nadiel and Master Ferribolt approached Jason from behind. Nadiel's blue cape billowed as his hand rested on the hilt of his sword. Master Ferribolt's orange robes shimmered slightly in the moonlight. Jason turned to face them both.

"Would you like to wait until morning to visit Grace Mountain?" Nadiel asked.

"No," Jason replied.

"Good. We shall take my carriage."

Master Ferribolt straightened his glasses. "I'll retrieve the Oracle Stone."

He was only gone a matter of minutes. When he emerged from the castle, he carried the Oracle Stone in both hands, wrapped in a thick, brown, cotton blanket. Even through the blanket, it was clear that the hue of the Stone was a shimmering white—a symbol that the one handling it had a pure soul.

The venture to Grace Mountain felt like ages. It was at the farthest edge of Eastern City, past the farmland that supplied the city with most of its food. The smells of livestock, corn, and wheat filled the clean summer air as the carriage jittered through the street. As they made their way through the district, children scampered out of their homes and dashed into the street, wanting nothing more than to touch the edge of a royal carriage. After all, it wasn't often that royalty passed through the farmland. Master Ferribolt leaned out to shake hands and smile, and he received smiles in return.

Ahead of them, Grace Mountain loomed sacred and quiet against the night sky. Jason couldn't think of how slow the carriage was moving. In contrast, where were the Ash? What was their next target? Were Barnabas and the others catching up to them? That was assuming that they were still alive.

Near the foot of Grace Mountain, a gated expanse of land stood to the left with grass that swayed in the summer breeze —Nezmyth City Cemetery. Tall iron bars guarded the perimeter of the grounds, but no soldiers patrolled them.

Jason remembered coming here during his Year of Decision, during a day when he was particularly discouraged. While he was there, he had ventured to the Court of Kings— the section where all Nezmythian Kings were buried. He sighed.

"At times like this I wish I could ask them for their wisdom," Jason said.

Master Ferribolt smiled. "That's precisely what we'll do."

At the very base of the mountain, the carriage lurched to a halt and the three of them piled out to make the rest of the way on foot. It was a steep climb, but Nadiel and Jason handled it in stride. Master Ferribolt was the only one huffing and puffing as time went on. They stopped to break twice for his sake. Jason offered to take the Oracle Stone off his hands, but Master Ferribolt refused.

At length, they arrived at the plateau of Grace Mountain— a flat courtyard of creamy white stone that overlooked Capitol Valley. From here, the three of them could see the whole city: the three market streets that form a giant triangle, Center Court in the middle, Upper City, the castle, and the outer walls.

The centerpiece of the Grace Mountain courtyard was a large, beautiful statue of the Sacred Dragon. It twisted Its strong, scaly body into undulating waves, and Its powerful claws clutched the edges of a square base. It snarled an inanimate breath, Its mouth wide open and Its wise, eternal eyes focused on the three of them as they approached.

Master Ferribolt took two steps forward and bowed, the Oracle Stone still in his hands. Then he reached out and carefully placed the glowing white orb in the Dragon's mouth. The white clouds inside began to spin and churn peacefully. Jason and Nadiel couldn't help but stare.

Master Ferribolt turned about. "Your Highness, would you like to offer the prayer?"

Jason swallowed and nodded. In unison, he and Nadiel unsheathed their swords, knelt down, and carefully laid them across the ground. Master Ferribolt knelt as well. All of their heads were bowed. Jason took a breath.

"Sacred Dragon," he began. "The kingdom is in dire need. We face an insurmountable enemy that wreaks a mighty wave of darkness and death. How can we defeat it? How can we defeat Nartikis and the Ash? Please, Sacred Dragon. Guide us."

They kept their heads down and stayed silent, waiting for an answer. It didn't take long.

"It's more complicated than you may think."

Jason's head popped up. He knew that voice—his mentor from beyond. Sure enough, the spirit of King Thomas stood next to the Dragon statue on its right side, smiling upon the party that knelt before him. The expressions that flew across Nadiel and Master Ferribolt's faces were similar—surprise, awe, then joy.

"Nadiel, Master Ferribolt, it's been a long while," King Thomas smiled.

"It indeed has," Nadiel said absently, his eyes wide.

"I wish the circumstances were better," King Thomas's smile quickly faded. "Master Ferribolt, you made the right decision. Bringing the Oracle Stone here to receive revelation was wise. I applaud you for your initiative." He looked to Nadiel. "Nadiel, your expertise of magical arts in battle and your patience with Tarren, son of Gulaf the stone mason, have been exceptional as you've prepared him to take on your mantle. Your obedience and sacrifice to your kingdom has been exemplary.

"And Jason," King Thomas locked eyes with him. "You responded to the Dragon's council, and not a moment too late. You're right, Barnabas will play a major role in winning this war, but he is just one piece of the puzzle."

Jason took a deep breath and let his gaze fall to the ground. The verbal confirmation—he had made the right choice. His feelings were true. Setting Barnabas free was the correct thing... but that didn't mean he had to enjoy it.

"Little is still understood of the Ash, correct?" King Thomas clasped his hands behind his back and took a step forward.

"Yes, sir," Jason said.

"Luckily for you, those of us who have passed through mortality get a panoramic view of Wevlia. We see the grass, the soil, the trees, the stone... how everything comes together to create a perfect whole. This means we even have an understanding of the intricacies of magic and how the Holy Dragon constructed it. That being said, we also understand how the Guardian of the Night counterfeited that magic for its own evil purposes.

"I want to remind each of you that *Tepnoh Edomah* is the single most nefarious entity the Guardian of the Night has ever created. It can devastate people and civilizations, but like everything the Guardian of the Night constructs, it is not absolute in its power."

Master Ferribolt and Nadiel leaned forward intently.

"Have you ever noticed the oneness in the way the Ash move?" King Thomas continued. "The way they carry out orders without a single word?"

"Indeed, sir," Nadiel said. Master Ferribolt nodded.

"This is because they all stem from the same source—King Nartikis himself."

"That makes sense," Jason replied. "He's the one that created them."

"Of course. They're all connected to the one soul that practiced *Tepnoh Edomah* to birth them," King Thomas said. "And since he is that person, when the Ash continue to kill and slaughter, it fills that dark reservoir in *his* soul even more, giving him more fuel to practice *Tepnoh Edomah*. With that fuel, more soldiers are made. Thus, we see the cycle. The Ash an entire kingdom away know this—they can *feel* it. Their life source is derived from the darkness in his spirit. As long as they can keep killing, they can keep growing."

"So we can slay all the Ash that we wish, but inevitably," Nadiel pondered. "As long as a single Ash survives to kill again, they can reproduce and spread."

"Precisely. Are you willing to hunt down every single Ash in Nezmyth for the rest of your days, just to be sure they'll never rise again?"

At this, the three of them were silent.

"It seems as though the force Nartikis created is nearly unstoppable," Nadiel said gravely.

"*Nearly* is correct."

"Wait," Jason interjected. "You said that all the Ash are connected to Nartikis directly. So if we… killed him… would that destroy all the Ash in turn? Since they live off his life force?"

King Thomas shook his head. "No."

"They would still *exist*?" Jason cried.

"Listen more closely, Your Highness," King Thomas said seriously. "The practice of the *Tepnoh Edomah* is the tainting of the *soul*. When you've killed a man, all you've done is rip his soul from his mortal vessel. The soul carries on! Spirits still live and thrive, obviously." He motioned to himself. "Additionally, when the soul is ripped from its mortal vessel, the state of the soul remains static—eternally evil or eternally good. If the Ash have a life source that is eternally evil, cast from its mortal body to dwell forever as a spirit, they've essentially acquired a life source that is never-ending. They could reproduce indefinitely."

Jason's blood ran cold. If Nartikis died in his current evil state, the Ash could reproduce forever. The thought made a shiver slide down his body. He couldn't help but grind his teeth behind his lips. What could possibly be done?

"You said the Ash are *nearly* unstoppable, correct?" Master Ferribolt echoed.

"Correct. Not entirely."

The three listeners perked up.

"As long as the darkness in Nartikis's soul survives, so do the Ash. If you can destroy or remove that darkness within his soul, the Ash would be obliterated. Gone. In one fell swoop."

Jason stroked his chin. *So in order to really destroy the Ash, we have to tear all the darkness from Nartikis's soul?*

"How would we even begin to accomplish a task as intricate as ripping the darkness from someone's very soul?" Nadiel said with narrowed eyes.

King Thomas almost smiled. "A Purge Ordinance."

Both Nadiel and Master Ferribolt met that response with wide eyes. They traded bewildered stares. Meanwhile, Jason couldn't help but ask, "An Ordinance? Is that some kind of advanced spell?"

"That's putting it lightly," Master Ferribolt breathed.

"Jason, you're considerable enough in your spellcasting," Nadiel said to the King. "But performing an Ordinance is far more complex and requires much more preparation— sometimes weeks, specific supplies, and multiple people."

"And this one is no different," King Thomas replied.

At this, Nadiel stood up straighter than he had before. Jason couldn't help but think that something had bubbled to this moment for him, almost as if he had been prepared for this. He would have smiled if he weren't hanging on King Thomas's next words.

"There are several components to accurately conduct a Purge Ordinance," King Thomas said, pacing back and forth in front of the Dragon sculpture. "First and foremost, the ceremony must be carried out by three Foreordained servants of the Dragon."

"So, it could be a King, Advisor, Patriarch, Chief Patriarch, a Blessing Scribe, or a Blessing Bearer?" Jason counted the positions on his fingers.

"It would be best if it were the King, the Advisor, and the Chief Patriarch," King Thomas said. "This Ordinance is one of the most powerful of all Ordinances, so it's fitting that the three individuals carrying it out are those Foreordained to the highest positions in the kingdom. However," King Thomas looked hard at Master Ferribolt, "I'm concerned for you, Master. The final stages of this Ordinance involve facing Nartikis himself, and in your advanced in years, I don't know if you would be the best candidate."

Master Ferribolt bowed his head. "I understand."

Jason narrowed his eyes irritably. "Who could possibly replace Master Ferribolt? He's a powerful magician and the purest person we all know—"

"Your Highness, restrain yourself," Master Ferribolt implored gently.

"No one is doubting his purity, Your Majesty," King Thomas said. "But the Ordinance is physically taxing for everyone, and you'll have to face Nartikis to perform it properly. Though we all know Master Ferribolt is a skilled magician, he isn't skilled in combat magic. We must find an alternative." He turned to Nadiel. "How is the boy?"

Nadiel perked up. "He hasn't succeeded me yet."

"Doesn't matter. He's still Foreordained as Advisor."

Jason considered the possibility of Tarren performing this Ordinance with them. The news would absolutely shock him. But he was the next best option.

Nadiel said, "He… is a very capable warrior. Learning intently about the magical arts, ever since he heard that he may be able to cure his mother."

"And his skills have been growing since his Year of Decision commenced?"

"Greatly."

"Then it appears as though the timing of his Year of Decision is impeccable," King Thomas said. "Master Ferribolt, I must commend you once again for your reception to the Dragon's wishes. Your spiritual attunement might have just saved the kingdom."

Master Ferribolt smiled gratefully, then clasped his hands together and bowed his head. King Thomas continued, "Next, the three Foreordained servants must consciously and actively work on the purifying of their own souls. Each of you will rotate meeting nightly on the top of this mountain to be mentored by a spirit from your past. None of you are to share your experiences with each other on this mountain until the Purge Ordinance is successfully completed."

"Are you going to be my spirit mentor, King Thomas?" Jason said.

"You won't know who your spirit mentor is until you arrive," King Thomas said. "And even after you meet your spirit mentor, keep that information to yourself. It's sacred."

When he said those words, though, his eyes twinkled a little bit. Jason smiled.

"In the meantime," King Thomas continued, "we'll need to collect three ingredients for a special potion. This potion must be drunk by all three Foreordained servants at sunrise on the morning of the Purge Ordinance. The ingredients are blessed healing water, a springlight flower, and a dragon scale."

"*A dragon scale?*" Jason echoed. "Dragons have been extinct from Wevlia for thousands of years! The blessed healing water is easy—any Patriarch can bless a container of water to give it healing properties. The springlight flower is a little bit more difficult since it only grows in small patches in the Eastern Mountains… but a *dragon scale?*"

Nadiel scratched his chin. "It will be difficult locating one. Even the merchants of rare goods across Wevlia have difficulty unearthing such treasures. We're fortunate, however. Nezmyth was one of the last kingdoms to have free roaming dragons before they were all slain preceding the Dark Era. There must be someone who is willing to part with one."

"Probably for a massive sum," Jason said darkly.

"As King, you must have a large reserve of Bars and Blocks, do you not?" Master Ferribolt inquired.

Jason shrugged. "I gave a lot of my wealth away when I became King so the kingdom could recover. Since then, I've tithed farmers, seamstresses, and other artisans to our needs. I never thought to reinstate any kind of tax."

Nadiel sighed.

"Once you have all three ingredients," King Thomas continued. "Mix them together and wait three days for the potion to cure. On the morning of the Purge Ordinance, come together to pray for the cleansing of Nartikis's soul, then consume the potion. You'll have until sundown to perform the Ordinance."

"So we must be absolutely certain Nartikis will be in a position to be Purged the morning we take the potion," Nadiel said with furrowed eyebrows. "He must be in person, among us?"

"Yes. It is the only way."

"And when we finally face him?" Jason asked. "What do we do then?"

King Thomas's eyes flashed. "That is what you'll discover in your coming lessons. Each Foreordained servant will play a different role, but each one is incredibly important. You will not discuss it with each other, but if you act with exactness the day of the Ordinance, Nartikis will be Purged of his darkness, and the Ash will be destroyed."

Jason stared at his boots and his sword that lay flat before them. As he stood there, processing everything that was just said, one missed detail jumped out in his mind.

"King Thomas," he began slowly. "If I'm supposed to be here at Grace Mountain every third day for my lessons, who will lead Nezmyth's army in battle?"

King Thomas smirked a knowing smirk. "You feel the need to ask?"

Puzzled, Jason's eyes hopped to Master Ferribolt and Nadiel, back and forth. After an uncomfortable silence, it finally came to him. The realization hit him like a lightning bolt to the brain. Immediately, his face got hot and his jaw clenched. He looked directly at King Thomas. Normally, he would hesitate to share his dissenting thoughts with his spiritual mentor, but this time, he couldn't help himself.

"No," Jason said with finality.

King Thomas's eyes narrowed. He replied with a tone that was calculated and controlled, but still fuming. "Jason—"

"Setting him free was bad enough!" Jason protested. "But having him lead our *entire army*? No. I won't allow it. He's killed thousands, including you! Think of how the people of Nezmyth would respond to that. He's still a criminal and he's not fit for—"

"And *you're* the one to make that judgment?" King Thomas was shouting now. Nadiel and Master Ferribolt shriveled a few steps away. "Jason, let's talk about *your* judgment as of late, shall we?

"You betrayed the warning feelings of your heart and ventured to Unbuntye's capital, resulting in the death of your father-in-law. You suppressed the impressions to free Barnabas earlier, resulting in the destruction of Treetown and Pinegrove, which added immensely to the Ash's forces. You've ignored Master Ferribolt and Nadiel time and time again, instead trusting your own wisdom. Well, look where *your* wisdom has gotten you! And yet you *still* have the audacity to defy the Sacred Dragon's orders when the shadow of destruction stretches over you! It's time to wake up and see your quiet arrogance for what it is!"

It was like a wall fell over Jason. The words assailed him like holy verbal arrows. He knew it, and he knew everyone there knew it. In that moment, he stepped outside himself and looked inward. It was easy to take a broken kingdom and watch it mend itself with the right push. But he had taken too much of that credit upon himself, and he had ignored those that had supported him along the way.

He couldn't help it. A lump grew in his throat and his eyes stung. He hung his head and stared at his boots again, not wanting King Thomas to see his face. The tears pushed through, and Jason fought hard to keep them back.

As he stared at his boots, he saw another pair of boots come up and stand across from his. Out of his peripheral vision, Jason saw King Thomas place his hand on his shoulder. He couldn't feel it, but he knew it was there. King Thomas bent down to look him in the eye. The tone of his voice was soft and calm now.

"All that being said," King Thomas said. "You *have* been the King Nezmyth needs. Unlike Barnabas years before, you really do love this people. The Holy Dragon has seen it. If you learn to let go and trust the wisdom of those around you, you'll be astounded at what can be done."

"Jason."

It was Nadiel. Jason sniffled, still not looking up. Nadiel marched up to Jason, then knelt on one knee.

"Despite of our numerous disagreements," Nadiel said. "I consider it an honor to serve Nezmyth alongside you. The Holy Dragon chose you well."

"That, it did," Master Ferribolt smiled.

Jason still didn't reply. He didn't particularly feel like a great choice at this moment. His chest was in a knot, and the lump in his throat was still there. Without a word, he wiped his eyes with the back of his hand. Nadiel stood and King Thomas stepped away.

"Gentlemen, this is all you need to know for tonight," King Thomas said. "Take up your swords. Leave this Mountain and remember the things that have been said. Nezmyth can win. Continue to search and listen for the instructions of the Sacred Dragon.

"Jason, you will be the first to be taught. Come here tomorrow night at sundown and your teacher will be waiting for you. Don't worry about wearing your armor or cape—dress as the commoner you once were.

"Farewell, my friends. May the Dragon bless you all."

With that, the personage of King Thomas faded.

24

THE WHISPER

Night had fully fallen upon the Western Woods, and a vast clearing teemed with a deathly chill despite the enormous bonfire that blazed in the center of it. Nearly a hundred dark figures moved quickly and feverishly around the flare as they threw a host of different animals into the heat, including wolves, foxes, and bears. The dark figures muttered to each other as they went. They didn't slow down. They didn't grow tired.

At the edge of a clearing, nestled on a tree branch dozens of feet in the air, Kalyk watched the proceedings intensely. Justice was perched on her shoulder. She sighed.

"I could have sworn this is where Pinegrove once was, Justice," she said. "Have they already torn it all down? Can they work that quickly?"

Justice clicked her beak. Kalyk sighed again. She closed her eyes and tried to focus magic to her ears. With it, she could hear the mutters of the Ash over the fire's blazing crackle nearly one hundred yards away.

"Work faster, you swine!" "Not enough humans..." "Bears are better than humans! They're stronger!" "Shut up, you!"

On the ground, concealed in the thick of the trees, over two dozen Nezmythian soldiers hunched to the ground, listening intently. They all slow burned a common stealth spell to muffle their footsteps and whispers. They could all slow burn that spell in bursts, not getting too tired if they burned and rested at ten-minute intervals. The Ash were so close, but they knew the mismatch was four to one. Revealing themselves would be suicide.

"Can ye 'ear any of 'em?" Chief Patu muttered, her towering frame hidden as she crouched behind a boulder.

A few feet to her left, Barnabas lay low to the ground. "No."

"Kalyk will 'ear somethin'," she said. She turned to him. "Why did yeh want t' pursue these things?"

Barnabas thought about it for a moment, then said, "They're my doing. It's my duty to destroy them."

"An' redeem yerself?"

Barnabas scoffed. "I'm far beyond the grasp of redemption."

"Then why are yeh really 'ere?"

Barnabas didn't know how to answer the question, so he didn't. His icy eyes stayed focused on the Ash congregating in the center of the clearing. He scanned his surroundings, taking in the trees, the brush, any signs of wildlife. They were outnumbered, but Nezmyth had conquered in battles similarly in the past. There had to be a way.

"Wha' is it?" Chief Patu could see the gears turning in Barnabas's mind.

Whump!

Kalyk suddenly leaped down and landed between the two of them. As soon as her feet touched ground, she shot her hand into her boot and procured a small piece of parchment. In her other boot, a writing stick.

"What did you hear?" Barnabas shot.

"There's no mistaking it," Kalyk said, frantically scribbling across the parchment. "They plan to attack Port Gala again. They'll build up their forces in the woods for as long as it takes, then launch a second assault on the city. Could take several days."

"We can't wait that long. We must destroy them *now*."

Chief Patu and Kalyk both looked at Barnabas. Chief Patu frowned. "What? 'Ow? There's four of 'em for every one o' us and they're stronger, faster—"

"We just need to keep them moving," Barnabas said. "When we allow them to nestle and stay in one place for long enough, they build a fire and make more. If we remain in the shadows and attack from the dark, they'll never get a sense of security. They'll move to a safer location, and we follow them. Then we can whittle them down over time until they're all destroyed."

Kalyk finished up the note and tied it to Justice's talon. "Sounds exhausting."

"If it's what saves Nezmyth, so be it," Barnabas said. "For now, I'll have our soldiers surround north half the clearing, climb into the trees, and fire arrows at the Ash. When the Ash escape the barrage, it'll drive them south—away from Port Gala. Then we wait an hour before we track them and attack again."

Chief Patu's eyes were stone, but she nodded, processing everything that Barnabas said. Kalyk finished tying the note around Justice's talon and set the bird free. She flapped her mighty wings and rose quickly into the air, clearing the trees, heading eastward. Kalyk straightened the bow on her back. "It sounds like as good a plan as any. It's better than just following them and letting them build their forces. Let's move."

Kalyk scurried to some other soldiers and passed along the orders. Then those soldiers told other soldiers. The orders rippled out until the whole camp, hidden and shrouded by stealth spells, knew the plan. They fanned out carefully, watching their every footstep. They climbed trees soundlessly, shifting from branch to branch as they ascended higher.

Meanwhile, the Ash continued to work, throwing more creatures into the fire. The smell of burning flesh and hair was pungent and filled the entire clearing. Many of the Nezmythians hiding in nearby trees scrunched their noses and tried to see through watery eyes.

It was only a few minutes, but everyone in the battalion managed to ascend the trees, all except Chief Patu. Due to her size, she stayed on the ground, concealed behind the boulder, weapon in hand.

Kalyk and Barnabas were nearly fifty yards away from each other in the tops of different trees. Satisfied, hearts thumping and ready to act, Kalyk released the signal. She pulled a small mirror from her pocket and tilted it carefully, making sure the moonlight would reflect to the tops of the trees. This light was seen by every soldier in the battalion, and when the twinkling moonlight reflected into their eyes, they knew to fire away.

The first arrow whistled into the camp. It skewered one of the Ash through the ear, toppling it immediately, its body half-consumed by the fire. The other Ash around it jolted horribly, turning about in every which way, their weapons flashing in the moonlight.

"Who's there? Show yourself?"

More whistling arrows followed, puncturing chests, arms, and heads. The Ash grunted and barked as they ran every which way. Their work ceased. It wasn't about throwing bodies on the fire anymore; it was about determining the direction of the assault. But it seemed to be coming from all around—at least every direction except south.

One Ash howled angrily and threw an ax wildly into the darkness. It found its mark in the tree trunk directly above Chief Patu. She gulped and tried not to breathe. A second later, an arrow found its mark between its eyes. The Ash turned about wildly, watching comrades fall around them. After less than a minute of madness, the forces uniformly, resolutely acted. They all turned and fled, heading southward, abandoning the fire and their dead.

The stampede shook the trees around them. Nezmythians clutched the branches in the treetops as the pine needles rustled around them. Sweating, their palms stained with sap, they listened for the receding sound of thundering footsteps growing quieter as they traveled south. After a few more minutes, the Nezmythians climbed down from the trees, landing on the cold soil beneath them.

The heat of the bonfire could be felt again. It was no longer shrouded by the dark chill of the Ash.

Barnabas and the rest of the battalion cautiously ventured into the clearing, melee weapons drawn, their eyes fixed on the remains of nearly twenty Ash carcasses. As they trudged closer, they found that the bodies were indeed dead—none of them sprung up in any kind of surprise attack. They lay with hanging jaws and wide eyes, their bodies punctured with arrows. Archers pulled the arrows from their bodies and stored them back in their quivers.

"It worked," Kalyk said, half-surprised.

"We shouldn' wait too long," Chief Patu said. "Dragon knows 'ow far they'll go 'fore they stop."

"Agreed," Barnabas sheathed his sword. "Search the bodies for whatever supplies we can carry."

"Father..."

The whisper was right next to Barnabas's ear, and it sent a cold chill down his spine. He tore his sword from his sheath and turned, ready to strike, but there was nobody there. Several nearby soldiers bristled and stared at him oddly. The hair on the back of his neck prickled, and Barnabas's eyes darted about the clearing, looking for anything. But the voice was gone. Almost as if it had never happened.

"Barnabas?" Kalyk frowned. "What's wrong?"

Barnabas didn't move. "I don't know." After a pause, he sheathed his sword again. "Let's get to work."

25

THE CAPTAIN

Master Ferribolt retrieved the Oracle Stone from the Dragon's mouth. Nadiel and Jason picked up their swords. But all the way down the mountain, the three of them remained quiet. It was mostly due to Jason. His heart was still racked with King Thomas's stinging rebuke. Every word played back in his mind like a cruel song. And he knew King Thomas was right about all of it. That was the worst part.

The carriage started up and the horses trotted back toward the castle. The stars twinkled overhead, dotting the endless black sky with their specs of light. The warm summer air lingered as if unaware of the danger that lay ahead. As the carriage crawled back to the castle, Jason stared at the Nezmyth City Cemetery.

"King Thomas was right," Jason finally said. "I've been arrogant."

"Others have been far more arrogant," Nadiel said.

"That's no excuse."

"Jason, King Thomas only wants you to become the best King you can be," Master Ferribolt said, leaning forward as he sat across from him. "Don't become discouraged. This represents an opportunity for glorious change."

Jason's eyes began stinging again. "He was right. All those lives that have suffered because of me... Nadiel, you warned me not to go to Unbuntye and I didn't listen. I felt for *ages* that Barnabas should be released, and I ignored it. Because I was so scared what my subjects would think of me. It was all pride." Jason turned to them. "I'm sorry. To each of you."

The rest of the ride was undisturbed. Nezmyth City was sleepy and still as the carriage made its gentle grind through the streets. The smells of livestock and fresh harvest melted away as they passed through the Eastern Market Street. Lanterns threw a soft, flickering orange glow, dimly illuminating their path as they traveled back through Upper City.

Jason spent most of the time either staring out the window or staring at the space between his boots. His eyes were glossy and vacant, and his mind churned with thoughts of guilt and regret. These thoughts plagued him even after they passed through the gates of the castle grounds.

As the carriage lurched through a stop, a weary Master Ferribolt rubbed his eyes and wished the King and Advisor a good night. In only the blink of an eye, he disappeared. Meanwhile, the guards hit the castle doors three times. They groaned open, and Nadiel and Jason marched inside.

The great hall was mostly unchanged. Torches lit the floors and walls since the sun had descended over the western horizon. Next to the throne platform, Saryan and Tarren sat at a small wooden table. They both stood up as Jason and Nadiel entered.

As they advanced up the red carpet, Jason's thoughts shifted to his wife and all that she had gone through recently. Garrit's death. Jason ordering her around. This was on top of all the times he had put her at a distance in favor of his royal duties. No wonder her fuse had been so short lately. He couldn't blame her for all the silence and distance.

"What did you find out?" she asked.

In response, Jason wordlessly wrapped his arms around her. He brought her in, holding her tight. Surprised, she held back for a second, keeping her hands free. She tried not to scrunch her nose.

"I've learned that I've been a fool," Jason said. "Saryan, I'm so sorry. So sorry for everything. I still have so much to learn. I've been awful and inconsiderate."

A knot in Saryan's chest, a knot tight from grief and pain, slackened just a little. She didn't scrunch her nose anymore. She slid her arms around her husband's shoulders and held him in kind. She didn't cry or shudder. She just sank into his arms and stayed there, allowing them to simply be.

They pulled apart, locking eyes. Deflating, Jason said, "He's meant to be the Chief Captain for the time being, Saryan. I'm sorry."

Saryan looked down. "I understand."

"He could never replace Garrit."

"I know."

Jason sighed. "First, I need to send a messenger hawk to the forces in the Western Woods, letting them know about Barnabas and his new position." Then he turned to Nadiel but cocked his head toward Tarren. "Do you want to tell him?"

"The Sacred Dragon has instructed us on how to obliterate the Ash," Nadiel said with confidence. "And you, Tarren, will play a major role."

Tarren's eyes grew wide. "*Me?* How?"

"I'll allow your friend to explain," Nadiel said. "As for me, I am diminished. I still haven't fully recovered from my magic usage at Port Gala. Your Highness, if I—"

"You're excused."

Nadiel bowed. "Goodnight."

"I'll go to bed, too," Saryan said. "You can tell me everything there."

"I'll be there as soon as I send this hawk. I promise."

Saryan half smiled, kissed Jason's cheek, and left the room.

A soldier delivered a writing stick and some parchment to Jason. He sat at the table and began drafting his letter to Barnabas, alerting him and everyone in his company that he was the new Chief Captain. When he was done, he signed the parchment, rolled it up, then stamped it with the royal seal. He handed it to the same soldier that brought him the stationary, and the soldier marched off to attach it to a messenger hawk.

"When do you think he'll get the message?" Tarren asked.

"By morning at the latest," Jason replied. "Hopefully by then, they'll have some news for us as well."

* * * * *

Birds didn't chirp as the sun climbed over the Western Woods. Sunlight shot through the cracks in the trees, casting fractured light across the forest floor. Barnabas and the rest of the soldiers made their way southward, searching carefully for the Ash's trail, but clues were few. The most telling sign was the air. It wasn't chilly, so the Ash couldn't be anywhere nearby.

As they walked, Barnabas stared cautiously on the ground beneath him. At one point, he saw an insect crawl under his boot just as he was about to step on it. He quickly sidestepped to avoid it, and the bug survived.

Behind him, two soldiers muttered to themselves, casting occasional glances at their leader. Barnabas ignored them both, instead focused on his feet and the Ash's trail. This went on for several minutes. Finally, one of the soldiers brought it in himself to approach Barnabas.

"Sir," he cleared his throat. "Forgive me for approaching you so casually, but my friend and I have heard… rumors. About King Jason."

Barnabas didn't look at them but kept trudging through the brush.

The soldier cleared his throat again. "Sir…" the soldier looked back at his friend, who prodded him forward. "Years ago, when he became King, how did he… defeat you? If you don't want to talk about it, I understand. But we've only heard rumors. It almost sounds like the stuff of legend."

Barnabas would never forget that battle. On the day of Jason's Ordination Ceremony, Barnabas nearly killed him in front of everyone at Center Court. But somehow, at the last second, Jason took on some sort of supernal power unlike anything he had ever seen. After an exhausting aerial battle, Jason held Barnabas at the tip of his sword. It was the first time he experienced defeat in decades.

Barnabas said, "The Holy Dragon gave him power."

The soldiers behind him stayed quiet, expecting more, but Barnabas didn't continue. Then, one of the soldiers said, "What kind of power? I heard he flew and shot fire from his eyes!"

"And I heard he roared so loud it shook the earth!" The other said. "Is that true? Any of it?"

Several feet away, Kalyk heard the conversation. "Leave the man be. This isn't relevant to the task at hand." She paused. "I've barely seen a sign of the Ash since they ran off last night."

"Aye," Chief Patu said as she swung her ax into a tree, lodging it. "The trail went cold hours ago."

"Dragon help us if they know we're tracking them," Kalyk muttered.

Barnabas frowned. His eyes continued to scan the woods all about him. He hadn't felt the Ash's chill since they drove them out of the clearing hours ago. Since then, they hadn't seen a hint of wildlife. No bears. No wolves. Nothing to hunt. The men and women in the company picked berries and fruit they found along the way to satiate their hunger, but it wasn't enough.

A flap of great wings came rustling through the trees. Kalyk didn't bother to hold her arm out. From the north, Justice cut through the branches and descended until she clamped her talons on her shoulder, resting comfortably. In her beak, she dangled a dead mouse. Kalyk held up her hand to block it.

"Don't swing that in my face, darling. Now that Port Gala has been warned, it's time to write King Jason."

Oddly, the flapping of wings didn't stop when Justice landed. Everyone looked to the east. Another hawk was descending through the trees, dodging branches as it dove for the ground. Soldiers scattered as the hawk flapped its wing one last time, landing gracefully to the earth. Around its leg, another note was wrapped. It had the royal seal on it.

Kalyk cocked her head. "A hawk from the King?" She stooped down to untie the note, and as she did, Justice and her mouse stooped down as well. The second hawk eyed the dangling mouse hungrily. When Justice noticed, she flew into the branch of a nearby tree to enjoy her meal alone.

The parchment crinkled as Kalyk unraveled it, and as her eyes traveled farther down the paper, her face hardened more and more. When she finished, she stared at Barnabas, dumbstruck.

"What is it?" One soldier asked.

"Yeah, what does it say?" Another shot.

Slowly, Kalyk handed the epistle to Barnabas. He pulled it to his eyes and read aloud:

My friends,

The Sacred Dragon has bestowed upon us great wisdom this evening. It is in full soundness of mind and resolution of soul that I appoint the former King Barnabas to the role of Chief Captain of the Nezmythian Army. From now on, he will have primary jurisdiction over

Nezmyth's armed forces, and he is no longer required to be guarded.

Messenger hawks have been sent to every village across Nezmyth to alert them of this change. The hawk sent to you will now be Barnabas's personal messenger hawk to use for giving orders across the kingdom. His name is Artemis, and his favorite snack is mice.

In the meanwhile, Nadiel and myself will remain in Nezmyth City to receive more sacred instructions on defeating the Ash.

May the Dragon bless us all.

—King Jason

Soldiers immediately started piping up. "You can't be serious!" "He's lying!"

"It's *true*," Kalyk said forcefully, stepping toward the crowd. "The letter had the royal seal. Barnabas is now Chief Captain, which, as I understand it, was the role that you held before you became King. So, Captain Barnabas..." Another pause. "What are your orders?"

Barnabas's head was swimming. Not two weeks ago he was captive in the darkest, loneliest cell in Nezmyth. Now, his former rank was completely restored. He wasn't going to be guarded for the first time in years. Not only that, but he was to *lead* a kingdom during a time of war. His square jaw tightened, and he couldn't help but look around blankly, unsure of what to think or feel. Artemis, his new hawk, ogled up at him with beady eyes and snapped his beak.

"I..." he stammered. "I... need to think for a moment." He straightened his back. "I'll return shortly."

At that, Barnabas turned around and marched away, trudging through the brush and soil. Kalyk and Chief Patu stole glances at each other. Kalyk nodded, then soundlessly leaped into a tree, ascending the branches to watch Barnabas as he skulked away.

Barnabas walked until he was out of sight and sound from the others. He began pacing back and forth. His hands rubbed together. He unsheathed his sword, looked at his reflection in the steel, and sheathed it again. The air pushing and pulling from his lungs was heavy. He swallowed.

"Captain…?" he muttered to himself. "Captain? I haven't been Captain in nearly twenty-five years. I was a prisoner. I still feel like a prisoner."

In his pacing, he pulled his hand back, charged a jeroki, and launched it at a nearby tree. The ball of gray light shot at lackluster speed, then dissipated as it connected with the tree, barely rustling its pine needles. Barnabas growled. He had practiced Dark Magic for so long before he entered isolation that he hardly remembered how to practice the normal way.

He didn't notice the person behind him.

"Captain? Quite a development indeed."

The voice was like ice sliding down his neck. Barnabas drew his blade and turned. The figure that stood before him almost made him drop his sword. It was like looking at a younger version of himself—the blue eyes, the hooked nose, the pale skin. But this young man was easily a foot shorter than him. Regardless, he looked back at Barnabas without a glint of intimidation. The black cape girded about him was ornate, royal even. Barnabas knew who he was.

"Hello, father," Nartikis said.

Barnabas had no words. His eyes stayed wide, staring his son in the face. He tightened the blade in his hand.

"It appears as though you have been presented with a monumental opportunity," Nartikis purred. "Not two weeks ago, you were rotting in prison, cast down from the throne. And now, King Jason in his astounding foolishness saw fit to grant you not only your freedom, but command of the *entire Nezmythian army*. I knew I acquired my cunning from you."

Barnabas still couldn't speak. Words fled from him. Nartikis's eyes were his own.

"Do you not see the opportunity in your circumstance?" Nartikis asked. "To regain the power you once had?"

"Of course I see it," Barnabas hissed.

"Then let me assist you," Nartikis sneered. "Let us take back Nezmyth. Together."

Barnabas didn't answer. After a silent moment, Nartikis bowed benevolently.

"I will give you time to consider it," he said. "But know that I will be watching."

Nartikis vanished in a puff of purple smoke. Not even a breeze whisked through the Western Woods. Barnabas stood for what felt like ages, stunned, suddenly paranoid. At last, he marched back to the group. From up in the trees, Kalyk saw Barnabas talking to himself, but no one else. Her eyebrows creased, then she hopped from branch to branch, reaching the company before Barnabas ever arrived.

26

THE INSTRUCTION

The outcry following Barnabas's release was as expected.

When the Nezmyth City guards announced to Center Court the following morning that Barnabas had been appointed to Chief Captain, a mob of people immediately stormed up to the castle and demanded an explanation from the King. They drew their weapons and banged their fists on the castle doors while the guards refused to let them enter. Jason and Saryan awoke to the sounds of it. By the time they had gotten dressed, Nadiel had already spoken to them. Those were his words, anyway. Jason suspected that his Advisor was much more forceful and frightening than he led on. No one came to the castle about it for the rest of the day, but the castle guards were still much more wary of approaching commoners.

That night, Jason climbed the trail to Grace Mountain by himself, dressed in commoner clothing as King Thomas requested. A warm summer breeze slipped up and over the Mountain. The stars twinkled in the black heavens overhead. Among them, two brilliant moons reflected its light onto Nezmyth. The sleepy Eastern Mountains stood majestic and silent in the far distance, carving dark edges out of the horizon where the stars abruptly stopped.

As he climbed, Jason's mind was awash with King Thomas's words from the previous night. King Thomas didn't confirm that he would be Jason's spiritual teacher for the Purge Ordinance, but he certainly alluded to it. The possibility of facing him again made Jason's climb all the more difficult.

The plateau of Grace Mountain looked just as it did last night. He moved his feet across the smooth white stone until he reached the statue of the Dragon. As he looked into the Dragon's mighty, inanimate face, he bowed his head and closed his eyes. He unsheathed his sword, set it on the ground, then took a large, cleansing breath.

"I'm ready," Jason said.

When he lifted his head and opened his eyes, sure enough, King Thomas was there, standing on the right side of the Dragon, leaning with his arm against it. He half-smiled. There was a hint of worry written across his face.

"I hope you're not too disappointed," King Thomas said.

"I'm not," Jason said. "You told me what I needed to hear. And I'm ready."

King Thomas pursed his lips together and he nodded. There was a twinkle in his eye, like that of a proud parent. "Thank you for your humility, Jason. A lesser man would be very bitter after the treatment I gave you yesterday."

"I never said I wasn't bitter."

Jason was smiling. King Thomas smiled back. Then he said, "Ready to begin, then?"

"Yes."

"Good. Let us sit."

King Thomas stepped in front of the statue and bunched his cape up as he bent down and sat with his legs crossed. Jason followed suit.

"What have you done to acquire the ingredients for the potion?" King Thomas asked.

"We already have the blessed healing water and the springlight flowers," Jason replied. "The water was easy to find, and the springlight flowers were expensive, but a florist on Northern Market Street was willing to donate them. As for the dragon scale..." Jason shook his head. "My guards visited every merchant on every Market Street. Nothing. They'll continue their search tomorrow. We'll likely find one in the hands of a private collector."

"Very good," King Thomas said. "And it appears as though the kingdom has reacted to Barnabas's position in a very expected way."

Jason rubbed his hands on his knees. "Yes. Nadiel had to quell a mob outside the castle today. And I was nervous about my carriage ride here tonight. We encountered some unfriendly faces on the way. My driver is cleaning the rotten fruit off the side of the carriage as we speak."

"I can imagine," King Thomas replied. "But Jason, this is how it was meant to be. You've done what's right."

"I know."

"Is there anything else that's been on your mind? Any concerns?"

It didn't take long for Jason to come to the thought. He asked, "Why wasn't my Knightly power enough to defeat Nartikis when we first met?"

"What do you think?" King Thomas said.

Jason shrugged. "Because I was putting off Barnabas's freedom? But the feelings weren't nearly as strong then."

"That's a part of it," King Thomas said. "But the answer is actually much simpler than that. The truth is that he was able to defeat you because his evil is stronger than your good. Nartikis has dug himself so deeply into a pit of *Tepnoh Edomah* that he's been completely consumed by lust and greed—more so than Barnabas ever was. You saw his kingdom. It's a wasteland. And it's all been because he's prioritized his own gain at the expense of others *that much*."

Jason scratched his head. "I see."

"You, on the other hand," King Thomas continued. "Are a very good person. You love the people of Nezmyth and you want what's best for them. Look, you distributed to the poor the wealth Barnabas accumulated and eradicated the Harvest Tax altogether! No leader in Nezmyth's history has done something like that! There's much good to be said of you, Your Majesty."

"Then why wasn't it enough?"

"Again, it comes back to pride. It's a universal problem. And I don't mean being proud of an accomplishment or someone you love—that's all well and good. Pride is pitting your will against that of the Sacred Dragon. And in your position, there can be no space for that. Your Foreordained position as King is directly intertwined with the will of the Dragon. When you start putting aside the Dragon's counsel and instead try to do things *your* way, it weakens your power."

"Oh," Jason stared at the ground. "So, the fact that I've been relying on my own wisdom for so long instead of seeking council from the Dragon is why I wasn't quite strong enough. That's why I was able to take down those ships in Port Gala but not defeat Nartikis back in Unbuntye."

"Correct."

"So now that I've freed Barnabas, would I be able to defeat him?" Jason asked.

"Perhaps. But remember, you're not trying to kill Nartikis. You're trying to rip the darkness from his soul. That will be much harder. Besides," King Thomas straightened his posture, "yours should be a constant quest for instruction and guidance from the Holy Dragon. Improve your connection. Always listen for instruction, then act on whatever impressions you receive. That will keep your pride at bay."

Jason nodded.

"Now," King Thomas said, "remember when we prompted you to control the weather back in Port Gala?"

Jason almost grinned. "Yes."

"You might need to do that again when you confront Nartikis," King Thomas said. "But before you can confront Nartikis, you need to put him in a position where you can meet face to face. How will you do that?"

Jason scratched his beard and stared at the ground in front of him. "I think it's a bad idea to go to Unbuntye. With Nadiel's help, we could transport ourselves magically across the ravine, but that kind of magic is taxing... we need to bring him here."

"I agree, and your Advisor would agree with you too," King Thomas said. "You have the advantage as long as he's here, Your Highness, and that's because he'll be on the *Dragon's territory*." He smirked. "Your Highness, Nezmyth is the last kingdom in Wevlia that practices the Old Ways. That means the Holy Dragon protects this land in ways that you can't understand. So again, how do you plan on bringing him here?"

Jason thought hard again. What has the war been like thus far? Nartikis has sent the Ash to do his dirty work. They made a beeline for the most influential hold in Nezmyth. Along the way, they ravished two towns with small defenses and built up their forces in the Western Woods. They needed to get the Ash *out* of the Woods. And they need to keep Nezmythians safe. What if...?

"This is a wild thought, but what if we brought everyone in the kingdom to Nezmyth City?" Jason said. "The Ash would be forced to attack one location. And I bet in Nartikis's arrogance, if I challenged him personally, he would arrive among the forces. Because if he kills me, Nezmyth would be ready for the taking." Jason let the thought twirl in his mind. "It might work."

King Thomas's eyebrows popped. "That's bold. Definitely something to consult the Sacred Dragon on—including your Advisor and Chief Captain."

That made Jason think of Barnabas and his battalion pursuing the Ash in the Western Woods. He had gotten an epistle earlier in the day from Kalyk, confirming that they got his message about Barnabas's new role, but they said they had lost the Ash's trail last night. That made Jason shiver. How do you lose the trail of over a hundred soldiers?

"I'll leave that to you," King Thomas said. "Now let's get to work. Stand up and call upon the Sacred Dragon for your Knightly power."

Jason did so. He pushed himself off the ground, took a deep, cleansing breath, then uttered a silent prayer. The Dragon granted him the power. His body burst into flames, the markings sprouted across his arms, and the Blade of Nezmyth appeared at his feet. Jason picked it up, still taking deep breaths, feeling every particle of air move in and out of his body.

"I thought I could only do this when evil was present?" Jason said.

"You're on the most sacred spot in the kingdom, being taught by a divinely appointed tutor," King Thomas said. "So, this is an exception. Now, I want you to bring rain over Nezmyth City. A nice little drizzle—just enough to water the daisies at the castle. I miss those."

In his elevated state, Jason looked the city in the west. His sword disappeared in a puff of smoke, and he lifted his arms in front of him, feeling the air move between his fingers. With his heightened senses, he could feel the moisture in the sky, the wisps of clouds as they drifted overhead. As he took it all in, he could feel their energy coursing in and out of his body, like ocean waves lapping on a sandy shore.

In his mind, he beckoned for the moisture in the sky to bunch into great clouds. What surprised him was that he could feel them—tiny flecks of air and water hanging high above him. When he got their attention, they dutifully shifted about, coagulating in large groups.

The move was gradual at first. The wisps expanded and thickened, forming great puffs that hung directly over the city. When Jason felt them bunched into large enough groups, he gently squeezed his hands as if wringing out a soaked rag. All was quiet, but as the seconds went by, Nezmyth lit up with the dull trickle of rainfall. Small streams of water carved through the gaps in the cobblestone. People scurried out of the street and found shelter in nearby shops. Rooftops pattered and the daisies back at the castle happily drank in the downfall.

King Thomas observed Jason's handiwork satisfactorily. "Very good. What did it feel like?"

"It felt almost like… a negotiation," Jason said wondrously, his body still glowing from his Knightly power. "As the clouds bunched together, it was almost like I was speaking with them. In my head. Asking them to bring rain."

"Indeed," King Thomas. "Your Highness, this is a kind of magic that Dark Magic or standard magic can never touch. This is a nameless magic that's only attainable under divine circumstances. You can practice it when you're a Knight of the Holy Order, but remember, the elements won't always bend to your will. They usually will, because they see you as a specially endowed servant, but not always. You can't just bring down rain, lightning, or hail willy-nilly. There must be a reason for it."

"What's the reason for this?" Jason motioned to the city.

"Education," King Thomas said. "And the next time you do it, it will be for the sake of defending Nezmyth. I'm sure the elements will be in favor of that." King Thomas clapped his hands together. "Well, I believe that concludes our lesson for this evening."

"Wait, that's it?" Jason protested.

Suddenly, his Knightly power vanished. The lesson was over, and his body returned to normal. King Thomas clasped his hands behind his back. "You've covered a lot of ground today, Your Highness. You're already searching for the ingredients for the Purge potion, you have an idea to run by your Advisor and Captain, and you've learned how to influence the weather." King Thomas paused. "Was there something else you were expecting?"

Jason scratched the back of his neck. "Well, yeah. What am I supposed to do during the Purge Ordinance?"

"That will be revealed in your next lesson," King Thomas said. "After we've had the chance to meet with Nadiel and Tarren. I'll be going now, Your Highness. I'll see you in three days."

He vanished, leaving Jason alone on the mountaintop. He breathed in deep, drinking in the clean air. The rain was letting up over Nezmyth City. The clouds parted and dissipated again, revealing the starry black sky that hung overhead. The moonlight rebounded off his blade and into his eyes. He sheathed it, then made his way down the mountain.

As he did, he thought of what might be happening in the Western Woods.

27

THE SONS

"Very good," Nadiel said. "Remember to breathe deeply and picture my face with the utmost detail."

Tarren strained as sweat gathered on his forehead. Inwardly, he was grateful he had drunk a magic elixir before his lesson, or this spell would have been impossible. He sat in Nadiel's study, surrounded by bookcases that covered every wall from floor to ceiling. Against the dark of his eyelids, he could see Nadiel's face and hear his voice, even though he was down the hall.

"I can tell you're not straining as much as earlier," Nadiel said. "You're improving. You may release."

Tarren opened his eyes and gasped. He took in deep breaths, his eyes adjusting to the candles lit around him. After a short minute, he heard Nadiel's footsteps approaching. When Nadiel pushed open the door, his red eyes were bright. He was even smiling.

"You picked up that spell remarkably," Nadiel said. "I am very proud of you, Tarren. As you master Ancient Nezmythian, your ability to perform these spells will improve in kind."

I'm very proud of you, Tarren beamed as he repeated the words in his head. "Thank you, sir."

"I do believe we've studied enough for tonight. His Highness will be returning to the castle shortly. You are excused if you wish to go."

The smile slid off Tarren's face. He scratched his knees and didn't move, but his face twisted in thought. "Actually, I've been thinking a lot about Barnabas the last few days. Since our talk about... Dark Magic... and his journey into it." Tarren stood from his chair. "Sir, I feel like if I'm going to be a good Advisor, I need to understand more about how Dark Magic works. It's clear that Barnabas would be the right person to teach me. He's been involved with it." Tarren stammered. "And maybe... if I understand his past, it'll help me put aside my feelings toward him."

Nadiel paced the room as he thought of Tarren's proposal. He folded his arms, nodded, then his face was intense. "Tarren, that may have been the wisest thing I have heard you say."

Tarren half smiled. "When he returns, I'd like to speak to him. And I'd like you to be there."

"Why wait? You can speak to him now."

Tarren's eyebrows creased. "Now? Wait... I communicated to you down the hall with that spell. Barnabas is halfway across the kingdom."

"With my help, you'll be able to reach him," Nadiel reassured. "Unless you'd prefer to try another time? I know this conversation might be difficult for you."

"No," Tarren said abruptly. After a long pause, he said, "I'm as ready as I'll ever be."

Tarren sat back down and closed his eyes. Behind him, Nadiel held his fingers and thumbs in a triangle directly over Tarren's head. Somehow, he could feel Nadiel's magical energy added to his own. It was *so strong*. It stretched from his toes to his fingertips and flowed through him like ocean waves.

He took a deep breath and pictured Barnabas.

As he strained, more things came into view. Trees. Stars. It was dark. Somehow, he was there in the Western Woods. His surroundings were blurry, but he could make out the conifers that spread all around him. Directly before him, Barnabas sat with his back against a tree, sharpening his sword.

Tarren swallowed. "Captain Barnabas, can you hear me? It's Tarren. I'm back at the castle."

Barnabas stiffened like a frightened dog. He brought up his blade and held it close, but when he heard Tarren identify himself, he let his guard down only a fraction. He scowled.

"How do I know it's you?" Barnabas spoke to the air. "And not some trick?"

"I—uh," Tarren stammered.

"I'm here too, Barnabas," Nadiel's voice came, "I'm helping the boy cast this spell. He wishes to speak to you."

"About what?"

Nadiel didn't answer, letting Tarren take the lead. Tarren cleared his throat. "Are you alone?"

Barnabas stole a glance to his right. Everyone else in the camp was several yards away, laying in the dirt and quietly eating up whatever berries they had found.

"Yes," he confirmed.

"I want you to tell me about... *Tepnoh Edomah*. Your story."

A flood of memories washed over Barnabas—most of them unpleasant. He set his sword down, letting the steel rebound silver moonlight onto his face.

"That," he said. "Is a long story. Are you sure?"

"Please."

Barnabas leaned his head against the tree and let his eyes soak in the starlight. He swallowed, nodded, and began.

"I was born into aristocracy. My father was a renowned jewel merchant that made many precious things for the King and Queen. My mother was a beautiful and tender woman, but she left my father when I was still very small, which led to his drinking deep and drinking often. To compensate for his shortcomings and his failed marriage, my father persistently pushed me to be the best—to find something and become dominant in it. It didn't matter what it was: trade, combat… he simply wanted me to be unrivaled. He told me that it that would bring me happiness and security. But I knew the truth: my success would be a badge of honor for him after the scandal of my mother's departure. I grew up knowing his love and approval came with expectations. It was conditional.

"All the while, Thomas and I were the best of friends. I spent every moment with him that I could, because it was in his company that I felt I was worth anything at all." He smirked. "We got into such trouble. He always hatched ideas for tricks we could play on the people in our neighborhood. All of that slowed down when we turned twelve and we received our Blessings of Fate. He was different from that point on. I knew he had been Foreordained to be something, but it was inappropriate to ask. I, however, was not. I could tell this disappointed my father. He labored under some vain hope that receiving a Foreordination would motivate me to work toward something. But alas, I wasn't called."

Barnabas paused and his eyes became vacant. Then he continued, "When I reached my manhood at age fifteen, I still wasn't sure what vocation I wanted to pursue. Most noblemen adopt the vocation of their families, but I had no interest in the jewel trade. Because of that, my father enlisted me in the Nezmythian Army without my knowing. I was shocked. Furious. We argued and screamed at one another that night—even more than the times when he had too much mead in him. But I couldn't change it. The deed was done. The next day, I started living in the barracks as a soldier.

"I lived and worked as a rank one patrolman for one year. Again, never showing any real talent or ability. It was during that time that my father became gravely ill. The Upper City doctors and healers didn't know what was causing it, or why his illness persisted. Every remedy they tried worked for a time, but this only prolonged his deterioration. He lost his ability to walk. His eyes lost their gleam. His bed became his permanent place of decay.

"In his final days, during one of my patrols, I was summoned to his bedside. I walked, alone, to his house in Upper City. One of the servants showed me to his room. As I stood at his door, his friends filed outside, dabbing their eyes and sobbing. I couldn't help but hate them. They didn't know him like I knew him—evidenced by their free-flowing tears and mournful countenances. They patted me on the shoulder and provided words of comfort. When they left, I walked into his quarters and closed the door behind me.

"As I pulled up a chair and sat by his side, he looked at me up and down in my guard's uniform. He didn't reach for my hand. He didn't smile. His eyes, like a ghost's, gazed upon me inside a face that glistened with sweat. His voice was hoarse when he spoke to me.

"'Barnabas,' he said. 'I'm sorry I couldn't help you more. You have the mind of a commoner trapped in the body of a nobleman. Despite all my success, my greatest failure was you.'"

Barnabas paused and pursed his lips. His chest rose and fell.

"He died the next day and was buried in the Nezmyth City Cemetery. If I needed comfort at that time, Thomas was the only one to give it to me. But I needed none. He was gone. I was rid of the crushing weight of his cursed gaze falling upon me. Free of the shouting. Free of the words that cut like knives in my heart. 'Common. Plain. Dull.'

"As I stood over his freshly filled grave, young, alive, and free, an ember burned inside me. I was my own man now. I didn't need his aggressive prodding to become something great. I could do that myself. And I would. Away from his watchful eyes. Away from the refined masquerade that he put on for his little friends. Away from his drunken buffoonery. I could become the *best damn soldier Nezmyth had ever seen*. And I would do it when his eyes would never have the pleasure of seeing it.

That would be the greatest revenge on his impudent attempt at fatherhood.

"From that point on, I stayed late into the evening and awoke early in the morning to run drills and spar. I cradled lantern light as I dove into books on warfare, strategy, leadership, and magic. My leaders began to pay attention. My comrades began to fear and respect me. And I won the admiration of the community as I volunteered more of my time and energy.

"The years went by and I climbed the ranks quickly. Before I was twenty, I was in charge of a garrison that patrolled the Southern and Northern Market Streets. By twenty-two, I was a Captain. And by thirty, I had achieved the illustrious rank of Chief Captain. I had become my own man. Without my father."

Barnabas's face darkened.

"By this time, Thomas had also been Ordained King, and shortly after his Ordination Ceremony, he asked me if I would accept the honor to serve as his Inheritor in the event that he pass before he found a wife. Of course, I was honored to accept. Not only was I overwhelmed to have granted such a rank of trust by my dear friend, but I couldn't help but think of my late father as I took the position. An *Inheritor.*

"But the years passed, and I found myself empty. I had become so consumed with rank and work that little else in my life mattered. I had achieved the highest rank in the Nezmythian Army. I had peaked, and there was nothing left for me. I wanted more. I needed something to show that I could be more."

Barnabas's face got even darker.

"I don't know the precise moment that I learned to use *Tepnoh Edomah.* I didn't begin learning it from a book or tome. I simply remember being alone in my home, wallowing in my emptiness. A rat scurried across the floor, and almost as a reflex, I shot it with a small jeroki. I killed it. I could feel something dark shift inside me, directly attached to what I was feeling. I had an idea to burn a jeroki in the palm of my hand and pour my resentment into it—the resentment that plagued my soul for years."

Barnabas closed his eyes as the memory engulfed him. He exhaled deeply.

"The feeling is difficult to describe. My anger was temporarily assuaged. My heart beat with excitement and soft waves of pleasure. The jeroki in my hand—purple instead of orange or white—pulsed with *strong* magical energy that made my entire body strong and resilient. I didn't know what that feeling was, but I couldn't hold onto it for long. It was gone before I knew it. What I did know was that I had to experience it again.

"I learned that I had more energy to perform this strange magic after I inflicted death on anything. I began small with insects, rodents, occasionally stray cats or dogs. The larger the creature, the more energy for the magic. I kept cages with mice and rats and killed them whenever I needed a rush. That got me by for years, but the rush was never enough. I began to rely on it to feel anything at all. When I wasn't practicing the magic, the emptiness inside me grew it became all I thought about.

"Thomas noticed the change in me over time. I was insistent that nothing was wrong, and I became more and more irritated every time he addressed it. I lashed out more. I began to lie. And my isolation grew.

"Over time, I became more jealous, envious, and angry. I often saw the decisions that Thomas made as King and thought about what I would do if it were me. That made way for more creeping thoughts: why should he hold a position of such power when he never worked for it? Why should it not belong to someone like myself, who fought and scraped and labored countless hours to achieve my rank? I pushed these thoughts away at first, disgusted at my own pride. After all, I should have been happy for my friend. But they kept coming back… especially after I would practice the strange magic.

"The day I found out what *Tepnoh Edomah* was, I was studying in the Ancient Nezmythian section of the library. I dropped a book, and as I bent down to pick it up, I noticed another book that had fallen behind a shelf. After some prying, I managed to wiggle it free. As soon as I touched it, I could feel there was something different about it. Something dark. But that dark feeling was familiar.

"Curiosity conquered me. I set down the other books and thumbed through this volume. The opening page had warnings —warnings of what this magic would do to me and those around me. That should have been enough for me, but it wasn't. I was Barnabas, Chief Captain of the Nezmythian Army. I was strong. Disciplined. I would be able to bend this magic to my will. I would never let it conquer me."

A long sigh left his lips.

"I tucked that book in my jacket and stowed it away until I got home, then, in my seclusion, I studied it. I learned to practice the tools of *Tepnoh Edomah* with more expertise and precision, and naturally, my practice of it increased. I became constantly angry and bitter. I allowed kingdom improvement initiatives to crumble to ruin. I thought about how I could attain more power, on how I could prove to the ghost of my father that I could become more than he ever was. Time went by, and I hatched the plot for my ultimate display of cunning. I would murder Thomas and seize the Throne of Nezmyth for myself."

Barnabas's jaw clenched and his eyes became misty, but no tears came.

"After the deed was done, I felt more empty than I ever had before. But even after I had the throne, I kept using *Tepnoh Edomah* to fill the void. I was still convinced that I was in control of it—that my occasional use meant I was still disciplined. Twenty years passed. It wasn't until I was succeeded by Jason and cast into the Vault of the Damned that my mind began to clear.

"The blessings and enchantments upon that cell kept me from going mad in my isolation and kept me from practicing *Tepnoh Edomah*. And there were many attempts. For weeks, I tried desperately to practice it in any way that I could, to feel that rush of power and pleasure sift through my soul. But to no avail. As the weeks turned into months and years, I understood that *Tepnoh Edomah* was in control of me. It turned me into a monster. It robbed me of the beauty I once saw in life and cursed me to an existence of constant need. It caused me to murder not just my one true friend, but thousands in the name of power and prestige. And for what? A jail cell in a Dragon-forsaken pit and a heart still racked with emptiness. And that… brings us here."

Silence. As the tale swelled in Tarren's ears, he found himself more and more in awe. Absently, he muttered, "Barnabas…"

That's when a burst of pain suddenly shot through Tarren's mind. Nadiel felt it, too—like a flash of terrible icy wind bursting through the door of their minds. The woods disappeared. Barnabas disappeared. They were back at the castle, surrounded by candles, clamping their heads between their palms, trying to push out the pain.

"*Augh!* What in the…!?" Tarren cried.

Nadiel overcame the pain quicker. He blinked the blurriness from his eyes, then scowled. Something pushed them out.

Back in the Western Woods, Barnabas suddenly heard a new voice. "That *was* quite a story."

No, Barnabas thought. *Not again.*

Barnabas jumped to his feet. Nartikis was standing only a few feet away from him, looking exactly as he did the day before. The pale skin, the dark regalia, the icy eyes. Barnabas felt the hair stand up on his arms and neck.

"Your friends will not need to be here for this," he said. "Have you considered my proposal?"

Barnabas frowned. "Yes."

Nartikis awaited more, but after an impatient moment, asked, "*And?*"

"And I believe you haven't thought it through."

For once, Nartikis's face wasn't flat. His eyebrows bent and his lips pressed. "Is that so?"

"You count yourself cunning, but you have not wisdom," Barnabas's chest puffed as he advanced on the projection of his son. "Did you not learn anything from my life? I *dabbled* in Dark Magic, yet it grabbed hold of me and consumed me until I was a husk of what I once was. You? The Ash are a witness that you've invited it fully into your heart. It's poisoned your mind just as it did mine. You've become drunken with arrogance and a lust for power that will cost you everything you know. If you do not withdraw your forces, King Jason and his Sacred Dragon will strike you down. Just as they did to me."

Nartikis tried desperately to contain himself, but his rage surged. His eye twitched. His lip curled. His pale cheeks burned red.

"I am *far* more powerful than you *ever* were!" Nartikis hissed. "The Ash are a testament to my mastery. And I'm far younger than you were when I took my throne. Jason defeated you? He *fled* from me! His Dragon and kingdom are nothing. Nezmyth will be mine. If you will not stand with me, then you will die along with him!"

"So be it," Barnabas said coolly.

Finally, Nartikis could take no more.

"*You weren't there!*" He bellowed. "I buried her alone! In her absence, I was left to rule Unbuntye as a *child!* And in my mercy, I gave you another chance. We could have ruled Unbuntye *and* Nezmyth as father and son. But no. You are no different from your coward father that cared only for himself."

His tone evened again. "Goodbye then, Captain Barnabas. Die now."

Nartikis vanished in a sheet of purple smoke. And suddenly, the forest was filled with a deathly cold. More puffs of purple smoke sprouted all around. The Nezmythians sprung up, weapons drawn, but by then, the growls and taunts of the Ash were all around them.

They were surrounded.

28

THE AMBUSH

The Ash didn't wait. They didn't stand around and sneer menacingly or harass their prey; they charged through the walls of purple smoke at full speed, weapons raised, red eyes hungry for blood.

It suddenly dawned on Barnabas where the Ash had disappeared to. *Nartikis transported them away and kept them ready for an attack. He knew what we were doing all along.*

Barnabas sprinted to join them. The camp of Nezmythians backed into each other in a large clump, facing outward—just over two dozen of them, scared and shaking.

"Orders, Captain?" Kalyk shouted.

There was no time. There was no more room for strategy or preparation—the two keys to victory. Barnabas was at a loss. The Ash would be upon them in seconds, and there were four of them to every Nezmythian. Nothing could be done. Nothing except—

"*Fight!*" Barnabas cried. "*For Nezmyth!*"

"*For Nezmyth!*" The battalion echoed.

And just like that, the slaughter commenced.

The forest filled with the clang of blades and cracking of bones. The pops of flying jerokis lit up the pines with flashes of light. The Nezmythians fought with all the fire they possessed, but they were still falling. Some of the soldiers cast barriers to separate the Ash from the wounded, but it was futile. There were too many of them. The Ash cackled and roared with delight as they broke bodies and shattered shields.

Kalyk expertly darted between the Ash and cut them down, but her face and arms bled horribly from the blows she took. Barnabas wasn't far away, disarming and gutting Ash with the expertise only a true warrior had. Justice and Artemis dove at the Ash, raking eyeballs and scraping faces as they careened through the air. Barnabas severed heads and slashed limbs that left the Ash useless, but all around him the men and women of his battalion fell to the earth, lifeless.

Several yards away, Chief Patu slammed the heads of two Ash together, crushing their skulls. She watched the scene with horror. Flashbacks of Treetown leaped through her mind. She relived her friends falling all around her. The blood. The screams. And Adria, fallen not a dozen feet away, the glimmer lost from her eyes.

Chief Patu's eyes stung as she tried to keep from falling to her knees.

Too many, she thought. *Too many…*

She roared and swung her ax, burying it in an Ash chest, and narrowly dodged the swing of another. She followed through and severed its arm, then its head. But around her, the other men and women weren't so lucky. Their bodies lay mangled and broken across the forest floor. It was hard to tell who was dead and who was wounded.

How could this happen in my beautiful forest? She despaired. *Will all these die for nothing? How can we possibly defeat—?*

Then the thought occurred to her. It was desperate. Futile. But so was their situation.

"*Lampi!*" She cried. "*Lammmppiii!*"

The onslaught continued without a hiccup, but only for a moment. The pounding of great footsteps came bounding from the north. It shook the pines and the dirt beneath them. Kalyk pulled her sword from an Ash corpse and looked up. So did Barnabas. In that miraculous moment, they saw a figure come barreling through the trees the size of a bear but with the speed of a gazelle. It had no neck or head; its face seemed to be part of its massive body. Its thick, furry arms and legs swung forward, and it stared down the Ash with righteous fury.

Kalyk stared with wide eyes. "By the Dragon..."

SLAM!

Lampi, the Guardian of the Forest, arrived for battle. As it sprinted into the camp, it swung its mighty arms and sent two Ash hurtling into trees with a roar that came from the forest itself. A group of Ash suddenly turned their attention from the Nezmythians and focused on Forest Guardian. They ran up like a swarm of wolves on a bear.

Lampi slammed bodies together. It threw bodies into the air. It stomped and punched and swung and bellowed full-gutted cries that made the earth tremble. The Nezmythians fought tooth and nail, swinging their weapons and howling through their battered and bleeding bodies. Lampi barely faltered from the stabs and cuts it endured at the hands of the Ash, but even the Forest Guardian was wearing down. More cuts and gashes were appeared on its fur.

After several minutes, both sides of the battle were diminished. Nearly all the Nezmythians were dead, and the Ash were losing steam. With Lampi protecting the humans, the Ash suddenly realized they weren't easy prey. Instinctively, the Ash turned their course of action. They holstered their weapons, scooped up the bodies of the dead Nezmythians, and sprinted westward.

"Oh no, you don't!" Kalyk shouted as she sheathed her sword and whipped out her bow.

She fired three arrows. Each of them found their marks in Ash heads and backs. But when one Ash fell, another one picked up the dropped Nezmythian body and kept running. The farther they ran, the harder it was to find a mark through the trees. Finally, Kalyk slung her bow over her back, defeated.

The few remaining Nezmythians were all wounded. Soldiers clutched their cut arms, legs, and heads, using what magic they could to heal their wounds, but many of them had expended their magic casting barriers and throwing jerokis during the fight. When Kalyk put her bow over her back, she grabbed her side. As she looked down, the side of her garbs were soaked with blood.

"Kalyk!" Chief Patu cried.

"I'll be fine," Kalyk grunted as her held her side.

Not far away, Barnabas cut some of his clothing to make a bandage that he hastily tied around his arm. He looked upon his battalion, massacred, now stuck in the middle of the woods.

"How are your healing spells?" he said. "Will they be enough?"

Many of the soldiers looked at each other doubtfully. Kalyk pressed her hand against her wound and started practicing a healing spell, but the wound was far too large. Barnabas frowned as he looked upon her.

I've seen wounds like that before, he thought. *Her magic should slow the bleeding, but if she doesn't get a proper healer soon…*

Suddenly, Lampi's massive, furry body shuddered, and it tumbled to the ground with a mighty *boom.* The forest shivered as everyone looked on, breathless.

Chief Patu was the first one to dart through the brush and reach its side. Lampi held up one of its furry arms, its hand outstretched. Chief Patu cradled her face in Lampi's huge, three-fingered hand. In that moment, their eyes locked. The Forest Guardian's were large, dark, and soft—full of silent wisdom and gentle warmth. But now they were tired. Fading. Chief Patu held Lampi's hand with both of hers, still cradling it against her face, trying to keep the tears from falling. After a long moment, her face melted from hurt to wonder. She nodded.

"I 'nderstand," she said.

She squeezed Lampi's hand one last time and placed it on its chest, which moved up and down with each uneven breath. She looked around, waving her arms, beckoning the surviving soldiers to come closer.

"Gather 'round! Quick!"

Every soldier limped over to Chief Patu and surrounded Lampi's body. Justice and Artemis found their spots on their masters' shoulders. As they all gathered in a circle, Lampi closed its eyes and held out its arms. Chief Patu took one hand while Barnabas took the other, and the rest of the soldiers formed a chain, holding hands until both ends connected in a semi-circle. As soon as they connected, every soldier was surrounded in warm, green sparkles. They felt their feet lift of the ground. Their insides felt calm. The darkness around them suddenly spilled into light.

As the image of Lampi quickly disappeared, Chief Patu tearfully said, "Thank you, ol' friend."

The light was now blinding. No one could see anything, but they kept their hands held tight. The light held steady and bright for several seconds, then it vanished. They felt crunchy soil beneath their feet—not the soft soil of the forest. And they could no longer smell the pines. Lampi had somehow transported the entire company somewhere. The large stone wall ahead made it clear where.

They were outside the gates of Nezmyth City.

29
THE CHALLENGE

The collection of trinkets and knickknacks before Jason was unlike anything he had ever seen. Artifacts from all over Wevlia were packed into every inch of the room. There were statues from the deserts of Mumbano, instruments carved from the palm trees of Kyne, and tapestries woven from the artisans of the Asgarath mountains.

He and two guards were led through the mansion of an Upper City merchant, not far from the castle. The town guards had searched the city for a dragon scale, and this was the only sure lead they could find. This man, a collector of rare and ancient artifacts, was said to be in possession of one. His name was Jimli—a shrewd, snaggle-toothed trader famous for his collection of antiquities and ardently disliked by everyone who had done business with him. His shoulders were always hunched forward, giving him the perpetual appearance of lurking as he walked.

"And *this*," Jimli said as he pulled back a tapestry leading to another room. "Is my Ancient Nezmythian room. Do be careful. Don't touch anything without permission."

Jason frowned. *Fairly audacious to tell a King, but fine.*

He followed Jimli into the next room. Jason stiffened his lower lip as he looked around. He had to admit it was impressive. Bookcases were packed with leather bound volumes he had never seen before, many of which had Ancient Nezmythian on the spines. The rug beneath their feet was from a graybear, a nearly extinct animal that resided in the Eastern Mountains. At the end of the room, there was a metal chest with no lock.

"*This*," Jimli said as he pointed out a dagger on a table. "Is the dagger of the last leader of the Night Hand—Lythe. Notice the serrated edges of the charcoal black blade? It reflects absolutely no light. It can only do that with a special enchantment that was lost after the Dark Era."

Good riddance, Jason thought. *I'd rather Nezmyth forgot about the era where the world was ruled by leagues of assassins.* "Interesting. Certainly rare."

"The rarest," Jimli puffed. "And *this*—" Jason couldn't ignore how he loved that word, "—is King Clements's personal joke book! All written by his own hand—nearly five hundred years old! I like to pull it off the shelf at times where my heart is grieved. The life of a high-profile merchant can be challenging, as I'm sure you—"

"This is all very interesting, Mr. Jimli, but we have more important matters at hand," Jason said. "I must see that dragon scale."

Jimli sighed and put King Clements's joke book back on the shelf. "Of course, My Liege. *That* remarkable artifact resides in that very chest." He pointed to the metal chest at the end of the room. "Feel free."

Jason strode up to the chest and put his fingers under the lid. He pulled up... but the lid wouldn't budge. There was no lock or latches keeping it shut. It just wouldn't move. Behind him, Jimli laughed a laugh that was somewhere between a cackle and a wheeze. He clutched his stomach, then after a few dusty coughs, walked up to the chest.

"I like to watch people try it themselves first," he said with another wheezy laugh. He pushed Jason aside (Jason frowned again) and put both hands on the chest, then closed his eyes. The area around his hands glowed blue. Jimli uttered the word *kimil*—Ancient Nezmythian for *open*. The lid popped up with a loud click.

Jason arched his neck as Jimli lifted the lid. He pulled out something the size of a dinner plate. There was no mistaking it —it was a dragon scale. The scale was dull as wood on the inner side, but on the outer side it shimmered like steel. Jason's eyebrows creased. It was definitely beautiful but not in a mysterious sort of way. Part of him was disappointed.

"Thank you, Jimli," Jason said as he reached out. "You have the gratitude of a kingdom at war."

Jimli reverently bowed and handed it to Jason, his eyes flashing. Everything happened in a fraction of a second. As soon as Jason had the scale in his hands, a quiet spark peeled through him. It wasn't wonder. It wasn't awe. It was a warning. Like something buried deep inside him shuddered. A single word slipped into his ear as if riding on a breeze: *fake*. The feeling was soft, but resolute and unmistakable. His face hardened.

Jimli rubbed his hands together. "Now, let us discuss the price of—"

"It's a counterfeit."

All color drained from Jimli's face. A nervous laugh hopped from his lips, then he cleared his throat. "Wh-what? Your Highness, I—"

"And you know it is, don't you?" Jason glared. "Why would you hold onto this? I thought you were a collector of rare artifacts. You wouldn't lie to your King, would you?"

Jimli's jaw quivered, then he dropped to his hands and knees. He bowed his head so low that his forehead nearly touched the graybear fur.

"Please forgive me, Your Majesty!" Jimli groveled. "Yes, I knew it was a fake! But real dragon scales are impossible to find! Please find the mercy in your heart and forgive an old man!"

Jason put his hand on his sword and rolled his eyes. Now that he thought of it, who knows what's real and what's not in this house? Maybe Jimli was expert at making fake artifacts to swindle other collectors.

"Jimli, I hope you understand the gravity of your lie," Jason said. "Finding a dragon scale is imperative to the victory of our kingdom in this time of war. And you just offered your King a counterfeit. What do you think the consequences would be if I were to walk off with this? Do you think Nezmyth would still prosper? You're as foolish as you are greedy."

"I know it! I know it!" Jimli's voice was muffled against the graybear fur.

"I'll give you a choice," Jason said. "You can sell everything in this house and give your proceeds to the poor, or you can go to the Nezmyth City Prison. What do you choose?"

Jimli froze. His eyes scooted around their sockets, admiring his trinkets and artifacts with undeniable longing in his eyes..

"Your Majesty, I—uh—can we, can we come to some sort of alternative?" Jimli forced out.

Jason raised his eyebrows. "I've set my terms. It sounds like you want prison."

Jimli's face hit the floor again as he bowed aggressively. "I'll sell it all! I'll sell every last piece! You have my word!"

"I must be honest, Jimli, your word doesn't mean much to me at this point," Jason sighed. "But I'll accept it. Sell it all. I'm sure the Dragon will bless you for your generosity."

"Oh, bless you, King Jason!" Jimli bowed again and again. "Bless you and your merciful heart!"

"Get up," Jason rolled his eyes again. He dropped the fake dragon scale, letting it clatter on the ground. Then he turned to his soldiers. "Let's get going, gentlemen. We have an infirmary to visit. The search for the dragon scale continues, I suppose."

* * * * *

The Lower City Infirmary was a small warehouse less than a mile from the Southern Market Street. There, a staff of a half dozen healers scurried about casting arrays of restorative spells alongside potions, sutures, bandages, and splints. Healing spells can speed up the healing process, but everyone knew true medicine could not be replaced.

Late last night when the moons were high, half a dozen people limped into the city walls, including Chief Patu, Kalyk, and Captain Barnabas. Lower City locals hoisted the wounded soldiers onto their own handcarts and hurried them to the infirmary, though rumor had it that they made Barnabas walk.

The infirmary had everyone bedded and treated before the sun rose. They even applied some new bandages to Barnabas, although begrudgingly. They stiffened at the sight of Artemis perched on the bed's headboard as they worked. Chief Patu needed two beds pushed together, and, even then, her feet dangled over the edge. Once they were treated, they slept all the way through the morning. No one stirred until early afternoon when the King arrived.

When King Jason entered, everyone stopped to turn and nod. King Jason nodded in return, his hand on his sword. Some of the injured began to rise from the beds and take their first steps. Their deep cuts and broken bones were healing well. Most of the healers said they should be free to leave by the end of the day.

Nadiel arrived hours ago and was sitting at Barnabas's bedside at the end of the room. They hardly spoke. Nadiel kept himself busy with a book and Barnabas stared at the ceiling with his hands over his chest. From across the room, Jason turned to the nearest healer. "How is Barnabas?"

"Well enough," the healer said darkly. "He had a few cuts, but not much more. Some of these others nearly died. Especially that one." She pointed to Kalyk. "She's lucky to have made it. She'll need to stay here another day."

Jason thanked the healer, and the healer nodded. Then Jason made his way to Barnabas's bed. Nadiel peered over his book and saw Jason approaching, then waved his hand and a modest wooden chair materialized. Jason sat in it.

Artemis turned his head sideways as he ogled Jason, clicking his beak. He smirked in reply, but his attention was on Barnabas. "Afternoon, Captain."

"Why would you choose me?" Barnabas said without breaking his gaze on the ceiling.

"I thought the letter made that clear," Jason frowned, "I didn't choose you, Barnabas. The Sacred Dragon did. I'm just following instruction."

That's when Barnabas popped up, swinging his feet over the side to face Nadiel and Jason. Nadiel looked up from his book. Barnabas had a way of towering over Jason even when he was sitting down. His forehead and bicep were bandaged, but that seemed to be the only damage he took during the ambush.

"You think the Dragon would reappoint a man like me to such a position?" Barnabas glowered. "A fallen King? A man of perdition? Are you sure you're not drinking from the dregs of madness?"

"Barnabas, if it were left to my wisdom, you'd still be rotting in the Vault of the Damned," Jason replied. "But the Sacred Dragon has commanded *you* to lead us at this time in our kingdom's history. So you will serve me and this people. That is final."

Barnabas was silent. After an uncomfortable pause, he said, "The soldiers fought bravely last night. Lampi saved us."

"You don't say," Jason leaned in, remembering his own rescue days before.

Barnabas nodded. "Chief Patu summoned it. Came flying through the trees like a runaway stallion. If it weren't for Lampi, we would have all been slaughtered."

"Their plan is to rebuild and assault Port Gala once again?" Nadiel asked.

"Yes, originally. But when Lampi started destroying them, they fled west."

Jason scratched his beard. "West? Why west?"

"I wasn't sure at first," Barnabas said. "But then I heard the Western Bridge was destroyed. Is that true?"

Jason and Nadiel confirmed it.

"My suspicion," Barnabas said. "Is that the Ash are rebuilding the Western Bridge. We could send a scout into the area, but sending anyone deep into the Western Woods at this moment is suicide." He turned to Nadiel. "Can you use your magic to spy on that area?"

Nadiel closed his book. "It is a possibility. I could not guarantee it. That kind of magic is very strenuous, and I would need some supplies from back at the castle."

"Such as?"

"Various herbs and potions. I have them."

"Then let's do it," Jason said. "But answer this: why would Nartikis want to repair the Western Bridge? He can teleport Ash wherever they need to be. We've seen it."

"In small groups, yes," Nadiel said. "But not a whole army. If he wanted to send an army of Ash large enough to destroy the entire kingdom, that would be too much. How many attacked last night? One hundred? Yes, transporting a group of Ash that large will likely put him out for days. If he can repair the Western Bridge, he can march as many Ash into Nezmyth as he needs. Nezmyth would be overrun in no time. That is, assuming this is even his plan."

"Then it's settled," Jason said. "We'll go back to the castle and have Nadiel look at the remains of the Western Bridge. By the way, the dragon scale I went to pick up was a fake. So the search continues."

Barnabas tilted his head. "Dragon scale?"

Nadiel and Jason spent the next few minutes filling in Barnabas on everything they learned two nights ago. Barnabas followed along carefully. When they brought up the spirit of King Thomas, Barnabas's eyes got glassy. Then they explained the lessons and the Purge Ordinance. When they were done, he was quiet.

"So you can just… rip the darkness from Nartikis's soul?" Barnabas breathed.

Jason nodded.

"Could you do the same for me?"

Surprised, Jason and Nadiel traded looks. Something flashed across Nadiel's face, it was hardly discernible, but Jason interpreted it as pity. He cleared his throat and said, "Do you still feel like there's darkness inside you?"

"It never leaves you completely," Barnabas muttered.

Jason straightened his armor. "Barnabas… we can discuss that another time. But for now, we need to figure out how to bring Nartikis to Nezmyth." His face sharpened. "And I think I have an idea."

That's when Jason explained his idea of bringing the entire kingdom to Nezmyth City. It would force Nartikis and the Ash to focus on one location. And if Jason could personally challenge Nartikis in battle, the dark king would surely rise to it.

"That is… quite an undertaking," Nadiel pondered.

"Yes," Barnabas agreed. "This city would be cramped and uncomfortable for everyone, and the unrest would be substantial. However," he stroked his beard, "forcing the Ash to focus on one location gives us the upper hand. But we would need to start fortifying the city heavily and immediately. Our walls aren't even half the size of Port Gala's. It won't be enough."

"We can order every stone mason in the city to cease their current projects and instead focus on the wall," Jason said. "And when more masons arrive from other villages, they'll join in."

Barnabas hummed. Nadiel nodded in the affirmative.

Jason stood. "I'll issue the decree. Everyone in Nezmyth is to retreat to Nezmyth City immediately. And we'll order every stone mason in kingdom to work on the wall. Today, we'll observe the Western Bridge, then we'll send a message to Nartikis."

* * * * *

They set up a pedestal with a basin of water in the middle of the great hall. Nadiel spent an hour meditating, then sprinkled the top of the water with various ingredients as he whispered phrases in Ancient Nezmythian. They pulled Tarren from his shop to come view this. He watched the proceedings with his chin on his hands.

The ingredients gliding across the top of the water glowed blue. Then the rest of the water glowed. Nadiel leaned over the pedestal, closed his eyes, and took a deep breath. When he opened his eyes, his entire body snapped rigid and he seemed frozen in time, gazing into the water's depths. Everybody in the great hall watched with anticipation. At long last, the water stopped glowing and Nadiel pulled his eyes away. His face was stained with tears after he hadn't blinked for so long. A soldier brought him a rag.

"The image was clear enough," Nadiel said as he dabbed his eyes. "I saw great dark shapes moving at the edge of the forest where the Western Bridge was. Many felled trees were nearby, and they had found some that were long enough to stretch across the remains of the bridge. It appears as though Barnabas was correct. They are rebuilding."

Jason folded his arms. As Nadiel described it, he could picture it in his mind: a legion of Ash working to repair that ageless bridge without rest or pause. Chopping down trees, lashing them together, laying them across the wide chasm that separated the two kingdoms. He frowned and shifted in his seat.

"What if we sent soldiers to destroy them and their efforts?" Jason asked. "That could afford us more time for preparations. Could you see how many Ash were working?"

"I cannot be certain," Nadiel said, still dabbing his eyes. "But there were many. Perhaps hundreds."

"So sending a force to snuff them out is out of the question?"

"Highly improbable, I would say."

Barnabas shook his head. "I wouldn't recommend it. It would take too long to assemble forces and march out there."

"So what do you suggest?" Jason said.

"We do as you've already decreed: gather everyone into Nezmyth City," Barnabas said. "Then we train and prepare for the incoming attack."

Jason flexed his hands and scowled at the space between his boots. "I hate sitting and waiting for them to strike. There has to be more we can do."

"We followed them into the woods before and that was a disaster," Barnabas replied. "This will be difficult, but necessary."

Jason twiddled his thumbs, his heart thumping hard and his face hot. "Fine. The decree has already been issued. Hawks have been sent to every city in Nezmyth, so people might begin arriving as soon as tomorrow. The next thing to do is bait Nartikis." He shifted his gaze to Nadiel. "Are you ready? Or do you need some time to rest and meditate?"

Nadiel heaved a sigh. "I'm too weary from that last spell. I suggest that Tarren conducts it for you."

Tarren was chewing on a morsel of bread when Nadiel made the suggestion. He nearly choked. After a brief cough, he covered his lips and said, "Excuse me?"

"I've seen your magical ability grow remarkably, my young friend," Nadiel said. "I believe you have it within yourself to cast one projection of Jason to Unbuntye castle, if only for a few minutes. I can assist you again."

"But that's across an entire kingdom!"

"You are ready. Trust me." Nadiel motioned to some guards. "Empty the contents of this bowl and fill it again. Fetch me dried snow berries, salt from the Eternal Ocean, and Western Woods pine needles."

The soldiers marched away to fetch the supplies, and Nadiel instructed Tarren to meditate. Everyone in the room watched earnestly as Tarren made his best attempt at meditation, but everyone's eyes on him made it difficult to focus. He squirmed where he sat, bending his eyebrows, never fully relaxing. In this state, Nadiel taught him the projection incantation, and Tarren repeated to himself frequently, trying to memorize it. After a few minutes, the guards returned with the supplies.

Tarren took the supplies in his hands, gulped, and brought himself to the bowl. He sprinkled in the contents, watching them float in the water, then he beckoned to Jason. "Your Highness, come stand on the other side of this bowl."

Everyone watched Jason as he put one foot in front of another, walking up to the pedestal and the basin. When he reached it, he gazed inside. Watching the pine needles and snow berries float around the surface was almost hypnotic. Jason could feel himself drifting, but he was oddly in control. Tarren breathed in deep and let the air pour from his nose. Behind him, Nadiel stood with his hands forming a triangle above his head.

Tarren began the incantation, and Jason could feel himself getting sucked in. His feet never left the ground, but somehow, he was being transported. The great hall melted around him, fading to black, then new surroundings came into focus.

He found himself in a room he had never seen before. It was large, constructed with charcoal-black stone in the walls, floor, and ceiling. The rest of the room was ornate. Everything was laced with gold or silver, from the spacious bed, to the wardrobe, to the mantle over a roaring fire. Numerous animal furs were spread across the floor. A large leather armchair faced the fireplace. What stuck out most, however, was a large golden statue of a snake's head mounted over the bed, snarling with a forked tongue.

In the bed, King Nartikis lay sprawled out, fully clothed, his face fixed on the ceiling. He didn't move or so much as blink. He just lay there, unaware of his uninvited guest.

"You seem to be quite fond of snakes," Jason said.

Nartikis gasped and sat up. As soon as he saw the projection of Jason, he launched a jeroki. Jason kept himself from flinching as the jeroki flew through him. He wouldn't show fear. Not to Nartikis. As soon as Nartikis launched the projectile, he slapped his hand to his forehead and steadied himself with his other arm.

"Barnabas was right," Jason said. "Transporting all those Ash took it out of you."

"Then they survived?" Nartikis hissed.

"A fraction of them," Jason replied. "I suppose that's what you get for sending a battalion of mindless monsters to do your dirty work."

That's right, Jason, he thought. *Lay it on thick. Goad him.*

Nartikis's lips quivered. "Give it time. I will lay waste to all of Nezmyth. As we speak, the Western Bridge is being rebuilt. And once it is, using magic will be unnecessary. I will send hundreds—*thousands* of them. Nezmyth will be overrun in days."

Jason's heart lurched at the thought. He pushed it down.

"Yes, and then Nezmyth will be ruled by the greatest coward since Barnabas himself," Jason said as he strolled over the fur carpets. "It's not surprising—cowardice obviously runs in your blood. A greater King would have the confidence to invade a kingdom himself, not concoct an army of disposable dead to scamper about. I pity you."

"Jealousy," Nartikis spat. "Jealousy of my power. You could not construct an army like the Ash after a lifetime of study."

"I think what it truly is," Jason sneered, as he stepped onto the bed, looking down on Nartikis, "is you are instead fearful of *my* power. You couldn't kill me before, and you still can't. So you're trying to stay as far away from me as possible. You fear what would happen if you faced me again."

At this, Nartikis smiled. He actually smiled. And it was awful. Two rows of yellow teeth curled into a twisted grin that could make the most weathered man shudder. Nartikis threw his head back and laughed a dusty cackle. "*Me?* Fear *you?* I would have squashed you like an insect if had you not fled. You speak of courage. Ha! It was your friend that displayed true courage. And oh, how he suffered for it…"

Garrit. The smirk dropped from Jason's face. He flexed his hands, but he tried to calm his rapidly beating heart. Nartikis noticed this and his eyes flashed.

"Oh yes," Nartikis purred. "We made sure he understood the true meaning of pain before we snuffed out his life. He made a fine Ash for a time. Ironically, you slew him yourself at the Battle of Port Gala. Drowned in the Wevlian Sea. Imagine that."

Jason's chest was in a knot. The rage must have been apparent, because the delight from Nartikis's face didn't fade. What was fading was the image of his room. Jason could see flashes of the great hall. The projection would be over soon. He had to act fast.

"Why do you want me in Nezmyth so badly?" Nartikis's icy eyes carved into Jason.

It was the only thing Jason could think to say, but between the knot in his chest and his shaking hands, he blurted it out: "Because I want to kill you myself."

Nartikis's lips curled into that horrible smile again. "It is mutual."

"Good," Jason said, "then I'll see you soon."

Nartikis's cold eyes were the last thing Jason saw before the room melted around him. He was back in Nezmyth. His eyes stung and his face was wet. Across from him, Tarren's face was coated with sweat. He would have collapsed if Nadiel didn't catch him. All eyes in the room were on Jason, silent and expectant.

Barnabas finally spoke up. "Well?"

Jason blinked the sting from his eyes. His heart was still pounding. His palms were sweaty. He could have ground his teeth into powder. He didn't even notice a soldier trying to hand him a rag as he thought of the last time he saw Garrit. The blood and soot covering his face...

That's when he caught Saryan's eyes from across the room. That was the moment it boiled over. He couldn't speak. He didn't answer Barnabas's question. Instead, he turned on his heels and bolted out of the great hall, leaving everyone bewildered and lost.

Jason's arms and legs pumped as he ascended the flights of stairs going to his chambers. Guards standing in the halls exchanged puzzled glances as they watched their King fly through the corridors. Jason suppressed the tears. His breathing came in labored bursts. Finally, he threw the double doors open and slammed them behind him.

He let the agony pour from him. He grabbed fistfuls of his hair and pulled as he screamed. He grabbed a chair and threw it against a wall, snapping it to pieces. He tossed jerokis into his wardrobe, shattering it and casting his clothes across the room. Finally, he collapsed to the floor, whimpering. He let the tears fall onto the stone beneath him as he shuddered, sobbing like he hadn't since he was a child.

He had never wanted to kill anyone before—not even Barnabas. Not until today.

30
THE COUNTDOWN

Jason stayed in the royal chambers for the rest of the evening. No one disturbed him except for Saryan, who crept up to the room after an hour of allowing Jason peace. When she emerged, she walked slower and folded her arms almost like she needed to hold herself. A handful of soldiers cleaned up the mess and replaced the furniture. As they did, their King silently lay in bed; they opted not to disturb him.

Meanwhile, Nadiel departed to Grace Mountain for his first lesson. When he returned to the castle, he found Tarren snoring in the study, an Ancient Nezmythian book draped over his lap. He smiled, then excused himself for the evening without waking his pupil.

The city guards scrambled throughout the night to prepare abandoned houses and buildings for incoming refugees. They chased out rats, swept through cobwebs, and tried to get everything tidy enough to be hospitable. By the time dawn came, many of the buildings in Nezmyth were ready for habitation so long as the refugees were willing to bring their own bedding and bunch together.

Sure enough, refugees began arriving by late that morning. The people that trickled in from nearby villages arrived to see every mason in town working furiously on the western wall. Scaffolding was in place to build the wall at least twenty feet high and three feet thick. But the wall surrounding the city was also several miles in circumference. It would take a miracle to get the whole city fortified before the Ash showed up again.

Barnabas spent the night at the castle—or rather, the castle grounds. Queen Saryan didn't want him staying under the same roof as her and the King, so an old tool shed on the farthest corner of the grounds was converted into his quarters. While Nadiel was at his lesson at Grace Mountain, King Jason ordered some soldiers to find another place to house the tools and to furnish the shed with some necessities. Barnabas walked in to find a cot, a rickety desk, and a stool with a water basin. He didn't use the cot when he finally laid his head that night. The Vault of the Damned had made him accustomed to sleeping on the ground.

Much to the chagrin of everyone around him, King Jason had Barnabas outfitted with the proper Chief Captain's armor: gleaming bronze shoulder plates, breast plates, knee plates, and a fine sword to sling around his waist. He wasn't sure what to expect when he watched Barnabas get fitted for the traditional uniform he once wore. He might have expected Barnabas to be more satisfied or proud. But when Barnabas saw his reflection, fully suited up, his face was as blank as ever.

As the refugees trickled into the city, soldiers peppered Barnabas with questions on how to handle the influx. Like a good soldier, Barnabas showed no fear and made no excuses. He fired instructions like the Captain he once was. He moved his desk outside so he could write notes and tie them to Artemis before he flew off.

By early afternoon, the soldiers were getting their handle on where to usher refugees, so the requests between battalions were becoming fewer. When Artemis came back from delivering the most recent message, Barnabas stroked the area under his beak. Artemis's head twitched, his large black eyes scanning the castle grounds.

"You've had a busy morning," Barnabas said. "You deserve to hunt for a treat. But be hasty."

Understanding him, Artemis flapped his massive wings and took to the sky, scanning the city for mice.

Barnabas took a large roll of parchment and spread it across the table, using small rocks to pin down the corners. It was a map of Nezmyth City. As he smoothed out the edges, he scanned every illustrated street. The focus, however, wasn't on the interior of the city. His eyes traced the circular wall that encased it all.

He frowned and scratched his beard. The Ash would no doubt come from the west, so that was the first section of the city that needed to be fortified. But would a twenty-foot wall be enough for who-knows-how-many Ash descending upon the city? Absolutely not.

Taking a writing stick in his hand, Barnabas made some rough sketches around the exterior of the western side. He scribbled some lines, stopped, tapped the writing stick on his lips, then scribbled more. As soon as he was done, he rolled up the parchment tightly and stood from his seat.

Barnabas marched through the grounds and headed for the castle. As he walked by, patrolling guards stood aside, nodded, and said "Captain." But there was no enthusiasm in their voices. It was tradition and responsibility. Nothing more. When he reached the castle doors, the soldiers didn't wait to be addressed. They took up the hammer and knocked three times. After a pause, the doors pulled open.

As Barnabas strode through, parchment in hand, he noticed that King Jason was in his throne on the opposite end of the great hall. Nadiel stood on his right side, shoulders back with his hands behind him. Standing in front of the throne platform, two commoners bickered and squabbled with one another. Their voices echoed through the great hall.

"He keeps branding *my* cattle!"

"Liar! Anyway, he keeps allowing *his* cattle to graze on *my* grass!"

In his throne, King Jason tried to appear cool and collected, but the drumming of his fingers on the armrest and his foul expression were unmistakable. Even Nadiel tried not to roll his eyes.

"Could you not just repair the fence?" Jason said while pinching the bridge of his nose.

"Of course, but *he* should pay for it!" one said.

"*Me?* Why, *you're* the one—" the other shot.

"Enough!" King Jason said, holding his hands in the air. "Both of you are going to pay for it! Fifty-fifty! Honestly, both of you are acting like children! I can't believe you brought this to my attention at a time like this. Go see to it and don't bother me with such trivial things again. Goodbye!"

Both of the farmers blinked, looked at each other, then strolled toward the castle doors shoulder-to-shoulder. Under their breath, they muttered things like "A tad irritable, don't you think?" and "Not as pleasant as I heard he'd be."

When they noticed Captain Barnabas, they glared and kept walking.

As soon as they walked out the double doors, Jason stood from his throne and dragged his feet over to Barnabas. He let out a long sigh and rubbed his face with both hands.

"If you want to take over this part for me, be my guest," Jason said.

Barnabas almost smiled. He bowed, then held out the map. "Your Highness, I'd like to extend my proposal for the city wall."

"What do you mean?" Jason said as he unraveled the parchment.

When he opened it, he found a map of Nezmyth City with several sketch marks just outside the western gate. There were long lines interspersed by square boxes. Jason gazed at each one with eyebrows furrowed.

"A twenty-foot wall is better, but it won't be enough," Barnabas said. "We don't know when Nartikis plans on attacking the city—could be days, could be weeks. My proposal, Your Grace, is that we focus on fortifying the western walls, as planned, while building an array of trenches and towers just outside the western gate. We should make it far more difficult for the Ash to reach the city walls."

Throughout the explanation, Jason's expression got harder. He kept looking at the expanse of long lines and boxes Barnabas drew.

"What you're requesting would take a substantial amount of man hours," Jason said. "There are dozens towers and miles of trenches."

"If we have all of Nezmyth in the city, Your Majesty," Barnabas said, "that alleviates the problem. It will decrease the number of residents inside the city walls. We can recruit thousands of people to work in shifts—some during the day, some during the night. With some luck, we can fortify Nezmyth City's western side in a limited period of time."

Jason turned to Nadiel. Nadiel stiffened his lower lip. Jason turned back to Barnabas. "If you think this can be done and you know how to get this going, you have my permission. I'm trusting you, Captain."

Jason handed Barnabas back the map and Barnabas took it again with a respectful bow. "Thank you, Your Majesty."

"Barnabas."

He looked up.

Jason took a quick look at him before he said anything— the King that could have been. The Barnabas full of drive and wisdom that existed before Dark Magic overpowered him. Nezmyth was building up its fortifications nicely in his hands.

With his help, and a miracle, they might be able to stop the Ash for good.

Jason said, "You're doing well."

Barnabas bowed and left the great hall.

* * * * *

"Barnabas presented a new plan to me today for the western wall."

"What is it?"

"He wants to build a series of towers and trenches outside the city—make it harder for the Ash to reach the gate."

"How in the world are we going to do that?"

Jason and Saryan sat together in the dining hall. A long table flanked by over twenty chairs sat before them. Above their heads, three crystal chandeliers hung in single file. Guards lined the edges of the room, but the royal chef stood off to the side, waiting to clean up after the King and Queen finished their meal. It was just them tonight. Nadiel was off meditating and Tarren was at his first Grace Mountain lesson.

"With everyone within the city walls, we'll have lots of people to help with preparations," Jason said as he chewed on some boiled carrots. "It'll keep the city from being so crowded, as well. I feel bad about putting so many of our people to work, but if it means ending the war and ending Nartikis." Jason jammed his fork through some steak. "So be it."

Saryan was pensive as she processed Jason's words. She carved her vegetables and steak delicately, then asked, "Do we know when Nartikis will be here?"

"No. We have no idea."

"What if he and the Ash arrive tomorrow?"

"I pray to the Dragon that they don't. We haven't even learned how to perform the Purge Ordinance, and we still haven't found a dragon scale."

Saryan continued to carve into her dinner. "We have to trust the Dragon."

"That's all we can do."

Jason chewed for a minute, looking ahead, his eyes vacant, when he realized that Saryan had stopped speaking. He looked over to see her frozen in place, her fork halfway to her mouth, not blinking. He quickly studied the room. All the soldiers and the chef were frozen in place, too. Jason jumped up from his chair and ripped his sword from its sheath, hunching down and clutching it with both hands.

Then he appeared. Nartikis, standing in full uniform, looking as icy and pale as usual. Jason glowered.

"Eight days," Nartikis said without feeling.

Jason's eyes narrowed. "That's it, then? Just eight days before you come here and face me yourself?"

"The Western Bridge will be repaired by then," Nartikis answered. "Then I march all of my forces straight to Nezmyth City. I know you are bringing your kingdom there—trying to focus my attention on the capital. So be it. You will all die regardless."

"Time will tell," Jason seethed.

"Indeed."

Nartikis disappeared in his puff of purple smoke. Then everything went back to normal. The clink of Saryan's silverware scratched softly from her plate. The guards and chef breathed again. All of them were visibly perplexed when they saw Jason out of his seat, facing the opposite wall with his sword in hand, all within the blink of an eye.

Saryan frowned and turned about, distraught. "Jason, what just happened?"

31
THE URCHIN

The sound of "eight days" put a cold shiver down the spine of everyone who heard the news. Eight days to find a dragon scale and concoct the Purge potion. Eight days to build the wall around Nezmyth City. Eight days to build the trenches and towers that Barnabas ordered. Eight days until destruction was upon them.

Immediately after Nartikis's appearance, Jason called a conference with Saryan, Nadiel, and Barnabas. He wanted to know if it would be wise to tell Nezmyth about Nartikis's eight-day challenge. The consensus was that although transparency is valuable, it would be unwise to tell the people. They would need all forces in Nezmyth City, and the knowledge would cause some to stay away from the city or, worse, flee the kingdom.

This also put tighter restraints on the dragon scale search. If the potion were to cure in time, they would have to find the scale in less than five days. Barnabas committed to double the guards' efforts. Jason invited everyone to pray to the Dragon for help.

Just a couple of hours later, Nadiel was sitting at a table in the great hall, reading a book and sipping from a goblet of cider. The day was winding down. Soldiers stood guard around the perimeter of the hall. Torches on the walls cast dancing orange light across the floor. The stained glass windows overhead let in no light. A calm stillness emanated from the night.

Nadiel licked his finger and turned the page. The silence was sweet nectar to his ears. Solitude was fertile ground for pondering and revelation. But he wasn't here to just study.

The familiar booms came from the castle doors. As they crept open, fresh evening air seeped into the great hall, and with it, a tall blonde man with purple eyes marching down the red carpet. Spotting Nadiel, he turned and made his way for the table. Nadiel folded his book shut and removed the reading spectacles from his eyes.

"Well?" he asked. "How went your lesson?"

Tarren sat down across from him, his hands together. His face was pale, and he didn't make eye contact. While staring at the grain in the wooden table, Tarren muttered, "I can't do this."

The glimmer from Nadiel's eyes left. "I beg your pardon?"

"I can't do this, sir," Tarren said, finally lifting his gaze. His eyes were swollen. "The Year of Decision, the Advisorship, the Purge Ordinance, everything. I'm not like you. I'm not wise and powerful and patient. I'm a Lower City boy. I'm not smart. I'm not clever. I've got by in life by trying to be strong and funny and working with my hands. This… this is the role for someone else. I can't… I'm not—"

"Tarren… we *need* you for the Purge Ordinance."

"No, you don't!" Tarren interjected. "You said it has to be done by three Foreordained servants! You could get any Patriarch, even a Blessing Bearer if you wanted!" His eyes teared up more. "What if, when the time comes, I can't do it? What if I fail and the Ash survive? What if—"

"Tarren, you must dismiss that kind of thinking *right now*," Nadiel shot. "Fear is the antithesis of faith. And in order to perform this Purge Ordinance, you must have that faith." He leaned forward. "You say you're not wise and you're not clever. A Lower City urchin. Even you are far more privileged than I ever was."

Tarren swallowed and forced back his tears. "What?"

"Have I never told you that I was abandoned as a young boy?"

Tarren shook his head.

"Please indulge me," Nadiel said. "If you know Barnabas's story, it stands to reason that you should know mine as well. After all, I am your mentor.

"When it comes to Lower City urchins, I was the lowest. I never knew my father. My mother abandoned me when I was seven years old. For years, I wandered the streets of Lower City and found my meals by pilfering fruit carts and bread stands. I knew how to hide in the shadows and steal what I could to get by. I even had my favorite hiding spots where I would sleep at night.

"When I was ten, a pair of soldiers caught me stealing a pair of shoes. They recognized me as the 'child with the red eyes.' As they prepared to beat me, a man walked by and hailed them.

"'There you are!' he said. 'Don't wander off like that! I was going to buy you those shoes tomorrow. Come here!'

"The mysterious man handed the shopkeeper two Bars and let me walk out with the shoes, but he didn't let me walk out alone. He gripped me by the arm and walked me down the street until we were out of earshot. Then he stooped down and looked me in the eye.

"'Don't steal anymore,' he said. 'I'm Will, the printer. My shop is just down the way. I'll give you a job. Come tomorrow morning at sunrise. I'll teach you how to print, and at the end of each day, I'll give you twenty Pieces.'

"When he said that, he let me go. I ran off with the shoes and decided to forget the man.

"But I couldn't. I didn't go to his shop the next morning. Days went by. I tried to ignore him, but every time I saw those shoes on my feet, I thought of him. I thought what it must be like to not hide in the shadows. To live free. To never look over my shoulder. The next morning, I mustered enough courage to enter his shop. He told me I was late, but he was smiling.

"Thus, I began working for Will the printer. He was an older man, lonely, with no wife or children, but yearned for such company. Every day I came to work, he gave me twenty Pieces, just as promised. I began buying food and clothing without guilt. We ate meals together, and he told me of his life. He was kind and patient, and I began to look to him as a father. That's when it delighted my heart one year later when he asked me to live with him as his son."

Nadiel's eyes sparkled and his lips pulled into a smile.

"I became his apprentice in the print shop. He gave me a gift for my eleventh birthday—I had never received a present before. It was a book on basic magic techniques. I was delighted. I learned to throw jerokis and heal simple cuts, and I couldn't resist showing him my progress. He was always supportive.

"When I was twelve, Will took me to our local Patriarch to receive my Blessing of Fate. When the Patriarch bestowed that sacred blessing upon me, Will and I were both shocked to hear that I was Foreordained to serve as a future Advisor. Me, an abandoned child. A thief. An urchin of the shadows. But amid the shock, something awoke inside me. A voice, you could say. It told me that I have purpose. That I wasn't disposable. That the Sacred Dragon saw potential in me. From that day, I swore that I would prepare myself to become a worthy Advisor."

Tarren's jaw was dangling now. Nadiel moved forward.

"Father Will encouraged me to go to the Nezmyth City Library to read as much as I could. He would allow me to leave work early to do so. I studied any book I could—books on Nezmythian economics, history, but especially magic. I was disappointed to learn that the most advanced magic was only possible through the language of Ancient Nezmythian, a language I didn't understand, and that Will couldn't possibly afford to teach me.

"So, the years went by. Will and I continued to work in the printing shop together. He passed away peacefully in his bed before I was twenty-five. I had him buried in the Nezmyth City Cemetery. It was a small funeral—only me and a few of his favorite customers attended. I kept the shop going, not knowing what to do about my Foreordination, and still disappointed that I would never learn Ancient Nezmythian. A few solemn years went by, then I met Rebekah."

At the mention of this name, Nadiel's eyes brightened.

"We met as I was performing some errands on the tail end of the Northern Market Street. She was a delight. Bright and articulate. Beautiful smile. I was immediately smitten by her. We formed a warm, rich friendship. She lived in Upper City with her family. During one of our outings, she discovered my desire to learn Ancient Nezmythian and took it upon herself to become my tutor. I, of course, was thrilled. So she taught me, and over a long period of time, I became proficient in the language. Even as a Lower City printer."

Tarren smirked and cleared his throat. "So... did you and Rebekah only remain friends?"

Nadiel's smile faded. "I was a coward. Yes, we only remained friends. I had wondered if she experienced similar feelings but was too nervous to pursue it. I assumed that she would never be romantically interested in a man such as me—a Lower City printer. I was plain and had nothing to offer her. And I didn't want the pursuance of romance to tarnish our friendship. So I let things be.

"Our friendship continued for nearly a decade, then she fell in love with another man, married, and moved out of the city.

I've always regretted not confessing my love to her. I never found a woman that matched her charm or beauty." Nadiel scratched at the table absently. "At the age of forty I was finally called to begin my Year of Decision. I worked with King Thomas during the last few years of his life. Then twenty years under Barnabas. And now four years of King Jason."

Tarren sat in silence after hearing Nadiel's story. He tried to picture a childlike version of Nadiel, without the gray hair but with the same stunning red eyes, dressed in rags and stalking fruit carts. It was such an outlandish vision, a direct contrast to the present—astute, learned, powerful, and wise.

"Thank you for your patience, my young friend," Nadiel said. "The object of my tale was to illustrate your *potential*. What you see before you is the result of an ungifted man taking himself to decades of study and practice. You yourself will make great strides in the future as King Jason's Advisor. That is, if you choose to accept your Foreordination."

Tarren didn't speak. He only shifted where he sat.

"It is your choice," Nadiel stood from his seat. "But I believe you would be doing a great disservice to the Dragon, this kingdom, and yourself by withholding your gifts from the Advisorship." He paused. "Goodnight, Tarren. Please try to sleep well."

Nadiel left the room, and Tarren remained where he sat, thinking. He didn't rise from his chair and venture home for a long while.

32
THE LAD

When Kalyk was released from the infirmary, she rushed to the castle and graciously showed her friends the long scar across her side. It made Saryan frown and Jason wince. Chief Patu, however, shouted and raised her fists with pride. As Kalyk carried about her typical duties, the scar often caused her to jolt and clutch her side. It hadn't fully healed yet, and the healers back at the infirmary were unsure it ever would.

Nadiel told Jason about Tarren's conversation from the night before—about Tarren's desire to renounce his Foreordination. It made Jason's heart sink, but he understood the feeling. Inside, he trusted that Tarren would have the grit to persevere through his Year of Decision, but at a time like this, who could know?

Throughout the day, there was no news of a dragon scale. Barnabas spent most of the day outside the city gates, overseeing the construction of the walls and the towers. It wasn't uncommon for travelers to arrive in Nezmyth City and immediately be put to work on the wall. It was tough, but necessary. Some citizens were understanding and eager to help. Many more protested, especially under Barnabas's supervision.

And with those protests came abuse. Barnabas ignored the majority of it; he expected nothing less. A few people had tried to attack him personally in a fit of anger and vengeance. Nearby guards stopped them before they could accomplish their purposes, and they were immediately thrown into prison. But that didn't stop the insults, spitting, and curses.

The guards also had their hands full with restless citizens. The once peaceful and unassuming Nezmyth City had become a hive of squirming unrest. With more people filling cramped living spaces, petty thievery and fistfights became common. Soldiers spent their days disciplining thieves, breaking up fights, solving petty squabbles, and trying to handle as much as they could without taking matters to the King. He had more than enough on his hands.

Amid all this, the people of Nezmyth City weren't near as happy or delighted to see the royal carriage as they used to be. As Jason made his way to Grace Mountain for his second lesson, the royal carriage was now rarely greeted with "Long live the King" or "All hail King Jason!" Usually, it was silence or murmurs.

The sun had nearly set as Jason made the climb up Grace Mountain. When he arrived on the plateau, he placed his sword before the statue of the Sacred Dragon and waited for King Thomas to arrive. It didn't take long. Jason knelt down, his face to the ground, and as soon as he looked up, King Thomas was there. The look on his face was something Jason couldn't quite decipher, but for some reason, he felt a twinge of guilt inside him.

"Good evening, Your Highness," King Thomas said cordially.

"Good evening."

"How fares the kingdom?"

Jason deflated. "You don't really need me to explain it, do you?"

"I'd like to hear it from your own mouth."

Jason rehearsed everything to him about the search for the dragon scale, the restlessness of the people, the preparations of Nezmyth City, Nartikis's warning, and Barnabas's regained position.

"My, it sounds like much has happened in three days," King Thomas said.

"Too much has happened in the last few *weeks*," Jason said. "I'm fearful for Nezmyth. Eight days is hardly time at all. It'll be a miracle if we're able to withstand the Ash, given the necessary preparations before they arrive."

"Luckily for you, the Sacred Dragon is a supplier of miracles," King Thomas said. "Now, before we get started, there is an important matter that we must get out of the way." King Thomas's tone darkened. "Your feelings toward King Nartikis."

Jason bristled. "What of them?"

"Let them go."

Jason laughed. He couldn't help it. Considering all King Nartikis had done to throw his kingdom into chaos over the last few weeks, forgiveness was the last thing on his mind. The bubbling, tense anger he felt inside every time he thought of the hundreds of innocent lives slaughtered... not to mention Garrit. No. He couldn't forget.

"King Thomas, I want *justice!*" Jason shouted. "I want him to atone for the thousands of lives he's destroyed! I want him to—"

"Don't mistake justice for vengeance, Your Highness," King Thomas cut in. "Justice will be dealt swiftly by the Sacred Dragon, don't you worry. But how it's carried out should not be for you to decide. Remember, if you're going to overcome Nartikis and destroy the Ash, your *good* needs to be stronger than his *evil.* How are you expecting to do that when your heart is flowing with anger? With the desire to *end his life?*"

Jason huffed. Once again, King Thomas was right. He was right and he hated it. "*How?* How can I just forgive the things he's done? How do I look at what he's done and dismiss it all?"

"That's not what forgiveness is, Your Highness," King Thomas shook his head. "It's not being dismissive of wrongs; it's allowing yourself to let go of the feelings attached to them. That anger you're harboring is what Nartikis wants. And that anger is the open door for darkness to seep into *your* heart. You need to let it go."

"You still haven't answered how," Jason murmured.

King Thomas paused, taking a deep breath. He looked Jason in the eyes and said, "Sit with me."

Jason bunched up his cape and squatted to the ground, sitting with his legs crossed. King Thomas did so in unison, sitting directly across from Jason about a dozen feet away.

"Breathe in deeply three times," King Thomas said. "In through your nose and out through your mouth."

Jason followed the order. He inhaled through his nose, then let the breath seep out through his lips. He did it once more. Then a third time. When he was done, he felt a little calmer, but the anger still lined his heart.

"Now, Jason," King Thomas said, looking directly at him. "Tell me what your heart feels *right now*."

Jason paused only for a moment, trying to put the words together. "I'm angry. More angry than I've ever been. I hate Nartikis. I hate this war. I hate that he's caused so much suffering. And I want him dead for it. I've never wanted anyone dead before… but with him, I do."

"Is that all?"

After another pensive pause, Jason nodded.

"Good," King Thomas said. "Your Highness, you've vocalized your feelings. Like oil collecting at the top of a pool, you've separated the anger and identified what's causing it. Now I want you to package it up and let it go. Breath again if you have to."

King Thomas breathed again to demonstrate. Jason closed his eyes and tried to copy King Thomas's relaxation, but with every breath he took, he couldn't help but think of the western wall. All those trenches and towers. Why? Because of Nartikis and the Ash. And what had they done? Slaughtered hundreds. Desecrated their bodies by turning them into Ash. Pitting them against their loved ones. He clenched his fists, then opened his eyes and stood up.

"King Thomas, I can't do this," he said. "I can agree not to kill him, but I can't forgive him. I can't look at—"

"*Sit down*," King Thomas commanded.

Jason tightened his jaw, huffed again and sat back down. King Thomas didn't speak. He sat quietly, his eyes closed, and stayed silent. Jason waited. After a long, expectant pause, King Thomas finally opened his eyes and looked hard at Jason.

"I just received permission to show you something. Something about Nartikis. It may help you understand your enemy a little better."

"By all means!"

"Very well then. Clear your mind."

Jason closed his eyes and went back to his meditative breathing. In his head, he started seeing images. In the darkness, shapes took form. As if awakening from a long sleep, Jason's vision became sharper. There was no sound, just moving images.

A small boy with pale skin and blue eyes sat on a black castle floor, drawing shapes with his finger. Not far away, a woman sat in a very tall throne. She was beautiful, slender, with sharp eyes and a contoured face. The gown she wore was ornamented with gold and lace, woven into a tapestry of elegance. In her hair, a delicate white flower rested just over her ear. Around the room, guards stood erect. They weren't Ash; they were human.

Suddenly, a guard marched into the room and said something. The woman's face lit up. The boy's eyes grew wide.

The woman immediately stood from her throne and rushed out of the room. The boy slowly stood, brushing his arm and following after the woman, his face fixed on the ground. After a moment, the woman came back into the room with a man. The man had a hooked nose, pale skin, pitch black hair, and the same blue eyes as the boy.

As the man and the woman walked together, the boy approached them. The woman scratched the boy's hair and smiled. The man looked down on the boy, patted his head dismissively, then said something to the woman and they walked off together. The boy watched them as they left, his eyes aching and his shoulders sagging. When they walked out of the room, he sat back down on the floor.

Jason's vision went dark. Then more images started to appear.

They were on a hilltop with prickly yellow grass. In the middle of a hilltop, a large stone tomb with a mouth the size of a carriage sat open, leading down to dark depths. Surrounding the tomb were numberless concourses of people dressed in black from head to toe. Their faces were covered. Just outside the tomb, a sleek black casket was being carried by six strong soldiers. Behind it, the boy with the blue eyes followed, slightly older than the vision from before.

The man with his same eyes was nowhere to be seen.

Jason's vision went dark again, then a new vision formed.

The boy hadn't changed out of his black clothing. He sat in the same tall, elegant throne that the woman once sat in. The room was filled with many older people dressed in expensive clothing, staring at him with a mixture of pride and grief. A man marched toward the boy with a cape in his hands. With reverence, he reached around the boy and tied the cape. As soon as the strings were tied, the boy's lips quivered, and tears filled his eyes. But the ceremony carried on. The crowd applauded. And on the throne, the boy cried.

His vision darkened. Then it lightened up.

The boy wandered in a courtyard, a soot-black castle looming directly overhead. He was followed by two guards. He swung a stick in his hand blindly, as if swiping at invisible foes. Then, he stopped. Something near the ground made him pause and stare.

In the courtyard, a small bed of flowers shuddered in the gentle breeze. They were white—just like the ones that used to be in his mother's hair.

The boy's chin shuddered. He swung his stick at the flowers with all his might. The delicate white pedals rained onto the walkway, empty and rootless, cast aside. When all the flowers in reach were destroyed, he turned to one of the guards behind him. He didn't look them in the eye. Jason couldn't hear the words, but he caught the boy's lips saying, "Did King Barnabas ever send word?"

The guard's face saddened and shook his head.

The tantrum continued. The boy screamed and tears poured down his face as he swung his stick at every flower in sight. The ground became a cascade of petals. Patrolling guards stopped and stared. In the boy's fit, a garden snake slithered out of some brush, trying to find cover. The boy noticed. He lifted his foot and brought it down hard, stamping the snake's head.

The snake's body curled horribly. Dead. The boy clenched his teeth and glared through stinging eyes, then surprise leaped across his face. He brought the stick up to inspect it. The end of the stick was burning with a flickering purple flame. His body stopped shaking, and the boy breathed with long, calm breaths. The purple flame reflected in his eyes almost like it were dancing. He couldn't look away. And he hadn't, even as Jason's vision started going dark again.

He could hear sounds again. When Jason opened his eyes, he was back on top of Grace Mountain, looking directly at the spirit of King Thomas. He hadn't noticed it, but his eyelashes collected a few droplets over the course of the vision. King Thomas didn't speak.

Jason took a long, quivering breath, then said half-angrily, "Don't make me pity him."

"Abuse comes from a place of great pain, Your Highness," King Thomas said softly. "Nartikis didn't ask for the life that was given him." He leaned in. "So learn to let go of your anger. When you defeat the Ash and Nartikis is purged from the darkness within, this will all be a part of the past."

* * * * *

Jason returned home that evening pensive and reserved. The hate that stirred inside of him had a new ingredient—pity. He detested it. It spoiled the whole concoction. He didn't speak much with Saryan or Nadiel before he readied himself for bed. The army would be upon them in just days, and that meant he had to learn to let his feelings go quickly.

As night fell and the city became still, Barnabas was having trouble sleeping. He pulled the blankets down to the floor and his back felt at home against the stone. Nevertheless, he lay awake, staring at the ceiling, breathing in the dust and watching the mice scurry back and forth through the low-hanging rafters.

He had a hard time putting aside the thoughts that plagued him ever since the forest. He had his old title back. Chief Captain—a position of supreme prestige and authority. It was just like the days before he was King. The days when his slip into Dark Magic was rapid and deep.

And as he remembered that magic, he couldn't help but stare at the mice scurrying back and forth above him. He could snuff out any one of them. They're vermin. Disposable. No one would know. He could kill one, then have enough to burn just a little flame on his finger. A small one. Just enough to help him relax. It would be so easy.

As if on cue, he felt a tickle on his arm. Without thinking, he slapped it. Then he looked.

The remnants of a small spider were smashed on his arm—its tiny, spindly legs detached from its smeared body. As soon as Barnabas saw it, his blood ran cold.

It was dead.

His heart rate picked up as his gaze slid down to his hand. He could do it. He could do just a little bit. He could hardly practice standard magic anymore, but after decades of use, the basics of *Tepnoh Edomah* were fresh on his mind. Just a little snap. A little purple flame could dance on his fingertip. He held his hand up to his face.

His heart raced as he stared at his fingers. It was like a slithering whisper in his ear, telling him to do it. And his heart wanted it. To feel that pleasure again. Any pleasure at all.

But then he remembered his cell in the Vault of the Damned. Jason fishing him out. Putting him here, in this new position. And now, he was just a twitch away from diving down that same rabbit hole he visited ages ago. The rabbit hole that got him locked away in the first place.

That thought was enough to shoot a jolt of fear through him. He popped up, threw the covers from off him, and stood. Shakily, he paced the room back and forth. He crossed the room and reached his hands into the water bowl.

Cupping his hands, he threw the water onto his face, rubbing his hair and beard. His breathing slowed down, and he stared at his reflection. But as the water settled and his reflection became smoother, he couldn't help but frown. His reflection seemed hardly his own. His hair was darker, without any of the grays around his ears, and his skin was younger.

Another bolt of fear shot through him. He wasn't looking at his own reflection. In the water, Nartikis sneered up at him.

"Hello, father," Nartikis said. The voice was inside Barnabas's head.

"*No!*" Barnabas cried.

It was too late. He was suddenly shrouded in darkness. Barnabas spun around, trying to catch his bearings. But everything around him was black. He was breathing heavily, and each breath seemed to echo for oblivion.

"You should not have turned away from me," Nartikis again was inside his head. "I am sure this looks familiar to you."

"Release me!" Barnabas shouted.

Nartikis laughed. "You cannot Overcurse me. You have not the strength to overpower a Dreamslayer spell—not in your current state. Suffer, then yield."

Suddenly, what felt like a million hot needles stuck into Barnabas's body. A giant snake materialized in front of him, with large, icy eyes. It slithered forward, as wide as Barnabas's wingspan, cocked its head back, and struck.

Barnabas could feel its fangs inside him. He knew this world he was trapped in wasn't real, but the pain... the pain was exquisite. His head was on fire. Thousands of insects crawled under his skin. His lungs filled with water, and he couldn't breathe.

"Yield," Nartikis said calmly in his ear.

The hot pinpricks around his body erupted into a splitting cold that froze him to the bone. The snake continued to strike at him, lacerating him with every strike. His body was being crushed—he could feel his ribs and spine breaking. He still couldn't breathe. He couldn't tell if he was burning, freezing, or drowning.

"I... I..." Barnabas stammered.

"Yield," Nartikis said again.

"I..."

"*Yield!*"

It was too much. He couldn't take another broken bone, another gasp for air, another burn. The snake's strikes tore at his flesh. The mountainous pain that waned and grew and made his body scream out. Enough. No more.

"I..." Barnabas said. "I... I yield."

33
THE PUPPET

Suddenly, Barnabas was back in his own body looking over the water bowl. But as he tried to move, he couldn't. Nartikis was in control. He yelped, but the sound echoed in his mind only. His lips didn't move. Nartikis laughed and went to work strapping on his armor, along with his sword.

"*Coward!*" Barnabas growled.

Barnabas felt the burning again around his entire body. But the pain only lasted for a moment before Nartikis let it up.

"I suggest you behave yourself," Nartikis said. "Unless you prefer the pain."

Barnabas watched his body exit the tool shed and stroll through the castle grounds. He stayed quiet. Never had he felt so completely powerless, not even in the Vault of the Damned. There had to be something he could do. But what? One thought crossed his mind, likely futile, but there were no other options. Barnabas took it and hoped that Nartikis couldn't hear his thoughts.

Dragon, if you'll listen to a wretch like me, Barnabas silently prayed. *Please warn the King. Warn Jason.*

Nartikis said nothing. Did he not hear it? Or maybe he thought it was so futile he wouldn't address it? Barnabas watched the whole scene with apprehension. As he approached the castle doors, the two guards addressed him.

"Captain," they nodded.

"Hm, I suppose I can't kill them now, can I?" Nartikis said in Barnabas's head. "I can't open these castle doors with your strength alone, so I need them alive. Even if I did have you kill them, the guards inside would surely hear the noise, then come out and kill you. No. I'll wait. But I'll let them take care of you *after* you've killed the King and Queen."

The guards knocked three times and the doors slid open. Barnabas's body strolled through, mechanical and stoic. Down the red carpet they went, until Barnabas's body stopped directly in front of the throne.

"Where are the King and Queen?" Nartikis asked.

Barnabas didn't answer. Then another searing bolt of pain shot through him.

"*Where are they?*" Nartikis commanded.

What's the point? Barnabas knew Nartikis could torture him as long as he needed until he gave him directions. So he did. Through the white-hot pain, Barnabas grunted out the directions to the royal chambers. Only then did Nartikis release him from the torture.

"Excellent," Nartikis said as he walked Barnabas's body toward a set of doors. "The next time I make a command, you will be wise not to hesitate."

Inwardly, Barnabas cursed Nartikis. He also hoped beyond hope that his prayer worked. He watched his body move through the doors, through a corridor, and up a set of stairs. All the while, Nartikis gloated freely in his head.

"I could have cast a Dreamslayer spell on Jason and had him kill himself, of course," the wicked king said. "That might have been simpler. But how much more *delicious* is it to have *you* kill the King and Queen in cold blood? The fallen King, exacting revenge upon his successor. The kingdom will be in an uproar."

Barnabas didn't speak. The night was as still as could be—King Jason would undoubtedly be asleep. As Barnabas's body passed through the halls, guards stepped aside and said "Captain." Many of them were perplexed to see Barnabas wandering the castle halls late at night and usually kept watching until they disappeared behind a wall.

At last, they turned on the hallway that led to the King's chambers. Barnabas watched with horror and despair as his body crept closer.

As his body approached the door, Barnabas was surprised to see that there were no guards nearby. Odd. It's standard practice to have at least two guards outside the King's quarters. But this didn't give Nartikis the slightest pause. Barnabas watched as Nartikis slipped his sword from his sheath. Barnabas's other hand moved forward to unlatch the doors.

He didn't get the chance. From the other side, they flew open with a *bang*.

Nadiel stood before them, fully armored. Over his shoulder, Jason and Saryan were out of bed, still in their night clothes. Beside Nadiel, a set of guards.

"Good evening, Captain," Nadiel said.

Nartikis lifted Barnabas's sword to strike, but he was too slow. Nadiel's arm shot forward, grabbing Barnabas by the forehead, his thumb and middle finger clamping his temples.

Everything went black.

Barnabas was out of his body and back in the dark room where Nartikis took control of him. Nartikis was there, too. But they weren't the only ones. Nadiel had arrived.

In a flash, Nadiel threw his arms forward and shot plumes of fire from his palms. Nartikis dodged them and threw his arms like windmills. Giant black daggers rained on the Advisor, but Nadiel lifted his arms to shield the blow, and the daggers bounced off an invisible shield.

Barnabas backpedaled, having no weapon and no magic to defend himself. He knew what he was witnessing—a duel of two master magicians, dark versus light.

Nartikis summoned giant snakes on either side of him. They slithered quickly toward Nadiel then reared their heads back, ready to strike. But before they could, Nadiel lifted his arms and clenched his fists. Immediately, each snake's head was severed from its body as if by invisible swords.

"*Release him!*" Nadiel's voice was deafening.

Nartikis shuddered before he regained his composure. Out of the corner of his eye, he spied Barnabas. Turning his attention, he dug his heels in and flew toward Barnabas at blinding speed. Barnabas flinched, waiting for the impact.

It never happened. Nadiel summoned a barrier that surrounded Barnabas like a giant barrel. Nartikis collided with it, rebounding off the barrier and skidding to a heap several yards away. He staggered to his feet.

"*Release him!*" Nadiel bellowed once more.

Nartikis breathed hard. His greasy black hair was matted and sweaty over his eyes. He roared horribly and, suddenly, his head sprouted long, curling horns. His eyes glowed purple. His arms and legs bulged, and his fingers turned into long, jagged claws. In his new form, he lifted his arms in the air, and suddenly the floor was covered with dark, decrepit arms reaching up from the ground as if stretching to escape a cold grave.

Several sets of arms grabbed Nadiel's legs. Even Barnabas, inside his shield, had arms grab him from underneath. They started pulling down. Inch by inch, Barnabas and Nadiel felt themselves sinking into oblivion. Meanwhile, Nartikis hunched down and bounded toward Nadiel, claws outstretched, hungry to rip and tear.

Through all this, Nadiel didn't flinch. He breathed deeply and held his hands together, bowing his head calmly. He began muttering a lengthy and complicated phrase, and as Nartikis barreled toward him at top speed, Nadiel's body radiated a blinding white light. Fire encompassed them from all around. Barnabas watched great flames fly by his shield, but he did not feel their scornful heat. The dark, disgusting arms shuddered and retracted into the ground. Amid it all, Nartikis howled. His body, overcome by the flames, swung and flailed through the onslaught, finding no relief.

"*Release him!*" Nadiel's voice boomed again.

Nartikis didn't listen. He growled and bared his teeth, pushing down the pain. He tried to open his eyes, tried to cast some other form of magic, but he couldn't overpower Nadiel. He sank back down to the ground, crying in agony.

"*RELEASE HIM!*" Nadiel demanded one last time.

And just like that, the black room was gone. They were back in the castle, just outside the royal chamber. Nadiel sank to his knees, gasping for air. Likewise, Barnabas collapsed to the floor, shivering and coated with sweat. The guards looked at both of them, shocked and confused at just happened. Several yards away, Jason knew.

"Bring them blankets!" Jason commanded.

Nadiel forced himself to his feet and made his way to a table just inside in the King's quarters. He sat in a seat, then lifted his eyes to a guard and said, "Please bring me a magic elixir. My strength is depleted."

"Yes, sir!" The guard nodded and left.

The other guard brought Barnabas and Nadiel their blankets, then helped Barnabas to his feet. Barnabas kept shivering, and his vision was blurry as the guard led him to the table where Nadiel sat. Barnabas bunched up the blanket around him. It was thick, but somehow did very little to warm his body.

"Did you Overcurse him?" Jason asked eagerly.

Nadiel shook his head while cradling his temples. "I cannot tell. The vision simply disappeared. If he were here, we would know for certain."

"So he might have broken the spell before you had the chance?"

"It is possible."

Jason sighed. "Captain, how are you?"

Barnabas continued shivering and kept his eyes down. "Lock me away when this war is over."

Jason's eyebrows pointed. "That's not your decision."

"*I* am the cause for *all of this*," Barnabas said through shivers. "Do you blame the people for cursing and scorning me? This is all my doing. Nartikis is *my* son. *My* bastard child." He paused. "I was so close to performing that cursed magic tonight. I'm always so close—teetering on the edge of a knife. I could very well become that man again. I could become a monster."

Everyone was quiet. Across the room, Saryan folded her arms and shuffled her cold feet. The guard returned with Nadiel's magic elixir, and Nadiel downed it. After he drank its contents, he looked hard at Barnabas and said, "Did you practice *Tepnoh Edomah*?"

Barnabas was quiet, but he shook his head. Almost imperceptibly.

"Well done," Nadiel said with a nod.

Barnabas didn't speak.

"Your fate is going to be decided by the Sacred Dragon, Barnabas," Jason said softly. "Where you go will be decided when this war is over."

The mention of the Dragon reminded Barnabas of something. "How did you... know... he was coming?"

Nadiel and Jason traded looks. Nadiel said, "A feeling. I was down the hall, reading in the library when I felt a dark presence approaching. Then, after a long moment, a single word came clearly into my head. *Dreamslayer.* I came in to warn the King, but he had felt the same thing."

By now, Barnabas wasn't shivering as much but was still sweating. The Dragon had heard him. Inside, he felt satisfied but also puzzled that the Dragon would listen. Barnabas forced himself to stand, still clutching the blanket around him.

"Please let me be excused," he requested.

Like a concerned parent, Jason nodded. "You are excused. Guards, please help Barnabas down to his quarters."

Everyone watched as Barnabas crept out of the room. He didn't regain his strength as he made the long walk through the castle grounds. The guards didn't follow him inside his tool shed. Barnabas closed the door behind him, painstakingly changed out of his armor, hung up his sword and wrapped himself in more blankets before he got too cold again. He even rested on his cot. He needed something soft.

He was about to drift off to sleep when a knock came to the door.

Barnabas clenched his teeth to keep them from chattering. Frowning, he said, "Enter."

The door unlatched. Queen Saryan entered, wearing a coat against her night gown. She closed the door behind her, then leaned her back against it, arms folded like before. She looked around at the Chief Captain's lodging, unimpressed and well aware that the arrangements were unbecoming of his status.

"If I were you," she said. "I would have named all the mice by now."

Barnabas forced himself to stand out of respect.

"Don't," she said.

Quick to follow orders, Barnabas plopped himself back down on the cot. His head swam. All he wanted was sleep. But he wasn't going to disrespect the Queen. Truthfully, he was shocked that she was even here.

"What you said up there, about being the cause of all of this," Queen Saryan began. As she started, she gave a long pause, searching for the right words. She opened and closed her mouth multiple times, then she said, "I think you're right. I think this is your fault. But... maybe that doesn't matter anymore."

Barnabas didn't respond. He wasn't sure what she meant.

"I've seen that my husband is trying to practice forgiveness, so I've decided to give it a try, too," Queen Saryan said. She locked eyes with him. Her chin shook. But she cleared her throat and forced herself to say the words. "Barnabas, I forgive you. I forgive you for the pain that you've caused me and my family. Tonight, I'm going to start letting go. I won't let myself hate you anymore."

Something was caught in Barnabas's throat. He tightened his jaw to control it.

"Just… stop giving the anger inside you a place to live," Saryan said. "I think… I think you can become the good man that you once were. Just… try."

She paused, awaiting a response. But Barnabas could give none. Her words assailed him in a way that didn't feel like an attack but exploded inside facets of his soul that he had forgotten he had. What was it? Why was she saying these things? He didn't deserve this. She knew who he was. So how? Why?

"Well, goodnight," Queen Saryan said. "May the Dragon bless you, Captain Barnabas."

She nodded, then slipped out the door, gently latching it behind her. Barnabas listened to her footsteps slip into the night as he turned over in his cot. He was still clenching his jaw, trying to suppress that feeling in his throat. He kept himself from blinking so he wouldn't stain his pillow.

34

THE GIFT

The morning after the Dreamslayer spell, Barnabas was awake and dressed before sunrise despite his exhaustion. He blinked and shook his head and tried to keep his balance as he readied himself for the day, but his head was light, and his body was weak. As he supervised the construction outside the city walls, he marched with dignity and poise. No one could tell how utterly exhausted he was.

Preparations on the wall were going slower than anticipated, even though the work never ceased. At dusk, the day crews retired to their barracks to get what rest they could, and the evening crews would emerge to pick up where the work left off. These crews were led by Kalyk and Chief Patu, who were accustomed to hunting prey through the night.

Along with the slow construction, a dragon scale was still nowhere to be found. Scores of guards visited every merchant and collector. Efforts were doubled and intensified. They visited every mansion, house, cabin, and shanty. But no one in Nezmyth City had a true dragon scale.

All of this led to mounting anxiety back at the castle. Jason lost even more sleep than usual. If they couldn't find a dragon scale, everything would be in vain. For this reason, those at the castle spent much of the morning supplicating the Sacred Dragon for assistance. Master Ferribolt joined them.

Meanwhile, the last of the refugees were filing into the city, dragging their tired feet along the dirt path that led through the construction. These were the farmers from the southernmost region of the kingdom—the plains near Dragonclaw Lake, Port Runoff, and the Eternal Ocean. Most of them were so poor that they walked across the kingdom carrying their possessions on their backs or in handcarts.

One of these families was no different. Two teenage girls with blonde hair and bright blue eyes pushed a handcart with their father sitting inside, the handcart wheels grinding through the dirt as they went. The man hated to watch his daughters carry his weight. He would have happily pushed the cart himself, but both of his legs were amputated from the knee down. So, he sat among the blankets instead, on hand on the remains of his knee and the other hand on a small wooden box.

The three cast their eyes about them as they approached Nezmyth City. Thousands of people were outside the western gate, digging trenches miles long. As they dug, they fastened sharpened logs along the edges, pointing upward and west like giant spears. Among the trenches, towers thirty feet high went up quickly, lashed together by thick cords. The tops were wide enough for maybe half a dozen men. Along the city walls, scaffolding was in place to build the walls at least twice as high and three times as thick. An army of burly masons worked on it, lifting stones, slapping mortar, and pushing rocks into place.

The father scratched his beard as he looked around. "So the Ash will have to climb over the spears and through trenches before they can even reach the wall. And from those towers, I bet they'll have archers and magicians fire down on them. Smart."

"I've heard nasty things about the Ash," one of the girls said.

"Yeah. I've heard they run like antelope, but they're strong like bears," the other girl said.

The father thought for a second. "Well, let's hope you heard wrong."

They walked quietly for a long moment, looking around at the construction. The sweaty-backed people deep in the trenches struck and hoisted out mounds of dirt, packing them tightly around the bases of the log-spears. Coughs and mutters were frequent. Soldiers patrolled with jugs of water and morsels of bread to give whatever nourishment they could. Through the crowd, one of the girls spotted a man—a man with broad shoulders and peppery hair, garbed with shimmering bronze armor, patrolling a trench with guards on either side of him.

"That's him, isn't it?" The girl nodded in his direction. "Barnabas. The fallen king."

The father followed his daughter's gaze and saw him. Yes, that was him alright. He had to stop himself from narrowing his eyes. Instead, he let out a long sigh.

"Yes, Helga, that's him," he said. "I recognize him from years ago. Dreadful man." The man let out another sigh. "Dragon knows what's going on in King Jason's head. But I want you two to remember—he is Foreordained by the Sacred Dragon to be where he is. If Barnabas is meant to be Chief Captain, King Jason must have been inspired to make it so. Understand?"

"Yes, Pop," the girls said in unison.

"All things happen in the Dragon's time," the father whispered as he looked down at the wooden box and gave it a pat.

Their silence continued as they passed through construction and approached the city gates. As they crossed the threshold into Nezmyth City, a small group of soldiers were there to greet them and the other refugees.

"Welcome to Nezmyth City!" one soldier shouted. "You'll be escorted to your assigned barracks. The King is in search for a dragon scale to assist in the war efforts! If any of you are in possession of an authentic dragon scale, you are required to make it known to the nearest soldier!"

The two girls traded wide-eyed looks, then looked at their father. He sat upright in the handcart. His heart rate picked up, but his soul was calm, and his mind was clear. He pulled the wooden box onto his lap.

"Hilda, go tell him!" The father whispered. "This could be it!"

Hilda nodded and hiked her dress up before she ran over to the soldier. The soldier stared her down. "Yes?"

"Sir, um," Hilda said. "*We* have a dragon scale."

* * * * *

Jason paced back and forth in the great hall. Nadiel sat at a table not far away, trying to read but finding concentration difficult. With no dragon scale and the battle days away, it was hard to think of anything else. Master Ferribolt was there, sitting across the table from him, his eyes closed, deep in meditation. Nadiel peeked over the top of his book just as Master Ferribolt opened his eyes.

"One more prayer, Master?" he asked.

"It was," Master Ferribolt nodded. "The Dragon will provide. I can sense it. But I don't know how or what else we must do."

Meanwhile, Jason was barely listening several yards away. He was beginning to worry that he'd wear holes in the carpet from all his pacing, but his beating heart compelled him anyway. Almost all of Nezmyth was inside the city, and a dragon scale still hadn't turned up. Maybe there's some merchant they hadn't checked with yet. Maybe there would be a nobleman that had missed the soldiers when they patrolled his street. After all, most of the Port Gala refugees arrived yesterday. Maybe they had one. That would make sense.

Boom boom boom

Jason let out a long sigh. If those knocks on the castle door were more commoners bothering him with another petty squabble, he might lose it. He didn't look to the doors as they creaked open and let in the afternoon sun. He just kept pacing back and forth.

Everyone else in the great hall watched two soldiers and three commoners march down the red carpet, though it would be more correct to say that only two commoners, both blonde girls, marched—the third, a middle-aged man missing his legs below the knee, was carried on one of the girl's backs. The other girl held a small wooden box and kept it close to her chest.

"Your Highness!" One of the soldiers said. "They have one! They have a dragon scale!"

Jason frowned. Looking over his three guests, he thought there was no possible way they could afford such a relic. The girls' dresses were eternally stained with dirt and grime, and their hands and shoulders were firm and strong—clearly farmers from the southern regions. They may think they have an authentic dragon scale, but these people rarely had anything in the way of possessions, let alone something so rare.

"It's authentic?" Jason asked seriously.

The three guests nodded.

"Well, let's see it then," Jason said. "Guards, bring this man a chair. What are your names?"

The man hanging on his daughter's back was the one to speak. "I am Rorik, son of Mikal the cabbage farmer, Your Highness. And these are my daughters, Hilda and Helga."

"Pleasure," Jason nodded. "Helga, if you'll bring me the box?"

Helga marched up to the King and handed him the box, a little perplexed at how underwhelmed the King appeared at their gift. She extracted a key from a satchel around her waist and handed that to him as well. By now, Nadiel and Master Ferribolt both left the table and arrived at Jason's side. Rorik and his daughters' faces lit up when they saw them.

"All three Foreordained servants of the Holy, Sacred Dragon!" Rorik reveled. "Master Ferribolt! The Chief Patriarch! It's an honor!"

A guard brought Rorik a chair and Helga set him down. Master Ferribolt graciously shook Rorik's hand with a glowing smile. He went on to shake each girl's hands as well, and they were just as delighted to meet him.

With a sigh, Jason unlocked the box and pulled the lid upward. If the dragon scale was truly in there, it was wrapped carefully in linen cloth. It seemed to be the right size, or at least similar in size to the fake one he saw days ago. Nadiel reached his hands into the box and took the parcel. Carefully, he unwrapped the artifact until the linen was completely removed.

As soon as daylight saw the dragon scale, fire ripped through Jason so suddenly that he gasped. He could almost hear a dragon roar in his ears as the scale reflected the light into his eyes. There was no question. It was magnificent. Unlike anything he had ever seen. Anything man made, no matter how ornamented and exquisite, would have been a cheap imitation to what he beheld. It was the size of a dinner plate but three times thicker. And it radiated a kind of energy that made everyone's inside swell warmly.

"My goodness," Nadiel said as he held it in both hands. "This… this must be authentic. I've never felt anything like this. It's as though I could… walk on fire."

Nadiel gingerly turned and handed the dragon scale to Jason. As he brought it closer, Jason could feel its aura more powerfully. And once he wrapped his hands around it, he felt the fire cascade through him once again. His magic reserves stirred inside him, like a beast as powerful as thunder but calm as a summer breeze. Jason inhaled deeply and let the breath pour out of him.

Rorik smirked from his chair. "You don't have to be so careful with it. It's nearly indestructible. I heard you have to know a special spell to break one, and I don't know it."

"Your Highness?" Master Ferribolt said. "If I may?"

Jason passed him the dragon scale, already missing the feeling it gave him. But Master Ferribolt's reaction was far different than either of theirs.

The moment Master Ferribolt got his hands on the scale, his body snapped rigid and he let out a sharp gasp. Jason's hand shot for his sword. Master Ferribolt didn't move. His eyes were glassy. He was present, but somehow seemed to be somewhere far distant.

"Master Ferribolt?" Jason called. "*Master Ferribolt?*"

Just as suddenly, the Chief Patriarch's body relaxed. He blinked, and he was back to himself. As he turned and looked at the concerned faces that surrounded him, his bottom lip quivered, and his eyes grew misty. Then, a smile. Everyone stared back at him, baffled.

When he spoke, he addressed Rorik, Hilda, and Helga.

"You... you have no idea how special this is, do you?" He breathed.

Rorik stumbled over his words. "Well, uh—I always thought a dragon scale was special, Master."

"*This,*" Master Ferribolt said, holding the scale up, "is a scale from Ugviir, the last Dragon King. The final Dragon King that ruled Nezmyth before the beginning of the Dark Era. I have just received a vision. Ugviir spoke to me." His lips quivered. "He has given us his blessing to use this scale. He wishes his beloved Nezmyth success."

Nadiel's eyes glowed. Jason was speechless. Hilda, Helga, and Rorik held each other close and rubbed each other's backs.

"Your Highness," Master Ferribolt said, wiping his eyes. "I'd like to get started on the potion immediately."

"You're excused."

"I shall assist," Nadiel said.

Master Ferribolt and Nadiel slipped away to begin the concoction, and as they did, Jason turned to his guests. Feeling silly and ashamed for his earlier thoughts, he said, "If you don't mind me asking… how did the three of you come in possession of this?"

Hilda and Helga turned to their father. Rorik's face beamed.

"It's been handed down through our family for generations," he said proudly. "As the story goes, my great-great-grandfather found it in a cave as he was out hunting. As soon as he touched it, he had a vision where he was told he should not sell it or use it for personal gain but must save it for when Nezmyth would need it most. Since then, it has been passed down." He paused. "It is our family's most valued possession."

"And… you're giving it to us freely?" Jason said.

Rorik nodded. "It is an honor to serve my kingdom and the Sacred Dragon, Your Highness."

Jason smiled. He couldn't help but marvel at this family's faith and dedication. He wished desperately that he could reward them, but he couldn't think of any prize worthy of their contribution. Regardless, he had no gold or treasures to give them.

Then it hit him. It brought pain to his heart, but he knew that this would be for the best.

"Well," Jason said. "You three have changed the tide of this war, and that's not an exaggeration. I wish I had more to give you, but I hope you'll accept this as a token of my gratitude."

At that, Jason unlatched the sword, sheath and all, and knelt down before Rorik. From his chair, Rorik gaped at Jason with wonder. Hilda and Helga's eyes were as wide as could be. Jason held his sword with both hands.

"I've had this sword since I was fifteen years old," Jason said. "Crafted it myself. Its silver hilt is encrusted with rubies from across the kingdom, and the blade is the highest quality steel. Ever since I birthed it, it's never left me. And now, it's yours."

Rorik was aghast. "Your Highness, I—I couldn't possibly —"

"It is *yours*, my friend."

Rorik's eyes shifted from the sword, to Jason, then back to the sword. He wrapped both hands around it, then brought it close to his heart. He pursed his lips and battled tears. He was able to mouth a single, "Thank you."

"You and your family have earned this one hundred times over," Jason said. "Do with it as you see fit." Then he turned to some nearby guards. "Create comfortable lodgings for these three and feed them a hot meal. They've served their kingdom more than enough today."

The guards nodded and escorted the family out of the great hall. Rorik, Helga, and Hilda blessed Jason and thanked Jason as they traveled back up the red carpet. They took turns holding the sword and inspecting it carefully, admiring every inch of it.

As they left, Jason watched them. Relief flooded him. Their prayers were answered, and they finally had the dragon scale. But his heart also ached for the loss of his sword. It felt somehow like watching a dear friend leave, never to return. Before the double doors closed, the sun hit the hilt in such a way that it gleamed light in Jason's eye for just a second— almost like a wink.

Jason smiled and said, "Goodbye, old friend."

Then the doors closed.

35

THE DESCENDANTS

Master Ferribolt used the Oracle Stone room to concoct the Purge potion; he said it felt appropriate. The ingredients were organized on a small wooden table pushed against a wall near the door. When Jason walked in, Master Ferribolt and Nadiel noticed the sword missing by his side. Their faces crumpled—seeing Jason without his prized sword was like seeing him without a limb. When Nadiel asked him where it was, Jason explained that he gave it to Rorik and his family.

"You gifted your blade?" Nadiel marveled.

"It's just a sword," Jason said, "I can always get another one."

Nadiel and Master Ferribolt slid each other looks. They knew how much that sword had meant to him. Giving it away must have felt like giving away a child.

In a large glass vase, the blessed healing water sat ready for the next ingredient. Master Ferribolt took the springlight flowers and sprinkled them in. The powder blue pedals floated along the water's surface along with their spindly green stems. Last was the dragon scale.

Master Ferribolt held it with both hands again, feeling its power. He sighed. "Such a shame to destroy something so rare and sacred."

Nadiel put a hand on his shoulder. "But necessary."

Master Ferribolt turned to his friends. "I might need your help with this one. Your Highness, if you would join in?"

Jason nodded and put his hands on both their shoulders. Nadiel and Master Ferribolt each put a hand on the scale, so the three of them made a small circle. Master Ferribolt and Nadiel recited a phrase in Ancient Nezmythian that not even Jason understood, and magical energy started seeping out of the three of them.

The dragon scale quivered, then rattled. Jason could feel the magic draining from him. He was getting weaker. At last, the scale snapped into pieces like a shattered plate. Jason released his hands from his friends' shoulders and rubbed his forehead, taking in deep breaths. Sweat had formed on his eyebrows, even after just a few seconds.

I was only a supplement to that spell and I'm already drained, Jason thought.

Master Ferribolt dropped the fragments of the dragon scale into the vase. As soon as he had dropped every piece in, the fragments bubbled and dissolved. Everyone watched in wonder as the ingredients swirled, bubbled, and transformed into a translucent blue.

Master Ferribolt clapped his hands and breathed deep. Then he put his hands around the vase but didn't touch it.

"*Baylohnin lah deelah*," he said.

After he said the words, a light blue barrier like a large eggshell encased the vase. It shimmered slightly in the torchlight. The Chief Patriarch turned to his friends.

"That will protect it until the time is right," he said satisfactorily. "Until then, I suppose we carry on with preparations as usual."

* * * * *

That night, Nadiel returned from his lesson at Grace Mountain without much to say. Tarren was waiting for him at the castle for another lesson on Ancient Nezmythian and history. Following their conversation days ago when Tarren voiced his discouragement over his position, Tarren ultimately decided to continue with his Year of Decision. Nadiel was happy to hear it. They studied by candlelight for a few hours before he sent Tarren home.

The following day was more preparations for everyone. Barnabas patrolled the trenches, unsatisfied with the progress. Trees from the eastern edge of the woods weren't shipped fast enough to city. Refugees, restless and hungry, often scuffled in the trenches, and guards had to break them up. The wall was the one bright spot on the city's preparations. There was plenty of stone to go around, and the masons were so accustomed to working long hours that the project felt like nothing new. The western wall would be fortified for nearly a mile by the end of the day.

Jason spent part of his day practicing with a new sword, although he never grew satisfied with its feel or weight. It wasn't that it was a bad sword, but it wasn't *his*. He had some satisfaction knowing his beloved blade was in the hands of someone who deserved it, but its absence still hurt.

Morning turned to afternoon. Afternoon turned to evening. And evening turned to night. Tarren left work, leaving his apprentice to lock up, and took his trek to the eastern side of town. He spent a just over an hour at his lesson at the top of Grace Mountain, then, when it was concluded, he made his way to the castle for his nightly lesson with Nadiel.

"Good evening, Tarren."

"Good evening, sir."

The two of them nestled into the library just down the hall from Jason's quarters. Nadiel had Tarren practicing intermediate healing techniques—ones that could heal broken bones and lace together deep slashes. They practiced on a wooden stick three inches thick. Nadiel would slice it in half with a sword, then Tarren would try to mend the stick, reuniting each wooden fiber with its original partner. Sweat coated his forehead and arms as he twisted his face, concentrating on it.

"This would be far more complicated with muscles and blood, of course," Nadiel mused.

"Not helping," Tarren grunted.

Finally, Tarren gave up. The stick was half-mended, with plenty of splinters and pricks sprouting from the side. He wiped his forehead. Nadiel didn't say anything as he allowed his pupil to regain his strength.

"Sir," Tarren said. "I've been wondering something. What happens if you try to perform an advanced spell and your body just can't take it?"

"You lose consciousness. Very similar to overexerting yourself physically."

"But I know that sometimes you can push your body too far. So much that... you can die," Tarren continued. "Is that possible with magic, too?"

Nadiel lifted his sword and slashed the wooden rod one more time. As the pieces split apart, he eyed Tarren. "What makes you ask, my young friend?"

Tarren shrugged.

In this instance, Nadiel's face showed his age. He let out a tired breath and nodded. "Yes, Tarren. It is possible."

"What would have to happen?"

Nadiel sheathed his sword. "Truthfully, you needn't worry of such things now. You do not have the experience or technique to perform a spell powerful enough to kill you. Those kinds of spells lock you into a sort of sequence that requires you to see it to the end. If you haven't sufficiently meditated or drunk magic elixirs to prepare, it *might* kill you. But it's far more likely that you'll lose consciousness."

As Tarren thought about his explanation, he hummed. Then he asked, "Is that all?"

Nadiel was quiet. He shuffled his hands and didn't look Tarren in the eye. "Yes. That is all."

* * * * *

Night came and went. It was now four days since Jason received his warning from King Nartikis, and four days until the Ash attack.

The sun hadn't crept over the mountains yet, but Tarren was awake. He marched down the Southern Market Street, nearly an hour before he would be at his shop to open up. He would normally sleep a little later since he lived above the shop, but he had other things in mind. Someone to see. And this person would be gone from their home by sunrise, so he had to wake early and get moving.

He left the Southern Market Street and traveled south along a road with some shabby houses. He eventually arrived at a house not a quarter mile from his shop. It was a small, one-room home, just down the path from Jason's old childhood home. As Tarren approached the door, he cleared his throat and tried to calm his rapidly beating heart. He lifted up his fist to knock.

Too slow. Before could reach it, the door swung open. Before him stood a burly man whose body filled up the entire door frame. His shirt was mercilessly stained with sweat, and the sleeves had been cut off to display thick, hairy arms. The top of his head was shaved. He carried a sack with some daily rations over his shoulder, and when he saw Tarren, his purple eyes popped open in surprise.

"Err—morning, Tarren," he said gruffly.

"Good morning, Father," Tarren croaked.

323

"Do you, uh… mind walking with me?" His father said. "I have to go to the wall."

"Um, sure. Sure, of course."

Gulaf the stone mason closed the door behind him and immediately made his way down the path, walking side by side with his son. Tarren was noticeably tall, but Gulaf was still slightly taller and wider. Tarren cleared his throat before piping up again.

"You know that Jason ordered all of Nezmyth to come to the city. So I was wondering… if you'd heard anything about mother."

Gulaf sighed loudly and shook his head. "No, Tarren. I don't think Lunli Village would come to the city. They're the kingdom's lunatics. The broken ones. They're expendable in a war like this."

"But Jason commanded *everyone* to come."

"And I'm telling you I haven't heard anything," Gulaf said. "You're free to search every barrack and building for your mum, but you'll do it alone."

"Father."

Gulaf stopped. Tarren looked into the eyes that mirrored his own.

"I think I might be learning some magic that could fix her. That could bring her back to normal. It'll take a lot of practice but with time I might be able to—"

A *tisk* leapt from Gulaf's lips. "No, you won't. No magic is capable of that. I've told you so many times, Tarren, *move on*. It's been nearly nine years. You needta let go."

Gulaf resumed his stride, but Tarren didn't move.

"Don't you miss her?" Tarren pleaded. "Don't you want to see her just once? She's your wife!"

Gulaf halted. "Of course I miss her! But no. I don't want to see her. You know why? Because that woman ain't the woman I married. That ain't your mother. She's broken, Tarren. Broken in her head! She's not coming back. Grow up."

Tarren's jaw tightened and he tried to push down the anger rising inside him. But for some reason, that verbal assault wasn't enough for Gulaf. He advanced on Tarren, his face pressed in a scowl.

"You remember why she's the way she is, don't you?" he growled. "You remember why they threw her in prison and what they did to her? It's all thanks to our new Chief Captain. The man your little friend decided to set free. And now I have to look at his face *every day* as he prances about in his armor, firing orders like he's King again." Gulaf scoffed, but his next line was a whisper. "I hope your position don't start until another King is called. Don't forget the past, Tarren."

Gulaf readjusted the sack and turned his back to his son, walking westward. Tarren stayed planted where he was, his fists tight, wanting to scream. But he didn't. He wasn't going to say that he would be an Advisor in less than a year, and he wasn't going to say he'll be proud of the opportunity to serve with Jason.

And he wasn't going to thank his father for helping him become the man he was. That was originally the plan, but he didn't feel like it saying it anymore.

$$* * * * *$$

"I'm sorry it's been so long since I've paid a visit."

"Don't apologize! With the war, you've had too much to worry about. We don't blame you in the slightest."

Kara always knew what to say to make Jason feel a little better. Jason sat in his parent's cottage not far from the Southern Market Street. This was the new cottage—the one that was rebuilt after Barnabas burned down the old one.

Kara filled a ceramic cup with tea and passed it to Jason. She and Tomm sat at a small circular table in the middle of the cottage. It was only one room, but cozy. Jason had made sure to furnish the place with certain comforts, but his parents insisted on nothing extravagant. A feather mattress was pushed into a corner. An iron stove was pushed into another. And a stone fireplace sat against the far wall and kept the cottage comfortable when winter came. The sunlight streaming through the open window made the floorboards glow.

"Many of our friends have been concerned about the return of Barnabas, though," Kara said.

"Yes, when he was first called, there were many questioning that you had gone mad," Tomm confirmed.

Jason couldn't help but laugh. "I don't blame them. I questioned it myself. But the Sacred Dragon wanted it."

"What is he like?" Kara asked with pointed eyebrows.

Jason held his cup of tea with both hands and stared into the surface. "It's... hard to explain. He's a broken man. He's told me multiple times that I need to put him back in prison when this war is over. Give him what he deserves. I want to. But I still don't know. It's up to the Dragon to decide."

Kara and Tomm exchanged looks. Then Kara spoke. "Well, I'm sure you'll do the right thing. Whatever it is."

"I sure hope so," Jason said as he sipped his tea.

* * * * *

Saryan's hand rested in the crook of Nadiel's arm as he escorted her through the Nezmyth City Cemetery. The only sounds were the crunching of their footsteps and the breeze rustling the grass and trees.

"Thank you for accompanying me, Your Highness," Nadiel said as he patted Saryan's hand.

Saryan merely hummed in the affirmative. Her tone was absent. Her eyes were filled with the reflection of the hundreds of gravestones that lay before her.

Nadiel led her through a journey of converging and diverging paths, not saying anything. In his hand, he carried a warm parcel that was slightly bigger than his fist, wrapped in a white linen cloth. Saryan could smell it, and she had to admit, it was lovely.

They only strolled for a few minutes before they reached a headstone looked no different than any of the others. It was the pinnacle of plain—a rectangular stone that wasn't elevated at all. Just a smooth, flat slab with three words engraved on it.

WILL THE PRINTER

Nadiel unwrapped the parcel in his hand. It was a loaf of bread—the kind that was rich with nuts, seeds, and oats. He tucked the linen cloth in his pocket and stooped down to set the bread before the headstone. When he did, he stayed down on his knees, gazing at the headstone thoughtfully.

"He always loved this kind of bread," Nadiel said with a smile.

Saryan half smiled. "How long as it been?"

"Forty-two years. No—forty-three." Nadiel almost laughed. "It amazes me how time passes. Every year travels a little faster."

"How did he die?" Saryan asked, then added, "I'm sorry if that's too personal."

"Not at all," Nadiel replied. "It was simply old age. Passed away peacefully in his bed." He looked up at Saryan. "How are you faring?"

Saryan let herself down and sat cross-legged next to Nadiel. She grazed her hand over the top of the grass as it swayed beneath her. "I don't know. Some days I still expect to see him roaming the halls of the castle, or the castle doors will open, and he'll walk in with some report. But then I remind myself that won't happen. He's gone. And the world keeps moving anyway."

"Death is never easy," Nadiel mused. "They say that time heals all wounds, but in retrospect, I disbelieve that notion. The pain is always there, but time simply allots us the will to bear it."

Saryan was quiet. She set her elbows on her knees and picked some grass by her feet. "I could definitely use that strength right now. My mother died when I was still young, but I never remember feeling this angry."

"Where is she buried?"

Saryan stood up and brushed her knees. "Not far from here."

Indeed, it wasn't far. Maybe only two hundred yards away. The dirt crunched beneath their feet again as Nadiel followed Saryan along the path. Eventually, they stopped at a headstone that came up to knee height, with a top level cut and angled at the sun. Around the name, there were inscriptions of flowers and mountains—very ornate.

The headstone was wide and intended to cover two graves. The right side was blank, but her mother's name was pushed to the left:

MELODY

"Melody," Nadiel read. "That is a beautiful name."

"I don't remember much from her, but I know she had a beautiful soul."

"I'm sure she still does."

Saryan smiled at Nadiel gratefully, then traced her mother's name on the headstone. "I still miss her sometimes… but I do find some comfort in knowing that they're together again." She smiled. "I can only imagine the look on her face when he ascended into the Third Life after sixteen years. I bet they gave each other the biggest hug. I wish I was there to see it."

Saryan coughed to cover up the shake in her voice, then she sniffed and wiped her eyes. Nadiel wrapped her arm around her shoulders and gave her a fatherly tug. She tugged him back and they stood there for a moment, soaking up the breeze and allowing themselves to feel.

"When this war has ended," Nadiel said. "We'll give Garrit a proper memorial. And the right side of this marker will be engraved beautifully."

Saryan smiled and coughed again. "I'd like that."

36

THE CONCLUSION

As Jason ascended Grace Mountain for his final lesson, he looked to the west. Nezmyth City was a dark lake of dancing candlelight in windowsills. Across the city, he could still hear the muffled clanking of hammers and the shouts of men working on the wall. The warm breeze nipped at his clothes. A large portion of the wall was fortified, but who could tell what it would be against thousands of Ash? He was starting to question if their fortifications would even matter.

He dragged his feet across the plateau as he made his way to the Dragon statue. When he reached the statue, he unsheathed his plain, uninteresting sword and set it on the ground. He breathed deep and bowed his head. The silence of the mountaintop echoed around him for a moment, then he heard the voice of King Thomas.

"That sword is different from the one you've had."

Jason lifted his eyes to see King Thomas sitting cross-legged at the foot of the dragon statue.

"Yes," Jason nodded. "I gifted my old sword to the family that gave us the dragon scale. It was their most valuable possession, so I wanted to return the favor somehow."

"That was very kind," King Thomas smiled. "You should know that many of your ancestors shed tears when they saw that. You made them proud." He paused and leaned in. "Have you learned to forgive yet?"

Jason's dipped his chin. "Not completely. But I'm trying. I really am. It's just… hard."

"That is enough," King Thomas said. "Keep searching your heart for that forgiveness and I'm sure you'll find it. The Holy Dragon delights in rewarding us for our earnest preparations, even when they fall woefully short."

He nodded toward the west—toward the preparations on the wall. Jason let out a long sigh through his nose. King Thomas put his hands on his knees and stood.

"Are you ready for your final lesson, Your Majesty?"

"Yes, sir."

"Good. Because this one is the most important. I'm going to teach you how to access the soul of Nartikis."

Jason stood up in kind. King Thomas's countenance was serious and stern.

"Take three deep breaths," he commanded.

Jason inhaled and exhaled three long, healthy breaths.

"Good," King Thomas said. "This technique is another technique that you can only access with sacred permission— much like controlling the weather. Drinking the Purge potion is vital in giving you the magical energy you need to perform this task, even as a Knight of the Holy Order. Hold your hands out like so."

King Thomas placed his thumbs and index fingers together so they made a triangle. Jason had seen Master Ferribolt and Nadiel do this before.

"You'll have to subdue Nartikis so you can perform this spell without interruption," King Thomas said. "But remember, *do not harm him*. It'll just make the rest of the Purge more difficult once you're inside his soul. I'd recommend a Paralyzing Curse."

"He's *really* strong with Dark Magic, though," Jason said, copying King Thomas's stance. "What if he can counter the Paralyzing Curse I try to put on him? And will the curse hold long enough for me to get inside his soul and do whatever I have to do?"

"Once you get inside his soul, time will become irrelevant," King Thomas said. "All you must do is subdue him long enough to put your hands over him and recite these words: *By the Dragon's Fire and Holy Breath, I claim your wretched soul from death, open the gates into your soul, that you may be Purged and renewed as whole.*"

Jason blinked. "A poem? And not in Ancient Nezmythian?"

"Remember, magic takes many forms," King Thomas said. "You used a song to cure your mother of the Ipoklime disease years ago. This part of the Ordinance is a poem. Recite it while your subject is subdued, and you will gain access to his soul."

"What do I do once I'm inside?" Jason asked.

King Thomas dropped his arms. "You will know once you're there. Every soul is different. And to be perfectly frank, Your Highness, I don't know how to prepare you for what you'll find in there. Nartikis's soul is something we cannot investigate."

"But as long as I can get inside and Purge him of all his darkness, the Ash will be destroyed?"

"Correct."

Jason nodded. The thought for a moment, then said, "But everything hinges on whether or not he shows up to fight me."

"Yes."

"What if he doesn't even come?" Jason said. "What if he sends his army of Ash and stays behind in Unbuntye? I did my best to goad him here, and I think he'll show. But what if he doesn't?"

To this, King Thomas nodded. "You must have faith, I suppose."

Jason waited for more reassuring words, but King Thomas didn't offer any. Finally, he said, "Is there anything more I can do to prepare?"

King Thomas half smiled. "You're already doing it."

* * * * *

The moons in the window meant that Nadiel didn't have to light a lantern in the study tonight. He just waved an armchair across the room and perched it next to the window. There, in the pale light, he sat with a book propped open in his lap.

He sat in silence for a couple of hours as Jason participated in his last Grace Mountain lesson. Silently, he wondered what he would be taught. He also wondered who his tutor was. He had suspicions that it was King Thomas, but Jason wouldn't confirm. If so, that first meeting must have been uncomfortable, given the verbal lashing King Thomas gave him the day before.

Nadiel soaked in the solitude, enjoying nothing but the soft moonlight and the crackling of a nearby fire. But suddenly, a knock came to the door. Half frowning, Nadiel blinked. He wasn't expecting Tarren for another hour, so the interruption felt misplaced.

"Come in."

The door opened just a crack, and in crept Barnabas, garbed in his Chief Captain armor. He stared at the ground as he slipped into the study and closed the door behind him. His armor clinked with each cautious step and he swung his arms unnaturally by his sides. All the while, he couldn't look at Nadiel.

Inwardly, Nadiel wondered if Barnabas were possessed again, but he didn't feel any dark aura in the room. It was just Barnabas, standing awkwardly at attention while keeping his gaze to the floor. Nadiel couldn't help but look on with scrunched eyebrows.

Barnabas cleared his throat. He looked around, scanning the bookcases that stretched from floor to ceiling. The crackling fire threw orange light on one side of his face. His arms were still swinging by his sides.

"Barnabas," Nadiel said with a nod.

"Nadiel," Barnabas replied, "erm… I remember this room. It used to be one of the treasuries, was it not?"

"Yes," Nadiel replied. "One of the rooms where you kept much of the gold."

Barnabas stiffened. "Of course, I remember. I didn't… read many books during my rule, so at the time, I'm sure I found it more fitting."

"That I remember."

"Yes, well," Barnabas shuffled his feet. "Perhaps if we survive this war and His Highness sends me back to my cell, he'd be kind enough to send me with a book or two."

"I'm sure that could be arranged."

"Wonderful."

More silence. Barnabas stood in the middle of the room, still not making eye contact, while Nadiel was half turned toward him in the armchair. Nadiel desperately wanted to continue with his book.

Where he stood, Barnabas kept shuffling his feet. He clasped his hands behind his back.

"Sir, how did you… stay your hand… all those years?" Barnabas forced out.

Nadiel blinked. "During your rule?"

"Yes."

"It was difficult," Nadiel said, "but time after time the Sacred Dragon confirmed to me that it was not my responsibility to end your rule. I was assured that soon a new King would be Foreordained, then it would be my duty to protect him."

"And that, you did," Barnabas said. "Jason is a fine King."

"That, he is," Nadiel said. A pause. "Barnabas, is that all you wanted to ask me?"

Barnabas shook his head. With his hands clasped behind his back, he mustered all his confidence. He lifted his chin, stood up straight, and tried to project as much Chief Captain energy as he could. He took a deep breath.

"No," Barnabas answered, "I came to implore you for forgiveness."

Nadiel's eyebrows popped. "Oh?"

"Yes," Barnabas confirmed. "For subjecting you to my awful rule for twenty years. You… you were a fine Advisor and you deserved better. You were wise and patient. And… and I was so… blinded by my bitterness and greed. You were always the first to taste of my cruelty. I owe you a great debt."

Nadiel took his thumb out of his book and set it aside. He leaned over in his chair, looking hard at Barnabas. By now, Barnabas's focus was on the ground again. Nadiel let the silence linger. He tapped his thumbs together, remembering all the times that Barnabas had served himself and let the kingdom rot. For years, Nadiel advised him against such matters, but Barnabas always ignored him. As the years went by, discouragement set in, and eventually Nadiel stopped advising him altogether. Instead, he wandered the castle like a ghost, finding solace from Barnabas and his corrupt soldiers in places like the library. But that was all in the past.

"Barnabas, you have my forgiveness," Nadiel said, "but this is how you will repay your debt—"

Barnabas lifted his gaze.

"Lead our kingdom to victory," Nadiel said firmly. "Lead as the Captain Barnabas that you once were. Fight in such a way that if this is the last thing you do—and it might be—that you will restore your honor, and the people of Nezmyth will look back at you as a hero that led us in our darkest hour." Nadiel's face hardened. "Will you do that, Captain?"

Barnabas's face radiated valor. He stood perfectly at attention, his eyes filled with fire, and said, "Yes, sir."

"Good. You are excused."

Barnabas spun on his heels and resolutely marched toward the door. Just as he unlatched the handle to pull it open, Nadiel said, "Barnabas."

The Chief Captain looked over his shoulder.

As Nadiel pulled his book back onto his lap, he turned to the former King and said, "Thank you."

Barnabas bowed respectfully, pulled the door open, and left the room.

37
THE REPLACEMENT

Jason couldn't dispel the awful feeling in his stomach. The Ash were only three days away, but the western wall wasn't seeing any significant improvements. It made images of the Ash flooding Nezmyth City too easy to imagine. Then it would be the screams and carnage of Pinegrove all over again. Jason found it hard to eat and sleep properly.

The good news was that the Purge potion would be done curing by this afternoon. It had been three whole days since they had found the dragon scale. Three whole days since Jason had gotten rid of his prized sword. He still hadn't gotten used to any other.

That morning, he ventured down to the western wall to see the progress with his own eyes. He couldn't help but frown when he saw the state of the trenches and the towers. Even with thousands of people working together, only half of the towers had been completed, and the trenches were far behind schedule. Barnabas had planned for three rows of trenches ten feet deep and fifteen feet wide, each several miles long. So far, only the first row was complete.

Barnabas himself escorted Jason along the trench. As they walked, many Nezmythians looked up from the rut to nod to their Captain and King. But just as many ignored them or looked up with shameless scowls—usually aimed at Barnabas. When Jason looked upon them, he saw dirty faces and blistery hands. They looked back at him with bleary and tired eyes, fraught with uncertainty and distress.

"Do they get many breaks?" Jason asked.

Barnabas shook his head. "As few as we can spare. We give them food and drink sufficient to carry out the task, but we're far behind." He looked over his shoulder at Jason. "I don't favor treating them this way, Your Highness. But this is war. And I intend to see Nezmyth survive."

Jason looked down into the trench again. He saw a man lean his hand against a dirt wall, panting heavily. As he wiped the sweat from his forehead, he smeared dirt across his hairline. The man next to him untied a canteen from his waist and shared it. The first man drank from it liberally, letting the cool water dribble down his chin.

Jason tightened his jaw and said, "I understand."

"You haven't been sleeping well," Barnabas said, tilting his head toward Jason.

Jason blinked hard and wiped his eyes. "I'll be fine."

"I hope you've been training sufficiently for battle."

It had crossed Jason's mind, but he also knew his primary directive was to Purge Nartikis of his darkness, not hurt him. For that reason, he had been focusing on meditation and magic instead of combat. "I've been preparing, don't you worry. The Purge potion will be ready today."

Barnabas nodded. "Very well. If I may make a suggestion, go back to the castle and get whatever rest you can. One of the soldiers will escort you back to your carriage."

And they did. Two guards escorted the King back to his carriage and it shuddered forward. Jason watched the city crawl by, thinking about what was to come in just a matter of days.

The townspeople that passed through the street were tired. Distant. Already defeated. He watched them with sadness until he noticed that they were coming up on the intersection of the Southern and Northern Market Streets. The driver was about to turn onto the Northern Market Street, but then, Jason had an idea.

Jason leaned his head out of the window and said, "Could you turn onto the Southern Market Street? There's a place I'd like to visit."

The driver complied, and they turned. There, Jason was struck with a parade of familiar sights. He had walked this street every day for years, and clearly it had changed for the better. The storefronts were cleaner and well kept. There wasn't as much trash strewn about. More vendors were out with carts and rugs strewn with goods to sell. It made him smile. But none of it made him smile as much as their destination.

The carriage stopped in front of Kristof's Weapons and Crafts—Jason's old shop. The King eagerly pushed the door open and hopped onto the cobblestone. In the window, a few swords were on display. There was also a full suit of leather armor. Jason hummed in satisfaction. He didn't ever remember making armor back when he was there. He marched directly up to the door and pushed it open.

The door didn't creak when he pushed it, which caught him off guard. He couldn't help but stand there, pushing the door forward and back again, impressed at how smooth the hinges were.

Wow, he thought. *Things really have changed around here.*

But the machines all sounded the same—their churning, sputtering steam filled his ears with delightful hissing and clanking. The air wasn't as humid as he remembered. Maybe they had fixed the ducts as well? The old coat rack was still in its usual spot. And the people... they were the same, too.

"Well, look who it is! It's King Jason, himself!"

It was Bertus—wide shoulders, ponytail, and all. He stood directly behind the counter, ready for whoever might walk in. Behind him, Jaboc dipped a blade into a barrel of water and lifted his eyes to see if it were true. Once he saw that it was indeed Jason, he creased his brow and went back to work. There was a third person in the shop that Jason didn't recognize—a boy that had to be twelve or thirteen, with a shock of blonde hair and a fair complexion. His jaw fell when he saw King Jason. But when Jason made eye contact and smiled, the boy quickly turned around and busied himself with some leather strips.

"That's Golan's nephew," Bertus said, noticing the confusion on Jason's face. "Started his apprenticeship a year ago when Golan left. How have you been, my friend? It's been too long!"

"It has been," Jason smiled, putting his hand on the hilt of his sword. "Golan opened up his own shop, right?"

"Yeah, Northern Market Street," Bertus confirmed. "Real classy setup. We don't hear from him much anymore."

"That's a shame," Jason said. "Jaboc, how are you? Settled down yet, or still chasing girls?"

Jaboc ignored him. Bertus cleared his throat and leaned over the counter to whisper. "He's a little sore about… our new Chief Captain."

The smile fell from Jason's lips. "Well, he's not the only one."

"So what can we do for—oh, I think I know. What happened to your old sword?"

"Remember how we were in search for a dragon scale?"

"Yeah."

"Some poor villagers from the Southern Plains had one. I wanted to pay them back somehow."

Bertus's lips pressed together into a grin. "There's the Jason I remember. So you'll be needing a new one? Something better than the royal guard standard issue?"

"Absolutely."

"I won't do it."

Bertus and Jason perked when Jaboc finally spoke up. His eyes were locked on Jason, white-hot, as he shoved another sword into a barrel full of water. Steam plumed into his face as his eyes drilled into the King.

Bertus put his hand on one knee as he turned to face Jaboc. "Come on, Jaboc. Jason is our—"

"He's not my friend," Jaboc fired back. "Not anymore. He barely comes by here ever since he became King. Thinks he's too good for us. And that's only the start of it. I won't craft a sword for a corrupt King that released a tyrant to start driving our people around like slaves. You used to work here? *Pfft.* I don't care. Need a sword? Go somewhere else."

The words were like daggers in Jason's heart. He remembered laughing with Jaboc all those years ago. Scraping through the hard times when the Harvest Tax nearly left them broke. Sharing bread at lunch time. Now, the eyes of a friend had no glint of kinship whatsoever. Jaboc's chest rose and fell with every hot breath. The churning of machines nearly ceased to exist among the conversation's tense silence. Near the far wall, Golan's nephew watched the exchange with mouth agape.

Bertus flipped around to face Jason. "Jason, he doesn't mean—"

"No," Jason said. "I think he does." He sighed. "Sorry to interrupt the lot of you. I'll be on my way then. Jaboc," he made hard eye contact. "I'm sorry I disappointed you. I hope you can someday forgive me."

As Jason turned to exit the shop, he heard Jaboc shout, "You can throw him back in prison where he belongs!"

The door shut behind him. He ignored the townspeople walking up and down the street ogling the carriage. After Jason climbed inside, the driver closed the door, climbed onto his perch, and snapped the reins. As the carriage jostled toward Upper City, Jason buried his face in his hands.

* * * * *

Jason told Nadiel about the exchange when he arrived at the castle. Nadiel was understanding and shared his sympathy. On the other hand, Jason knew better than to share the experience with Saryan. If he told her, she would probably take the carriage down there personally and order them to make him a sword. At this point, Jason didn't care that much about the sword. Losing the trust of a friend was far worse.

The afternoon hours crept on, and Jason tried to ease his nerves, to no avail. He practiced a myriad of magical techniques in the back courtyard including healing spells, fire beams, lightning strikes, and even transfiguration. They did a lot to tire his mind and body, but the unease that oscillated through him would not be denied.

As the sun fell, Jason sat with Saryan and Nadiel in the dining hall. Jason sat up straight, trying to appear unperturbed as he speared some vegetables with his fork. Saryan stole glances at him out of the corner of her eye, studying him as she ate. Finally, she couldn't resist.

"What's wrong?" she said. "You're upset about something."

Jason set down his fork and knife. "This war. Everything."

"There's more. Tell me."

Jason blinked at her. "How do you do that?"

"I'm your wife and I can read you like a book. What's going on?"

"I was… I just…" Jason said, spearing more vegetables. "The preparations on the wall. They're far behind. It's got me concerned."

Saryan's eyes narrowed to slits, digging into her husband. Jason didn't return the glance. He kept keenly focused on his food. In response, Saryan turned to Nadiel. "Is he lying to me? You *have* to tell me the truth, Nadiel. You swore an oath."

Jason eyed Nadiel threateningly and shook his head. Nadiel returned the gaze with utter defeat—trapped. He swallowed what was in his mouth, then cleared this throat. "Jason went to his old shop today to get a new sword made. They wouldn't do it because he freed Barnabas."

Saryan slammed her silverware on the table and stood up, pushing her seat back. Without another word, she stomped toward the dining room door.

"Don't tell me you're going down there," Jason said despairingly.

"Oh, I'm going!"

"Saryan…"

"You are the *King!*" Saryan shot. "You were acting out the Sacred Dragon's orders! They should know! They're going to make you a better sword than the one you had before, or they'll have to—"

Boom boom boom. The castle doors rang.

"Can't it wait?" Saryan hollered.

"Thank goodness," Jason muttered as he bunched up a napkin and threw it on his plate.

Jason, Nadiel, and Saryan could hear the castle doors creak open before they even entered the great hall. Down the red carpet came a single man, escorted by a couple of soldiers. The setting sun turned him into a silhouette, but as he walked farther and farther down the red carpet, Jason finally recognized who it was. His face lit up.

"Thomas! Thomas the blacksmith!" Jason said, his hands outstretched. "What a surprise on this dreary day! How are you, friend?"

The last time Jason saw him, Thomas was bandaged up back at Fort Abernath after the defeat at Pinegrove. Now, Thomas had a black eyepatch where the bandage once was. He smiled broadly and shook Jason's hands with one of his own. With his other hand, he clutched a long parcel against his chest —a parcel wrapped thickly with twine and cloth.

"Your Highness, it's an honor," Thomas said, bowing a little. "I hope I didn't catch you at a bad time?"

"Perfect timing, actually," Jason said. "What brings you here?"

"This," Thomas said, holding the wrapped parcel with both hands. "I hope you don't mind. Word travels fast of everything you do, and I heard that you gave your sword to the man who had a dragon scale. He was a poor farmer from the Southern Plains. Is that true?"

"Yes, on both accounts," Jason said.

"Well," Thomas said timidly. "I wanted to give you something as a token of my gratitude. You helped preserve my life and kept the promise you made to my dear Emilee. I hope this will suffice."

Thomas held the parcel out with both hands. Jason's smile touched his ears. He took the package from Thomas and held it carefully. It felt about the right weight… could it be? Jason went to work untying the string and unwrapping the cloth like a birthday present. Saryan and Nadiel both watched from several feet away. When the parcel was unwrapped, Jason's eyes grew.

A stunning, magnificent new sword. The hilt was a shimmering white metal Jason had never seen before, and the grip was wrapped in braided leather. A ruby was encrusted in the pommel, and the cross guard was two dragon heads snarling in opposite directions. He ripped the sword from its sheath and held the blade to his face. The steel sang as it reflected the light's surface. It felt perfectly balanced in his hand—the work of someone with decades of experience.

"Thomas, this blade is exquisite," he marveled. "What kind of metal is this? I've never seen a white handle before. It's beautiful."

"It's something of my own invention," Thomas said. "I haven't even a name for it."

Jason's chest swelled and his smile touched his ears. He slipped it back into its sheath. His gaze shifted to Thomas, who looked just as happy with his work as Jason was to receive it.

"This is the finest blade I've ever handled," Jason said. "You give this to me freely?"

Thomas bowed. "It was an honor to craft it, Your Majesty."

Jason smiled, still admiring the work as it rested in its sheath. "You know, most blades of this craftsmanship have a name. What would you have me call it?"

"Well, Your Highness," Thomas said, rubbing his hands together. "I would be lying if I said I hadn't thought about it. You are one with the Sacred Dragon... eager to do good and cast out darkness... the kind of King that makes the Guardian of the Night tremble. For that reason, I would call it Nightbane."

Jason held the sword up to his eyes again. Beaming, he said, "A fitting name. Thomas, please kneel."

Thomas knelt before Jason and bowed his head, clasping his hands in front of him. Jason slipped Nightbane from its sheath and stretched it forward, tapping each of Thomas's shoulders.

"From now on," he said. "You will no longer be known simply as Thomas the blacksmith. You will be revered as Thomas, Forger of Nightbane."

After Jason conferred upon Thomas his new title, Thomas rose to his feet with a smile so wide it could have made his whole body float. Jason sheathed Nightbane, then threw his arms around Thomas. The two embraced. When they let go, Jason said, "Thank you for this beautiful gift. I'll never forget it."

They exchanged more pleasantries, then Thomas, Forger of Nightbane, walked down the red carpet and exited the castle. By then, Jason had already slung Nightbane around his waist and thrown the other sword to the nearest soldier to take it away. Over and over, he tore Nightbane from its sheath and swung it around like a child with his new favorite toy.

Saryan slouched in the throne, folding her arms, looking over her husband with a smirk. "Well, at least your friend saved me a trip to the market."

* * * * *

Night had fallen on Nezmyth. Just hours ago, Nadiel had returned to the castle from his third lesson on Grace Mountain. Tomorrow, Tarren would ascend for his final lesson, then the three of them would be fully prepared to conduct the Purge Ordinance. Until then, work continued on the western wall.

Outside the gate, the night crew was hard at work in the trenches. Above them, guards patrolled the newly widened wall and stayed posted in their towers, looking to the west. Each guard was equipped with a standard issue telescope enchanted to see far distances even in the dark.

Two of these guards, stationed at the tower just above the gate, conversed as they looked on the trenches below.

"Just over two days before they arrive," the first guard said. "These trenches won't be close to ready."

The second soldier spoke through bits of guabo in his mouth. "At least we're not down there working in them, covered in dirt all day."

"I dunno. Standin' around here every night kinda makes me wish I was put to more use. It's nice to get dirt under your fingers sometimes."

"Says you."

"Besides, it's a little chilly tonight. That kinda work keeps the blood flowing. Keeps you warm."

"I'll take a patrol job over manual labor any old day, friend."

The first soldier smirked. He unclipped his telescope and extended it to the horizon. He adjusted the focus as he pointed the lens westward, and as he did, his shoulders snapped and his arms sprouted in goosebumps.

"No…" he breathed.

Leaning over the side, he adjusted the lens more. After a long, taut moment, he lowered the telescope and snapped it shut.

His face pale, the second soldier said, "Don't tell me."

He could see it. Bolts of terror tore through him, making his hands shake and jaw chatter. It was time. Everything they had worked for amounted to this. The war, the struggle, the death. And in the night, it moved swiftly eastward, stampeding toward them. His mouth was dry, but he managed to force out two words:

"They're here."

38
THE ARRIVAL

The first horn sounded. Then more throughout the city. Within minutes, all of Nezmyth City was alive with the blaring of war horns. The Ash were spotted coming out of the edge of the Western Woods. With their speed, they could be upon the city in just over an hour.

Construction on the wall and trenches were abandoned. The workers fled into the city. Everyone strapped on whatever armor they had and armed themselves with their weapons of choice. Along the wall, every guard and soldier in Nezmyth positioned themselves to be the first line of defense against the Ash.

Back at the castle, Saryan and Jason jumped out of bed as a flurry of soldiers invaded their room to get them dressed for battle. Jason had only slept for a few hours, but fatigue fled from him. Adrenaline pumped through his system and his face burned red.

"He's *two days early!*" Jason roared. "Why was I such a fool to assume he'd told the truth? Our defenses aren't even close to finished!" He turned to one of the soldiers suiting him up. "Go get the Purge potion! Alert Captain Barnabas! Prepare the coach!"

As the soldier ran out, Nadiel marched into the room. He was fully suited up, his sword at his side. "The day has come, Your Majesty."

"Two days too soon!" Jason growled. Then it hit him. "Our instructions were to drink the potion at sunrise. How many hours until then?"

Nadiel clenched his jaw. "From now… perhaps three or four."

"This ruins everything," Jason mumbled.

Across the room, Saryan never spoke a word. Her armor was nearly on, and her silver eyes burned with an intensity Jason rarely saw. When she was fully suited, one of the soldiers passed her staff to her and she slung it onto her back. She tightened her bracers, then she looked at her husband.

Something like a flicker of a smile passed over her face, but it disappeared as quickly as it came. Jason's heart grew then sank. His armor wasn't done yet, but he crossed the room and held Saryan's face in his hands. He leaned forward and planted a sweet kiss on her lips, then stared deeply into her eyes.

"Whatever happens today," he said, "just know—"

"I love you too," Saryan said.

"You know you don't have to fight. You're the Queen. No one would blame you for staying behind. You're the Inheritor."

She pulled his hands from her face. "I'm going to the wall. Father will be with me."

Jason nodded. "I know he will."

They kissed again, then Jason's guards went back to work finishing his armor. Their fingers worked nimbly as they tightened every strap and buckled every buckle. After a few quick minutes, he was ready—bracers, breastplate, cape, and all. The finishing touch was latching Nightbane to his waist. Jason did it with pride, and he withheld the temptation to rip it from his hip and look at it once more.

Everyone hurried down to the great hall. There, a soldier waited with the Purge potion in hand. He and another soldier carefully poured its contents into three separate flasks. Jason took one and put it in a pouch by his waist. Nadiel took the other two—one for him and the other for Tarren—and hid them both away in a similar pouch. It was then that another soldier hurried into the hall from the outside. The castle doors were wide open.

"Sir, Captain Barnabas has already left for the gates!" the soldier said. "He took a horse minutes ago!"

"Good, he'll be organizing the soldiers," Jason said. "Let's get Tarren then! Quickly!"

The three of them loaded into the royal carriage, and the crew went barreling down Upper City. All around them, people poured from their homes with armor and weapons, running toward the western wall. The carriage driver snapped the reins, and the horses whinnied. He blew a horn of his own to alert the people passing through the streets. Civilians rushed out of the way before the carriage came flying down.

They veered left onto the Southern Market Street and struggled to get through the crowd as it became more congested. When the driver pulled up to The Cranny Musical Instrument and Repair Shop, he yanked on the reins with all his might. The horses let out a cry and slid to a stop.

They arrived just in time. Tarren came running down the stairs from his flat and was about to join the rest of the city heading for the wall. When he saw the carriage, he knew what to do. He ran for the door and hopped inside. Jason beat his fist against the wall once Tarren was in. The driver got the message. He flipped the carriage around and made for the western wall.

Inside the carriage, Tarren was panting heavily. His eyes darted about. Nadiel handed him a flask full of the Purge potion. Tarren held it with one hand, looking down at it. His face white as a sheet.

"I haven't had my third lesson," he breathed.

"That doesn't matter now," Jason said.

"No, it *does* matter!" Tarren shouted. "I was supposed to be taught something really important tonight! Something about finalizing the Ordinance!" He stared hard at the flask shaking in his hands. "Guys, we might be done for. I don't know if I can do my part. What if this falls apart and—"

He didn't finish his sentence. Next to him, Nadiel grabbed Tarren's chin and forced him to look in his eyes. Nadiel's searing reds had rarely been that intense.

"Tarren, you listen closely," he said. "The Sacred Dragon will provide a way today. Nezmyth will not be defeated. You will do your duty, and that will be enough. You will help us achieve victory."

Tears rapidly filled Tarren's eyes. "Sir, I don't know—"

"Wipe that fear from your heart!" Nadiel barked. "It has no place here! The Sacred Dragon has foreseen this and will provide a way! Will you stand with me at this hour, Tarren, Advisor of Nezmyth?"

Tarren's lip quivered, and his chin tightened. Battling tears, he nodded.

At that, Nadiel looked up. "Holy Dragon, grant us the strength to Purge Nartikis from the darkness inside him. Help us defend Nezmyth."

The carriage bumped and jostled horribly as it careened through the streets. The city's war horns had subsided as legions of people flooded from their houses, but the horn from the carriage was loud and clear as people made way for the King. At length, they got close to the western wall, but the crowd of people was so thick that the carriage couldn't push any farther. Jason and the others filed out, and as they moved through the crowd the people parted, turning to stare as the King and his friends made their way toward the wall.

Barnabas had already arrived in full armor, Artemis perched atop his shoulder. As he stood on the top of the wall, he fired orders to the guards and townspeople, ordering them into groups and instructing them on where to stand and what to do. Archers started climbing onto nearby rooftops. Magicians stood inside the gates. And at the gates, people threw whatever they could against the massive wooden doors, fortifying them with anything that could possibly hold them shut.

At the base of the stairs leading to the top of the wall, Kalyk and Chief Patu stood at the ready. They nodded to Jason as he got ready to climb the steps with the others.

"Ladies," Jason said. "Today is the day."

"It certainly is," Kalyk said darkly.

Chief Patu was quiet, but she stood with her feet planted and both hands on her battle ax. Jason was about to keep walking, but he noticed something on the ax that he had never seen before. The word *Adria* was crudely engraved on its head. And it looked fresh.

His eyes flashed, and he brought his gaze up to meet Chief Patu. She didn't need to speak. He already knew exactly what was going through her mind. He narrowed his eyes, smirked, and nodded to the village chief. In return, she returned the nodded with stinging eyes, holding the ax tighter.

With that, Jason and the others climbed the wall, reaching for the platform where Barnabas stood. As they did, Barnabas greeted them with nothing but a head nod, then continued to fire orders. Two other soldiers were there, though—the ones that saw the onslaught coming from the distance. They straightened their posture and nodded Jason as he approached. Jason's face was hard.

"You're positive it's them?" Jason said.

"Yes, Your Majesty. See for yourself."

One of the soldiers handed Jason a telescope. Jason immediately extended it and put his eye to the lens. Through the telescope, the hills were as bright as noonday. He could see everything. And just outside the western forest, he could spot them. Like a sheet of roaches crawling thunderously toward the city. He scanned left to right, trying to spot where the forces ended.

Jason sighed and handed the telescope back to the soldier. "And they'll be upon us in less than an hour?"

"That's what we speculate, sir."

Jason nodded, his eyebrows still pointed. His eyes darted to the towers that had been erected outside the walls. There had to be two dozen of them spread across five miles, staggered in position. Each one was manned by half a dozen magicians wearing heavy plate armor and equipped with several flasks of magic elixir. Then Jason spotted a small battalion of villagers sprinting along the edges of the trench. Jason put his hands on the edge of the wall and stared down at them.

"What are they doing down there?" He shot. "Get them up in the towers!"

"They're planting runes, Your Highness," one of the guards said. "They're more of our magicians—Upper City folk that know Ancient Nezmythian. Some of them said they can make runes that explode when stepped on. When they're done, they'll climb the towers and join the rest of them."

Jason frowned. "Very well."

Next to him, Nadiel, Saryan, and Tarren gazed over the hills. Each of them had a different mixture of emotions upon their faces. Saryan's mind reflected the memories of the father that was taken from her. Her eyes were like iron as she scanned the landscape, and Jason couldn't help but see a reflection of Garrit in her. Nadiel was resolutely focused on fulfilling his duty and carrying out the Purge Ordinance. Tarren had to clench his teeth to keep them from chattering. His shoulders sagged as if they had the very weight of Nezmyth upon them. Jason understood the feeling.

They hadn't noticed it, but Barnabas had stopped firing orders to the crowd behind them. He placed a hand on Jason's shoulder.

"Your Highness," Barnabas said. "I think it would be wise if you gave a word to your people."

Jason looked over his shoulder. There below them, a large crowd of chattering, nervous Nezmythians had gathered. His people. All armed with whatever they had, looking up at him, expectant. His heart lurched inside him and he dragged his feet to the edge of the guard tower.

As he looked over his hometown, with its sea of cottages and cabins, his heart swelled. This was home. This was Nezmyth. From the shanties of Lower City, to the warehouses and shops of the Market Street Triangle, to the mansions and castle of Upper City, this was home.

The chattering of the crowd died. Jason looked down into worried, tired faces. All was still. He breathed deep, let out a cleansing breath, looked up to the black sky, then down to his people. Behind him, Nadiel cast a quick spell to amplify his voice.

"My friends," Jason began shakily, "my fellow Nezmythians. Today, we face a foe unlike any other. Unlike anything this kingdom has before seen. The Ash are ruthless. They are tireless. And they have a singular mission: to destroy all of us."

The crowd stayed deathly silent.

"But I believe that the Holy Dragon above us smiles upon us this night," Jason continued, "and as I stand atop this wall, looking over our beautiful city… I can't help but think of my love for each of you. I've seen your faces in the streets, and I've come to know many of you by name. You're my people, and I love serving you."

The people of Nezmyth stayed still.

"But there are many that have not lived to see this day," Jason's eyes stung, and his lips quivered. "There are many who should have been with us *now*. Treetown. Pinegrove. Fort Abernath. These people were murdered by a King that wishes to rule over you. I have seen his face, and I have felt his darkness. He is not benevolent—he is evil, bitter, and greedy.

And he wants to have dominion over you. People of Nezmyth, *do not give him the satisfaction!*

"We are free! We are strong! And by the Dragon's Fire we shall prevail! As Nartikis casts a looming shadow of death upon us, let us raise our voices and shout as one that *we will not fade into the night!* We will not bend or sway in the face of death! We will *fight!* Here, we end this war! Here, we stand for life and truth! Here, we avenge the deaths of those that Nartikis so wrongfully took from us!"

Saryan's silver eyes stung. Among the crowd, Chief Patu blinked the tears from her eyes and bared her teeth. Next to her, Kalyk let the memories of Treetown flash before her.

"Today, *Nezmyth remains free! Will you fight with me?*"

There was quiet, then Nezmyth roared. The people held their weapons in the air, crying with a single voice. It was deafening. On the ground, Chief Patu was probably the loudest. Up on the wall, Jason controlled his stinging eyes. Through the roars, he softly said, "Dragon help us."

With that, the roar died down, and Barnabas went back to firing orders. At this point, the Ash were probably swimming over the Nezmythian River several miles out. Jason hoped that their armor and weapons would weigh them down and drown them, but with an army made from Dark Magic and dead bodies, he doubted it would have an effect.

One of the passing soldiers gave Jason his telescope, and he checked it frequently. As the minutes passed, the army in the distance grew closer. Their stampeding footsteps sounded like a distant waterfall increasing in strength over time. Just a few feet away, Nadiel and Tarren both meditated. They sat with their legs crossed, facing each other, eyes closed, their hands on their knees. None of the passing guards disturbed them.

All the while, Jason's heart thumped in his chest. They were here. They were coming. Two days early. The trenches and towers weren't done. The fortified wall was a few miles wide— the stone masons had done a terrific job—but so much was still unprepared. Was his speech worth anything? Could Nezmyth survive in circumstances like this?

Everything depended on the Purge Ordinance. It had to work.

The Ash were almost there. They were close enough now that you didn't need a telescope to see them in the distance. A sheet of sickly gray masses, hurling themselves into the wind, numberless in size, a torrent of footsteps like a great storm.

All the guards in the city lined up on the wall, shoulder to shoulder, ready for the attack. They anticipated that they wouldn't stop, but head straight for the gates, running like frenzied animals. That's all they had always done, and so it would be here.

But the Ash were upon them now. It was still dark out. The sun wouldn't rise from the east for nearly two or three hours. On his hip, the flask full of the Purge potion rested at Jason's side. On his other hip, his hand rested on the hilt of Nightbane. He prayed today that the sword would live up to its name.

Finally, the Ash arrived. With them, a chill like winter. Everyone shivered where they stood, their armor clinking and rattling. And when everyone saw the size of their forces, there was no way to hide their fear.

There were thousands upon thousands of them, stretching for miles. Sheets of gray, shifting masses armed and hungry for death. They carried no banners. They carried no drums. They hardly wore any armor—just animal skins around their privates. But each of their bodies were slashed with red paint, and every hand held a weapon.

With a telescope, Jason could see him in the very back of the pack. Nartikis. He sat in an ornate chair of ebony and gold that rested on the shoulders of six Ash. He sat perfectly straight, both hands on his armrests. Aside from that, Jason couldn't get a good look at him—he was just too far away.

But he could hear him.

"Greetings from your new King."

Nartikis's voice sounded clearly in everyone's ears, almost as if he were standing next to them. There was no echo or booming reverberation off the buildings—just a casual drawl slipping into everyone's ears. They could almost feel his breath.

"Your Foreordained King, Jason, brought this upon you," Nartikis said. "I gave him the choice to step down from the throne without bloodshed and without struggle. But he declined. Now, death has arrived at your walls. Surrender when you wish—I do not desire to rule an empty kingdom. Until then, prolong your inevitable demise as you wish. Farewell."

The Ash charged.

39
THE WALL

Ash roars filled the night. Their charge shook the ground as tens of thousands of legs pumped for the wall. Red eyes glowed inside their sockets, filled with bloodlust. Their forces stretched for miles on either side, moving toward the city like a mudslide. On the wall, the people of Nezmyth held their breath, waiting for what was to come.

Jason bowed his head and closed his eyes.

Sacred Dragon, give me the Knightly power—

Not yet.

The answer was immediate. His eyes popped back open and suddenly he knew why. His Knightly power wouldn't last all these hours. He had to wait until sunrise—wait for the time to take the potion. Until then, Nezmyth would have to survive.

As the Ash stampede thundered closer, the magicians in the towers braced themselves. They launched an assault of spells Jason had never seen before. Tiny red projectiles shot from their palms until they found their marks at the Ash's feet.

As soon as the projectiles touched ground, they erupted into pillars of fire. Ash were sent reeling, hurling dozens of feet through the air. They lost their weapons and landed on their comrades. But the Unbuntye forces careened forward, oblivious or uncaring of their dead.

Eruptions of fire continued to light up the field, flashing red heat against the dark. As the Ash approached the trench, they scrambled up the long dirt mounds that blocked their way. They moved like a horde of spiders flailing against the hills. But before they could reach the tops, they passed over the runes that the magicians left earlier.

More fiery explosions plumed from the mounds as more Ash were sent hurtling through the air. Nezmythians cheered and hollered from the wall as they watched the spectacle. Some on the wall conveyed the sight to those on the ground. The townspeople perched on roofs or manning the gates looked up with a mix of hope as the scene was described.

But those on the wall couldn't rejoice too much. They could see what was coming their way—an insurmountable army thirsty for their blood, sprinting tirelessly toward them. And they could be upon them in minutes.

The runes were used up quickly. The horrible, mangled Ash bodies fell in the trench or on top of the Ash behind them, but the onslaught barely hiccuped. They climbed up the mounds of dirt before reaching the giant spears blocking them from the trench. Some of the Ash tried to chop them down. Some tried to climb them. It stopped their forces for a few minutes, but then the logs began cracking and snapping.

Bit by bit, those fortifications were torn apart. The Ash came cascading down the other side of the mounts and into the trench. The first wave tried desperately to climb out, but the incoming forces squashed them in, pinning them down like squirming gray masses.

Jason almost smirked at the sight, but the humor of the moment was lost. As more and more Ash tumbled into the trenches, the Ash behind them stepped on top to move forward. It was only a matter of moments before the trenches were filled with broken, squirming Ash bodies, used as a bridge for the thundering forces behind them. The Ash sprinted across the trench almost as though it was never dug at all.

The Ash several ranks behind fired arrows up at the towers, and magicians dodged out of harm's way, narrowly missing arrows whizzing passed their ears and shoulders. They launched more fireballs. Then, the towers started to shudder and shake. At their bases, the Ash splintered their hands and knees as they climbed while others hacked at the beams with swords and axes. The towers cracked, shuddered, and began to tumble.

The magicians were prepared. With what energy they had, they ran to the edges of the platforms and leaped off. They let the air pull them, gliding the distance to the city walls. The people of Nezmyth cheered and hollered as they soared and arrows followed them, whizzing through the air as the magicians soared toward refuge.

One magician got hit just before she reached the walls. The arrow stuck through her stomach. In the air, she faltered, her eyes closed, and her body fell into the flood below, disappearing under the stampede. She wasn't the only one. Dozens of others didn't make it back. Their bodies dropped like fallen birds shot from the sky.

Jason's fists tightened as he watched. The magicians that did make it back stumbled and collapsed onto the wall, their bodies drenched in sweat and their bodies scraped with arrows. Many of them downed elixirs and refused to leave the wall. They faced their enemies, breathing deeply.

Yards away, Captain Barnabas fixed his gaze on the west as if his very eyes could force a retreat. His thick chest rose and fell and the muscles in his arms twitched. He didn't blink. He watched the Ash rush upon the wall with blazing intensity, calculating.

"*Fire!*" Barnabas shouted.

From around and behind him, a volley of arrows whistled through the air. They soared through the night until they found their marks in the bodies of the Ash. Many missed their marks, lodging themselves in the ground, but others found torsos and heads, toppling the Ash and forcing the ranks behind them to trample them.

The forces still moved with frenzied speed. The moonlight reflected their molten red eyes. Another volley of arrows fired. Just like before, some found marks while most didn't. All in all, the Nezmythians might have killed one or two percent of their forces. But there were still mighty gray sheets of Ash that stretched into the hills. They could keep coming for hours.

How long has it been? Jason thought. He looked over his shoulder to the east. No glint of sunrise.

"Away from the railing!" Barnabas shouted.

A slew of soldiers echoed Barnabas's command all down the wall until it carried to the very edges. Everyone stepped back. Jason hadn't even thought of the metal railing that was installed just off the side of the wall's edge, but as he looked below, he noticed that it stretched to the very bottom. And the bottom had long metal barbs sticking out.

It was at this moment that the onslaught of Ash arrived at the wall.

BOOM

They collided with tremendous force. The very mortar between the bricks shook, and everyone staggered. The Ash leaped up, scratching for handholds, but were unsuccessful. The magicians from the towers stepped up to the edge of the wall and gripped the metal railing. They exchanged glances with each other, nodding with resolution.

"Now!" Barnabas shouted.

Each magician released a lightning spell through their hands. Sparks shot down the railing before they fanned out in massive fingers from the barbs below. For a brief moment, the bottom of the western wall was illuminated with a hair-raising blue light. The Ash nearby convulsed, then fell to the earth, bodies smoking. The magicians pulled their hands off the railing, fanning them, steam rising off their palms.

"*Ready again!*" Barnabas commanded.

The Ash kept coming. Wave after wave, the magicians electrocuted those that reached the foot of the wall. And with each wave, the pile of bodies reached higher. The Ash scrambled and clambered over the smoking, charred bodies of those that came before them, growing closer and closer to the top of the wall.

They were close enough to look in the eyes now. Their huge bodies rippled with muscle. Their awful, rotting teeth dripped with saliva. They growled and snarled and roared with the smell of Nezmythian blood so close. They still leapt at the wall, bending their fingernails backward as they scratched and searched for handholds, desperate to climb.

"I'm waiting."

It was Nartikis's voice. Jason could hear it in his ear. He looked around to see if anyone else was hearing it. No. He ignored it. He had to wait for sunrise. He just prayed that Nartikis wouldn't be impatient and attack first. Hopefully, he'd want to watch the onslaught from the back of the pack.

The electrocuted Ash bodies were piling up, but hordes of Ash moved toward the walls in long, uniform rows. They were carrying things. Jason had to squint to see what they were at first. When he realized what they were, his heart sank.

Ladders and a battering ram. It was just like Port Gala all over again. And this time, the walls weren't near as high.

"*Ladders!*" Barnabas roared. "*Wooden ladders!*"

The guards on the top of the wall readied their weapons. The magicians hurried and downed more magic elixirs. Just like at Port Gala, the battering ram was made from a gigantic tree trunk carried on the backs of eight bears. And it was bounding straight for the western gate. Meanwhile, the Ash stuck the feet of the ladders into the ground behind their fallen comrades. With grunts and roars, the tops swung forward like giant axes.

They slammed against the wall, their long hooks latching onto the city wall making them impossible to push over. The Ash scrambled up each rung, hungry and quick. As the ladders shuddered with every step, the magicians leaned over the edge and shot fire from their palms. They were aimed at the Ash, but more importantly, they were trying to ignite the ladders.

Jason drew Nightbane from its sheath. Nadiel stood next to him, hands sparking. Tarren stood next to him likewise, a dagger in one hand and his other hand flickering with fire. Saryan waited with a calm vengeance, clutching her staff in both hands.

When an Ash reached the top of the ladder, the magician would quickly step away and a Nezmythian would jump in to cut it down. The bodies would fall to the ground below, and the magician would step in to keep burning the ladder. Dozens of yards away, Barnabas kept watching with fixed intensity.

Boom

His gaze shifted down to the battering ram at the main gate. Every ten or fifteen seconds, the wall shuddered horribly as the battering ram slammed into the doors. With the size of the ram and the speed of the bears, it should have splintered the gate on first impact. But the gates on the opposite sides had been reinforced so heavily with large objects and barrier spells that the gates held. In the back of his mind, Barnabas prayed that the reinforcements would hold until the Purge was complete.

Boom

Another shudder. Inside the city, a host of archers and magicians with shaking hands and moist foreheads perched atop roofs, waiting for the moment when the gates broke and the barriers shattered. Less than a hundred yards behind them, cannons lined the streets—carried all the way from Port Gala. Among them stood Kalyk and Chief Patu, weapons drawn, listening to the clangs and the shouts above.

Chief Patu set her hand on Kalyk's shoulder. "I'm glad to be fightin' 'ere with ya, friend."

Kalyk put her hand on hers. "I feel the same, my Chief. For Treetown, the forest, Adria, and Nezmyth."

"Aye," Chief Patu's eyes glistened. She turned her ax so the word *Adria* reflected in the moonlight. She grinned.

Boom

The battle continued for what felt like ages. Over time, the magicians burned and charred some of the ladders enough fall apart when climbed. Still, some of the Ash made it to the top of the wall, but they were quickly cut down by the soldiers manning their posts. Their bodies encumbered the walkway as they fell. They were too heavy to push over, and the walkways were hardly wide enough to navigate.

However, the Nezmythians weren't without casualties. There were so many Ash climbing that they couldn't all be killed. Some broke the ranks, and those that did carved out swift death. Bodies fell onto the street below, bleeding and maimed, while the forces on the ground watched.

Boom

The gates splintered. The battering ram was about to break through. Kalyk and Chief Patu held their weapons tighter and thought of their home. The clangs and crashes of weapons sang from the wall. Barnabas continued to fire orders, and the bodies kept piling up, particularly outside the wall. Most of the ladders had been destroyed, but gray, mangled bodies had accumulated so much that the Ash could nearly grab the wall's ledge with their fingertips.

Soldiers leaned over and launched jerokis aimed and heads and torsos. If anything, this just caused the Ash to stumble on the unstable bodies beneath them. It was a filthy, putrid mess. From the air, it looked like a giant mass of gray was pressed up against the wall, squirming and stretching higher inch by inch.

And overhead, the black sky became dimly tinted with blue.

Boom! Crash!

The main gates finally gave way. They splintered and groaned open, sending the bears and the battering ram barreling into the first blue barrier. They crashed into it heavily, causing the whole thing to crack and spread. They reared back and made another charge, then broke through the first barrier. Then the second. The third was the last one. Archers and magicians readied themselves with shaking hands. On the street, the cannons were loaded.

At the wall, the Ash could now hoist themselves over the edge. Guards and soldiers sliced at their fingers and arms, but there were always more Ash ready to climb back up. More Nezmythians fell. Jason and the others went to work assisting, reaching over the wall and hacking away whatever they could. Nightbane glistened in the moonlight, thrilled to cut away the forces of darkness.

Amid at the destruction, Jason heard the voice again.

"I am growing impatient, Your Majesty," Nartikis said. "But alas, I am enjoying the spectacle. I will be sure to kill you last."

Jason bared his teeth and tried to suppress the anger that bubbled inside him. Had to let it go. Had to *try* to forgive. But as he looked upon the fruits of Nartikis's conquest…

He swung at heads and torsos instead of outstretched arms and fingers now. They were getting higher. The Ash still clambered over their dead comrades, crawling with vigor and thirst. And stretched out to the west, there were still thousands more of them.

Crash!

Down below, the third barrier broke. The gate was open. The bears and battering ram charged into the street.

Nezmyth City was now open to the Ash.

The archers and magicians unleashed a rain of arrows and fireballs. The invaders crumpled under the slaughter, and the battering ram fell onto the street, but swarms of Ash flooded through the gate. As the archers knocked more arrows, the cannons fired, blasting Ash to bits, sending shattered bodies and severed limbs careening through the streets. Clouds of dust filled the air. The roof forces and street forces took turns attacking, just as they did in Port Gala. Meanwhile, the forces behind the cannons waited for more to break through.

They didn't have to wait long. With the sheer volume of the incoming Ash, the cannons were soon obsolete. Their dark footsteps thundered through the gate. The Nezmythians abandoned the cannons and took up their weapons. Shouts and crashes filled the city as the Ash continued to pour in, running amok.

Jason saw it over his shoulder. They had broken through. They were in the city. Beneath him, his people would be fighting the Ash face to face, battling for their lives—exactly the last thing they wanted. With their size and speed, it would be a massacre. But in that same moment that his heart sank, a jolt of hope rocked through him.

Just over the Eastern Mountains, an orange sliver was rising just over the mountains. The sky was turning bluer.

"*Sunrise!*" He bellowed.

Tarren and Nadiel didn't hesitate. They fumbled with their flasks and quickly drank.

It only took a second, but Jason felt magical energy rock through him like a tidal wave. Ugviir's scale supercharged him with a fire and serenity he had never felt before—like he could command the sun and stars if he wanted to. And with that potion coursing through his system, he felt a sharp, strong voice echo through his mind.

Now.

He uttered the silent prayer. His body burst into flames. The markings formed on his arms and legs, and his eyes burned orange. Nightbane disappeared from his hand, instead, the Blade of Nezmyth shimmered with its radiant orange blade, eager for battle.

Jason faced west, feeling Nartikis in the far distance.

"I'm coming," his voice rumbled.

He planted his foot on the wall and jumped.

40

THE ORDINANCE

Arrows whizzed past him as he shot through the air, soaring over the Ash that crowded the wall below. He dipped and dodged as arrows punctured his cape or bounced off his armor. His vision was razor sharp; he could see Nartikis a mile away.

Nartikis saw Jason shooting toward him in the distance, and when he did, his icy blue eyes lit up, and a smile slithered across his face. He stood from his throne.

Jason brandished the Blade of Nezmyth as he soared closer. He reared it back, ready for a strike. From Nartikis's hands, two long, curving blades materialized out of purple smoke. As Jason flew down to the ground, the grunts and roars of the Ash became louder. And Nartikis waited with wild, eager eyes.

Clangg!!

Their blades met in a mighty flash. Instinctively, every Ash darted away from the two to make a giant circle. Nartikis wanted Jason for himself. The Ash knew it.

In this moment, Jason got to see Nartikis like he had never seen him before. He had practiced so much Dark Magic that his eyes had sunken into his skull, surrounded by dark marks. And across his pale face, skin cracked and splintered with shallow purple cuts. His body shook, teetering on the edge of an implosion. A raw nerve.

Silently, Jason wondered how this would affect his combat. But there was no time for that. The point was to Purge him, not kill him—no matter what ill feelings he was still fighting in his heart. On that note, Jason thought of his lesson at Grace Mountain. He thought of his training on controlling the weather. Silently, he petitioned the clouds to form.

And they did.

Dark, swirling clouds formed in the pale morning sky. They churned and spun overhead. Scores of Ash and Nezmythians stopped fighting to witness the spectacle. The wind picked up until it became a furious gale, and the Ash near the two Kings struggled to stay on their feet. As they ran away, many of them fell over, losing their weapons and cursing.

Clouds continued to billow, focused on the spot where Jason and Nartikis stood. Flashes of sparks leapt across the sky, hissing and banging through the air. As the clouds gathered, a long, thick finger of gray stretched down, twisting and writhing as it went. Its enormous gray cylinder stretched and expanded until it was nearly one hundred yards wide—a cyclone. And inside it, Jason and Nartikis faced each other, paces apart. Their capes snapped, and their eyes locked on each other as the wind was deafening around them.

Outside the tornado, nothing could enter. The weather bent completely to Jason's will.

A mile away on the western wall, Nadiel and Tarren stared with wonder. Nadiel put his hand on Tarren's shoulder.

"Are you ready, my friend?"

Tarren's mouth was dry, but he swallowed and said, "Let's go."

As soon as he confirmed it, the world around them went dark. Tarren and Nadiel felt weightless. On the wall, they vanished. Their vision both became blindingly white, and then things came into focus. They were surrounded by a swirling gray mass and the sound of a hundred raging waterfalls. The wind snapped at their hair, and they had to squint their eyes to see. Nadiel had transported them both inside the tornado.

The two Kings' swords clanged and crashed as they sparred. Nartikis was on full offensive, while Jason skillfully parried each blow, but never injured the dark King. Nadiel and Tarren wordlessly bolted to opposite edges of the tornado, shielding their faces as they ran. The wind became more intense the closer they got to the edges, but no debris reached them.

As they reached the opposite edges, they both faced the center and planted their feet. They muttered complex phrases in the ancient tongue. Tarren silently prayed that his would work. When each of them had muttered their spells, they held their hands up. Transparent blue film stretched from both of their hands and grew throughout the interior of the tornado, forming a gigantic dome. Nartikis and Jason watched as the blue film rippled through the air and eventually closed in the middle, encapsulating them both. Mysteriously, the wind and gust still snapped at their hair and capes, even inside the dome.

Nartikis, narrowing his eyes said, "What magic is this?"

Jason ignored the question. "Yield, Nartikis! There's no escape!"

Nartikis laughed awfully. Long, curling horns grew from his head. His eyes flashed completely purple. He smiled wickedly, then charged at Jason, swords drawn. Jason planted his feet.

Clang! Crash! Shing!

Nartikis released a barrage of blows in the blink of an eye. He was so *fast!* Jason dodged and ducked and parried, struggling to keep up. Through it all, Nartikis never lost a step.

Jason leaped into the air and Nartikis followed. In the air, their blades sang and flashed. With one mighty swing, Jason deflected one blade and knocked it out of Nartikis hand. It tumbled to the ground until it disappeared into smoke. While Nartikis was distracted, Jason shot forward and tackled him, careening to the ground below.

They slammed into Nartikis's throne, shattering it into a shower of gold and ebony. As the pieces littered the ground, Nartikis shook his head to regain himself. On top of him, Jason lifted his palm and tried to cast the strongest Paralyzing Curse he could muster.

It failed. He could feel the Paralyzing Curse settle on Nartikis, but as soon as Nartikis recognized it, he nearly Overcursed Jason. He felt the power of the curse rebound on him and start to seize his limbs and muscles.

With that, Nartikis saw the opportunity. He swiped at Jason's throat. Jason flew backward but couldn't dodge the blow completely. A thin cut three inches long slipped across his neck.

Jason's heart jumped into his throat as he retreated. Nartikis floated back onto his feet. The blade disappeared from his grasp. He stretched out his hands, and immediately Jason was consumed in a tunnel of darkness. There was nothing, just he and Nartikis at the end.

His head felt weak; his knees trembled. A rhythmic, thumping pulse grew inside his mind, and Jason smacked his hand to his temple to stop it. But he couldn't help it—he was getting dizzy. The vision of Nartikis dozens of yards away was swaying and fuzzy.

Tarren and Nadiel witnessed it from outside the dome— Nartikis with his hands outstretched, Jason standing not far away, staggering like a drunken man. Both watched with wide eyes and hearts full of worry. They wanted to help. But they couldn't. Duty bound them to their roles in the Ordinance. If they didn't perform it to exactness, everything would be for naught.

Tarren's forehead was coated with sweat, and his knees knocked together. He clamped his teeth to keep them from chattering. Nadiel held steady on the opposite side of the barrier.

Jason couldn't fight the dizziness. His body felt like it was clenched in an enormous fist. Nartikis's body was just a faint black outline now. Despair gripped him. His Knightly power started to flicker and fade.

Help, he thought.

"We're still here," the voice of King Thomas came. *"We always are."*

He snapped back to reality just in time. Nartikis wasn't fuzzy anymore. Jason could see clearly. And in that split second, Nartikis dug his feet in, leaned forward, and launched himself at Jason.

Reflexively, Jason felt something rise inside him. The Blade of Nezmyth disappeared and he threw two hands forward. Just before Nartikis reached him, blades raised and ready to strike, an invisible blast shot from Jason's palms and launched Nartikis backward. The evil king flew until he slammed into the edge of the barrier halfway across the dome. Then he slumped down to his knees, clutching his forehead.

Jason growled. *Can't hurt him too much. How do I Paralyze him without getting Overcursed? He's so powerful right now.*

"You have to be patient," King Thomas's voice came in his head. *"Under this dome, his Dark Magic powers are limited. There's only so much he can do to you. Just hold on and you'll be able to Paralyze him. Don't hurt him!"*

Nartikis stood up. He didn't dash at Jason like he did before. Instead, he focused his hands together, forming a ball of black energy hovering between his palms. Jason watched with squinted eyes. When the ball finished charging, Nartikis cocked it back and thrust it into the ground. The dome suddenly turned dark as night—filthy, thick, and endless.

And with that darkness, a heavy feeling. Jason jumped into the air, trying to soar away, but even as he floated, he felt himself pulled down. And it wasn't just his body—his mind and heart were sinking into the abyss. Memories of the recent dead bubbled up inside him. Treetown. Pinegrove. Fort Abernath. Garrit. His insides trembled with rage and shame. He knew it was Nartikis's fault, but he was also to blame. The dark cloud overshadowed him and refused to let go.

Then the anger took control. Each breath became labored and hot. He wanted to break Nartikis. He wanted to destroy him. He wanted recompense for every life he had destroyed.

But that was when King Thomas whispered, *"It's okay to feel that pain, Your Highness. You can accept it. But do not allow it to be your master."*

Jason's eyes stung and, he swallowed the lump out of his throat. He closed his eyes and breathed deep, letting a tear form on his eyelash. He let out a cleansing breath, allowing the tension to slip away. Smoke billowed from his nose. In his heart, he knew Dragon would bring justice. Patience.

With that, Jason not only let himself get pulled down to the ground, but he stomped when he reached it. A ripple of fire swept out from his body, dispelling the darkness around him. Nartikis's eyes popped. Jason took several sprinting steps toward him, every footstep creating a small circle of fire over the abyss. Then Jason stomped his feet one last time, and streams of fire shot from his palms.

Nartikis had to shield himself from the flames with a dark barrier, but he couldn't stop the heat. Sweat drenched his forehead and arms. It was hard to breathe. Drops of salty sweat dribbled from his neck and down his chest.

Outside the barrier, Nadiel and Tarren continued to watch the battle with awe. Nadiel held steady, his arms rigid, feet planted firmly. A hundred yards away, Tarren struggled under the weight of the dome. His entire body shook, and the sweat from his forehead dribbled into his eyes.

"I can't do this…" Tarren muttered in despair, "I can't… I'm not strong enough…"

"Yes you are!" Nadiel's voice was somehow right next to him, despite the gale. "Pray to the Dragon for strength, Tarren!"

"*I have been!*" Tarren said, tears mixing with the sweat. "I'm using everything I have! Even with the Purge potion, I don't know how much longer I can last... I can't..."

"Just stay with me a little longer," Nadiel said softly. "You have no need to fear, Tarren. Don't you give up. I am with you."

Inside the dome, Jason stopped shooting fire. Nartikis barely had time to look over his shielded arms to see Jason hurdling toward him. He tackled Nartikis into the edge of the dome, then took him in both hands and threw him into the center. The dark abyss was gone now—back to grass but scorched with fire. Nartikis tumbled and fell onto his back, and Jason took a chance with another Paralyzing Curse.

He thrust his hands forward and flexed them, focusing. He could feel Nartikis resisting from so many yards away, but Jason's Paralyzing Curse was working—incrementally. Nartikis's muscles were seizing up. His arms and hands were pressing to his sides. Jason kept his focus taught and his arms outstretched, mustering every ounce of magical strength he had.

Then Nartikis's resistance grew stronger. Jason felt his own hands and arms starting to seize as Nartikis tried to Overcurse him. It started at his hands. Then moved up his arms. His legs started to buckle. Just as Jason was pushing the Paralyzing Curse on Nartikis, Nartikis was pushing back on him, getting closer and closer to an Overcurse.

No, Jason thought. *It ends. It ends now.*

Jason mustered whatever heavenly strength he had and let out a colossal roar. The ground shook—even the tornado seemed to shudder at the sound. The roar was like one of the great Dragon Kings of old, all-powerful and all-encompassing. And with it, a column of fire sprouted around Nartikis, ascending nearly to the top of the dome, throwing brilliant orange light all around.

That did it. Nartikis let out a horrible howl as the heat encased him. The Curse rebounded. The flames surrounding him extinguished in a hiss, and Nartikis fell to the ground, rigid and unmoving.

But now, Tarren was struggling more mightily than ever.

"Nadiel…" he breathed. "Nadiel, I think I'm about to pass out…"

"Stay with me, Tarren!" Nadiel commanded. He paused. Some part of him hoped it wouldn't come to this, but he knew it was inevitable. He took a deep breath. "I hope you'll forgive me, but I wasn't perfectly honest with you the other day."

Tarren struggled to stay erect and conscious, but he uttered, "What? How?"

"There is another way you can perish through magic. You separate your spirit and your body to strengthen someone else," he said. "It can only be done by a very powerful magician. And that, my friend, is what I'm going to do for you."

Tarren's eyes shot open even as his vision continued to darken. "*What?!* No! Please don't!"

"Tarren, I made this decision during my first lesson on Grace Mountain," Nadiel said. "The Sacred Dragon has prepared me for this moment. With your succession, my role in mortality is fulfilled."

"Nadiel, don't!"

"I hope you'll forgive me—"

"*Stop! I still need you!*"

"Farewell, Tarren, Foreordained Advisor of Nezmyth. I am very proud of you."

"*No!*"

It was too late. Tarren couldn't see it, but Nadiel smiled. As he did, his eyes rolled back into his head, and he fell to the earth. A sudden wave of strength flooded over Tarren. He stood firm, he stopped shaking, and his vision stopped darkening. But through it all, bitter tears poured down his cheeks and dripped from his chin.

He was gone. Nadiel. His master. His mentor. The Foreordained Advisor of Nezmyth. So soon and so sudden. Why did it have to be so? Why couldn't Nartikis have attacked one day later? Perhaps his extra training could have saved him. Tarren fought the lump in his throat and the tears in his eyes.

But somehow, he could feel a hand on his shoulder.

"Do not fear. I'm still with you."

Tarren looked over his shoulder. Surely enough, it was him. Separated from his body, still clothed in his Advisor armor, but with a smiling, beaming face devoid of the wrinkles he was accustomed to. He was magnificent—glorious even. Tarren stared through his tears in wonder. Nadiel's eyes sparkled.

Swallowing, Tarren said, "Stay with me to the end?"

"To the end," Nadiel nodded.

Inside the dome, Jason was upon Nartikis. Over his Paralyzed body, he held his hands out, forming a triangle. Then he said the words:

"By the Dragon's Fire and Holy Breath, I claim your wretched soul from death, open the gates into your soul, that you may be Purged and renewed as whole."

Everything around him disappeared.

41

THE SOUL

It all happened in the blink of an eye. Jason's eyes shot open. The gust of the tornado and the sounds of battle disappeared. All was quiet. Serene. He found himself in a place that he had only visited once before in a vision: the courtyard behind Unbuntye castle.

Lovely blue and purple flowers sprouted throughout the garden, shivering in a breeze that Jason couldn't feel. As his boots trudged along the stony path, they made no noise. He wasn't even sure if he was breathing right now. Is there air inside someone's soul? No guards patrolled the garden, either. As far as he knew, he was the only one there. All was quiet, empty, and still.

He looked down. The markings were still on his arms and hands. He was still in his form as a Knight of the Holy Order. In a flash of white smoke, the Blade of Nezmyth appeared in his hand. Then Jason jumped and ascended into the sky.

Jason didn't stop flying until he reached the peaks of Unbuntye castle. Here, he could see all of Unbuntye. He expected to see the Unbuntye capital beneath him, with hundreds of shanty houses and Ash soldiers patrolling, but no.

The castle was surrounded by miles of endless wasteland. There were no other people, houses, animals—nothing. Just the castle.

Jason allowed himself to fall back to the ground, but he slowed down before his feet touched the surface. Again, his boots made no sound when they touched the stone walkway. Not a single person was anywhere to be seen. He couldn't feel anyone else's presence, either. As far as he knew, he was the only one here. But Nartikis had to be here somewhere.

He looked over his shoulder at the castle. Then he took a deep breath and allowed the Blade of Nezmyth to disappear in a puff of smoke. Straightening his shoulders, Jason turned and marched toward the nearest castle door.

When he approached the door, he grabbed the handle and thrust it open. Like everything else, it made no sound. Light poured into the corridor of the dark castle, and as Jason closed the door behind him, he had no difficulty traversing the dark path. It was like he could see every fiber and particle of mortar between the stones. He soldiered through cautiously, ready to summon the Blade of Nezmyth at a moment's notice.

The first room he came to was large and long—obviously the great hall. He recognized it from the vision he had days ago. Nearest to him was the dais, where a tall, golden throne, highly ornamented and finely crafted sat empty and alone, not even a single guard in place. Jason could easily retrace the steps of the Queen, Nartikis, and Barnabas from his vision. A small shock of pity surged through him, but he largely ignored it.

Through another corridor he went—this one feeling a little more familiar. In a moment, he knew why. He had stumbled upon the dining hall, the same place where he conversed with Nartikis, and where Garrit met his demise. He flexed his hands angrily and tried to let go as his eyes scanned the long dining table and black walls. He marched through the dining hall and exited through another door.

More hallways and corridors. He found a sparring room, a room for alchemy and spells, and multiple libraries with shelves covered in cobwebs. Surprisingly, most rooms were barren. Just empty black walls. No furniture. This was clearly a castle made for one.

"Where is everyone?" He muttered.

At length, Jason found himself trudging through a hallway on one of the upper floors. As he turned a corner, he noticed a doorway at the end of a hall with a trickle of light seeping out. He bent his eyebrows and the Blade of Nezmyth flashed into his hand. He crept forward, barely breathing.

As he got close, he slid his eye up to the crack in the door. Through the slit, he could see discarded toys strewn about the floor. There was a brightly colored chest low to the ground— clearly a child's room.

Clutching the Blade of Nezmyth, he bent down and pushed the door open. What he saw made his skin pale.

In the center of the room, a humanoid creature sat in midair. It was naked, covered by nothing but slick purple skin. It had to be nearly eight feet tall, not including the curling horns protruding from its forehead. Its eyes were glowing black slits, and a sickly, sharp-toothed smile stretched along the width of its head. Its hands were long and flat, topped with fingers like tent stakes.

By the creature's side lay a boy wrapped in chains that covered his whole body. They culminated in a large leash that the creature held with one hand. The boy in the chains was obvious—fifteen years old with pale skin, a hooked nose, and blue eyes that were absent, defeated, and disconnected. Nartikis.

Jason shivered at the sight, but he swallowed and entered the room anyway. The creature smiled when he did.

"Jason, the Foreordained King of Nezmyth," the creature purred. "What an honor."

"Release him," Jason commanded.

The creature laughed. "No."

"Release him, *now*."

"Now, Your Highness," the creature said. "Is that any way to make an introduction? Not very hospitable of you, I should say."

"You're hardly one to speak of hospitality," Jason said, nodding to the chains.

The creature laughed again. It made Jason's bones shiver. The creature crossed its legs as if it were enjoying an afternoon cup of tea.

"Your Highness, if you plan on Purging the darkness from poor Nartikis's soul, you must be prepared to do it on my terms," the creature said. "I am his Keeper, after all."

Jason's eyes narrowed. "Keeper?"

"The one assigned by the Guardian of the Night to tend him," the Keeper said. Then it leaned forward. "Who do you suppose *your* Keeper is?"

Jason raised the Blade of Nezmyth to the air, hoping it would flash some sort of worry across the creature's face. "Release him, *now*, Keeper! Unless you'd like to see the might of the Sacred Dragon and the Blade of Nezmyth!"

The Keeper slapped its hand to its mouth. "Oh, my! The Blade of Nezmyth! Please. Do you not think I remember that Great Battle in the Life Before? I remember when that wretched blade was *forged*. We have our ways of dealing with your toy. I would advise you not to become overconfident."

For a fraction of a second, Jason saw hundreds of dark spirits surrounding him inside this very room, all nearly identical to Nartikis's Keeper. Their eyes were locked on Jason. It made his blood freeze and his jaw clench. When they all vanished, and it was just the three of them again, the Keeper sneered.

"My. Terms." the Keeper repeated.

Jason let the Blade of Nezmyth vanish. "What is it you want?"

The Keeper smiled. "You."

"Explain."

"Darkness cannot be merely driven out, Your Grace," the Keeper proceeded. "It must have a place to go. Did they never tell you that in your training?" It floated back down to the ground and stood. "I will release Nartikis on the condition that you transfer the darkness from his soul to yours. It is the only way."

Jason frowned. *He could be lying. Why should I trust this demon, who works for the father of all lies?*

"Nonsense," Jason said. "Just like shining a light in a dark room, darkness doesn't need to travel somewhere else to be whole. Darkness is always overcome by light. All you are is an absence of light. Nothing more."

The smirked faded from the Keeper's face. "You are in the world of spirits now. Things are different here. If you want to Purge Nartikis's soul, you must offer yourself as recompense. Those are the terms. There is no other way."

Jason scrunched his eyebrows. Should he trust anything the Keeper has to say? Its whole job was to follow Nartikis and influence him to do wrong. He could very well be doing the same thing to Jason. And what would the Keeper have to gain from overcoming the last King in Wevlia that follows the Old Ways? Everything the Guardian of the Night could ever want. This had to be a trap. There had to be another solution.

He wanted to say everything he was thinking—to call the Keeper's bluff. But he couldn't help but think of the hundreds of dark spirits surrounding him just out of sight. He was on their territory. Could they have the power to destroy him where he stood, even with the Blade of Nezmyth and his Knightly powers? He couldn't know for sure. Not until he tried something drastic. The Guardian of the Night's tactics were founded on distraction and fear—so perhaps those spirits were a lie as well?

The Keeper was growing impatient. He pulled Nartikis's leash tighter.

And that's when it struck Jason. The chain. The thing tethering Nartikis to his Keeper. Maybe that was the key to breaking Nartikis from the darkness inside him. The Keeper embodied Nartikis's reliance on *Tepnoh Edomah*. Perhaps if he broke the chain… that would be the final act of the Purge.

The Keeper must have saw this on Jason's face, because its reaction was immediate.

"You cannot have him!" The Keeper wailed. *"Give yourself to us!"*

That was the confirmation Jason needed. He sprinted for the chain, but as he did, the room disappeared, replaced with endless black on all sides. The Keeper and Nartikis flew backward as quickly as Jason could run. With his Knightly power, his feet left the ground and he soared toward them through the black, gaining on them inch by inch.

Hundreds of evil spirits suddenly appeared around Jason. He commanded his body to catch flame as he careened through the endless murk. The spirits flew at him. Any spirits that he couldn't ward off with the Blade of Nezmyth passed through his body as they wailed and howled. And as they passed through him, they made his insides cold and clench. His eyes became blurry. His disorientation increased with every passing spirit.

He gritted through the pain of the dark spirits blasting through him. He was almost close enough to reach Nartikis— he could see his fuzzy outline. He swung the Blade of Nezmyth, but he missed by inches. His Keeper continued to soar through the endless black, wailing a high-pitched shriek that scraped at Jason's ears.

Jason kept swinging, but he was still too far away. He fought off the spirits that assailed him. He forced his body to burn brighter and hotter to keep the spirits at bay, until finally, the fire around his body transformed into a radiant light. The

Keeper shielded its eyes, and the evil spirits dissipated. Jason was close enough.

Gripping the Blade of Nezmyth with both hands, he took one last mighty swing.

Shiinngg!

The chains broke and disappeared into a glimmer of white light. And as they did, a barrage of memories and emotions assaulted Jason.

His soul and Nartikis's became one. And for somewhere between a few seconds and fifteen years, Jason felt and experienced everything that Nartikis had. The anger. The betrayal. The loneliness. The abandonment. He saw his childhood. He saw the loving but distracted Queen. He saw and felt the anger in the wake of a father's absence. He saw and felt the anguish of burying his mother alone. He felt the euphoria and despair of Dark Magic. He saw the desperation for love and connection that transformed him to a monster.

And when it was all over, Jason was left gasping for breath. Warm, salty tears streamed down his face. He and Nartikis were both surrounded by white light, and they sunk to the ground.

For some reason, the action felt natural. The anger that lived inside Jason was no longer there. After all, how can you hate someone you understand perfectly? Through the Purge, Jason not only accepted Nartikis, but he loved him.

He wrapped his arms around Nartikis and held him close. Through his tears, he said, "It's okay. You're free."

42

THE AFTERMATH

When Jason opened his eyes, he was bathed in the light of a summer sunrise. The tornado and the blue dome were gone. And to the east, a sea of gray. Not moving, not armored or grunting or roaring, piles upon piles of gray ashes scattered for miles, mixed with discarded weapons and scanty animal furs.

In the far distance, Nezmyth City cheered.

Dozens of yards away, Tarren fell to his hands and knees, gasping. Tears still dripped to the end of his nose and onto the soft, cool grass. Before him, the spirit of Nadiel crouched down so he could look him in the eyes. Tarren shivered as the tears continued to fall.

"You did wonderfully," Nadiel said. "I couldn't be more proud. I'm off to rest, but I have a few favors to ask of you before I go."

Tarren's voice shook as he looked up at his mentor's face. "Anything."

"Bury me next to my father," Nadiel smiled, "next to Will the Printer. I want a small funeral—just my friends, including you. Second, please continue in your studies. The castle's wealth of knowledge is available to you. I know you'll make a fine

Advisor. And I have faith that you'll heal your mother just as you hope to."

Tarren nodded. "I'll do it."

"Splendid," Nadiel said. "Now, I hope you don't mind, but I haven't seen my father in over forty years. I'm eager to feel his embrace."

Tarren nodded again.

"Adieu, my young friend. I never had a son, but if I did, I would imagine he would be something like you." He smiled. "May the Dragon bless you."

And just like that, the spirit of Nadiel, son of Will the Printer, disappeared. Tarren pushed himself onto his knees and wiped his eyes, sniffing loudly and letting out a long, cleansing breath. He forced himself onto his shaking legs and trudged a hundred yards to Nadiel's body, sniffing and wiping his eyes as he went.

Nartikis was unconscious in Jason's arms like a sleeping child after a long day. Jason rested his chin on Nartikis head and squeezed his shoulders one more time before gently letting him down on the grass. His Knightly power was still upon him. He stood to his feet.

Lifting his arms, Jason felt every particle of ash scattered across the hills and Nezmyth City. He took a long breath, and the wind picked up. The endless piles of ashes swirled in happy cyclones until they gathered in a giant gray cloud. Then, in one mass, the ashes were sent over the Western Woods. There, they could fertilize the soil to bring new life to the parts that had been destroyed. While he was at it, Jason filled the trenches with the dislodged soil outside the city gate—the whole thing.

His Knightly power faded. No more markings, waving orange hair, or orange eyes. Nightbane was by his side once again. The Blade of Nezmyth was gone.

Nartikis stirred where he lay. But it was in this moment that Jason noticed Tarren over by Nadiel's body. He scrunched his eyes and ran over to meet them.

While he ran over, Tarren lay Nadiel on his back, slipped his eyes shut, and put his hands on his chest. When Jason arrived, Tarren popped up to his feet. Without saying another word, he threw his arms around his friend, holding him tight. Immediately, Jason knew what it was. An embrace of grief. As he looked down at Nadiel, seeing his shut eyes and hands on his heart, he knew.

"He's gone," Tarren's voice shivered. "He gave his life to help me finish the Ordinance."

Jason's heart sank, and he felt his own throat tighten. He held his friend in return and pushed his face into his shoulder, letting himself feel the sadness. They embraced for a while, sniffling and shaking until they finally let go. Through misty eyes, Jason said, "We'll give him the warrior's farewell that he deserves."

Yards away, Nartikis groaned, and his eyelids fluttered. Jason gave his friend one final hug before striding over to Nartikis. He bunched up his cape and plopped down next to him; his arms rested on his knees as he looked to the city. Gradually, Nartikis came to himself. He forced his eyes open, straining in the sunlight. Then he leaned up on his elbows, still blinking. The purple cracks were gone from his skin, and the darkness around his eyes had lifted. A little bit of color had even seeped into his pale face.

Before them, the sun had risen over the Eastern Mountains. Brilliant light poured over the kingdom, and the air was crisp and cool. Jason breathed in the morning, drinking it in.

When Jason was sure Nartikis was awake, he said, "Quite the sunrise, isn't it?"

Nartikis responded in the tone of someone who was half asleep. "It is." He gathered enough strength to sit. And as he did, he rubbed his hands together and gazed at his fingers with incredulity. "It's really gone, isn't it?"

"Yes. All of it."

Nartikis gazed upon the sea of scattered weapons and Ash clothing, along with the toppled towers and scars along the Nezmyth City wall. Breathlessly, he said, "I can't believe I did all this."

"You weren't yourself. Darkness had overtaken you."

Nartikis couldn't tear his eyes away from the destruction. "Are you… going to throw me in prison?"

"I probably should."

"I deserve it. I hurt a lot of people. *A lot.*" His voice started to shake. "All I wanted was to feel good. To feel something."

His shoulders shuddered as he tried to hold in a cry. Jason wrapped his arm around him.

At this moment, two carriages came bustling out of the western gate, heading toward them. It weaved through the remaining Ash armor and scattered bits of guard towers until it finally arrived where Jason and the others sat. Out of the first carriage came Captain Barnabas and Saryan. Out of the back carriage, Kalyk climbed out with a bandaged thigh. All of them were covered in soot, their armor was scuffed and scraped, and they all suffered from cuts and gashes.

Nartikis's eyes shot to the ground when Captain Barnabas approached.

Barnabas scanned the scene—a hundred-yard circle stained with burn marks and gashes. And he noticed Jason sitting with Nartikis. His eyes got serious and full of wonder.

"So it worked then?" he breathed, "You did it?"

"Yes," Jason confirmed, "your son is fine."

Nartikis kept his gaze fixed on the ground. As he looked upon his son, Barnabas seemed like he wanted to say something—opening and closing his mouth multiple times. But nothing came. Finally, Saryan broke the silence.

"The Ash made it as far as Center Court," She said. "Half of the city was covered with them. It was awful. But they all fell apart before the city was completely overrun."

"Are there many dead?" Jason asked.

Barnabas nodded. "We haven't been able to count yet."

Scanning the group again, Jason said, "Where's Chief Patu?"

All eyes were on Kalyk. She didn't look up. She pursed her lips together and shook her head. No one spoke. It would be hard to imagine the woods without the giant heart of Chief Patu. Every Treetown refugee would be mourning today. Everyone dipped their heads out of respect.

Jason's tone darkened. "We have one, too."

Everyone turned to see Nadiel's body. Tarren knelt by it reverently, gazing into the face of his mentor and friend, aching for just a few more minutes with him.

"Come on," Jason said lowly, "let's get his body into one of the carriages. Saryan, Kalyk, Tarren, come help me."

Barnabas was slightly taken aback that Jason didn't ask for his help, but he soon realized why. Once the others were carefully carrying Nadiel's body into one of the carriages, Barnabas was left alone with Nartikis.

Nartikis's gaze didn't rise from the grass. As Barnabas looked down at him, it felt like a reflection of distant memories —the memories of Barnabas's ventures to Unbuntye to see the Queen. Nartikis would do little things to try for his attention, like bring him a toy or ask him a question, but largely Nartikis was left sitting alone on the floor somewhere. Just like he looked now.

Barnabas's heart rate picked up and he cleared his throat. He felt himself pulled to Nartikis while simultaneously repelled —the desire to make amends and the desire to run away. What could he possibly say after all this? How could he possibly heal these wounds? He rubbed the back of his neck, cleared his throat again, then meandered over to where his son sat. Bending like an old man, Barnabas let himself down on the grass beside him.

For a moment, they sat in silence, not even looking at one another. Barnabas opened his mouth, then closed it again. Then he sighed and cleared his throat one more time.

"It… feels a lot better, doesn't it? Your mind is clear."

Nartikis didn't reply right away. But after a moment, he nodded.

"I remember feeling trapped like you," Barnabas continued. "Angry and bitter all the time. King Jason had to lock me in a magic cell for years before I was healed." Barnabas paused. A defeated sigh left his lips, then he turned to his son. "I don't know… what I can do. But… I'll try to be better than I was. From now on, I'll try."

Surprisingly, Nartikis met his gaze. Those blue eyes were swollen and wet. In his face, Barnabas saw himself in more ways than one. Not just the nose, eyes, and pale skin, but the pain. They were the same, just decades apart. Finally, Nartikis nodded.

"Okay," he said.

They loaded Nadiel's body into the first carriage; Tarren and Jason insisted on keeping it company. Everyone else climbed into the second. The drivers yah'ed, and the carriages lurched to a crawl, heading back into Nezmyth City.

✳ ✳ ✳ ✳ ✳

The entire kingdom celebrated that night. The inns and taverns were filled to capacity. People sang and drank and danced in the streets. But those up at the castle took no part in the revelry. Master Ferribolt prepared Nadiel's body for burial. Jason slept, as did Saryan. Tarren assisted Master Ferribolt with the preparations, then studied late into the night. In Barnabas's shack, he and Nartikis talked for hours before he escorted Nartikis quietly to the Nezmyth City Prison, where Nartikis retired willingly to the Vault of the Damned. No one in the city knew that King Nartikis was still in their kingdom.

The next day, people gathered their things and began leaving the city, headed for their homes, wherever they were. For a typical royal funeral, they should have stayed in town at least for the afternoon. They should have lined the streets leading from the castle to the Nezmyth City Cemetery, tossing flower pedals as the casket went by. But that's not what Nadiel wanted, according to Tarren. And no one questioned it.

The breeze was gentle around them, and the sun was brilliant. It wasn't too hot—just a beautiful summer day. Garrit's funeral was first. There was no body recovered, so no burial was needed. Master Ferribolt placed his hand on the headstone next to Melody's name, and Garrit's information was magically engraved—Captain Garrit, Chief Captain of the Nezmythian Army. Everyone took turns exchanging words. Jason played a song on his flyra. When it was done, Saryan's shoulders squared like a weight was lifted from them. She looked up to the sky and let the breeze kiss her, like the lips of a loving father on her forehead. That was enough.

Nadiel's came next. They found the headstone of Will the Printer. Nadiel's casket floated above an empty grave next to it —Master Ferribolt held it there magically. The Advisor's small group of friends stood in a circle around it: Jason, Saryan, Master Ferribolt, Tarren, and Kalyk. All of them wore their best formal attire. Barnabas stood several paces back.

Just like Garrit, they all took turns exchanging words. Saryan spoke of Nadiel's insights on the Ancient Text and his dry sense of humor. Jason spoke of his wisdom and patience in the face of his arrogance. Master Ferribolt and Kalyk spoke of his kindness and intelligence. Finally, it was Tarren's turn.

"Tarren," Jason said. "You only knew him for a few weeks, but you almost became the closest to him. Would you like to share some words?"

Tarren's eyes glossed over as he remembered the nights of studying by lantern light with Nadiel. The practicing of magic. The carriage rides to and from his flat. His chest swelled and deflated. Then he said, "Nadiel is the greatest man I've ever met. He was abandoned, but through study and grit became strong. When I felt like I couldn't do anything right, when I felt like things were hopeless, he never pushed me down or made me feel small. He tried to make me see myself as something great. Because that's just what he did—he made everyone else around him better. He was smart and kind and good. I thank the Dragon that I knew him. And I'll thank the Dragon every day until I see him again."

Tarren nodded at Jason. He was done. Then Jason sniffed and cleared his throat as he prepared to recite the Servant's Farewell.

"May the Hall of Servants ring with praises as they welcome you home in a blaze of majesty, Nadiel, Advisor of Nezmyth," Jason recited. "May the Sacred Dragon bathe you in its Holy Light as your spirit ascends to its Eternal Rest. May the forces of Darkness look upon your deeds with fear and tremble, for a mighty spirit has risen to Paradise. You were and forever shall be a scholar, a hero, a mentor, a warrior, and a friend. To the Sacred Dragon, we release you."

As Master Ferribolt lowered the casket into the empty earth, Jason pulled his flyra from a pocket and played a somber, whistling tune. The notes bent and swayed with sadness and love as the coffin found its rest in the earth. Master Ferribolt pushed soil over the opening, filling the hole. With another wave of his hand, a body of white flowers sprouted where the overturned earth was.

Tarren stepped forward. He placed his hand in the center of the flowers and concentrated for a moment as Jason continued to play. When he lifted his hand, a single red flower greeted the sunlight where Nadiel's heart would have been. Everyone smiled.

When the proceedings were done, everyone began to shuffle away. Jason caught Kalyk out of the corner of his eye.

"What's your plan for Treetown?" Jason asked.

"Rebuild," Kalyk said. "Make the town as beautiful and charming as it once was. We'll bury those that we lost in battle yesterday… including our Chief. She'll be buried next to Adria. It's what she would have wanted."

"Send Justice to us to let us know what we can do," Jason said. "Thank you for your assistance in this war. Your service will never be forgotten. May the Dragon bless you, Chief Kalyk."

Kalyk bowed to her friends, then slipped inside her carriage and drove off, jittering westward through the streets of Nezmyth City.

Meanwhile, Tarren was still kneeling by Nadiel's grave. Master Ferribolt put his hand on his shoulder and said, "I'll be in my carriage. Take as long as you need." As he got up to walk to his carriage, he passed by Jason and Saryan. "I would greatly enjoy if you two would stop by my home soon for tea. The Dragon knows we need a time to unwind and savor the friendship that we still have."

Saryan smiled warmly. "We'll come visit tonight. Thank you, Master."

Master Ferribolt smiled in return, then climbed into his carriage.

Jason let his mind hover on those he loved for a moment. Saryan. Master Ferribolt. Tarren. How remarkable it is that life is so fragile and time so finite. Master Ferribolt was right; things must be savored while they can.

His arm was around Saryan's waist. He pulled her close. "I think it's time for us."

"For us to what?"

He looked into her eyes. "To try for a child. Just like you wanted."

Saryan's eyes sparkled, but she ogled at her husband skeptically. "You're sure?"

"Yes. I think I'm ready."

"What changed?"

Jason kissed the side of her head. "This war. Everything. I love you. And I want to add more love to our family. I think I'm ready."

She grinned and her eyes sparkled brighter. "Okay then."

They both noticed Tarren by Nadiel's grave, now sitting instead of kneeling, appearing deep in thought. They exchanged looks, then Jason asked, "Did you want to stay out here for a little longer, Tarren?"

"Yeah. I think I do. Master Ferribolt will give me a ride back to the castle."

Jason trudged over to him and squatted down next to him, putting his arm around him. "We'll all see him again someday. And… he was truly proud of you. I hope you know that."

"I do."

Jason gave his shoulders a squeeze before he stood up. As he walked over to take Saryan's hand, he noticed Barnabas still standing a little ways off. "Barnabas, did you want to stay a while, too?"

"I might," Barnabas said. "There are some items of business I would like to address here."

He craned his neck to look at Grace Mountain just over his shoulder. Jason said he understood. Then he and Saryan climbed into their carriage and traveled back to the castle.

As Barnabas left the cemetery, Tarren sat at Nadiel's grave, letting the sunlight soak over him and the breeze waft around him. When he looked behind him, his eyebrows furrowed. On Will the Printer's grave, a whole loaf of grainy bread sat just in front of the headstone. He cocked his head sideways.

"Flowers, I understand," he wondered out loud, "but what kind of person leaves a loaf of bread on a headstone?"

* * * * *

Captain Barnabas ascended the switchbacks to the top of Grace Mountain, and by the time he reached the peak, his legs were sore. Amazingly, no one else was on the plateau—remarkable for a beautiful summer day like this. He looked out to the west. He could still see the wreckage from yesterday's battle; the stone masons hadn't yet started repairs on the wall yet.

It had been years since he'd been on the top of this summit —decades. He had almost forgotten what it looked like. The cream stones beneath his feet seemed to never wear or fade, and the Dragon statue several yards away was still as majestic and terrible as ever. He straightened up and took a deep breath as he approached it.

When he reached the Dragon statue, he extracted his sword from its sheath and lay it on the ground. He knelt down, looking into the Dragon's eyes only briefly before his gaze fell to the stone again.

"I… do not know where to begin," Barnabas uttered. "It's been… it's been a long time. I would say I've made a lot of mistakes, but that's putting it far too simply. This, you already know. You know it all. I just… I just want to let you know… Sacred Dragon… that I'm trying. And please, if it is not too much to ask… please… give my apologies to friend, Thomas. Perhaps you know a way to articulate the feelings of my heart better than I can."

The Dragon was silent. Nothing but the sun and the breeze responded to him. Barnabas sighed. He took up his sword, slid it into his sheath, and turned his back to begin the descent down the mountain. But then a voice came.

"The Holy Dragon thought you should tell me yourself."

Barnabas jumped. There he was. King Thomas. With his curly black hair and his full royal regalia, just as he remembered him. He was smiling a full, toothy grin—his dark eyes glistened. Barnabas just stood there, completely stunned.

King Thomas smiled wider. "It's been a long time, my friend."

Barnabas finally found words in himself. He scoffed, and through stinging eyes he said, "How can you call me that? After the treachery and the betrayal—"

"Barnabas."

"After I stole your throne to satisfy my petty desires—"

"Barnabas."

"For *twenty years* I ruled and nearly destroyed what you built. You were loved, and rightfully so! You were benevolent and wise. Then I snuffed out your life and reigned with malice and hate. I am not worthy to be called your friend. Please don't rack my soul with your mercy."

King Thomas advanced on him until they were only a few feet apart. Barnabas's eyes continued to sting, and a lump in his throat grew. Through it all, King Thomas gazed upon him with unfiltered pride.

"Barnabas, *look at you!*" He said delightedly. "You're Chief Captain again! You fought and defended Nezmyth at its time of greatest need! Through your efforts, the Dragon has granted you miraculous results! Don't you believe that says something about you?"

Barnabas shook his head. "I do not understand."

"Understand what?"

"How can you freely forgive someone who has done so much wrong? I was dreading the day that I would see you face to face, but you greet me like a brother."

"Because you've allowed yourself to be healed," King Thomas said. "You've abandoned the wretched thing that you became and have reemerged into something greater. Nartikis's darkness was Purged from his soul, and during the same time, you were Purged in your own way. And I couldn't be happier. The way I see it, my old friend is back." King Thomas smirked. "Remember when we we snuck that cat into Mrs. Taraphil's bedroom window?"

Barnabas laughed as he wiped his eyes. "And she startled it so badly that it broke half of her porcelain dolls?"

King Thomas smiled wider. "Oh, what a wretched woman she was!"

"Just awful. All the children hated her."

"Almost as much as the adults!"

They both laughed together, cleansed by the sparkling memories of the past. When their laughs died down, King Thomas shimmered once more with pride.

"Barnabas, I feel as though there are still great things for you to accomplish," King Thomas said. "I'm sure our friend Jason will be with you along the way."

Barnabas half smiled and looked down on the castle in the distance. "Part of me feels as though our destinies are intertwined. He elected not to send me back to Prison, so I want to serve Nezmyth with the utmost of my ability until my body is laid to rest. Only that will be recompense for my crimes."

"You'll fulfill your duties well, I'm sure," King Thomas said. "And when you're done, I'll be the first in line to throw my arms about you when your spirit ascends to the Third Life."

Barnabas's heart swelled and a grin graced his lips. "I don't deserve you, Thomas. I never did."

"Sometimes, brothers don't," King Thomas winked. "Carry on, dear friend. May the Dragon bless you."

SOME YEARS LATER

The two moons over Nezmyth were shy to shine their light tonight. Nezmyth City had fallen under a somber hush in the wake of today's events. News traveled fast, and when people heard the whispers in Center Court and on the Market Streets, their hearts sank, and many wiped a tear.

Soldiers patrolled the area between the castle and the Nezmyth City Cemetery, making sure everything would be free and clear for tomorrow's procession. The soldiers spoke in low tones to each other. Even Captain Barnabas, who was famous for containing his emotions in the most pressing circumstances, felt no need to suppress his grief. His hand rested on his sword as he conversed with a pair of soldiers on the edge of the Northern Market Street.

"Are the southern gates open?"

"Yes, sir."

"Good," Barnabas said. "The Advisor should be returning from Lunli Village soon. He cut his trip short when he heard the news." He paused. "Thank you. Carry on."

The soldiers saluted and marched away. Barnabas put his hands on his hips and looked up to the sky. Somewhere up there, the spirit of his friend ascended to the glistening halls of the Third Life. He took a handkerchief and dabbed his eyes.

"Sir."

Barnabas quickly coughed and stuffed his handkerchief away. He turned to see a woman marching up to him, her armor clinking as she went. A sword was slung around her waist, her steely blue eyes reflected the moonlight intensely, and her bright blonde hair was tied in a tight bun. Somehow, the long scar stretching diagonally across her left cheek didn't hinder her beauty in the slightest. Behind her, a small battalion of soldiers followed closely.

"Captain Kierli," Barnabas sighed. "I can always count on you for good news."

Kierli almost grinned, but kept her poise. "All of Center Court has been cleaned of any trash. On our way, we found an urchin attempting to break into a Northern Market Street shop and apprehended him. A couple of my guards are taking him to the prison as we speak. I've sent a few more of my guards to make sure the grave site is clean and prepared."

"Excellent work, Captain, as usual," Barnabas nodded. "Well done. If you'll excuse me, I need to go follow up with the other garrisons."

With that, Barnabas marched away. The soldier just behind Captain Kierli leaned forward and whispered, "At this rate, Kierli, you'll be up for Chief Captain when Barnabas is ready to retire."

Kierli actually smirked this time. "Only if you chumps continue to make me look good."

All her soldiers chuckled in admiration. She turned to face them.

"You all have done great work tonight," she said. "You're excused. Be ready for the procession tomorrow at sunrise."

The soldiers in Kierli's battalion gave their "yes ma'ams" before marching away. As they dispersed, Kierli made her way to her barrack just off the Northern Market Street. This Market Street, along with Center Court, was her battalion's responsibility, the most sought-after position in the whole city.

Kierli's soldiers maintained it like a fine machine, and it was something she was very proud of.

When she reached her private barrack—furnished with a feather mattress, full body mirror, hardwood chest, and bear rug—she quickly undressed and hung her armor on a wooden mannequin by the door. But she kept her boots on. After she donned her nightclothes, she laid her sword by the bedside.

Her boots clomped across the floor as she made her way to the hardwood chest. She unlatched the lid and pulled it open. Inside, pushed into a corner, was a small cage filled with lizards flicking their tongues and crawling over each other. When she reached in, they scurried away from her hand. But she managed to grab one.

She dropped it to the floor. The lizard instinctively knew what was coming and tried to dart away, but no. Kierli brought her boot down on it, mashing its body into the hardwood.

Kierli sighed. She put the cage back into the trunk, took off her boots, and made her way to the bed. After she slipped under the covers, she folded her arms so her hands were on her heart. Her palms glowed purple and quiet waves of euphoric pleasure rippled through her body.

ABOUT THE AUTHOR

Aaron N. Hall is the author of The Wevlian Chronicles, the Hammerfist Series, and multiple collections of stories and poems. When he's not writing (which isn't often), he's doing nonprofit work, exercising, reading a book, or sipping a cup of tea. He lives in Utah.

For updates on future books, visit **aaronnhall.com**